Praise for *The Covered Deep*

We at the Christian Writers Guild couldn't be more proud of Brandy Vallance. Let her debut novel transport you to a time and place where you'll soon forget you're turning pages and find yourself riveted to the destinies of characters who will leave a lasting impression on your heart.

—Jerry B. Jenkins,
New York Times best-selling author

I love a good romance! I'm so happy that new author Brandy Vallance has given us one filled with adventure, truth, and grace!

—Stasi Eldredge,
coauthor of *Captivating*

Superb historical romance, with a spiritual theme woven seamlessly throughout. I much enjoyed *The Covered Deep* and look forward to more from its author!

—James Scott Bell,
best-selling author of The Trials of Kit Shannon series

Ripe with history, romance, and suspense, *The Covered Deep* by debut author Brandy Vallance is fast-paced fiction at its finest. Readers will thrill to the picture-perfect descriptions of the Holy Land and touches of humor from Vallance's skilled pen.

—Elizabeth Ludwig,
author of *Tide and Tempest*

The Covered Deep is a lovely debut that pushes every emotional button as its sigh-worthy hero and plucky heroine struggle with vagaries of the heart, honesty, trust, and forgiveness. I laughed, caught my breath, nibbled my nails, got teary-eyed, and sighed. Bravo, Brandy Vallance!

—Tamara Leigh,
award-winning author of *Lady of Eve* and *The Unveiling*

The Covered Deep is a decadent, mysterious, and absorbing debut, with brilliant dialogue and a cascade of well-thought plot twists. Through a story infused with history and the expert weaving of faith, I was captured to the very last page. Vallance's debut is Christian fiction at its finest, a stunning novel every historical reader will devour and keep on their favorites shelf for years to come.

—Kristy Cambron,
author of *The Butterfly and the Violin*
and *A Sparrow in Terezin*

A promising debut for a talented new author, *The Covered Deep* is an engaging tale that spans America to Victorian London to the Holy Land. When soon-to-be spinster Bianca Marshal wins an essay contest, her first place prize not only sets off a long-hoped-for romance but mystery, intrigue, and danger as well.

—Kathleen Morgan,
best-selling, award-winning novelist

In *The Covered Deep*, debut author Brandy Vallance examines a compelling question: what can true faith withstand? Set against the backdrop of the Holy Land, Vallance shapes believable characters whose past mistakes threaten their future hopes. With every turn of the page, I found myself more intrigued by this novel, and I'm already looking forward to Vallance's next book.

—Beth K. Vogt,
author of *Somebody Like You*

From the first page until the last, *The Covered Deep* felt like falling into another world where the author's words were as evocative as the plot. I was swept into the story and tumbled along with every bump in the long road between the first blush of hope and the breathlessly gorgeous final scene. Brandy Vallance's beautifully written tale made me forget everything, including sleep, in order to immerse myself in the story. I will not soon forget this book, nor will I miss reading anything else this talented author writes.

—Kathleen Y'Barbo
award-winning historical fiction author

The Covered Deep

Brandy Vallance

WORTHY®
PUBLISHING

Published by Worthy Publishing, a division of Worthy Media, Inc.,
134 Franklin Road, Suite 200, Brentwood, Tennessee 37027.

Worthy is a registered trademark of Worthy Media, Inc.

HELPING PEOPLE EXPERIENCE THE HEART OF GOD.

eBook available wherever digital books are sold.

Library of Congress Cataloging-in-Publication Data

Vallance, Brandy.
The covered deep / Brandy Vallance.
pages cm
1. Young women—Appalachian Region—Fiction. 2. Self-actualization
(Psychology) in women—Fiction. 3. Americans—England—London—
History—19th century—Fiction. 4. Americans—Palestine—History—
19th century—Fiction. 5. Christian fiction. 6. Love stories. I. Title.
PS3622.A476C68 2014
813'.6--dc23
2014019347

Scripture quotations are taken from The Authorized King James Version.
Public domain.

This is a work of fiction. Any similarity to persons, living or dead, is
entirely coincidental.

For foreign and subsidiary rights, contact rights@worthypublishing.com

ISBN 978-1-61795-375-0 (paperback)

Cover Design: Smartt Guys design
Cover Image: pixelworksstudios
Interior Design: Christopher D. Hudson & Associates, Inc.

Printed in the United States of America
14 15 16 17 18 VPI 5 4 3 2 1

In memory of Hester Cropper and Paul Cole, two of the greatest storytellers who ever graced this earth. And dedicated with utmost respect to my father, Tim Cole. Thanks for teaching me that with God all things are possible. Also, to my grandmother, Minnie Cole. Your love and prayers have made all the difference.

Call unto me, and I will answer thee, and shew thee great and mighty things, which thou knowest not.

—Jeremiah 33:3

Chapter 1

At seventeen, most ladies of fashion expect to receive proposals. If they do not marry within a few years, they have a mortified sense of having lost time. Inevitably, they become an object of sympathy. The next few years are often a period of subdued vexation. During this time, the sweetness and contentment of the lady's original character is impaired. As the unwholesome state of spinsterhood approaches, a lady finds herself soon to be restricted in social pleasures and more.

I am inclined to believe that with good temper, pleasing manners, and respectable connections, a lady need not despair. Herein are the facts: Between the ages of twenty to twenty-four, a lady has a 52 percent chance of marrying. Between the ages of twenty-five to thirty, her chances are 18 percent.

The book slipped from Bianca's hands, the pages fainting on her bedroom desk. Words. Reminding her of all the ways she'd never fit in. She collapsed in the chair, her cotton dress limp against her. "When the sun rises tomorrow, my chances of marrying will drop thirty-four percent." She breathed, in and out, slowly. "Spin—" The word felt like cod liver oil on her tongue.

"It doesn't matter that my twenty-fifth birthday's tomorrow." She slid her hand underneath the desk and pressed the small, metal button. The secret slot popped open, sending a spray of dust over her sleeve. "When going into battle, planning is often the most important thing." Saying the words calmed her, as did the feel of the hidden paper. She unfolded it and scanned the first few lines.

Soul mate must be
(1) a true believer in Jesus Christ
(2) devastatingly handsome, with a slightly wild look in his eyes
(3) brilliant and humorous like Mark Twain
(4) a foreigner, possibly a disgruntled duke
(5) able to quote Bible verses and Shakespeare
(6) a more than capable kisser
(7) adore me completely.

"Yes, well." She drew her eyebrows together as she considered. "Perfectly reasonable I thin—"

"Bianca! You'd better be lacin' up your boots." Mama's voice was a crescendo crack, the kind of noise one hears when alone in the woods and a big tree falls. "Girl, don't you make me late."

Bianca shoved the list back into its hiding place, but the secret door wouldn't shut. She pushed harder. Nothing.

"Are you ready to go or not?" Mama rapped her knuckles on the door, like the battle march of a soldier's drum.

"Coming." Bianca stood and put her weight against the warped side of the drawer. "Just a moment."

Mama jiggled the door handle. "I told Mr. Rutherford we'd be there by four o'clock. It is now precisely 3:09."

A hairpin came loose, and a piece of Bianca's dark auburn hair fell over her eyes. "Guts griping harpy!" The drawer slammed shut. The large bottle of ink tipped. A waterfall of black spread over her books, seeping into the pages like hungry poison.

"What is going on in there? Open this door."

"I'll be out momentarily." Bianca fought to level her voice. "I'm just tidying things up." Papers flew off the desk. Pens hit the floor.

She sent up a whispered prayer. "Oh, please, not my new books. Lord, don't let all the pages be ruined." She flipped though *Inquire Within: Things Worth Knowing.* The pages were soggy clumps and witching-hour black.

The floorboards in the hall groaned. Bianca heard the sound of a drawer opening. Mama was going for the keys.

The lock turned. The door hit the baseboard.

"What have you done to your hands?" Anger rippled in Mama's blue eyes, as cold and distant as Pike Lake. "Child, look at the floor."

Bianca dropped her gaze to the polished oak floor and then back to the ruined books. "I was clumsy . . . Daddy went all the way to Cincinnati for these books. My early birthday presents."

"More books you don't need." She scowled at the ink-stained covers of *Ancient Society* and *The Wreck of the Grosvenor: An Account of the Mutiny of the Crew and the Loss of the Ship When Trying to Make the Bermudas.* "More money wasted on your fancies." Mama took her by the shoulders. "You will see Mr. Rutherford today."

Bianca tried to pull away. "Little good it will do. I won't marry someone who has the imagination of a butter churn. If he's anything like his sermons, I'd die of boredom."

The lines around Mama's eyes deepened. "Your Aunt Sally says he can just look at a person and tell if they're right with the Lord. Wouldn't you want a man who has that kind of power?"

"No, I wouldn't," Bianca said matter-of-factly. "That's not something anyone can tell simply by looking at a person." She waited for a reaction Mama didn't give—a common ground they'd never had. "'Man looketh on the outward appearance, but the Lord looketh on the heart.'"

Mama threw up her hands. "All your friends are married. Some have two babies by now. Either the man's too dull or his profession is." She looked her up and down. "As if you had a lot to offer." Her gaze went to the many scattered books. "You'd rather read than do anything useful. Those men you read about in those novels of yours, there's a reason they call it fiction."

Bianca's gaze went to the secret drawer in her desk. "I haven't found my soul mate yet." Her voice faltered, as if she'd said the words too many times. "I will not marry just because."

"Soul mate." Mama's lips pinched. "Marriage is hard work. I've told you that before. It's not some unending fairy tale where a man fulfills your every dream. It involves a great deal of will." She chopped at the air with her hand. "You find a man who you can build a life with. Love comes later, after sacrifice has made it grow."

"Is that what you and Daddy have? Is that why you're both so . . . *happy*?" She knew she shouldn't have said such things, but she let the words hang, suspended in the air like an ugly decoration that everyone ignored.

Mama's forehead creased ever so slightly, then she walked to Bianca's brass bed. "You really shouldn't fold your quilt down like this. Always up, that's what I say."

"What's wrong with the way I fold it?" Bianca's voice rose, as did her ink-stained hands. "King Louis the sixteenth had his bed made this way at Versailles."

"Oh, did he now?" Mama tucked the quilt under the mattress like she was killing something. "The only Versailles I know about is the one across the river in Kentucky. Your father continues to fill your head with such strange notions and strange people." She punched down the feather pillows and made them flat. "I told him all them books would make you restless. Make you long for things you shouldn't have."

Bianca focused on the gray hair that painted Mama's temples and alternated through the strands of red. Sadness washed over her, and all she could do was pity Mama. For the limited way that she thought. And the romance Daddy would have given her, if she'd been different. "I'm very thankful for the life I have here. It's just that . . . I'm not so sure I'm meant to be here forever." Bianca bit the corner of her lip. "Is it so wrong to want to see the world that God created? Is it so wrong to want to marry someone outside of this little town?"

"You ought to be content." Mama opened the dresser and rearranged Bianca's nightdresses. "You've always got to be different. Always got to be fancy." She narrowed her eyes and seemed to have a revelation. "You're a selfish girl, not proud of your heritage." She shoved the dresser drawer. The bottles of honeysuckle wash clanked together. "You come from plain, good people. There is safety here, Bianca."

"Do you know how much history is in Europe? Can you even comprehend how much I could learn? All those museums—"

"Are nothing but a collection of idols. Dens of sin glorifying the heathen nations."

Bianca winced as if Mama had slapped her. "Do you know where your traveling preacher, Mr. Rutherford, gets his theology?"

"From God Almighty."

"He's affiliated with Victoria Woodhull. Remember when she ran for presidentess of the United States five years ago?" Bianca lowered her voice. "That woman has no respect for the marriage bed."

Shock splashed over Mama's features. "How dare you speak about such—"

"During the War of Rebellion she worked as a clairvoyant—a professional charlatan. She knew exactly what to say to get people's money." Bianca stepped across the faded rug, anger swelling like muddy water in the rain. "Who knows, maybe she even swindled our Ash—"

"Don't say his name. Don't you ever say that name."

The air changed—a pulsing heat, suffocating. Bianca turned to the window.

Mama moved behind her, a constant shadow. "Every man I've chosen for you, you've turned away. You're too high and mighty, that's what you are."

Bianca focused on the oak tree outside and the branches straining against the wind. The tree swing drifted backward and the seat lifted—as if a ghost child sat there, enthralled with the way the dust swirled and mingled with the clouds.

Bianca took a deep breath to try to alleviate the crushing weight in her chest. "I'm sorry you think that about me, Mama."

"I think I'll go see Mr. Rutherford by myself today." Mama licked her finger and rubbed the ink smudge on Bianca's cheek. "I'm sure he's going to give me some very good advice. And regardless of what you think, he would make you a good husband."

Bianca kept her gaze on the tree swing.

"There, now." Mama ran her hand down Bianca's back. "I hope you'll be more agreeable when I return."

And then Mama was gone.

Bianca didn't know how long she stood by the window. The old clock on the bookshelf ticked on, not caring that her marriage prospects were slipping away as quickly as the fading afternoon light. *Help me, God. Forgive me for the way I spoke to Mama. I believe You gave me these desires. Make something of them or take them away.*

A movement caught her eye from outside. Daddy crouched alongside the bushes by the potato shoots in the garden.

Relief flooded her. She opened the window.

Daddy held up his thumb and Bianca returned the sign. "Mama's about to go to town," she whispered. "For a while, I think."

"Good." Daddy gave her a grin full of conspiracy, hiked his leg over the windowsill, and climbed into the room. "Because I know she wouldn't approve, as usual." He shook a folded newspaper between them and then sat. His mustache turned upward, just as his lips did, but then it fell. "Here, now, have you been crying?"

"It doesn't matter." Bianca tried to give him a convincing smile. "What do you have?"

"What happened at your desk?" He scanned the puddles of ink. "Reenacting the ink massacre of sixty-three?"

"Very funny."

"Your enthusiasm for reading is incomparable, daughter. Perhaps next time a less cataclysmic approach? Now, to the point." He slapped the newspaper. "I've been waiting for this advertisement for a long time."

"Have you?" Bianca reached for it, but he snatched it away. "What's it about?"

"Guess." He wiggled his thick, brown eyebrows. "This advertisement happens to come from a very old place."

"Old?" She felt her smile growing.

"Yes. This country has a large affinity for tea and a certain queen whose name starts with the letter *V*."

Bianca widened her eyes. "Surely not. England?"

"Ah, you've guessed it. Clever girl. But I suppose I made it too easy for you? No matter." He tapped the edge of the newspaper on her mason jar of foreign coins. "It's time to acknowledge the corn."

"You're giving up? Just like that?" Bianca placed her hand on her hip. "You normally have me guessing for a straight fifteen minutes, at least."

"Yes, well . . . You've had me catawamptiously chawed up of late." He twisted the corner of his mustache. "Ever since your theory on the moving stones in the old Shawnee Forest. I'll place your triumph there."

Bianca curtsied, hand over heart. Her voice took on the tone of a seasoned actress. "Thank you."

"I may be able to redeem myself soon, have no fear." He handed her the newspaper.

Sir Adrian Hartwith, Knight Grand Cross of the Order of the Brazen Crown; Attached to Societies Musical, Societies Medical, Societies Philosophical, Societies Sociological, and Societies General Benevolent throughout Europe, wishes to announce a contest of the most venerable kind.

Being a seeker himself, Sir Adrian wishes for those who seek to join him on an expedition to the Holy Land. Four personages will be chosen to walk where the Lord walked, stand on the exact spot where He was crucified, and hear the music of almost nineteen hundred years ago.

If chosen, all expenses will be paid. Furthermore, £300 will be awarded to the contestants who complete the journey.

To be considered, compose an essay highlighting your inter-ests, personal goals, religious beliefs, and a regret from your past. Begin the first sentence by choosing words for this acronym: T F S L A H B T T H S E B T I S.

The winners will be notified by post on or before the 1st of June. If applicable, tick-ets for transportation to London will be included. The fortunate party will depart London the 5th of August by ship.

"Three hundred pounds!" Bianca looked over the advertisement again. "Daddy, how much is that in American currency?"

"Close to five hundred dollars, I'd say."

Bianca's mouth gaped open. "With such money, you wouldn't have to work at the shoe factory anymore." Excitement wove through her body like the beginnings of a summer storm. "We could traipse around the world like gypsies. Drink chocolate in Paris. See the ruins of the Temple of Artemis in Ephesus and afterward, walk where the Great Apostle proclaimed the Living God."

"Indeed." He looked at her poignantly. "Such a thing could be accomplished."

All the conversations they'd had over the years echoed like bells. "Do you think it's a genuine offer?"

"Of course it is," he said without reservation. "This advertisement cost Sir Adrian a fortune. Why would he go to such lengths for a farce?"

Bianca touched the indentation of the black, printed words and furrowed her brow. So many dreams had been lost already. So many times Daddy had tried to make things different for them and failed. "How did you know to expect this advertisement? This is the *Columbus Dispatch*."

Daddy cleared his throat. "A gentleman I associate with delivered it to me."

Bianca narrowed her eyes. "Daddy, did you go up to Raven Rock again?"

Daddy sat straighter in the chair and crossed his arms. "My dear, the Brotherhood of the Shrouded Tree can hardly meet in your mama's parlor."

"If Mama found out . . ." She shook her finger at him. "You're going to get yourself killed. The path up that hill isn't safe."

"Ah, but Bianca, the view." Daddy smiled, that old, winsome smile. The one he saved for summers that slipped away too soon. The one he smiled when he sat on their porch and he was lonely, always just before she joined him to listen to the pound of the rain and watch the white streams of water falling from the tin eaves.

Bianca knew what words would come next, so she said them for him. "You like to see the river winding like a silver snake through the hills. To be in the place where Daniel Boone escaped the Indians by taking a daring leap from the rock, into the mist and onto a tree."

Daddy nodded as if she'd said the truest thing in the world. "In such a place, a man believes he might be more. Troubles can be hung on the limbs and left there for the golden eagles to carry away."

Bianca closed her eyes and could almost see it— Daddy and his deep-thinking friends sitting high above Portsmouth as the sun set, the steamboats looking like toys slipping away on the white sliver of river.

Daddy's voice was gentle, the timbres of all their tomorrows. "When I first got wind of this contest, it sounded perfect for you, but of course I was leery. After all, how could I send my only daughter across the perilous sea?"

Bianca studied the intensity in his eyes. "Me? You want me to make an attempt?"

"I've thought about this quite a lot, Bianca. And I've prayed. Every time I get the same answer—you ought to try." His expression was conflicted, as if he couldn't believe the words he'd just spoken. "For months I've been writing letters, checking references, and asking questions about Sir Adrian. I have a stack of replies hidden in the smokehouse. Would you like to see them?"

"Of course. But Daddy, you ought to go." Bianca thought of Mama, and as much as she wanted to drift into the air and never see this place again, she thought of all the ways it would break Mama's heart. "Couldn't someone take your place at the factory while you were away? Surely Mr. Selby knows how hard you've worked. Your ideas alone have improved—"

"Listen to you. You've already assumed my entry would be a winner."

"And why do you think it wouldn't be?"

"Oh, your love for me is far too biased, Bianca. I can't do everything, you know. I get a day here and there for my efforts, but I can assure you, Mr. Selby is not that lenient. There's a string of men in line for my position."

"Well, how am I to go if you don't? Assuming that I win, how would it be proper for me to travel all that way alone?"

"I could go with you as far as New York Harbor. Sir Adrian is wealthy enough; he could no doubt supply a chaperone. In fact, I would insist upon it. However, I'm sure traveling alone is the last thing on your mind." He gave her a fatherly stare. "I know about your excursions to the woods outside of town."

Bianca raised the newspaper to hide her face. It would not do to let him see her smile.

"Did you see anything interesting out at the Indian mounds?"

"Just a few artifacts. You wouldn't be interested."

He pushed the newspaper down. "Wouldn't I?"

"Pots, fragments of bone." Bianca leaned forward. "And a ceremonial pipe. The earth was worn away from that last gully washer. I didn't touch anything, of course."

A slow smile spread across his face. "Afraid of Indian spirit revenge?"

Bianca raised an eyebrow. "'There are more things in heaven and earth, Horatio, than are dreamt of in your philosophy.'"

"I wonder if I shall ever pass a day without hearing you quote Shakespeare. Here now, you're getting me off the subject." He stood and paced the room. "If you win this contest, as soon as you reach London you'll be with Sir Adrian's party. That will grant you a great deal of protection."

"But we don't know anything about him. He could be a complete lunatic." Even as she said the words, she was drawn to this stranger. A noble. The thought of meeting such a man—of being in London and the Holy Land—some things glittered too bright to be strung into words. And this advertisement . . . Here was a door to ten thousand possibilities.

"The man's a genuine blue blood, to the manor born. He has more than enough credentials to testify of his good character."

The creak of the front door hinges sounded through the house.

"Mama must have forgotten something." Bianca fought the urge to throw the newspaper under the bed. It was only a paper with some printed words. How dangerous could it be?

Daddy hurried back to the window and climbed outside. "What are you standing around about? Has the spit and vinegar gone out of you all of a sudden? Don't you have an acronym to ponder?"

Bianca clutched the newspaper to her chest and felt a strange sensation. It felt like hope. "Yes ... It would seem I do."

Fog from the Ohio River seeped through the Bottoms like a wispy mourning veil. Errant clouds slid across the moon, casting shadows upon the long grass and the soggy ground. Bianca curled her toes until cool mud squished between them.

Daddy peeked over the cattails, lifted the lantern, and hunched back down. "Sure enough, it's a big one." He cocked his head toward the pond. "You ready?"

Bianca nodded and picked up a makeshift spear. Rusty nails and twine held the metal to the wood. "Should I use the four-pronged or the three?"

"I'd use the four. You'll have a much better chance of success." Bianca grabbed the four-pronged spear with both hands and moved to stand. Daddy's hand shot out and gripped her arm. "Don't forget—fast and hard, just like a tribeswoman in the Amazon."

"I ... am a tribeswoman ... in the Amazon." To her ears it was like a life-altering mantra. She tucked the edge of her skirt tighter into her belt. The wet fabric looped between her legs and clung as scandalous as pantaloons. Mud painted her calves like hippopotamus beauty cream. In the reflection of the moon on the water, her hair resembled a lopsided corn pone and clung to her face in the humidity.

Daddy chuckled and covered his mouth.

"Just what is so funny?"

"I was thinking that you do rather resemble an Amazonian at this moment. Your mama would kill me."

Bianca tilted her head, causing more hair to fall from the loose pins. "I suppose it's a good thing someone told Mama I was canning tomatoes at Aunt Sally's."

"A stroke of genius."

Bianca bit back her smile and rose a little higher.

The buzz of the cicadas increased. An owl hooted just beyond the still, dark trees. Daddy raised the lantern. The bullfrog's eyes were glowing orbs in the darkness, stunned by the light. "Steady now."

Bianca wrapped her fingers around the rugged wood until her knuckles turned white.

"Slowly."

She waded deeper, wet grass tangling around her ankles.

"Now. Spear that undeserving croaker!"

Bianca jumped and shoved the spear down like a bona fide man. A great splash arced above her, drenching the rest of her clothes. Pieces of lily pad and mud slid down her face. She blinked. "Did I get it?"

Daddy wiped pond water from his eyes. "I don't know, dear, you have to pick up the pole and see."

Bianca held the spear aloft. The frog's arms grasped and twitched. "I did it!"

"By Jove, you did."

The frog's slick, green skin glinted in the light of the moon. Its golden eyes were still captured in Daddy's lantern light. Bianca frowned.

"Are you going to cut its legs off when we get back to the house? It's one thing cooking it when I've brought it to you. Quite another when you've killed it yourself."

Bianca stood straighter and waded to the bank, pushing the lily pads aside. "If I can kill a chicken I think I can handle a bullfrog. Opossums might be a different matter."

Daddy held out his hand and smiled. "Let's take a break. You've done well." He tossed the frog into the basket and laid down her spear. "Shall we listen to the crickets play us a song?"

"I'd like that." Bianca sat down on a rock, hugged her knees, and studied a moonbeam that shifted to a patch of jewelweed.

"What are you thinking, Chickabiddy?" He brought the lanterns closer and added a few more candles from the basket he'd brought.

Bianca hesitated. "Well, tomorrow's the first of June."

Daddy leaned back on the bank. "Now that you mention it, tomorrow is the first of June. What happens on the first of June?"

Bianca rolled her eyes and took the handkerchiefs that he offered. "Nothing of consequence. I was just thinking." She dabbed at her legs. Pale white began to show under the streaks of mud.

"The beginning of each month always brings about a reverie for me as well. The first of June . . ."

She rested her chin on her knees and stared into the blue-white mist rising from the pond.

"That date does somehow seem familiar. Oh, I know, the sale at the sundry shop begins tomorrow. Are you thinking of getting a new fountain pen?"

"No, Daddy."

"Is it the quilting bee at Mrs. Lunsford's?"

"No, that's on the seventh. And I don't think I'm going to go this month. All those women do is try to marry me off."

"Well, I can see how that would be tiresome. Who was it last time? Jesse Smikes?"

"No." She sighed, and she felt the weight of it in her bones. "Rufus Smith."

"The grocer's son? Now I am insulted. Why didn't they just suggest those bootlegging fools who live up Brush Creek?"

"Oh, don't despair, I'm sure they'll get to them eventually. At least Rufus can read. That's more than I can say about the last two they suggested. I overheard Mrs. Lunsford say I was running out of options."

Uncharacteristically silent, Daddy stared into the lantern light. "I can't believe I'm about to say this, but Mrs. Lunsford might be on to something."

"She might?" Bianca sat up straighter and tried not to look offended.

"My dear, you've waited a long time for your knight in shining armor, and he hasn't come."

There it was, plainly spoken, as transparent as the silver haze around the willow trees and the glow of the lightning bugs playing above the water.

"He hasn't come to you as I'd hoped he would. I'd always imagined he'd be passing through town on the railroad and get delayed. Maybe he'd be an inventor or a musician . . . Never mind." Daddy cleared his throat. "You mentioned June the first."

"Yes."

"I know very well what June the first is to you. It's the last day to hear from Sir Adrian about the contest. From your sudden lack of enthusiasm I'm guessing you think you didn't win."

She breathed deep and focused on the thick blades of grass between her toes. "You're going to tell me I have to settle and marry, aren't you? You're going to say that since I didn't win I need to lower my expectations."

"No, quite the opposite." Daddy smiled and reached into the basket. "Do you have any interest in reading a letter from London? It just arrived today."

"What did you say? From London?" The word played at the edges of her mind, like a melody long forgotten.

Daddy's smile widened. He brought the letter closer to the light. "If I'm not mistaken, this is very fine paper. Must have come from the desk of an aristocrat."

"Read it." Her words came out in a whisper. "Please."

He broke the seal, slowly, reverently. The noise of the crickets and the frogs dimmed.

Dear Miss Marshal,

Out of one hundred and twenty-three entries from America, you are one of two that I have chosen. Enclosed you will find a ticket for your passage to England. Per your father's request, I am sending Mrs. Gavina Sheighly to be your chaperone for the Atlantic crossing. I first met her in Scotland whilst doing business. I believe you will find her to be amiable, and everything a lady such as yourself might wish.

When you reach Victoria Dock, my coach will be waiting to bring you safely to Hartwith House. I look forward to meeting the woman whose charm is so evidently and gracefully penned upon the page. Prepare yourself for the adventure ahead, and leave all thoughts of mediocrity behind.

Kind regards,

Sir Adrian Hartwith

"There you have it," Daddy said simply. "You're off to London and the strange beyond."

Bianca reached for the letter, but drew back just before touching it. "It's real, isn't it?"

"Yes. Now, dear, back to my earlier train of thought about a husband."

Bianca's hands shook, along with her shoulders. She could save Daddy now from the life he despised. The pond and the night bent and changed, everything shone brighter. Now she had a chance to find him— the one her soul longed for. The man she ached for night after night without even knowing his name.

"I know your husband's out there beyond these hills, no matter what your mama says. You might meet him on the ship or walking through Trafalgar Square.

Maybe you'll even meet him in Palestine. I trust you. You have very sound judgment."

Bianca stood and paced, hot and cold rushing over her body. "You may live to regret this decision. I could come back with a Bedouin camel breeder."

Daddy laughed. "I doubt it. You'll know him when you see him, I'm sure."

Bianca closed her eyes, and she let the music of the crickets lift like a song of praise. "Thank You, Lord Jesus." Her voice strained in her throat. "Daddy, do you mind if we go home now?"

"Not at all." Daddy tucked the letter into the basket. He picked up the spears and the buckets with the frogs. They walked in silence, the grass path soft beneath their feet. "Bianca . . ."

"Yes?" The fog rose around her. It danced in the dark. It pulled her toward her destiny.

A shimmer of tears laced his eyes. "I knew you'd win."

Chapter 2
London, England

The coach swayed, rocking with the rhythm of the horses' hooves, moving over cobblestones flooded with golden morning light, turning around Westminster bends and the spiry Houses of Parliament. Big Ben resonated as they passed, loud and low, marking the moments that would nevermore be the same. She would meet him soon, the man who would hold all her tomorrows and give her his name. Bianca knew, deep within her, that it was so. The shifting of the light as they drove by Kensington Gardens was like a beacon urging her on. And, when the coach passed Chesterfield Street, Bianca picked up the faint smell of biscuits, just like the ones her grandmother made. The last time she'd been to Grandmother's house, they'd talked of great romances.

So there, it was settled. Nothing happened by accident.

Bianca felt her smile grow, and her voice came out with as much awe as she felt. "I will meet him today."

Gavina Sheighly glanced up from her novel, *Les Diaboliques*. "You're excited about meeting Sir Adrian, then?" Her thick Scottish accent trilled and dropped, like a defining moment in a song. "You won't be disappointed."

Bianca bit her bottom lip. She was excited about meeting Sir Adrian, but something within told her he wasn't the one. Maybe it was the way she'd studied his letter over and over again by the light of a candle. Things could be known by a man's handwriting, at least the women back home said as much. But those same women also looked down wells on May Day to discover the identity of their future husbands in the shades of rippling water.

One thing was certain, she had poured out her heart in prayer for years. Such utterings were bound to make a difference. Such words rose to the throne of God like incense. She would know him when she saw him, Daddy said. And between this moment and all the moments yet to come, every eligible man would be compared to the list.

More's the pity she hadn't found someone on the ship to meet her requirements. It seemed only long-eyebrowed codgers and whelpish rakes desired to travel to England. But then again, there was the consideration that Gavina had kept her so entertained she hadn't had much chance for examination of the husbandly sort. Gavina had talked about scandals, and romances, and Scottish Highlanders who were wont to carry a woman away in the middle of the night and marry her.

They hadn't talked much of Gavina's husband, which Bianca thought strange, or of how Gavina knew Sir Adrian. But those small details had slipped away in the light of midnight tales of conquest and everything forbidden. Bianca had neither laughed so much nor been so enraptured in all her life. Gavina never told Bianca whether her stories were autobiographical, but there was always something very knowing in her indigo eyes.

Truly, the woman was not like any chaperone Bianca had ever read about. Weren't they required to be matronly? Drowsy on occasion? Extremely dull and have a propensity to knit?

Ah, well, Sir Adrian certainly knew more about the requirements of society than she.

Gavina played idly with her dangling amethyst earring. The sunlight hit the gem, casting shifting triangles of lavender upon the coach ceiling. "You might want to take in the view." Her Cupid's bow mouth stretched into a smile. "The approach is always my favorite part."

Bianca leaned against the window. "I can see why." They passed sprawling townhouses and people who looked like they'd stepped from *Harper's Bazaar*. She'd seen the magazine once, years ago, and, oh, how she'd stared.

The coach turned a corner and entered Mayfair, the wealthiest district of London. Although she hadn't thought it possible, the houses stood larger on every passing street—palaces and playthings of the nobility.

Bianca tightened her hold on the velvet-lined armrest. She was moments away from meeting the man who had brought her to England. The thought pushed her somewhere between the vapors and a summer concerto, at least what she imagined a summer concerto might sound like.

She placed her other hand against her chest and willed her heart to slow. It disobeyed, as usual. Unrealistic, romantic, sensational, dramatic thing. It reacted to the slightest bit of provocation, like the calmness of the paved New York City street after the jarring of a dirt road. The sight of a pink and orange sunset on the water when she'd boarded the ship. The flap of the sails of the smaller boats, like flags of exultation. And, most of all, as she'd turned and waved to Daddy, his expression that said things far too deep for tears.

The coach stopped, and for a moment, Bianca was sure it would move on. The windows of the house were taller than the governor's mansion in Ohio. The curtains looked like they were made of spun gold.

Bianca opened her mouth to speak, but no words came.

A white-wigged footman opened the coach door and held out his hand.

"Come along, then." Gavina gripped the man's hand and descended. Her skirt rustled behind her, billowing out in the gentle roll of the London wind. Not one snag on the coach stairs. Not one falter in the way she walked. However did she manage to look so elegant with a bustle the size of the state of Virginia?

On the porch, a tile mosaic spread out beneath the door. Two gryphons held a raised *H* between their talons—a blue and white hue. Perhaps they were moonstones, like in Wilkie Collins's novel. The Romans thought moonstones were formed out of moonlight. In Eastern cultures, they were the stone favored for love. Was it a sign?

Bianca glanced up at the footman, expecting him to relate a similar story.

"Is everything all right, Miss?"

Since words seemed elusive, she hoped the grin on her face, which must be completely cockaninny, was an adequate reply.

The concern on his face deepened. He opened the door and bowed.

Music wafted through the marble columns in the entrance. It reminded Bianca of the fiddle, but it was deeper, soothing. The sounds stretched to a domed mural above a velvet-blue night sky. Chandeliers of gold were suspended like stars, reaching from the realms of the faux-painted night, welcoming visitors like heavenly emissaries. The music slowed and strained; it had within it such longing, as if it were pleading.

As if it were saying words a young lady should not hear.

Gavina smiled. "Look there. A cello."

Everywhere Bianca looked she saw the best, the finest, the oldest, the most resplendent. Wetness sprang to her eyes, and the blues and golds blurred. "It's like stepping through a gate I've always known existed. The sights. The sounds . . ."

The footman peered down as if she might need to be leeched and locked in a coal cellar.

"I knew you'd like the house." Gavina winked like they were schoolgirls and placed her hand on Bianca's shoulder. Her white-laced fingerless glove was a definite contrast to Bianca's plain cotton bodice.

A shadow stretched upon the checkered floor. An older man stepped into the entranceway, his long gray hair tied back with a ribbon. "Mrs. Sheighly, how nice to see you again."

"Julius." Gavina bowed her head toward him and then whispered to Bianca. "The butler."

"And this," he drawled out, "must be Miss Bianca Marshal from America. Regretfully, Sir Adrian had a matter of business to attend to, but he left you this." His hand came quickly from behind his back with a letter of crisply folded parchment between his long, white-gloved fingers. Bold, dark strokes on the envelope formed Bianca's name. "Sir Adrian has employed a lady's maid for you. She's an excellent seamstress." He looked Bianca up and down, then cleared his throat. "If you should have any need."

Bianca felt her cheeks redden. "I see Sir Adrian has thought of everything."

"He always does." He slid his gaze to Gavina.

Gavina nodded, as if some unspoken message had passed between them.

Julius raised his chin. "You will find yourself pleasantly occupied while you're here. Boredom at Hartwith House simply isn't allowed. It should be . . . How would you say it in America? As scarce as hen's teeth."

Hearing such a phrase from such a man really was something akin to bliss. Bianca stifled a smile. "Spot on."

Julius looked horrified. Either that, or he realized he was about to smile.

Gavina took Bianca's hand and led her toward the stairs. "I'm sure you'd like to see your room. Shall we?"

Bianca wanted to ask her how she knew her way around Sir Adrian's house so well, but thought better of it. The answer would probably involve some social rule she didn't understand.

As she climbed the stairs, Gavina slid her hand along the wide handrail in back and forth motions like petting a cat. "Don't let that stuffy man intimidate you. He's wound tighter than tree bark, to be sure, but harmless. In the letter you're holding, there is an invitation to dinner. That gives us just enough time to make you magnificent. Not that you aren't already. Most women would put up with a tinker's curse to get thick hair like you've got."

"A tinker's curse?"

"Aye. A gypsy. Don't you have any of those where you're from?"

Bianca laughed. "You know the answer to that. It might be more interesting if we did."

"It might be more interesting if you had three handsome Highlanders living in Portsmouth, Ohio. But then again, we all have our wishes." Gavina stopped before a tall mahogany door. "Here's your room."

Inside, the painted wallpaper held knights and ladies in scenes of courtship. Thick, red curtains draped the bed, hung from a wooden canopy. A plush carpet stretched nearly wall-to-wall. The bright, intricate threads made the design of a garden.

"So, what do you think, Bianca? Can you endure the hardship?"

Bianca walked to the marble fireplace and traced the beak of a carved peacock. "Words can't possibly do this room justice." On the mantel sat a silver box. She lifted the lid.

Beautiful dreamer, out on the sea... Mermaids are chaunting the wild lorelie... Over the streamlet vapors are borne... Waiting to fade at the bright coming morn...

"It seems odd hearing something so American this far from home." Bianca turned so she could see Gavina's face. "It's 'Beautiful Dreamer.' Are you familiar with the composer, Stephen Foster?"

"No. But that melody certainly puts a body away in a dwalm, doesn't it?"

"A dwalm?"

Gavina's eyes held a far-off look. "A dwalm is our way of saying a daydream in Scotland. Tell me about this American composer."

"Well, he was very popular before the War. He used his songs to make people feel compassion for the slaves. One of his songs, 'Bury Me in the Morning, Mother,' will haunt me forever, I think." Bianca paused, pushing away the images that always came when she spoke of the War. "He died in a hotel room when he was only thirty-seven years old." Bianca gently closed the music box. "'Man is born unto trouble, as the sparks fly upward.'"

"You're very good with facts, aren't you?"

"Detail is everything, don't you think? I'm sure detail is everything to God."

Gavina held herself as if she was cold. "You haven't seen your sitting room yet or the bath." She opened the second door. "How'd you like to lose yourself in that slipper tub for an hour or two?"

The bedroom door opened.

"Good morning. My name's Mary." Her black dress, white apron, and white cap were starched to perfection.

She looked Gavina up and down. "You're in proper hands now, Miss Marshal. Proper. Don't worry about a thing."

Gavina returned the woman's scrutiny with a smile. "I'll just go see about some tea."

"You do that." Mary's gaze followed Gavina out.

Bianca furrowed her brow. "Is something wrong?"

"There's a lot wrong with the world, Miss." Mary looked like she wanted to say more but only smiled. "Right now I imagine you'd like to get some of the traveling dirt off." She emptied the contents of a small cloth bag into the bathtub. "Sir Adrian's done nothing but talk about how perfect he wanted everything to be for you."

"Did he?" Bianca couldn't help the smile that came.

"Yes, indeed." Mary turned the handle on the tub. The clean water came out, along with beautiful, glorious steam. Not only did the house have indoor plumbing, but a hot bath on the second floor!

Bianca was captivated by the smell of the bath salts—spicy and sweet at the same time. There was lavender and peppermint. Maybe cloves.

"Now, let's get you out of those clothes."

"Get me out?" Bianca backed up until her legs hit the edge of the bathtub.

Mary ignored the way Bianca held her arms across herself and began unbuttoning Bianca's bodice. She slipped it off.

"I've no wish to offend you, however, I'm quite—" Mary turned her. Bianca curled her fingers around the edge of the bathtub. Surely the woman didn't mean to undress her completely.

The buttons on her blouse came undone.

Bianca stared into the water at the reflection of her stark naked shoulders. Surely now Mary would discreetly walk away.

Hope was a futile thing.

Her blouse slipped lower.

"My goodness, I haven't seen a corset in this style for years." Mary laughed. Like it was actually funny.

Bianca returned the laugh but the sound was high-pitched. "Yes, well." She swallowed, not sure if she should divulge the next part. "It used to be my mother's." Bianca remembered in horror that the corset had a stain. If Mary lowered the blouse any more, she'd see. She felt her face on fire.

They had dressing screens in England, didn't they? Didn't the heroine of *Death by Dagger* use a dressing screen in chapter 2? Recollection dawned as the bath steam hit her full in the face. The book had been written fifty years ago.

The corset loosened. And fell.

Mary tugged Bianca's skirt off, then clutched the hem of Bianca's chemise.

"Great Jehoshaphat's garters." The words escaped Bianca's mouth as she lifted her arms. The chemise disappeared. She crossed her arms again, and it wasn't in the least bit comforting.

"Did you say something, Miss?"

"Nothing." Some things are always similar, even in fine London houses—breezes, being one.

"Shall I remove your necklace, Miss?"

Bianca touched the small, silver locket. "I normally . . ." What should she say? She normally didn't take a bath this deep. Or stand raving naked in front of a stranger. "I always keep it on. No, I'd best take it off. It's very precious to me."

"Very good, Miss." Mary unlatched the locket and laid it on the side table. A long pause ensued. "Miss, you can get into the bath now."

Bianca plunged herself in as deep as she could, spilling water over the side. Bath salts were a wonderful thing. Bath salts meant clouded water.

Mary busied herself with something in a cabinet.

Bianca searched for something to say so Mary wouldn't think she was a complete uncultured fool. "You could make a fortune in America selling this salt concoction."

"Well, I suppose when you experience my shampoo you might think you've gone to the great beyond." She lifted Bianca's hand and scrubbed with a sponge.

Bianca scooted lower, until her chin touched the tip of the water. "I'm sure it's much better than the honeysuckle paste I'm used to."

"My word, do they still use shampoo pastes in Ohio?"

"Is there something better?"

Mary took the pins out of Bianca's hair. "Excuse my forwardness, Miss, but you may need a proper London education."

A proper London education? Perhaps *improper* should be the word of the hour.

Daddy's words came back to her. *Now, Bianca, things are going to be a lot different from what you're used to. Instead of thinking someone is right smart of a ghoul, give them a chance. When in Rome . . .*

Mary poured water over Bianca's hair and massaged something into her scalp that tingled. Bubbles slid down and floated on top of the water, reflecting rainbows and tingling against her skin.

Slowly, Bianca started to relax. She stretched her legs and was amazed to find that her toes didn't reach the edge of the bathtub.

"I'll leave you to soak for a while. There's a lovely dressing gown behind you and some slippers under the chair." Mary opened the door. "Oh, good, the tea's here now. Cook sent some pastries and tarts."

"I don't suppose there's any clotted cream to go along with it?"

"T'wouldn't be tea without it, Miss." Mary winked and then slipped behind the door.

Bianca scooped up a mound of bubbles, slathered them up her arm, and laughed. Perhaps a proper London education wasn't so improper after all.

Bianca scrutinized herself in the tall mirror. Had Mary really transformed her best Ohio dress and made it look as if it belonged in London? As if she belonged in London? Where simple pleats had been, ribbons made clusters of flowers. Velvet trimmed the sleeves. And the neckline! She had considered it lovely before, but now...

Bianca placed her hands upon her waist. "I can't believe what a new corset and a few alterations can do." She actually looked pretty. Not harsh and plain like Mama always said.

Gavina came into the mirror's view and beamed like a schoolmarm who'd just seen her pupil advance. "There are many tricks available to women. I would advise you to learn them all."

"Tricks for what?"

Gavina lowered her gaze and smiled. The clock on the mantel struck seven thirty. "It's almost time." She went to the window and pulled back a corner of the heavy curtain. The glow of gas lanterns shone on the cobblestones.

Bianca turned. "Where's your cloak? We don't want to be late."

Gavina let the curtain fall back into place. "There's something I've been meaning to tell you."

Bianca slid on her gloves. "Yes?"

"I'm not your chaperone for the entire journey."

"What? But why—"

"It's best." Gavina held up her hand. "Your chaperone for the rest of the journey is a fellow contest winner. You'll meet her tonight."

"I don't understand."

"There's not much to understand, really. Sir Adrian paid me to be your chaperone for the Atlantic journey. Now, the woman you'll meet tonight will fulfill the rest of the obligation."

"But, we get along so well."

Gavina reached for Bianca's hands. "Indeed we do." Her smile was a little too perfect, the edges of her lips too high.

"There's so much more I hoped to talk with you about. What if I don't even like this other woman?"

Gavina tsked. "What if the sky suddenly starts raining crumpets? Truly, Bianca. I thought you were braver than this."

"I am." Bianca narrowed her eyes. "It's just that you could have told me sooner."

Gavina took a deep breath. "I would go to dinner tonight, but I have a miserable headache. Besides, I'd just be a third wheel."

"You've been acting very strange today. What am I supposed to make of all this?"

"Make?" Gavina laughed. "You're supposed to enjoy yourself, that's all. And above all else, be yourself. You do want to meet Sir Adrian, don't you? And go to the Holy Land?"

Horses' hooves echoed on the pavement outside.

"Of course."

"Then away with you." Gavina adjusted the ribbon on Bianca's sleeve. "It isn't far, but Sir Adrian wants to keep it a surprise. Just a few minutes, and you'll be there."

Bianca walked to the archway but then turned. "Will you be here when I come back?"

"Absolutely. I wouldn't miss hearing about your first impressions."

Bianca smiled and felt a little better. "Any parting words of wisdom?"

"Yes." Gavina said the word slowly. "'All the world's a stage, and all the men and women merely players.' Bianca, play your part well."

Chapter 3

*D*arkness hung like a forgotten cloak draped carelessly. Folds of it blacker in some places—over the Regent Street shops laid out as a stone crescent moon, in the round open space of Piccadilly Circus, and on Great Russell Street, just before the fog bled in.

Bianca took a deep breath, at least as deep as the whale-boned corset would allow.

The coach sped up, following tall, black spires of iron. The fence blurred, pole after pole softening into shadows.

Bianca flipped open her fan and waved it like smelling salts beneath her nose. "Just don't start sweating," she murmured quietly to herself. She held her arm aloft, closed her eyes, and fanned hard enough to put out a brush fire. What if they thought she was only a country simpleton? She lowered the fan and considered asking the driver to stop. So she could vomit, right there on the street.

"What would Daddy say?" Bianca let his voice slide from her memory, his strong drawl blending with the passing gaslights and the red bricks of the buildings. *"Chickabiddy, if you want to whip your weight in wild cats you've got to have wits like greased lightning and be as smart as a steel trap. Just be yourself and you'll be fine."*

Be yourself. The same thing Gavina had told her.

"I'll be fine." The words didn't ring true. Bianca thought of a favorite Bible passage, *"Trust in the Lord with all thine heart; and lean not unto thine own understanding. In all thy ways acknowledge him, and he shall direct thy paths."*

The driver shouted a muffled command to the horses and the coach slowed. Light cast flickers of orange upon iron lions that guarded a massive gate.

The coach pulled through. Tall, fiery torches flanked the driveway. The flames bit through the fog and taunted, their long orange fingers beckoning. The glow extended to a fountain and, past that, to columns holding a pyramid roof carved with animals and people in robes.

Bianca's breath hazed the coach window. She drew a heart on the glass. The torchlight set the heart on fire.

"I can do this. It begins now."

The footman opened the door. "Welcome to the British Museum, Miss."

Bianca peeked around the brim of his tricornered hat. "This is the British Museum?" She took his hand and stepped down.

"Yes, Miss." He took a step backward and stirred the fog around them, like heaven's soup—a moving carpet made of eternity.

A small laugh escaped her lips. Only a few feet away were treasures from all around the world, things she never thought she'd see. The torch flames leapt higher and licked the night, casting shadows on the massive columns, dancing in and out of crevices and carvings in stone.

They climbed the steps and the footman put his hand on the door. He cracked it just a little. "Sir Adrian will be waiting at the end."

"The end?"

The wind blew the feathers on his hat. "You'll see."

Bianca narrowed her eyes. Did he really mean for her to go by herself? First Gavina, now the footman. Was there some sort of conspiracy to ensure she meet Sir Adrian alone?

She glanced back at the coach. She could simply get back inside and insist that she be taken to the house. That's what she should do. It was proper.

Something she wasn't.

She hadn't come this far to flee. Perhaps *he* waited within—her perfect romantic hero. Just a doorway. Just a little dark. A small brush with impropriety.

And no one would know.

A breeze blew through the courtyard and the torch flames snapped in the wind.

Bianca took a breath, then stepped inside.

More columns were all around her, just like in Sir Adrian's foyer, but on a larger scale. This time they were like the arms of God. And she was just a mote beside them, a speckle of green dress embellished with silk roses. Her footsteps echoed, telling the vastness of the hall.

When her gaze lowered, she saw an Assyrian winged bull. Bianca moved to read the plaque. "Built for King Sargon II, more than twenty-five hundred years ago." She tilted her face upward—to the long stone beard, the cold unseeing eyes. The light from the outside torches still flickered in—a shadow here, a wedge of light there.

And then she saw it.

"The Rosetta Stone." She took a few more steps, then stood with her hand over the writing, hardly believing she was this close. "If only I had more light."

The footman held the edge of the door, but he was letting it slide. The light on the floor shrank; she stood in its orange, outstretched hands.

"Wait." Bianca stepped toward him.

He held the door by one white-gloved finger.

"Where do I go?" The hands of the light folded. Bianca's voice rose. "How do I find them?"

The footman had an odd look on his face—as if he knew a secret, and she was the last person he would tell.

"Wait!"

The light shrank to a needle. The door fell against the frame. Air reached for her, and then it fell, cut off from the outside. Darkness circled her, heavy and thick, pressing itself against her, sliding its fingers against her cheek.

"Hello?" She reached for something—anything. A shadow moved to the left. "Is anyone here? Sir Adrian's at the end of what?" Her pulse was in her ears. She drew back her hand because it trembled.

Darkness noticed.

Bianca swayed, her heart pounding. She squinted and took a few steps. A little light shone to the right. She felt for the wall and exhaled when smooth, cold stone met her palm. Around the corner, more light shone. A path of candles had been laid out upon the floor. Rows of small flames danced in the dark, curving around display cases and leading up the stairs ahead. Hundreds of glass globes sparkled, melding into one long river of light—a molten invitation.

When she had reached the top of the stairs, the deep tones of a man's voice wafted from a faraway room. Laughter followed and the soft notes of a harp.

A smile curved her lips and a warm glow surged though her body. Finally, life was here and now. Not across the cornfields where she'd walked through the stalks and imagined, feeling the dry leaves crumble in her hand. Bianca gathered the side of her skirt and walked on.

In the next corridor, Greek statues stood as if they'd been frozen by Medusa. The marble shone luminescent in the flicker of the candles. Each strand of hair was meticulously carved, every indentation accented. The hems of the women's robes fell in perfect folds around their naked ankles.

Bianca smiled at the sight. Mama would be completely scandalized.

Further on, the smell of old leather and pages drew her. With each step, the scent fell around her as summer rain falls—soft and warm, comforting like a friend. Thousands of books lined the balcony, the lower shelves, and the desks.

Bianca closed her eyes and turned her face into the perfume of wisdom. She twirled, like she was dancing. "I could spend my entire life in here."

"I've often thought that exact same thing."

"Who's there?" Bianca stopped and scanned the darkness just beyond the light.

"Forgive me." The figure of a man moved across the room. Bianca couldn't see his face, but his high, white collar glowed from the light of the candle. "Allow me to introduce myself. Paul Emerson, a fellow contest winner."

"Oh." Relief floated her shoulders down. "I see." But she couldn't see anything. She smiled into the darkness and felt like a fool. He was only a shadow, walking by the display cases, just out of the reach of the light.

"Might I inquire if you are Miss Bianca Marshal, from America?" His voice was smooth and cultured, thick with tones that bordered on velvet.

"I am."

His footsteps echoed across the marble floor, measured and precise; they came around the bookshelves, washing over her. "Welcome to England, Miss Marshal. What a delight that our journey begins tonight."

She'd be delighted if his face matched his voice. Bianca bit back another smile. Two cockaninny smiles in one day would just be too excessive.

The shape of him materialized. He was tall. Excellent. After all, what romantic hero was ever short? Bianca pretended to care about the last button on her glove. "I can't tell you how much I've longed to see your country—and the Holy Land as well."

"You pay us British citizens a very high compliment. I hope you won't be disappointed." The candlelight flickered, stretching toward him. The midnight black of his evening clothes separated from the dark.

Bianca dropped her gaze to the candles. That's what demure young ladies did, wasn't it?

"And the Holy Land . . . We'll definitely have something to write home about, I am sure." He reached the candles in front of her.

Bianca lifted her gaze slowly to his cravat, his chin. She felt her cheeks flood with heat. His face was smooth and strong, and his eyes—deep green. To say that he was handsome was like saying the sun had a little bit of shine. "How do you do?" The words stumbled out, regardless of the fact that they'd already been through a short conversation. She extended her hand clumsily.

Mr. Emerson took her hand and bowed over it. "Enchanted, I am sure." He lingered there, looking into her eyes. "This is the King's Library, dedicated in 1857. You were admiring it, I believe, before I was so impertinent as to startle you."

"Yes. I confess I'm not used to such . . ." She swept her gaze over his face again. "Possibilities."

He stood and pulled his hand away. "I take it you are fond of books?"

"I am more than fond of books, Mr. Emerson."

His scrutiny became more acute. "Have you been to the Reading Room yet? It's much larger."

"No. There are more books in the Reading Room?"

"Tons." The word dropped tantalizingly from his lips, like something forbidden. He stepped to the side and peered into the dark. "At the moment, we're expected in the Egyptian Gallery. Your chaperone is not with you?"

Bianca cringed. "She had a horrible headache. The truth is, she was only supposed to accompany me to England, and not to the Holy Land."

"I don't understand."

Neither did she. Bianca took a deep breath. "Apparently, my new chaperone is a fellow contest winner. I'm supposed to meet her tonight." She closed her eyes, waiting for the rebuke that would surely come.

"Well, then." His voice was gentle. "I would be pleased to escort you to her."

"You would?"

"Of course." He clasped his hands behind his back. "The candle path is the scenic route. However, there is a shorter way."

"I don't mind." A radiant anticipation echoed somewhere around the region of her heart. "That is, if you don't mind. I'd like to see everything I can."

"Very well."

They passed marble busts of gentlemen from centuries past, their long curls and intellectual stares amplified in the light of the candles.

When she looked back to Mr. Emerson, he was watching her. He quickly turned his scrutiny into a smile. "Do you enjoy history, Miss Marshal?"

"Very much."

He seemed to be thinking. The muscles at his jaw tensed and then relaxed.

Her heartbeat picked up its pace. She couldn't help but wonder if he might fit her romantic hero list. She searched for something useful to say, anything of significance. "I've read that your city has quite a lot of fog. I admit, I thought the author was exaggerating."

"I've only fallen into the river twice, so I count myself lucky."

Bianca's laugh echoed in the vast darkness.

"I'm not joking." His expression grew serious, but just as quickly his lips turned up in a smile. "I'm sorry. I couldn't resist. We're used to the fog, I suppose." Mr. Emerson led her up a staircase. "And the rain . . .

The only thing that can cut our gloominess is a good, strong cup of tea. So, drink plenty, or you shall be in danger of falling into an irreversible depression. Or perhaps the river."

Bianca bit back another smile. "I did have the opportunity to sample your good, strong tea earlier."

"And did it meet with your approval?"

Bianca studied the strong curve of his jaw and the way his hair curled slightly over his ears. She mentally checked off a few of her requirements for a soul mate—devastatingly handsome, slightly wild look in his eyes, humorous, a foreigner. "Everything has exceeded my expectations."

"Excellent." Mr. Emerson turned his face toward the windows. "The museum does have to close sometimes because of the fog. It's most inconvenient."

So, he was definitely familiar with the museum. A man who loved history was very hard to find. "I live very close to the Ohio River, in Portsmouth, Ohio."

"If memory serves me, Ohio is an Iroquois Indian name meaning 'good river.'"

"Does it?" She had never heard that information. Obviously Mr. Emerson was very learned.

A draft wafted through the next corridor. It touched the candle flames and shifted them, casting shadows in the opposite direction.

Mr. Emerson lowered his head, as if he were imparting a secret. "I must confess that these candles make me a little nervous. The director almost had an apoplexy when Sir Adrian told him what he wanted to do. Sir Adrian, however, can be very persuasive to say the least. In the end, it was the large donation that changed the director's mind." He held his hand out toward a display case of Roman cameos. "Luckily for Emperor Augustus, the director has posted guards with water buckets in each room."

Bianca searched the shadows. "I thought I was alone before you came."

"Look just there," Mr. Emerson whispered.

Bianca saw the shadow of a man standing in a corner. He did indeed have a water bucket beside him. "Did Sir Adrian tell you his conversation with the director?"

"No." Mr. Emerson looked slightly embarrassed. Or humble. Bianca couldn't tell which. "I am the museum's historian and whatever else they happen to need at any particular moment."

Bianca glanced up at him and knew that keeping her cockaninny grins to just one a day was absolutely impossible. She mentally checked off "brilliant" from her list as well.

They entered a great hollow hall. Their footsteps echoed like shots in the dark.

"I was just coming back from my office when I met you. Sir Adrian asked to see something from my personal collection." He stopped and withdrew a small, blue cloth from his jacket. "I acquired it last year on a dig in Egypt." His gaze softened as he looked at the hidden object in his hands. "We have a few minutes before dinner. Would you like to be the first one to see it?"

"Does the Queen like tea?"

It looked as if he bit the inside of his cheek to keep from laughing. "I take it that's an American way of saying *yes.*"

"Yes," she repeated, astounded at her lack of poise.

He unwrapped the blue cloth and revealed a little hawk made of gold. "This dates before the New Kingdom in Egypt when bellows were invented."

"It's so beautiful." Bianca moved closer to his outstretched, gloved hand. "The detail on the feathers is exquisite. I've never seen anything from Egypt before." She looked up, gratefulness overtaking her. "This is an extreme honor. You have no idea."

"Would you like to hold it?" Mischief seeped into his eyes. "Normally I wouldn't allow it, but I think you can be trusted."

"Please." Wonder and awe swirled in the dark around her.

Mr. Emerson watched her face as he lowered the hawk onto her glove. His voice became hushed and reverent. "You are perhaps only the third person who has held it in over three thousand years."

The green of Mr. Emerson's eyes had taken on an excitement that drew her in even more.

"I wonder whose hands held the hawk before yours and mine?" He stepped closer and seemed to be looking at the bird for the first time. "A priest? A pharaoh? A princess? What secrets would it reveal if it could speak to us now? In all the millennia it was locked in that dark tomb, what disclosures from the spirit world did it hear? What whispers came from the hieroglyphics painted on the quartz stone walls?"

Candlelight on a three-thousand-year-old artifact was certainly a sight to behold. Candlelight in the eyes of a man who just happened to be a historian, and distractingly handsome... well. "You do paint a very vivid picture, Mr. Emerson. You almost make me feel the hot sand and smell the sweet scent of lotus flowers." She handed the artifact back to him, willing herself not to stare into his eyes like a fool. "Do you write your charming rhetoric in articles for the museum?"

"Sometimes. Although I don't think my prose has ever been called *charming* before. A critic of my last book said the word *exhausting*, I believe." He held his hand out to the candle path. "Shall we?"

Their walking was slower than before.

"Your last book? May I ask the subject?"

"The Italian Renaissance."

She struggled to recall a fact that might please him. It had been so long since she'd read about the Renaissance. "You no doubt touched upon Petrarch, the father of humanism."

"How could I not? He alone took up one hundred pages. I explored the lives of Castiglione and Machiavelli in the latter section, right after architecture such as the Duomo."

The room was far too hot. Apparently the English didn't believe in ventilation. "I'd love to read it."

"Then I will make sure you have a copy before you leave tonight."

Bianca allowed herself the liberty of looking directly into his eyes. She was frightened, suddenly, but forced herself not to glance away. "I'll look forward to it."

"You're very kind." Mr. Emerson turned into another corridor. "Here is Sir Hans Sloane's collection of seventy-one thousand objects that formed the museum in 1753." His gaze shifted to the locket at her throat, then back to her eyes. "The Egyptian Room. It's just this way."

Bianca took a quick look at his left hand as he slid it along the staircase rail. If only he'd take off his glove, she could end this madness. Not knowing if he was married was causing her mind to fray.

He opened a large door, and they stepped outside into a courtyard. The buildings of the museum surrounded them, the stars a ceiling of ink black-blue. The candle path curved around a circular building, and the flames moved gently in the wind.

"The Reading Room I told you about earlier."

"Oh." Moonlight smeared the many windows.

"Was—"

"Have—" She held up her hand. "I'm sorry."

"No, please. I was only going to ask you if your Atlantic crossing was pleasant."

"Yes. It was my first time on a ship." She looked at the ground, realizing how unrefined she must sound. The smell of his shaving soap—sandalwood and citrus—was driving her to distraction. "And I was going to ask if you've always been interested in Egyptology."

"Yes, I have."

"What fascinates you most about the Egyptians?" Bianca clenched her fan. She must be sweating, but if she used it he'd know.

Mr. Emerson blew out his breath as if trying to decide. He opened the next door, bringing them back inside. "Have you heard of Professor Piazzi Smyth? He's the Astronomer Royal for Scotland."

"No." Bianca shook her head and a curl came loose. The pin tinged on the floor.

"Please, allow me." Mr. Emerson knelt and looked from stretching shadow to candlelight. He pulled on the edges of his right glove, took it off, and then reached for the pin. He stood.

He was mere inches away. And, oh, what a difference that made. Like falling into the deep end of the sea.

Bianca moved closer, just a step. The candlelight shone on his hair and turned it the color of burnished mahogany. She looked into his eyes and could barely breathe.

"Your hairpin," he whispered. He placed it in her hand without touching her.

Bianca stepped back, embarrassed, and slid the pin into her hair. "My pins never want to stay in . . . My hair's much too thick." She cringed again. "Were you asking me a question?"

"I was wondering if you'd heard of Professor Piazzi Smyth." He spoke the words like she was indeed a foreigner and translation was needed.

"No." Bianca raised her hand to her temple and took a deep breath.

Mr. Emerson gestured to the next room. "You asked what fascinates me most about the Egyptians. To answer that, allow me to tell you about Professor Smyth." He was purposely holding himself away from her, not standing as close as before. "About ten years ago he made an astounding discovery—that the Great Pyramid was located on the thirtieth degree of north latitude, and that its four triangular sides faced exactly the four points of the compass."

Bianca keenly felt that she had offended him. What had she been thinking, standing so close? "Did he do this by exterior measurements?"

"Yes. And interior." His scrutiny of her was acute. "Smyth also discovered that when the Great Pyramid was built—around 3500 BC—the descending passage pointed to the star Alpha Draconis, the chief star in the constellation of the dragon." A faraway look crossed his face. "Excuse me." Mr. Emerson reached into his frock coat. He withdrew a small leather journal and flipped it open to where a ribbon held a page. "*Thuban* in Arabic . . ."

He wrote a long sentence in another language. "Forgive me. *Draconis* means dragon, which is translated *thuban* in Arabic. I've been working on this subject recently, as you can see." He turned the journal toward her. "This shows the constellation Orion. The three pyramids together map out an exact duplicate of it here on earth."

"How is that possible?" Bianca stepped closer again and couldn't help herself; she ran the tip of her finger along the drawing.

"That's quite a good question, Miss Marshal. I'd like to know the answer myself."

"From the looks of this page, I think you soon might find out." For a moment she forgot his opinion of her, whatever that might be, and let the words draw her in. "May I?"

"Of course." Mr. Emerson handed her the journal, seemingly glad to have a barrier between them. "But come into the light over here. I think we're in danger of going blind where we stand."

Bianca followed him to an archway where long-legged cranes were painted, their beaks holding fish. Candles were stacked like a shrine.

He slid his hands into his pockets. "You asked what intrigued me about Egyptology. The questions do, and all the secrets yet to be discovered. All history is like that, don't you think?"

"I agree." Bianca put her finger under the next page, but lifted her gaze for his permission.

He nodded his consent.

More drawings and multiple languages scattered the page. "Daddy and I often talk for hours about the mysteries of history." She tried to count the languages, but stopped at seven. "It's strange to find something so familiar this far from home." A candle hissed and then extinguished. "What do you make of the Sphinx, Mr. Emerson? I've always thought there must be some great mystery there."

"You're very clever," he said slowly. He closed the distance between them and turned the journal back two pages. There were drawings of the Sphinx from every angle—the head, the tail, the paws. Random notes were scribbled at different slants—*Faces due east. Stares straight into the sun on day of spring equinox. Dedicated to the constellation Leo?* And there, down by the drawing of raindrops, he'd written in large letters— *SHOWS CLEAR LINES OF GREAT WATER EROSION.*

The strange music began again. Bianca looked up, jarred from reading and taken out of the ancient world. "I could spend a lot of time reading this."

Unease crossed his face, but just as quickly he pushed it away. Mr. Emerson lifted the journal from her hands and closed it. "At least you didn't say it read like a *McGuffy Reader* . . . The Sphinx is on the sand. The sand is hot. The Sphinx is old. Good-bye, Sphinx, good-bye."

Bianca's laugh sounded louder than she'd intended. "Quite the opposite. I'm beginning to wonder if you're capable of dull subjects."

Mr. Emerson slid his journal, and all its secrets, back into the silk of his elegant frock coat. His gaze was as erratic as a summer storm.

"What is it?" Bianca asked.

When he spoke, the velvet tones had returned. "Nothing of consequence . . . I was only thinking that I shall enjoy this journey . . . very much."

Chapter 4

*A*lthough Mr. Emerson had said it with a gentlemanly sort of deportment, there was something uncertain behind the words. Something unspoken.

Something Bianca desperately wanted to know.

She looked past the crisp fold of his collar to the hieroglyphics on the archway. She could feel his gaze upon her; it was conflicted warmth—like shivering in summer rain. Bianca parted her lips to speak, wanting to ask him if he was fond of Shakespeare, or, more importantly, if he was a Christian. Her smile brushed the questions away. "The Egyptian Gallery . . . It must be through here."

"Did Amun-Ra give it away?" He lifted his eyes to the Egyptian statue looming behind her that she hadn't seen.

She tried not to cringe for the umpteenth time. Or laugh like she was fit for Bedlam.

She wasn't successful.

"Do all the young ladies in southern Ohio blush as much as you do?"

"No. It's a talent I've had to cultivate over the years."

Mr. Emerson's gaze softened and indiscernible thoughts crossed his features—the lifting of the corner of his lips, concentration on his brow. His eyes took on a shade of darker green, magnified in the glow of the candles. "Time well spent."

The sound of footsteps echoed down from the corridor beyond.

"That must be someone from our party coming." Mr. Emerson inclined his head toward the doorway. "We should go."

A biting draft flowed past the hieroglyphics.

The candle flames shrank like minions and bowed against the dark. Shadows shifted. The shape of a man materialized from the outer darkness beyond the Egyptian reliefs. "Ah, here you are." His voice held the commanding tones of emperors and kings. His hair was the uncommon shade of red and his eyes, sapphire blue. Over his evening clothes, the man wore a long velvet robe the color of blood. He held a silver walking cane and ran his finger lightly over the handle, an elaborate ram with jeweled eyes.

"Sir Adrian, may I present Miss Bianca Marshal. I had the pleasure of meeting her in the King's Library. We were just on our way back when we stopped for . . ." Mr. Emerson quickly glanced at Bianca and then the hieroglyphics. "A bit of admiration."

Sir Adrian assessed them both and then stepped forward. "Miss Marshal, how long I have waited for this moment." He reached into the air, moved his fingers, and produced a white rose from nothing. He handed it to her. "For new beginnings. How far you've come, and how much farther we all still have to go."

Bianca's mouth gaped. "Thank you." The rose was perfection, not one leaf bent or petal damaged.

He held out his hand. "May I steal her from you, Mr. Emerson? I must admit that I revel in the idea of getting to know our American guest by discussing pith and moment . . ." His gaze swept over her. "And whatever else happens to come along."

Bianca glanced over her shoulder.

Mr. Emerson turned a scowl into a smile. Just barely.

Sir Adrian led her into the corridor. "I trust you were treated well at my home."

"Yes, thank you."

"Excellent. I have a pseudo tour of Egypt planned for us all tonight." Sir Adrian lowered his voice so only she could hear. "I hope that pleases you."

Even if he'd announced they'd be eating turkey gizzards she would've been pleased. She decided to spare him from that information. "This is the greatest experience of my life. I'm so grateful you chose me."

"The choice wasn't hard at all."

They came to a reconstructed temple flanked by more candles. The walls were almost as high as the museum ceiling. Sir Adrian surveyed the large, smooth stones. "I had the temple made for the purposes of our little soiree. Are you quite ready to pass from the darkness into the light?" He lifted one of the candles and held it before them. The glow stretched into the black void of the entrance.

"Lead away." Bianca remembered the words from his congratulatory letter. "I'm ready to leave mediocrity behind."

Recognition dawned in his blue eyes. He smiled.

And then he led her into the darkness.

The passageway was narrow, a maze of rights and lefts. More hieroglyphics were painted on the walls—scenes of death and life—struggles for the eternal.

Bianca turned again and could barely discern the outline of Mr. Emerson.

Sir Adrian noticed her pause. "It's very fortunate for us that you happen to be home this time of year, Mr. Emerson." He lowered his voice and leaned toward Bianca. "Can't keep the man in England, I've heard. Always something new to bring back from some remote corner of the world. Had countless adventures, that one."

The passageway opened up to a great expanse, much larger than the earlier corridors. Egyptian statues lined every wall. Glass cases framed the room.

"Great Jehoshaphat!" The words from home came tumbling out. Never, never, never did she think she'd be standing in such a room as this—a real Egyptian Gallery. The ages poured from every artifact, every papyrus on the wall, every case full of scarabs made from jasper, amethyst, and carnelian. Her imagination soared and she covered her mouth with her hand to keep from gasping. Moses himself could have worn the ring directly in front of her when he was a prince of Egypt. He could have run his fingers over the hieroglyphic tablet when he was learning to read as a boy.

Sir Adrian seemed pleased by her reaction. He gestured to a gargantuan stone face to the right. "You see there Ramesses II. Isn't he magnificent?" They all moved to stand beneath the statue. "Such a colossus. Observe that crack just there. I'd say he took a nasty fall from the look of his headdress."

Mr. Emerson moved to stand beside Bianca. "He's also known as the Younger Memnon. The statue was found in 1816 at the King's Mortuary Temple at Thebes. The snake on the head cloth was thought to spit fire at his enemies."

Bianca studied the intensity in Mr. Emerson's eyes. Even though he was probably familiar with every galley, every artifact, he still seemed profoundly affected.

They stood in silence, all three looking up at a face thousands of years removed. The music grew in volume—sounds of Egypt, Bianca supposed. In the corner, four dark-skinned men wore long, white robes. Their eyes were lined with kohl. They played tambourines and drums, and other instruments she couldn't name. The sound was mysterious and strange, as if falling through time.

"This statue was the first piece of Egyptian sculpture to be recognized as a work of art by connoisseurs." Mr. Emerson's voice was shrouded in mystery, as if every detail was a key that would unlock the pharaoh's secrets. "Before that, the connoisseurs made judgments by the standards of ancient Greek art."

Sir Adrian turned to face them. "I, for one, have never cared much for what connoisseurs say." His expression was veiled and noble, like the face of Ramesses II. "Finding out things on one's own is half the fun."

The music rose and fell in a frenzy. Bianca opened her fan and forced herself to concentrate. Thoughts began to blur. The corset laces felt entirely too tight. "I think that's the wisest course of action, Sir Adrian. Taking other people's opinions as gospel can only lead to ruin."

"Very well put." Sir Adrian placed her hand on his arm and led her away from the statue. They crossed the polished floor, weaving in and out of candlelight.

Bianca gripped Sir Adrian's arm tighter. The night had not even begun and already she was feeling faint. She breathed, forcing her ribs to expand. The corset protested. Vehemently.

"Speaking of gospel… Did you know, Emerson, judging from her essay, our Miss Marshal's quite the believer in the old-time religion, not at all a scientific or modern approach." His smile didn't quite reach his eyes. "Which is why our trip to the Holy Land will be that much more of an experience for her, I am sure."

"Yes—" Bianca's shoe caught on the hem of her dress. Her hand slipped from Sir Adrian's arm.

"Gad!" Sir Adrian reached for her, but missed.

Mr. Emerson's shoes skidded on the floor.

The display cases blurred, as did the Egyptian statues. Her skirt twisted around her legs.

Just before she hit the marble floor, an arm was around her back.

Bianca looked up and saw nothing but Mr. Emerson's face above her. Her heart beat like a wild thing, a creature set loose from its cage.

Mr. Emerson's eyes were full of relief. "Are you all right?"

"I'm . . . just a bit clumsy sometimes."

Sir Adrian reached for her hand and helped her stand. "My dear, you almost gave me an apoplexy. Do take care. You're very valuable to me. I won't have you killing yourself before our journey's even begun." He consulted the heavy, gold pocket watch at his side. "The other two contest winners are running late. I'll go and see if I can apprehend them." His dark blue eyes locked onto Mr. Emerson. "Will you watch after her for a moment?" Just before he reached the rear doorway, he turned and smiled. "I assume you to be a man of honor. And that you can be trusted alone with a lady." His blood-red robe fanned out, the gold edging sliding into the darkness behind him.

Bianca moved to withdraw her hand from Mr. Emerson's. Their fingertips lingered, and then fell away.

"Shall we go to the table?"

Bianca nodded, shame flooding her like a gorge.

Mr. Emerson pulled out an elaborate chair draped with the skin of a leopard. He reached for the water pitcher, filled her glass, then sat down.

The music eased into soft tones.

The cold drink of water helped the squeezing around her waist, but she found that she wanted to cry. She'd wanted to act with poise and deportment. Instead, she'd soundly passed herself off as a Henny Penny. "I'm so embarrassed."

"Please, don't be. In fact, this gives me the opportunity to tell you something." Mr. Emerson reached for the bottom of his right glove and took it off.

"Yes?" Bianca stared at his left hand.

"Before you fell, Sir Adrian mentioned that you're a Christian." He reached for the bottom of his left glove.

"Yes. I am." She was sure he would ridicule her now, sure that to work in a place such as the British Museum he must be a man of science with no room for faith.

"I also share your belief." Mr. Emerson's bare wrist came into view. The glove slid over the bottom of his palm. "The Gospel of Jesus Christ is very dear to me. Two years ago, I became a Christian. Not just in lip service, and not in the general sort of a way that the English like to consider themselves to be."

His removed his thumb from the white glove. His forefinger. "Actually, it was the American evangelist, D. L. Moody, who brought everything about. He spoke at Her Majesty's Opera House. His sermon that night changed my perceptions."

The words spun themselves like fine gossamer. They settled somewhere near the region of her heart. "How wonderful," she said before she smiled.

Bianca allowed her gaze to falter. To the flower arrangements. The stuffed birds on the high platter. The gold-edged plates.

Then she let her gaze slide back to his left hand.

And the ring finger that was blessedly bare.

Chapter 5

*T*he pluck of the harp came suddenly, shuddering through the air like the ache of something born. The atmosphere in the Egyptian Gallery floated and fell, surging with hopes that sang though her heart by memory. Thoughts came to Bianca, a million possibilities that she saw in Mr. Emerson's deep green eyes. He took the time to study her as well, and that knowledge brought a shiver akin to being wrapped in hot, white light. The room faded away, the artifacts and musicians gone. Looking at his gentle smile was like breathing deep after lacking air too long, plunging through the surface of what had been into what could be.

Mr. Emerson leaned toward her. Words fell from his lips, soft and low. "Most came to the opera house that night out of curiosity. I admit that I was one. Advertisements had been posted around London for months but I hardly paid them any mind. After a particularly . . . difficult time, a particularly difficult day, I decided to walk home instead of taking a coach."

"Yes?" Bianca forced herself to stay back against her chair. She so wanted to lean in as he had done. "Please, do go on." Every nuance and gesture was like a page turned, something revealed about him—the way he held his hands in his lap told her he was patient. The way he looked her in the eyes as he curved his lips around his words, that indicated he was honest.

"The wind here can be temperamental at times, such was this day. A paper for the revival meeting was blown against me. I stood on the corner. Left was the direction of the opera house, straight ahead was my home." His intense gaze strayed to the floor and a shadow crossed his face. Perhaps he was thinking of what would have happened to him if he had walked on. "Before that night, I am ashamed to say that I had never given much thought to the condition of my soul. I thought religion was enough for salvation—that if I did my duty and went to church, abode by the rules of morality . . ." His eyes closed as if the words were hard. He took a deep breath. "I thought on many things differently than what I do now."

"So did I." Bianca's words surprised her, but he looked as if he'd been embarrassed and she wanted to alleviate that pain. "Daddy—My father read me stories from the Bible for as long as I can remember. But it wasn't until later that I discovered the power in the words. Before the awful war in our states, I used to go down by the creek and read the Bible for myself. As I read, it was like I wasn't alone." Her smile grew at Mr. Emerson's look of excitement. "God sat beside me on that bank, whispering things into my soul. And when I got to the Gospel of John, it was like Jesus was standing there waiting with an outstretched hand."

Bianca looked away, aware now that the musicians were still in the corner. They still played their beautiful music, and how she had forgotten about them, she had no idea. Perhaps she should not have shared such intimate things with Mr. Emerson. Her cheeks reddened once again and she wanted to get up and walk away. What must he think of her talking about creeks and God talking?

"Exactly so." The rich tone of his voice was like the sweetest comfort—a blanket that had been hanging by a fire to ward off the cold, the rays of the sun after a long, lonesome winter. "I felt that too." He disarmed her with his smile. "Except perhaps in my situation it was somewhat terrifying. The entire opera house was filled with the best of London. And here was this American preacher saying it was time for the invitation, whatever that was. We had no idea. One organist began to play, and then hymn books were passed around."

Bianca did lean forward then. "What did you sing?"

Mr. Emerson took a drink from his water glass. "'Come ye sinners poor and needy, weak and wounded, sick and sore. Jesus ready stands to save you, full of pity, love and power.'" He spoke the words like the purest, deepest thing. "'I will arise and go to Jesus, He will embrace me in His arms. In the arms of my dear Savior, O there are ten thousand charms.'" He paused and refilled her water glass. "I'm sorry I don't remember the rest. At that point I left my seat to go forward. I knelt amongst the gold leaf and red velvet curtains and cried out to God. I asked for forgiveness and confessed my belief in Him. When I rose, I was quite changed, Miss Marshal."

Bianca nodded slowly. If she had thought Mr. Emerson to be a perfect romantic hero before, now he shone beyond reason. He had looks that would make a woman weak—like Mr. Willoughby of *Sense and Sensibility*—but his words rang as true as Colonel Brandon.

Mr. Emerson drew his eyebrows together. "Is something amiss?"

"Not at all." Her voice sounded wispy. "I'm sorry . . . Perhaps I'm not quite recovered from the fall." She waved her hand in the direction of where she had fallen, trying to clear her head.

An odd man stepped out of the temple passageway. He wore a worn-out suit and his beard was much too long. Dark circles rimmed his eyes. He scanned the room and then jerked back every few steps as if he could see what lay beyond the shadows—things of dust and decay, malevolent phantoms perhaps.

Bianca narrowed her eyes. "That must be the third contest winner."

"I expect so." Mr. Emerson stood, then hesitated. He, too, seemed to be studying the man's strange way of walking—pulling back and pressing forward. The man paused at a display case holding ancient sandals made of gold. Mr. Emerson stepped forward. "You must be Mr. Tabor, Sir. From Boston, I believe."

"Indeed I am." He looped his thumb under the lapel of his faded formal coat. "Joshua Udolphus Tabor." He flung the words together—jabbing and punching the syllables. Some he didn't bother with at all.

Bianca stood and walked toward them, the sound of her shoes blending with the music.

Mr. Emerson introduced himself, mentioned his position at the museum, and explained Sir Adrian's whereabouts.

"And who is this delightful young thing?" Mr. Tabor stepped around Mr. Emerson.

Mr. Emerson raised an eyebrow. "You have the honor of addressing Miss Bianca Marshal. Also an American."

"An American!" Mr. Tabor shook her hand like he might wrench it off. "What a happy little party we'll be. It is *Miss* Marshal, isn't it?"

"Yes." Bianca pulled her hand from his grasp.

"That's wonderful. Quite wonderful." Mr. Tabor spread his arms wide. "And here we are. Gee whiz. What a place!" He put his finger to his thin lips. His eyes were so light blue they looked gray. "Your accent... You're not quite from the South, but..."

"Southern Ohio."

"Ohio?" He took a breath. "For a minute there, I thought you might be from Kentucky."

"No." Bianca smiled out of courtesy she didn't feel. "But we can see Kentucky from across the Ohio River."

Mr. Tabor nodded slowly, as if a thought was suspended in his mind. A thin sheen of sweat seeped along his hairline. He withdrew a handkerchief and wiped his brow. "It's been a long day."

"Please," Mr. Emerson said, gesturing to the table. There was wariness in his eyes. Once again he pulled out Bianca's chair. "Sir Adrian should be along directly."

Mr. Tabor ran his palms along the tablecloth. He followed the lines of it down, on either side of his legs. "Oh, yes, this is fine." He straightened his fork. He flicked the tip of his water glass.

Bianca folded her hands in her lap, hoping Mr. Emerson would start some semblance of conversation.

Mr. Tabor picked a piece of lint off his jacket.

The tambourine shook, ending another song.

"Very fine, indeed. But not quite the caliber of the Union Oyster House." Mr. Tabor straightened his napkin. He unfolded it. He folded it back again. "I don't suppose we'll be having chowder tonight?"

Mr. Emerson stared at the cloth. "I have no idea."

Bianca leaned forward, trying to discern the meaning of "chow-dah." "May I ask what your occupation is in Boston?"

Mr. Tabor shook out the napkin and placed it on his lap. He folded the corner. "I operate a horsecar. The finest there is."

"We call them trams here." Mr. Emerson still scrutinized the napkin. "In some parts of our city, steam is replacing the horses."

"Steam?" Mr. Tabor laughed and reached for his water goblet. "You Brits are nothing if not ambitious."

"What do you mean?" Bianca asked, not liking Mr. Tabor's tone.

Mr. Tabor looped his arm over the back of his chair. "Oh, I don't know . . ." His gaze slid to the musicians. He frowned at their tanned, oiled skin, their shaven hair. "The English seem very intent upon blending people. Covering the entire world with their empire." He tapped the side of his nose. "We had best take care." He laughed again, his beard parting into a wide, toothy guffaw.

"Excuse me?" Heat raced to Bianca's cheeks. "We are guests, Sir, of an Englishman. May I remind you that you are sitting next to one now?"

"So I am." He smiled as if they were talking about the proper way to prepare Indian pudding. *Not too much molasses, dear. And make sure you butter the dish.*

Mr. Emerson tapped the table with his finger, slowly, as if trying to decide on what to say. "I can assure you, Mr. Tabor, you are quite safe from any artifice here." His voice dripped with restraint. "You will find no secret plotting beyond which spices to use in the food."

Bianca lifted her fan. Tension stretched in the air like a tight, shaking cord. She searched her memory for a snippet from *The Ladies' Book of Etiquette*. Perhaps the chapter on how to diffuse an argument . . .

"I'm sure you're right," Mr. Tabor said. "I meant no offense. You'll have to forgive this Bostonian. I feel a bit out of place in your city." He raised his gaze, taking in the shadows against the ceiling. "Since you're a historian, tell me . . . What do you think of my city's history?"

Bianca exhaled, a little too loudly. Even though it happened a hundred years ago, surely the man was not so lacking in social grace that he would discuss the history of Boston with an Englishman.

"Boston has a brave and glorious history. It is very much a part of your esteemed heritage."

Mr. Tabor smirked.

Mr. Emerson placed his forearm on the table. "I'm sorry. Is that not what you expected me to say?"

Bianca closed her eyes. Chapter 8 from the book of etiquette came to mind. *"When strife ensues, distract gentlemen with a handy fact."* "Did you know that the most remarkable echo in the world is at the Castle Simonetta, two miles from Milan? It repeats the echo of a pistol shot sixty times."

As if cued, the music stopped.

Mr. Tabor covered his mouth with his hand and laughed.

Bianca waved her fan faster, sure they were going to come to blows. She looked at the doorway where Sir Adrian had disappeared, then back to Mr. Emerson. He looked like he'd tasted something rotten. With a drizzle of spoiled milk.

Mr. Tabor pulled a lily out of the flower arrangement, then pushed it back in. "Oh, you're top rail, Mr. Emerson. First class, indeed. What a shame you aren't wearing red this evening."

Bianca lowered her fan. A redcoat. Surely she'd heard him wrong. She was delusional. Imagining conversations. This corset really was laced too tight and affecting her brain.

Mr. Emerson turned to Bianca, disbelief clearly written on his features.

Only one phrase came to mind for cases such as this. *Great Jehoshaphat's britches.*

"And here we all are." Sir Adrian stepped from the corridor and into the room.

Bianca caught his eye and inclined her head toward Mr. Tabor. Surely he would do something to ease the tension.

Sir Adrian only smiled and strolled leisurely forward, a beautiful woman holding his arm.

Apparently, Bianca's chaperone.

Bianca took a second look. The woman was a little older than she, but not by much. The woman's black hair was pinned to perfection, violets woven into it like a coronet. One long curl swooned over her shoulder. She held herself like a queen, chin tipped up, dark, sultry eyes looking bored and amused all at the same time. She was perfect.

And the woman knew it.

Bianca suddenly felt very foolish. Like a child who had been caught dressing up in her mother's best clothes, stumbling in shoes too big.

Mr. Emerson had gone pale. He gripped the edge of the table. His stare was fixed.

Bianca felt the blood drain from her face. The room felt hot and cold at the same time.

Clearly, Mr. Emerson was attracted to this woman.

Bianca's throat felt tight, her breathing too shallow.

The woman locked eyes with Mr. Emerson. Her smile was bold; her lips all pout and suggestion.

"Allow me to present our last contest winner." Sir Adrian led the woman to the table. Even he took her in with his eyes, tilting his head in admiration. "Mrs. Madeline Greene."

The woman was married. Bianca laughed in relief, but covered it up as a cough.

"Widowed last year, poor dear."

Bianca frowned. Shakespearian phrases were handy in situations such as these—*spleeny reeling-ripe minnow*, for one.

"Hello, all." Mrs. Greene flung open her fan.

The snap made Bianca jump. She stood.

"Of course, you're Bianca Marshal." Mrs. Greene stepped forward and embraced her. "We'll get along famously. And I'll take excellent care of you. You'll see."

Bianca cringed. Compared to Gavina, Mrs. Greene was even more unconventional as a chaperone. And, it seemed, her competition.

"Ain't this grand?" Mr. Tabor stood and shook Mrs. Greene's hand. "Pleased to meet you." He said his name, just the same way he'd said it before. More's the pity.

"Such exuberance." Mrs. Greene near-glowed when she laughed. It was infectious and warm.

Like influenza. Bianca propped up the corners of her mouth and hoped it passed for a smile.

Mr. Emerson's chair scraped the marble tile. "A . . . surpris . . . ing . . ." The words were thick and choked, barely discernable at all. "Pleasure."

Mrs. Greene's smile grew, ever so slowly. Her lips parted, the corners tipped, her eyelashes bowed, just for a moment—until she raised them to Sir Adrian. "What a wonderful host we have." She held her hand out and fanned it to encompass the room. "He's gone to all this trouble, just for us."

Sir Adrian pulled out Mrs. Greene's chair. "My dear Mrs. Greene." After she sat, he continued, "Now that I have met all of you, I can honestly say you were worth the planning. Now, let's begin." He nodded to a servant standing near the door.

A deep gong sounded. A steady march of footsteps sounded outside the corridor. Men, also dressed as Egyptians, carried in trays. Five women walked behind them, holding long poles tipped with ostrich feathers. They stepped behind each chair and fanned.

One of Bianca's curls brushed her ear, and gooseflesh rose on the back of her neck. The servants kept their eyes cast down, as if they actually belonged to the ancient Egyptian millennium.

Sir Adrian lifted his hands slowly into the air, in time with the music. His slid his gaze to each one of them and finally locked eyes with Bianca. That startling blue ran deep into her soul and probed. Right before his unapologetic stare became unbearable, he snapped his fingers. Bowls erupted with fire on a table behind him. Heat rolled into the air and dropped like a *whoosh*.

"By jingo!" Mr. Tabor jumped from his chair and propelled himself under the table. His muddy boots stuck out from under the cloth. "Don't advance! The primer has failed!"

Bianca leaned down and widened her eyes. "Mr. Tabor?"

Mrs. Greene shrieked but then smiled. She fanned herself, moving her loose black curls against her shoulder.

Mr. Emerson hadn't moved at all. It was as if he was in a trance, his face pale, his eyes fixed upon Mrs. Greene.

Sir Adrian laughed and clapped slowly, seemingly happy with his display. "Forgive me, I couldn't resist. I do love a good surprise. And timing is always key. Mr. Tabor, are you quite well to get up off the floor, man?"

The tablecloth shifted. A grunt came from under the chair. "Sir Adrian, I do most humbly apologize. I have completely lost my scruples." He sat and attempted a laugh. "My scruples sometimes have a way of going straight out the window and ending up on a train to Georgia. You do understand?"

"Of course." Sir Adrian lifted his glass. "To all of us— may we find our heart's desires on this journey . . . and have the cleverness to conceal our motives if we do."

Bianca paused before she drank. Why would anyone want to conceal their motives?

After a long swig, Mr. Tabor snatched up a piece of bread and ripped it apart. "I don't know how I'll be able to sleep from this moment on. To think that I, Joshua Udolphus Tabor, will be sailing to the ends of the earth . . ." He stuffed the bread in his mouth, stifling whatever direction his thought had been heading.

"Not quite the ends of the earth." Mrs. Greene's gaze traveled slowly around the table and settled on Mr. Emerson. "Sir Adrian told me you do quite a lot of traveling. Have your endeavors ever taken you to India?" She tilted her head, as if she was hanging on his expected words.

Bianca remembered seeing such a look in a ladies' magazine. Apparently, Mrs. Greene had flirting perfected. *The harpy.*

"I was in India a little over two years ago." Mr. Emerson's gaze clung to Mrs. Greene's. "Quite frankly, my experience ranked somewhere between rickets and the plague."

Mrs. Greene pouted at him, as if to say "poor dear." "I only ask because I lived there." She turned her eyes on the rest of them. "My departed husband was a merchant. For a short time we lived in Benares." She closed her fan and put it on the table. "Very near the Ganges River."

Sir Adrian placed his hand over Mrs. Greene's. "As I told Miss Marshal in the corridor, I hope this journey will be the start of many new beginnings." He sat back and moved his fingers casually, feeling his many crested and jeweled rings with his thumb. "I have put quite a lot of thought into the coming weeks. I can assure you, you won't be bored." He looked at the ceiling as if seeing into all his past days upon the earth. "Boredom for me is the ultimate sin."

Bianca remembered Sir Adrian's butler's words—boredom at Hartwith House was not allowed. Who was this man? And how, with all the other possibilities, had he chosen her?

"Why, Miss Marshal, you look quite shocked."

"No." Bianca managed a smile. "Not at all."

Sir Adrian looked down at his plate and smiled secretly. "Do any of you care to know who solved the acronym correctly?"

"I know it wasn't me." Mrs. Greene smiled sweetly before sipping her drink. "I think Sir Adrian took pity on my sad attempt, and that alone got me here."

Sir Adrian clucked his tongue. "You're too hard on yourself. There's to be none of that. There is only one requirement on this journey—that you all be at ease and be completely yourselves."

"Top rail." Mr. Tabor shoved in figs until his cheeks were fat.

If Sir Adrian noticed, he made no recognition. He held his hand out toward Mr. Emerson. "Here is our acronym solver. The master of the cryptic. Bravo!"

Bianca clapped with the others and caught Mr. Emerson's eye. "Congratulations."

Mr. Emerson didn't look nearly as pleased as he should be. "Thank you, Miss Marshal." He dropped his eyes to the food on his plate, which he hadn't touched.

"I'm dying of curiosity," Mrs. Greene said. "Tell us how you solved it." When he didn't answer, she lowered her spoon and sat forward. "How clever you must be. I imagine you're a man of quite some reputation."

"The acronym was Proverbs twenty-seven, seven." Mr. Emerson worked the muscles at his jaw. "A principal verse from the teachings of the Rosicrucians from the sixteenth and seventeenth centuries."

Sir Adrian twirled his hand. "Which is?"

"'The full soul loatheth an honeycomb; but to the hungry soul every bitter thing is sweet.' When Sir Adrian called himself a Knight Grand Cross of the Order of the Brazen Crown in his advertisement—that phrase set me on a mad search for any Rosicrucian documents that I could find."

Sir Adrian smiled. "Those of you who think yourselves clever might as well abandon the thought now." He raised an eyebrow, as if they should pay particular attention. "Emerson thrives upon challenge, or so I've heard. A quality I appreciate—Are you all right, man? You look a little put off. You're not ill?"

"I—"

"Oh, posh." Mrs. Greene scowled. "We simply cannot have you being ill. After all this waiting, that would be too tiresome for words."

"I admit I am not feeling quite myself." Mr. Emerson lifted his water glass and drank deeply. "Forgive me."

"A good, strong tonic might be in order." Mr. Tabor nodded, his earlier panic returning to his face. "I've taken the liberty of packing a few. I'd be happy to make them available to you. One can never be too prepared."

"You're quite right." Mr. Emerson took another large drink of water. "One should always be prepared . . ." His gaze slid to Mrs. Greene. "For the thing one least expects."

"Well," Sir Adrian said. "Perhaps a good night's sleep is all you need. You did tell me earlier you've been distraught over that shipment of Roman ossuaries that arrived broken."

"Oh, no." Bianca set down her fork. "That's terrible."

"Yes, terrible." Mr. Emerson put his fingers at his temple like he had a headache. "Irreplaceable, of course. Unable to be salvaged."

"Tragic," Mr. Tabor said. "But in a different way than the Great Boston fire of seventy-two. Burned for twelve hours." His expression fell. He boosted it up again.

Sir Adrian cleared his throat. "Perhaps you are all wondering why I chose Miss Marshal. To be quite honest, it was the innocence of her answer."

Bianca's gaze faltered. "I think you're giving me more credit than I deserve. After three days of thinking, it was simply the best thing I could come up with."

"See everyone." Sir Adrian leaned forward. "I am nothing if not a good judge of character. Innocence—she blushes."

The blush deepened.

"What was her answer?" Mr. Emerson asked softly.

Sir Adrian made his fingers into a pyramid by his chin. "Let me see if I can remember . . . Ah, yes. 'Truth found sweetly lies asunder, harrowing; but truth thought holy sings eternal between tunes in seraphim's songs.'"

"Beautiful," Mrs. Greene said.

Mr. Tabor pointed his fork into the air. "It does have a certain ring."

"I couldn't pass up such a poignant statement—truth found sweetly becomes harrowing—a synonym for painful, tormenting, heartbreaking." Sir Adrian tilted his head. "It set me to thinking, I can assure you. Such a statement might indicate that truth found out the hard way—let's say by experience—becomes something we really listen to. Truth given to us freely, left unheeded, brings us pain."

"Very nice." Mr. Emerson's voice held tones of strain. "Well done, Miss Marshal."

"Thank you." Bianca wished they could go back to the moments before everyone else had arrived. He had been so at ease then. Now . . . Now she had no idea what was bothering him, only that it was keenly so.

The others fell into conversation—observations about the room, the food, the music. Mr. Emerson ate a little, but hardly much to speak of. He laid his napkin on the table and leaned toward her. "Tomorrow I'll be speaking at a special exhibition at the museum. We have a painting on loan from the Louvre. I'd be honored if you'd attend."

"I'd like that very much."

"That does sound wonderful." Mrs. Greene amplified her voice. "I do hope that invitation extends to me, your fellow traveler."

"Of course." Mr. Emerson locked eyes with her. "You must come too."

The servants cleared the dishes away. Sir Adrian unfolded a map and called the men over to join him.

Mrs. Greene rolled her eyes and turned to Bianca. "Finally. Now we can talk." She scooted her chair closer. "Have you purchased a copy of Baedeker and Cook's guidebook to the Holy Land?"

"No. I've not even heard of it."

"Oh, good. Here you are." She opened her reticule, fringed with long black beads, and handed her the book. "I've already read it twice."

"Thank you." Bianca flipped through the first couple of pages.

> *The mystical and the exotic await travelers from the West. The East promises to fulfill every desire from the spiritual to the profane . . .*

Mrs. Greene sighed. "I could definitely use some of my desires fulfilled. How about you?"

Bianca closed the book and glanced at Mr. Emerson. "I suppose everyone would like to see their dreams come true."

"Aren't you a cautious one? That's good." Mrs. Greene puckered her lips. "It will save you some trouble in life, I think. I was the exact opposite in my younger years."

"You weren't cautious?"

She gave Bianca a reserved smile. "Let me give you some advice—never marry a man who doesn't keep his shoes clean... No, don't laugh, I'm serious. If a man pays attention to such a small detail as that, he'll pay attention to the other details of life such as how to romance a woman *after* he marries her."

Bianca ran her finger along the spine of the book. "And here all I thought I had to worry about was finding a man who is my soul mate in every way."

Mrs. Greene laughed. "I think we're going to be great friends. Would you call me Madeline? This journey is going to be far too long for formalities. It's a hard world, women have to stick together."

Bianca sighed. It was a hard world. And she did need a friend, desperately. Just because Mrs. Greene was beautiful, and Mr. Emerson might be interested in her, she'd already judged her. Unfairly. And that was not who she was. "Yes. Please call me Bianca."

The men were deep in conversation about the route they'd take to the Holy Land. Sir Adrian spoke of the luxury of the ship. Mr. Tabor spoke of Old Ironsides and alluded to the War of 1812.

Bianca closed her eyes, embarrassed again at Mr. Tabor's lack of tact. She opened her eyes at Mr. Emerson's voice. He spoke of the customs of the Arabs and the Jews.

Madeline reached for her fan and opened it, concealing her face from the men. She brought her voice to a whisper. "Isn't Mr. Emerson one of the handsomest men you've ever set eyes upon?"

So, she'd noticed. *Reeky ratsbane! Mewling folly-fallen giglet!* Other Shakespearean insults came to mind, but she pushed them down. "I come from a very small town, Madeline. I can't say I have a big point of reference."

Madeline peeked over the lace of the fan. She took a good, long look at Mr. Emerson. "Sir Adrian told me about him as we walked." Her voice was dream-like. "I imagine he's quite something—exploring the continents, acquiring priceless artifacts, blending in with the people."

Bianca allowed herself the foolishness of staring. Mr. Emerson held the map now, and she overheard him speaking of trade routes and Ottoman kings. As the moments waxed on, he spoke of places to be avoided once they reached the Holy Land.

"And such a voice, laud." Madeline's eyes shimmered in the candlelight; so many different shades of brown, any painter would weep for lack of matching the color. "He speaks multiple languages. Can you imagine? What would they sound like, whispered in a woman's ear?"

"I . . ." Bianca dropped her gaze to her bare ring finger. Anguish slid its arm around her shoulders. It patted her back. It leaned against her like a friend.

Paul Emerson had never been one for hiding, but now, as Miss Marshal's coach pulled past the museum gate, he stood in the portico shadows like a fool. How could he wave good-bye as if everything was fine? As if the past hours hadn't been torture.

Excruciating in the extreme.

The moon bled through the fog in patches. He walked, opening his palms to the scattered shafts of light.

Secrets had come out to play. His ship had come in.

He crossed into an alley, black as a heathen's last words. A flash of wild grief ripped through him as he realized he couldn't go to the Holy Land now. Even after it had been his heart's desire since the night of his conversion to God.

Miss Marshal must think him the worst sort of man, talking about Jesus one moment and barely coherent the next. The way she had looked at him with questions in her remarkable hazel eyes ... Never in his life had he been at such a complete and utter loss. He slipped between the brick buildings and emerged on Gower Mews. He'd even forgotten to give her his treatise on the Italian Renaissance. He never forgot. It was something he simply did not do. What must she think about such blatant disregard?

Sir Adrian spoke about surprises and the importance of timing. Well, the man had that much right.

Madeline. The name brought a sickness he hadn't felt in two years. But how had she come to be there? It had to be Sir Adrian.

The only thing that had kept him from walking out of the room was Miss Marshal. She made him feel so many things—dangerous things he had locked down, packed away, and given up on hoping for. As soon as he had seen her face and bowed over her hand, it had been like being run down by a coach on Oxford Street. Standing in the dark with her was not a good idea at all. Flirting with her outside the Egyptian Gallery was worse. He crossed his arms and tried to ward off the coming cold.

"Father, after all I've done . . ." He couldn't even pray the words. He couldn't ask God for that which he most wanted but didn't deserve—the perfect wife. "Would you give me . . ." Still, he couldn't form the word. And, as expected, no answer came. The only sound was the sound of his footsteps. The only thing moving was the fog.

"Why couldn't I have met her yesterday?" He kicked a bottle against a building and shattered it. "Any day but today. In any context but this trip!"

A dog barked in the distance.

He should disappear for a while. It would be easy enough. Borneo—he could bring back the dragon's blood pigment for the tribal exhibition. Singapore—he could buy the ancient stone fragments from the river . . .

He'd see Miss Marshal tomorrow at the Rembrandt exhibition. He'd be insane to get on that ship but . . . The way her face lit up when she talked of history . . . Her smile, so warm, unlike any other woman's. Her wit and gentle way . . . And then there was the conversation that couldn't be ignored—their mutual faith.

Paul ran his hand over his face, exhaustion claiming him once again.

Tomorrow he'd decide.

Chapter 6

*B*ianca hadn't slept. How could she? Sleep was the fickle instrument of the practical. Not for those on the verge of great romance. Conversations would ensue today that would alter her destiny, she was sure of it. And how heady was that feeling, like standing on the rafters of the barn in Ohio, ready to jump into the haystacks. Her fingers would loosen bit by bit. Her toes would curl over the edge. Below it was dizzying, but oh, how glorious the fall. Looking up at the British Museum now, she realized that feeling was similar to this. Wishing and caution were gone, left behind in the Egyptian Gallery.

From the moment Mr. Emerson had excused himself after dinner, to this moment, her mind had wandered. To being his wife. A life in London. Loving him every day. She'd sat in the bedroom at Sir Adrian's house and wrapped her lips around the possibility of saying Paul Emerson's name every day. When she had spoken it, the effect had made her shiver, although there had been no cold. Prayers came like breathing, all enveloping the same words. *Please, God, only You can do this.*

Now, Bianca stared at the doors of the museum, which were tightly shut. Just like the secrets Mr. Emerson said the corridors held within. Just like the contents of his journal, so many mysteries yet to be discovered.

Two young men guarded the entrance, dressed in seventeenth-century attire—woolen hose, lace collars, velvet doublets. They stared straight ahead, avoiding eye contact.

Bianca's stomach lurched and a sudden chill played up her spine. In only ten minutes, she would see Mr. Emerson. And he was probably only being kind to her last night. Once again, she glanced at Madeline, standing beside her. Her dress was a perfect mix of blue velvet and ruffle—sophistication and all the things Bianca wasn't. Candlelight did have a way of softening features. Next to Madeline in the daylight, she wouldn't even compare.

"Are you all right?" Madeline placed her hand on Bianca's arm. "You look a little pale."

"It must be the city air. Or perhaps the food last night didn't sit well." A wave of nausea ripped through Bianca's stomach. She clamped her lips shut and closed her eyes.

"I should take you back to Sir Adrian's house."

"I'm fine." She squeezed the handle of her parasol. The fringe on the canopy trembled.

Madeline scowled. And even that looked perfectly well done. "Perhaps you need a doctor."

"Once we get inside, I'll be—"

"My lords, ladies, and gentlemen." One of the guards tapped his pole upon the stairs. "Welcome to The Rembrandt Hour." The guards pulled open the doors. A sudden wind plunged over the roof and dove into the crowd.

The guards' purple capes snapped and flared.

The capes reminded Bianca of something. *Shakespeare. Antony and Cleopatra . . . "Purple the sails, and so perfumed that the winds were love-sick with them."* "Lovesick." The word came out in a whisper. There was nothing wrong with her. She was just lovesick over Paul Emerson.

"Oh, this wind." Madeline brushed her hat veil away from her lips. "Did you say something?"

Bianca brushed away a stray curl and covered her smile with the back of her hand. "Nothing of importance."

The crowd pushed in toward the door, some three and four at a time. Ladies held the rims of their hats and tried to secure their shawls. Men put their hands on the top of their bowlers. Stray papers flew past—a page from the *London Times*, a calling card.

Bianca opened her reticule and reached for the ticket Mr. Emerson had handed her last night.

This ticket entitles Miss Bianca Marshal to a sight of the British Museum at the hour of two o'clock on Saturday the 4th of August, 1877. No money is to be given to the servants. Special reception follows.

She studied Mr. Emerson's handwriting—bold, straight lines, which reflected his strength of character. Flourishes at the beginning and end of the words, indicating his passionate nature, she was sure.

Madeline raised her voice over the wind. "Mind your parasol, I think it's about to go topsy-turvy."

Bianca's parasol flipped inside out with a *thwump*, poking its spines into the wide backside of the woman in front of her.

"I beg your pardon!" The woman fell against her companion.

"I'm so sorry." Bianca's grip on the parasol faltered. The ticket trembled in the wind. Within seconds, the small rectangle was as high as the second-story window. "I won't get to see—" She almost said Mr. Emerson. She stopped herself. "I won't get to see the Rembrandt. What will I do?"

"My dear Bianca, we're women." Madeline raised her chin a notch and smiled. "We'll improvise." She clutched the side of her skirt, flared it out, and headed for the stairs.

A man stuffed tickets into a copper box. "Tickets, please." Questions came from the crowd. "Yes, Sir, we are running a bit behind schedule today but everything's in order."

When it was their turn, Madeline gave him a smile that would have melted the hardest of men. "I have my ticket here, as you can see. However, my friend has had the misfortune of losing hers to the wind."

"I'm sorry, Madame. No ticket, no entry. The rules are strict."

"Are they?" Madeline pouted, and with her lovely eyes and full lips, the effect was perfection. "Perhaps you'd be so kind as to alert Mr. Emerson of this predicament."

"Why would I bother Mr. Emerson?"

"I think he would want to know." She deepened her pout and lowered her lashes. "We're traveling with him, you see. Tomorrow. To the Holy Land."

The man's expression softened. "Mr. Paul Emerson?"

"Exactly. Now, if you would be so kind . . ."

"Hmmm?" His hands fell to his side. He grinned like a backwoods drunkard.

The people behind them murmured. Complaints filtered through the noise of the wind.

"Mr. Emerson?" Madeline repeated.

The man's gaze fell to the people waiting on the stairs. His cheeks reddened. "Yes, of course. One trifling moment, Madame . . . Just a—" He scurried off to the left, his coattails flying behind him.

Madeline folded her hands and gazed at the ceiling, looking as if she were waiting for paint to dry.

After a few minutes, the man appeared with a smile. "It's quite all right, ladies." He tipped his hat and opened the small gate. "Mr. Emerson is expecting you, and he sends his compliments."

"Thank you, Sir." Relief washed over Bianca, and then euphoria.

Madeline granted the man another smile, then laughed when they were out of earshot. "And that, my dear, is how it's done."

The clock in the corner struck two. The crowd clapped. The burst of applause grew louder until Mr. Emerson appeared. He stood next to the covered painting, looking like it was the most natural thing in the world to be dressed like he came out of an Alexander Dumas novel.

Bianca sighed. Blue velvet doublet, buckled shoes, scabbard, and sword. She remembered something from *The Three Musketeers*: *"Well, and by my faith," said Athos, "it must be acknowledged that this Englishman is worthy of being loved. I never saw a man with a nobler air than his."*

"You are clever," she whispered to herself. "Chapter nine, I believe."

Madeline leaned toward her. "My dear Bianca, I can't hear you when you murmur."

"I'm sorry. It's nothing." She suppressed a smile.

Mr. Emerson bowed to the crowd, sweeping his hand into the air. "I give you one of Rembrandt van Rijn's most profound paintings—*Return of the Prodigal Son*." He pulled a tasseled cord. The heavy curtain fell to the floor.

The crowd gasped and clapped again.

He waited for the applause to die down. "Rembrandt enveloped all his subjects in an aura of mystery. This was intended not to conceal, but to reveal. If you look closely enough, you'll always find some surprise in his paintings. In the shadows, sometimes just beyond—a glass, a vase, a person. These discoveries are part of the wonder that he left behind."

He walked to the right and picked up a metal coat of arms. "The standard of Leiden, Holland—two crossed keys. Rembrandt was born in Leiden on July 15th, 1606. Earlier that year, the trial of Guy Fawkes began for the famous Gunpowder Plot or the Powder Treason, as it was known at the time." He paused and stepped nearer to the crowd, lowering his voice. "Other things happened in 1606. Those of you who did more in school than dipping girls' braids in ink might remember."

The crowd laughed.

"On February 26th, the Dutch navigator Willem Janszoon made the first confirmed sighting of Australia by a European. Shakespeare's *King Lear* was performed at court. And let's not forget April the 12th when the Union Jack was adopted as the national flag of Great Britain."

"God save the Queen!" The crowd erupted in cheers.

Mr. Emerson smiled and gave a nod, then he stepped back to the painting and seemed to be studying something. "Rembrandt wanted to get to the bottom of things—the depth, the passion, the feeling he wished to portray. Unfortunately, this view ultimately counted against him. In his fashionable town house in Amsterdam, tragedy struck again and again. Three of his children passed into eternity. His wife, Saskia, also died. After that, there were even fewer commissions. In 1657 he had to stand by and see the collection he had built up throughout his life sold at auction. Money became such a concern that he resorted to selling his wife's tomb."

A hush descended upon the crowd. Mr. Emerson joined in it, marking the tragedy. He walked slowly across the stage. "Rembrandt's only surviving son, Titus, saved his father from complete destitution. He formed a company to protect his father from his creditors by officially employing him and selling his paintings."

Mr. Emerson moved to a marble table and lifted a cloth from a small painting. "Titus." He said the name almost as if he mourned the young man immortalized in pigment. The deep browns in the background of the painting, and even the umbers of Titus's clothes caused an unearthly effect. The face of Rembrandt's son near-glowed with emotion, almost as if he could step from the painting and move among them.

"You can see the love that Rembrandt had for his son—the soft way he accented his eyes here." Mr. Emerson held out his gloved hand. "Look at the shadows there. He stares at us over the centuries with a combination of levity and kindness that must have been woven into his personality as intricately as threads in a Persian rug." Mr. Emerson crossed his arm, still staring down at the painting. "Titus died tragically of the plague in 1668, six months after his wedding."

Bianca felt how he shifted the mood of the crowd with his words. And he did it all so effortlessly—a pause for effect, a poignant look. She took a breath, more to assure herself she wasn't dreaming. She could hang on his words forever; listen to him talk about the patterns of sheep herding and still be enthralled.

He went on, speaking of all the seventeenth-century displays in the room—textiles, weaponry, manuscripts, and jewels. Then he moved back to center of the stage. "We are proud to have these two masterpieces on temporary loan. Take your time today and enjoy everything the British Museum has to offer." His gaze met Bianca's. His smile was as intimate as a kiss.

Bianca's cheeks flashed with heat. She knew she should look away. That would have been the reasonable thing to do—what decorum expected.

Decorum always was a dull maid.

He bowed, his eyes never leaving her. "Thank you so much for coming."

The applause was like rain on a tin roof in June.

Mr. Emerson disappeared, slipping past the paintings and stepping off the stage. Her gaze followed the back of his white lace collar as he walked through the crowd. She hoped he would come toward her. He did not.

People mingled, some pushed closer to the paintings, some gathered around display cases.

Madeline tapped Bianca's arm. "Sir Adrian just arrived. Fashionably late, I see."

Heads turned. Whispers drifted their way.

"There he is," said one of the two elderly ladies who stood to Bianca's right.

The other woman pretended to be examining a musket, just so she could turn her head to better see him. "Still unmarried."

A young man with a long mustache whispered to his friend. "Worth twice as much as his father."

The second man adjusted his monocle. "Have you heard about the trip he's taking to the Holy Land?"

Sir Adrian strode forward with something akin to predatory grace. The crowd parted, and they didn't reserve their stares. Bold and open, they looked him up and down as if he was one of the things displayed in the museum. His fine clothing did stand out from the rest of them—the gleaming gray of his frock coat, the pronounced silver stripes in his tie—even the snowdrop flower in his buttonhole. Bianca searched her memory for the significance. Snowdrops were flowers that only bloomed in spring. Being as how summer was currently raging, that one small detail must have cost him a great deal.

Sir Adrian reached them. He inclined his head. "Mrs. Greene."

"Sir Adrian." Madeline returned the gesture.

"Miss Marshal, I was remiss." He lifted her hand and kissed it. "And now you must forgive me."

Everyone stared. Bianca's cheeks reddened again. "Whatever for?"

"For being unable to take breakfast with you, and then not being able to escort you here."

"That's all right." Bianca brought her hand back to her side. "Madeline is my chaperone, after all. And a very good one, I might add."

"Oh, you're so sweet." Madeline placed her hand upon her heart. "The fates truly have been kind to bring us together. What perfect orchestration our personalities are." She laughed like she was musing. "It almost seems premeditated."

Madeline was right. When they had talked earlier, conversation flowed easily. Laughter had been in abundance, and, once again, Bianca had to chide herself for being jealous. Madeline had proved herself worthy as a chaperone. She wouldn't even be at the exhibition if it weren't for Madeline. God was in the details. That was certain.

"Still." Sir Adrian held up his gloved hand. "I had to put business before you. That was unpardonable. I'm sorry."

Bianca smiled, hoping it eased him. "There's nothing to forgive. I'm sure you had very important things to do."

His expression softened. He leaned in. "You're just like I knew you'd be." His voice turned husky, waves of emotion lingering behind the tones. "I do regret that I was preoccupied with last-minute details for our departure tomorrow—a favor for a friend. Someone I shall introduce you to when we arrive in Jerusalem." He stood straighter and scanned the crowd, indifference back in his eyes. "I believe refreshments are being served. Shall we, ladies?"

Madeline stood on her tiptoes, trying to see. "I'd like to inspect the lace on display over there." She took a few steps but then looked back. "I won't be long. Please. I'll join you momentarily."

"It would seem lace is preferable to tea and cakes. Imagine." Sir Adrian offered Bianca his arm. "If you will allow me."

"Of course."

The conversation in the room grew to a frenzy—laughter and voices mingled, then tore away. People pressed together, anxious to reach the antechamber. Sir Adrian shielded Bianca with his body, walking just so to keep her from harm. It was charming and it made her feel something she hadn't felt in so long—special.

More whispers followed in their wake.

"That's her, the American." The voice was very near Bianca's left shoulder. She turned but no one was looking her way. She turned back.

"Traveling with three men alone."

Bianca raised an eyebrow and gripped Sir Adrian's sleeve tighter.

"Well, there is that other woman."

A laugh followed. "She can hardly be counted—"

Sir Adrian looked over his shoulder and glared.

The conversation stopped abruptly.

When he turned back to Bianca, he smiled like an emperor who'd just been crowned.

Bianca leaned toward him and lowered her voice. "Were they talking about Mrs. Greene?"

"Let them talk." His aristocratic mask was firmly in place. "They always do. They'll still only be talking while we're the ones crossing the ocean, uncovering secrets, and delving into the unknown."

Bianca saw the mirth that lay just beyond the veiling in his eyes. "What kind of secrets?"

"Only the best kind."

"And whose secrets will we be revealing, pray tell?"

He pretended to be studying the Rembrandt painting that they'd easily moved in front of. "The captain, perhaps? Or the cabin boy? Maybe they're in cahoots to pollute our minds on the ship. Or perhaps murder us in our beds."

Bianca giggled, then turned her expression to mock seriousness. "Really?"

"Absolutely. And then there are the fig mongers in Jaffa. No telling what tortures they'll devise."

Bianca laughed in sheer joy and felt more carefree than she had in years. She didn't know how it was possible, but she knew they were going to be very good friends.

An older man cleared his throat, lowered his spectacles, and eyed her like she was a two-headed cow.

Bianca narrowed her eyes and pretended to be scrutinizing the painting of Titus. Then she didn't have to pretend. It truly was beautiful. Just like Mr. Emerson had said. She lifted her chin and looked over the horde of people.

"Looking for someone?" Sir Adrian examined his gold pocket watch and then wound it.

"Yes." She considered lying to him, but then pushed the thought away. "Mr. Emerson was just here. I thought I would say hello."

"Ah. Indeed you should." There was something a little too knowing in his smile. "Shall I go and fetch him for you?"

"Oh, there's no need—"

"Nonsense. I shall go directly." Without another word, Sir Adrian parted the crowd again, and disappeared into it.

Bianca placed her hand upon her hip. "How extremely odd."

Madeline came around a flower arrangement. "Find a man who doesn't have odd tendencies and you'll find yourself in a graveyard."

Bianca smiled. "I do enjoy your sense of humor."

Madeline looked back from where she'd come. She focused on someone Bianca couldn't see. She turned quickly in the opposite direction, opened her fan, and ran her fingers across the lace.

A woman moved through the crowd.

Madeline gasped and threw out her hands. Silks, bows, and feathers blended in an embrace.

"Bianca, this is Mrs. Seraphina Wake, my dear friend from childhood. My goodness, we've not seen one another for how many years?"

"Too many." The woman looked like a pixie with her turned-up nose. There were tears in her eyes.

Madeline grasped Bianca's hand. "Dear, would you excuse us for a moment? We have a bit of catching up to do. Married life talk and such." She scrunched up her face. "You wouldn't be interested. I'll just be over there."

"Of course." Bianca forced a smile.

Madeline and Mrs. Wake moved a couple of steps away, bending their heads low like conspirators.

The way Madeline had touched her fan seemed oddly familiar. Wasn't there a language of fans? Bianca ran her thumb over the ivory handle of the fan Madeline had allowed her to borrow. She could just see the women of Portsmouth talking about the evils of communicating in such ways. Because if a lady could communicate with her friends, she could surely give a gentleman a message as well. Bianca opened the fan and experimented. *Why hello there, Mr. Emerson.* She waved the fan near her left cheek as she had seen Madeline do outside the museum. A giggle escaped her.

"Miss Marshal, how wonderful to see you again."

Mr. Emerson's voice washed over her, as waves of a tempestuous sea. She turned and tried to look pretty, smiling what she thought was her best smile. "And you as well. Thank you for inviting me."

"It was my pleasure." His gaze went to Mrs. Greene and Mrs. Wake in the corner. "What do you think of our little exhibition?"

Bianca weighed her words, not wanting to seem too forward. "Few things have given me greater enjoyment or greater anticipation." It was the honest truth, and he was free to interpret it any way he liked. "May I compliment you on your costume? It adds a wonderful touch to the day."

"Thank you." He dropped his gaze, a hint of a smile on his lips. "I like to make history appear alive, not dead, as some would have it. Last year a few of us dressed like Roman soldiers—helmets, swords, and greaves. It was for the unveiling of a collection of coins and weapons from that period. Some of the papers called it scandalous."

"Scandalous?"

"Some of the reporters said we were defiling London, traipsing about in skirts."

Bianca laughed. "Men wear kilts on a regular basis not very far from here. I hardly see the difference."

"I think the reporters chose to ignore that fact. Some Englishmen like to forget about our Scottish neighbors to the north." He paused and drew his eyebrows together. Thoughts passed upon his face, none of which she could discern. "I promised you a copy of my book." He revealed a beautiful leather volume from behind his back. "I was not quite myself last night." He closed his eyes as if he regretted the words. "Later in the evening, that is." He took a breath and extended his hand. "If you are still interested in reading my drivel on the Italian Renaissance, it's yours."

Bianca opened her mouth to speak but found it hard to choose what to say. She reached for the book, knowing how many hours he must have labored over it—how much of his soul must be reveled in the prose. When she closed her hand around the cover, it was like closing her hand around a key. "Thank you." They were the only words she could manage. She wanted to hold the book to her chest, but instead she kept it respectfully in her hands.

"You're very welcome." In his eyes were rivers of tomorrows, things converging and things falling away. He opened a black portfolio that he'd also been holding. "These lithographs are by David Roberts. You have heard of him perhaps?"

"Oh my, yes. His work is well-known in America. I've only seen his pictures of Europe, though." Bianca slowly lifted each page of scenes from the Holy Land—the Pillar of Absalom, the Pool of Siloam, Tiberius on the Sea of Galilee. The detail was extraordinary. "If I remember correctly, his journey to the Holy Land in 1838 proved to be the most rewarding of his career."

"You surprise me again." Further intensity resonated in the deep green of his eyes. "You must be a very extensive reader."

Bianca nodded, hardly knowing what else to do. Her legs felt weak, and her lips quivered. "I've heard these are very hard to find."

"All the more reason why you should have them. Your family will want to see where you have been, I am sure."

"You want to give these to me?"

"If you will allow it. A gesture of goodwill for the journey."

Bianca ran her palm over his book and the portfolio. "I do accept. With pleasure."

Voices rose across the room. A few hands lifted above the crowd.

Mr. Emerson frowned. "I see the reporters have arrived. The director gets nervous, and he always says the most bizarre things. Unfortunately, they all manage to make their way into the *Times.* I'll have to deal with them. Perhaps we can talk afterward."

"I would like that very much."

"As would I." Mr. Emerson bowed to her and turned toward the reporters. At his first remark, they flipped open their notebooks and began to scribble, looks of concentration etched upon their faces.

Just then, Madeline was beside her again. "I'm sorry. That took a bit longer than I anticipated. Was that Mr. Emerson?"

"It was."

"And he gave you something?"

"He did." Bianca realized her voice sounded a bit detached, like a floating flower on the wind. She cleared her throat. "Lithographs of the Holy Land. A gesture of goodwill."

Madeline raised her eyebrows. "Goodwill?"

"Of course. What else would it be?"

Madeline rolled her eyes. "I'm sure I have no idea. Come along, all this excitement has given me quite a thirst."

In the courtyard, wisteria vines made a canopy of purple and green. White wicker chairs littered the space. A long table boasted pastries, sandwiches, and tarts. Servants poured tea. The sun came down in patches through the lattice, checking the sandwiches and the high-stacked plates.

"This looks lovely." Bianca placed Mr. Emerson's gifts under her arm and then reached for a teacup. Was there ever a more beautiful day?

A petite blonde moved to stand beside them. Her dress was deep hues of rose, lighter accents of pink, and white ruffles. "Are you Bianca Marshal?"

"I am."

Madeline looked curiously at the woman. "And you are?"

"Amelia." The woman stepped closer. "How I envy you, Miss Marshal."

"Envy me? I'm sorry . . ."

"For being one of the contest winners. Everyone's talking about it."

"Oh, I see." Bianca took a sip of tea. "I can hardly believe it myself."

"How delightful it will be for you—seeing all those exotic places, eating all that strange food—being in the company of Paul Emerson."

"Excuse me?" Madeline snapped her fan shut.

Bianca stood a little straighter. "I'm sorry. Do you know Mr. Emerson?"

"Oh, yes. He's quite the catch, you know." The woman's small mouth puckered into an obscene smile. "It took me ages to finally snag him."

Madeline's eyes widened. "I think you'd better leave."

"We're engaged." The words slipped out of the woman's mouth and forced their way into Bianca's heart—splintering, shattering, boring into her soul.

Madeline took Bianca's teacup from her. "Are you quite all right?"

"Whatever is the matter?" Amelia placed her hand on Bianca's arm.

Bianca took a step back, ripping the woman's grasp away. Mr. Emerson's book slipped. The lithographs fell to the floor. She pushed through the crowd, wiping her eyes with her hands.

Sir Adrian stepped forward and caught her arm. "My dear Miss Marshal, how can I be of assistance?"

Bianca reached for his arm and held on. To keep from falling, she stared into the quiet watchfulness of Sir Adrian's eyes.

Chapter 7

*B*eyond England's shores lay many dangers for a man. Once leaving the russet waters of the Thames, the intermingling seas were never predictable. The foreign shores those waves lapped upon were even less so. Life could be snuffed out in a moment, taken by disregard and greed. Ambitions that were once noble sometimes became twisted in remote corners of the world. Within the far reaches of the Crown the rules bent. Sometimes out of necessity, sometimes not. If a man managed to survive these temptations, he was among those most fortunate.

But, oh, how deep the scars.

Paul Emerson stepped out of the coach and shielded his eyes against the sun's glare on the Port of London. Vessels littered the water—gliding rowboats, lumbering barges, and great behemoths of steel. The wind held the smell of all things undiscovered; it rippled through the sails and filled him with familiar longing—knowledge to be gained, cultures to unlock, artifacts to hold in his hands.

As historian of the museum, he'd been on hundreds of ships—seen hundreds of ports—and yet, it was the steamer at the end of the street that caused his blood to pound as if it were his first expedition.

The ship's whistle sounded, long and shrill. Steam billowed over the roofs of the warehouses and into the sky. Paul looked back to the hackney driver. "You couldn't have gotten me closer?"

"As you see, guv'nor." He gestured to the crowd of carriages and hansom cabs. "That lane's tighter than Victoria's purse."

"I'll go on foot." Paul flipped a sovereign coin to the driver. "Can you manage the luggage? Try going 'round the warehouse. There may be a chance."

"I'll try." The driver widened his eyes at the gold coin. "That is, I can manage it."

The whistle sounded again. Through the crowd, Paul saw the crew walking toward the ship's ropes. He looked back at the driver. "What are you waiting for, man? Drive like Jehu!" The biblical reference was lost on the man. "Make haste!"

The driver snapped the reins and Paul ran, his coattails flying out behind him. Hordes of people flooded through the street, pushing their way in and out of warehouses, loading deliveries, and passengers still trying to get through. Maneuvering around the delivery carts was easy, the labyrinth of cargo boxes spilled upon the street was not. The crates were marked—spices, tea, silk—too many to observe.

Finally, he was through, but the dock was no less crowded. Paul pushed his way up the ramp just as the ship's bell rang.

Sir Adrian stood staring at his pocket watch. He looked up, relief flooding his expression. "Quite a way to begin the journey, Emerson. I almost required smelling salts."

"My apologies." Paul took a few breaths and held his side. He cast a glance over his shoulder. Far below, the driver who'd brought him was just arriving with his luggage. Curse it all, it was going to be dashed inconvenient wearing the same clothes. On the side of optimism, at least that was preferable to the tribal grass he'd had to wear in Tuvalu. He squeezed the handle of his leather satchel. At least he had his books.

Sir Adrian peered over the rail, careful to hold his gray top hat firmly in place. "Your luggage perhaps?"

"Unfortunately, yes."

"A great pity, that. One moment." Sir Adrian walked across the deck to a man dressed in uniform. As he approached, the fellow widened his eyes and stood straighter. They exchanged words, none of which Paul could hear. After a moment, the man hurried up the stairs as if his trousers were aflame.

Sir Adrian strode back along the promenade as if he owned it.

Stewards rushed from the upper deck and lowered the ramp again.

Paul raised an eyebrow. Perhaps he did own it.

Sir Adrian smiled casually. "Shall we repair to first class? I'm sure you're anxious to be settled, and the others will want to know that you are here."

A wave of unease flowed through his body. "Of course."

The wood of the promenade deck was polished to a high gleam. Wicker chairs held plush white cushions and matrons keeping their daughters close. Already, some were journaling or drawing the view. A club of ladies had formed in a circle of chairs. Talk of Venice, Greece, and Rome filtered through the blast of the ship's horn.

A notice hung on the carved doors of the main gathering room. A mock trial was to be held, as well as nightly charades and games of whist. A sewing circle, a choir, and collaborative journal writing had already been organized. Separate lounges for gentlemen and ladies were diagramed. Daily prayers and hymn exultation were to be held in the upper cabin. It was highly encouraged to visit the garden room where plants from around the world were on display.

Sir Adrian perused the rest of the paper. "Will it be enough to keep us occupied, do you think?"

Paul took a breath and nodded. It certainly wasn't boredom he worried about.

Inside, the walls were of dark wood paneling, as fine as any one would see in the West End of London. Modern gas lighting hung from the walls. The chairs were of leather and tapestry.

A cloud passed over the glass dome in the ceiling. Shadows moved over the people, the globe in the corner, and blotted the columns by the stairs. Madeline, Mr. Tabor, and Miss Marshal stood next to the fireplace with their backs turned.

Miss Marshal's smile fell when she saw him. She turned and walked away.

The sound of the anchor being lifted reverberated through the ship. The urge to flee hit him full force.

Weariness bled into his bones. Weariness like he'd felt in India.

He ran his hand over his face.

Madeline could destroy everything.

It wouldn't take much.

All she'd have to do is tell Miss Marshal the truth.

HMS Vignette was a beautiful ship, but beauty was a hard thing to admire now. Throughout the night before boarding the ship, Bianca had managed not to think of Mr. Emerson once or twice. She'd managed not to think of him when she'd torn her *Requirements for a Husband* list into a hundred scraps. When she'd thrown those jagged fragments into the fireplace at Hartwith House, not one inkling of his perfection entered her mind. When those shards of words had caught fire and collapsed upon themselves—*believer, handsome, wild*—when only the heartless ash remained, she'd not thought about him at all.

Not one bit.

Bianca wrapped her fingers around the ship's cold rail and squeezed. The bow of the ship dipped into the endless sea. England fled away, shrinking into nothing but a shadowy strip of green.

"He'll never bend his head to whisper in my ear. I'll never be kissed. Not by him. Not by any man. Not ever." Bianca bit her lips to control her sobs.

Time passed, numb as the hour of death. She shouldn't have let Madeline convince her to get on the ship. She should have gone home. What was the point of delaying her inevitable spinsterhood?

She leaned her head against the ship's thick rigging rope. She should go and find the others. But what would she say when she saw him? The rope shook with the intention of the wind. Bianca closed her eyes. "Mr. Emerson, I met your fiancée yesterday. What beautiful children you'll have together. I'm sure they'll all be endowed with your charm, your love of history, and your deep green eyes. Did I mention your smile? Me? Am I crying? Oh, heavens, no, it's merely the salty air, I am sure . . ."

Needing a handkerchief, she snapped open the latch of her carpetbag. *Shakespeare's Sonnets* nestled in the corner, pretending to be innocent. Bianca's lips trembled. "You did this." She clutched the book and held it above the water. Her pinkie finger lifted, her fourth finger, her thumb.

The book floated in the foam, and then sank, taken by the waves.

Bianca took a shaky breath and lifted her gaze to the half day-lit sky. It insulted her by being beautiful, pretending that everything was good and right and pure.

A seagull hovered above, crying sorrowful laughter.

"Exactly so," Bianca said, numb as an old battle wound. "I completely agree."

The bird studied her with its yellow stare, dipping its wings, daring her to dance. Bianca sneered and closed her eyes again.

"The sea is quite lovely, isn't it?"

Bianca bent under the weight of his voice. Her eyes opened to a blurry vision of the rolling sea. "It's amazing." She forced the words out, like pouring something costly upon the ground. "Such untouched beauty."

Mr. Emerson was silent for a moment, his presence as radiating as the waves. He joined her at the rail. "Yes, untouched." He locked eyes with her but then tempered his boldness and looked away. "The way the sunlight barely shines just there—it's remarkable. And that color of blue, well, how could one possibly describe it?"

"I've no idea." The words drifted absently from her mouth, as if they came from another place—a place where dreams weren't shattered on a whim.

"It reminds me of a poem . . . 'The Sea-Limits,' by Dante Gabriel Rossetti." He leaned against the rail and stared at the horizon. The sun pushed farther, cut itself on a cloud, and bled. "Would you like to hear it?"

She wanted to tell him to go away, to leave her to her grief. Her lips formed the words but then betrayed her. "Yes." She closed her eyes again as the word fell.

"Consider the sea's listless chime: Time's self it is, made audible—the murmur of the earth's own shell . . . Secret continuance sublime is the sea's end; our sight may pass no furlong further. Since time was, this sound hath told the lapse of time."

His voice lulled her, struck her, plunged into the secret parts of her soul.

"Gather a shell from the stormy beach and listen at its lips; they sigh."

The pain twisted. Bianca gripped the rope tighter.

"The same desire and mystery, the echo of the whole sea's speech . . . And all mankind is thus at heart . . . not anything but what thou art; and Earth, Sea, Man, are all in each."

Only the churning of the tide remarked at the ending. Bianca forced a smile that failed miserably.

"Miss Marshal, I think something is bothering you. Would you tell me what it is?"

He would laugh at her if she did. And instead of that, she would rather die. "I might be a little seasick."

"You should have said something." He gently put his arm around her shoulder. "Perhaps if you sat down."

Bianca's breath caught at his touch. She lifted her hand to push away his arm, but only brushed the tips of his fingers.

He led her to a deck chair. "May I bring you some water?"

"No, thank you." Having him so near was a sharp kind of pain; it was inward and outward all at the same time. She found she couldn't breathe, for when she did, she was tortured with the smell of sandalwood, his shaving soap. And, worse than that, was the smell of his fresh linen shirt, and the leather satchel at his side. They were smells that wouldn't become familiar. Just fleeting things for a memory. Like the blanket from a baby who had passed. Or a pressed flower in a book, shriveled and crumbling with age.

"Is there anything you require? Tell me and I will get it for you."

She wanted to tell him to get her love. But that was impossible. Especially for spinsters like her. "I require nothing, Mr. Emerson."

His brows drew together. "Everyone was wondering where you were. I was wondering where you were. We've all been searching for you."

Bianca dropped her gaze to the planks. Why would he look for her? So he could flirt with her while being engaged to another woman? "After I settled into my cabin . . . I went exploring. I wanted to see the ship."

He brought his head down to her eye level. "Exploring? On your own? Did you think that wise?"

"I know I'm too curious, but I've never been called unwise." She wanted to laugh. The sound would have been full of irony if she could've managed it. She was both too curious and unwise. If she hadn't been, she wouldn't be sitting alone on the ship's deck with Mr. Emerson. She wouldn't be a lot of things.

"I seem to recall you wandering alone in the museum's corridors the first time I saw you. You could have gotten into all sorts of trouble—fallen down the missing staircase, locked yourself in the mummy sarcophagus, cut yourself on the collection of torture devices on the second floor. It could have been horrible." He contorted his face into a look of mock horror. "If I hadn't been there to distract you with that golden hawk business, you might have never been found."

"Wouldn't I?"

He sighed dramatically. "Yes, lost forever . . . It's a very big place, you know. I can see the headlines now—'Poor Misfortunate American Meets Her End Amongst Shrunken Heads and Zimbabwe Masks: Against Better Judgment She Had to Touch the Spears.'"

"I don't think you have very much confidence in me."

"Is gallivanting around every nook and cranny something that you do often?"

"Occasionally." Daddy's words came back to her about the episode at the Indian mounds. "In my defense, my wandering alone in the museum was part of the ambience that Sir Adrian wanted—all of us arriving at separate times, all of us finding our way through the half-light." She thought of that half-light where she'd first seen him. She took a slow, deep breath and pushed her lips shut so she wouldn't cry again.

"May I take you to see the ship's doctor? Miss Marshal, please." He lifted her chin with the tips of his fingers.

His touch burned like forbidden fire. "There isn't any need for you to . . ." Her hands shook.

"Any need for me to do what?"

"Stay." As she looked into his deep green eyes, the intention changed. She wanted him to stay forever, to tell her he wasn't engaged.

Breathing was no longer important. She felt herself slipping, sinking. Her body swayed. Black laced the edge of the sky.

"Miss Marshal?"

Her fingers slid from the arm of the chair.

"Miss—"

She felt his arms around her back and under her knees. And then he lifted her.

The last thing that she heard before she fainted was the strong and steady beating of his heart.

The next morning, a knock came on her cabin door. The ship's doctor—a serious, whiskery sort of a man—had just finished taking Bianca's pulse.

Madeline looked up from *Godey's Lady's Book*. "I wonder who that could be?"

"Allow me." The doctor snapped his medical bag shut and went to the door.

Sir Adrian stepped through, a look of concern upon his face. Shaded glasses were pulled halfway down his nose, the gold frames an elaborate scroll. "How is our damsel in distress?"

Bianca managed a small, tentative smile. "Better. Just a little cold."

"A common side effect of the laudanum," the doctor said. "I gave her the tiniest bit last night so she could sleep." He reached for the doorknob. "And now I shall take my leave."

"Thank you, Doctor." Bianca slid her feet off the chaise lounge and onto the floor, careful not to reveal anything higher than her boot laces.

Sir Adrian tapped his walking stick on the carpet. The handle was a silver wolf. "I was going to see if you felt up for a walk, but since you're cold . . ."

"No, I'd like to walk. Some fresh air would be nice. Don't you think so, Madeline?"

"I do." Madeline stood and gathered their hats. Her movements were too quick. She knocked over a picture frame on the writing desk.

"Is everything quite all right?" Sir Adrian asked.

Madeline met his stare. "This journey . . ." Her gaze faltered. "May be too much for her."

A muscle tightened at his jaw. "All is right where it should be, Mrs. Greene. Have no fear." He looked over at Bianca. "You heard her yourself, she is feeling a little better."

Bianca rose, trying to draw strength from somewhere. She gazed through the crack of the bedroom door. Her Bible still lay on the bed.

Sir Adrian opened the cabin door. "You were sorely missed last night and the only topic of conversation."

"Indeed you were." Madeline laced her arm through Bianca's. "Mr. Tabor seemed to think you might have contracted a rare disease brought on by English aphids. He proceeded to tell us the habits of the creatures until we were ready to do ourselves in."

"Aphids?"

"Yes," Sir Adrian said dryly. "Seems he has more than a passing interest in insects—a fact I didn't know when I chose him. Poor Mrs. Greene tried to change the subject to African exports of ivory, but that just reminded him of the dung beetle."

Madeline closed here eyes, as if in pain.

"I'll spare you the details, but after dinner my head was reeling all night, I can assure you." Sir Adrian climbed the stairs to the promenade deck. "Actually, I don't know if I shall ever recover."

Bianca laughed, but the wind of the deck stole it away.

"And then there was Emerson . . ." Sir Adrian donned his top hat and adjusted his scarf.

"Yes?" The mention of his name made her throat ache. She'd cried enough tears to fill the Jordan and still felt the need for more. She hated herself for that. She was supposed to be strong.

"Well, when Emerson wasn't staring out the window, he was constantly asking after your welfare. There wasn't any other conversation to be had from the man. He sounded like a rusty squeeze-box."

The information didn't help. In fact, it made no sense at all. Why should Mr. Emerson care that much about her? "I've never fainted before. I feel like a complete ninny. What must you think of me?"

"No worse than I thought of you before." Sir Adrian gave her a gentle smile. "We all have moments of weakness."

"I was definitely not myself yesterday."

"Obviously." Sir Adrian opened the glass door of the atrium, and the light inside made his red hair glow like fire. They walked past a canopy of vines and a collection of orchids. "But now that you're recovered, you will be yourself and not faint again. I forbid it."

Madeline bent to smell a flower. "I forbid it too."

"I shall do my best." Thoughts of love came like the dampness in the air—too warm, too thick, and too much illusion of beauty.

"Are you all right?" Sir Adrian stopped.

"I'm tired."

"Please." He fanned his hand toward an iron bench, then sat with her.

Madeline wandered down the tropical path, disappearing behind leaves as big as elephant's ears.

Sir Adrian took off his shaded glasses and dangled them by the round earpiece. "May I be bold with you?"

Bianca's body stilled.

"Just a thought, if you will allow me to venture it."

"You may say anything you like."

"You weren't really seasick yesterday, were you?"

"No." She didn't know why the word slipped out so quickly. Perhaps it was the intensity in his eyes. "Would you grant me the liberty of a guess?" Thoughts seemed to be turning over as rapidly as the glasses in his hand. "You'll forgive me if I'm wrong?"

"All right."

"I think you're quite smitten with Paul Emerson."

Bianca squeezed the edge of the bench.

"Silence is often considered to be consent."

She turned her face away.

"So is aversion."

When she found her voice, it sounded foreign to her, like some other woman wielded it. "Much good it will do me. He's engaged."

"I see." Sir Adrian gazed at the floor. "And how do you know this information?"

"His fiancée approached me at the Rembrandt exhibition."

"She approached you, how interesting. Did she give her name?"

"Amelia, I think."

"She gave you her Christian name?"

"Yes."

"And did she tell you her surname, er . . . last name?"

"She didn't offer it."

"She didn't offer it. And she introduced herself, alone." He flung his gaze to the high-pitched glass ceiling. "And that doesn't strike you as odd?"

"I never thought about it before now."

"What exactly did this Amelia say to you?"

"She warned me to stay away from Mr. Emerson."

"Ah." He looked like he was listening to an old, tiresome song. "A complete stranger comes up to you with no introduction and threatens you . . . If Emerson is engaged to this woman I feel sorry for him. She obviously has no possession of social grace. Seems to me that in his position, he would need a woman who does."

Bianca let the thought simmer. "What are you saying?"

He locked eyes with her. "Do you feel very deeply for Mr. Emerson?"

The question brought a wave of emotion—tides pulling as old as the sea. "From the first moment I saw him, I just knew . . . I thought I knew."

"You were attracted to him."

"It was more than that. In the King's Library, I heard his voice before I saw him. It was like my soul stirred within me and took note—*There he is*, it seemed to say—the one I'd been searching for. God help me, but I believed it."

"What does God have to do with it?" The aristocratic mask was back again—the hardening of his eyes, the lift of his chin.

"Quite a lot, actually. He brought me here for a reason, and I thought that reason was Mr. Emerson."

"I brought you here." Sir Adrian lowered his voice. "Unless you think God influenced me."

"Of course He did." Through the atrium glass, she saw a gust of wind catch the sail; it trembled against the wide sky. "God knows how many hairs we have on our head. His thoughts toward us are more than all the sand in the world."

The corner of his lips turned up. "I see your faith is intact, even after your bit of horrid news."

"My faith wouldn't be very strong if that's all it took to shake it."

"I thought as much." Something secret glimmered in his sapphire eyes but he locked it away. "Here, let's be done with all this theological discussion, shall we? Back to Emerson . . . The way I see it, there's only one thing to be done."

"Can anything be done? I thought I'd found my soul mate, and he's unavailable. I will live out my life as a spinster."

Sir Adrian chuckled. "You are nothing if not dramatic." He slid his dark glasses back on. "He's never mentioned a fiancée to me."

"Just because he hasn't mentioned it doesn't mean it's not true."

"Just because a woman comes up to you and says she's his fiancée doesn't mean that's true either. People do lie—especially in my world."

"Why would she lie?"

"Apparently, you don't know much about London society." He rested his elbow on the back of the bench. "How could you?" His shaded eyes raked over her face. "Look—I have learned to adapt, to be as formless as water, to be what the situation calls for. With these sorts of situations, you have to know how to play the game."

"The game?"

"Master the art of indirection—the rules of a courtier, per se—and they are many." He waved his comment away as if he'd wished he hadn't said it. "It comes to this—I don't think he's engaged, and I'm going to find out for you."

"But how?"

"My dear, that is my affair. You must leave it to me."

"Surely you won't tell him—"

"You wound me, truly you do." He placed his hand over his heart and took on a French accent. "Mademoiselle, I am a master of discretion. I will not fail you."

Bianca leaned back and they stared at each other. It was odd, but she felt so comfortable with him, like she'd known him her entire life.

"Trust me. I've brought you this far, haven't I?"

She studied his expression before answering. "Well, you did choose my acronym."

"Yes."

"And you have already given me the greatest experiences of my life."

"Excellent, go on."

"And I have no reason not to trust you."

"A logical deduction. Sherlock Holmes couldn't have done any better."

"Yes, then."

"What was that? My ears are a bit fogged, it would seem."

Her smile grew. "I said yes. You have my permission to speak to Mr. Emerson." She rolled her eyes. "Not that you needed it."

"Good." He pulled her to a standing position. "Now that that's settled, let's have a bit of fun, shall we?" He looked across the room and spoke louder. "Where the devil has Mrs. Greene gone?"

The tops of the tall ferns swayed. Madeline's voice wafted across the potted banana trees. "Just getting a closer look at these heliconias." The sharp sound of a pot breaking echoed off the glass walls.

"I'm glad to see my choice in a chaperone has paid off. I could have completely corrupted you by now." Sir Adrian winked, then lifted his chin. "Have you noticed that monkey in the corner? Look past the miniature palm trees."

"I've never seen a real monkey."

"There's a revelation, Miss Ohio."

She took a risk and smacked him on the shoulder. "Be good."

His smile tripled. "But that's so unlike me."

"Unfortunately, I believe you."

"You should." He grabbed her hand and pulled her toward the monkey's cage. "Let's do an experiment. Ten guineas say the little fellow will go straight for that woman's hat."

Bianca peeked through the foliage. A woman dressed in absurd shades of yellow and brown had just come through the door of the garden room. "Surely you're not serious." Bianca moved closer to the cage. The creature bared its teeth and panted like a dog.

"Am I not?" Sir Adrian reached for the latch.

"What if it's vicious?"

"Then we'll die a brutal death." He turned the latch slowly, mischief etched into his smile.

The monkey shrieked like a banshee.

Bianca covered her ears and raised her voice. "What if it overtakes the ship and ransacks every cabin?"

"Then, my dear, at least we'll have something to talk about over lunch."

Sir Adrian stifled a laugh as he passed the usual gawkers on the promenade deck. A real laugh . . . He indulged it, slowly at first, and then it grew.

He pictured the look of terror on Bianca's face when the monkey plopped into her arms like a sulking child. She'd turned as pale as sea foam. "What a little charmer," she'd said, trying to pull her face away from the creature's hands that smelled suspiciously of the apple tart he'd given it earlier that morning. In the end, the monkey had curled its tail around her arm and settled in for the duration.

How was she ever going to survive? Completely full of dreams and twice as naive.

Just like he'd hoped.

To be the man she loved . . . He stopped and closed his eyes, feeling the wind on his face like smooth fingers. No, that privilege was not for him.

That was for Paul Emerson.

And, as things stood, Emerson seemed to be only a handbreadth away from falling in love with her completely.

And it only took two days.

A twisted smile pulled at his lips.

Knowing just by their contest entries that Bianca and Paul might be a good match was one thing. Out of all the entries, theirs were so similar in thought that even a fool could have seen it. Such stuff as dreams are made on.

Paul Emerson—an icon in his field, a sought-after bachelor, more of an adventurer than most people knew. Even he had been surprised by the candid words etched in response to "a regret from your past" on the contest entry—*I regret India*—just three little words.

It hadn't taken much digging to find out why.

Sir Adrian stopped by the ship's rail and focused on the hazy outline of Spain. Maybe he should leave it alone. Bianca was so innocent.

He thought about hating himself for a moment.

The thought passed, as errant as the wispy ocean fog.

No. This was too important. And he hadn't waited this long just to give up before he had his answer.

He strode through the library doors.

Paul sat in a leather chair across the room. The man's face looked rumpled, as though he'd slept in his thoughts all night.

Excellent.

Sir Adrian slid into the opposite leather chair. He dropped his expression into one that was unassuming.

The game was set. Now it was time to put the pieces into motion.

Chapter 8

*T*he ship's library was a comfortable place, full of dim corners and elaborate nooks where one could disappear. The hand-painted wood paneling and the carefully selected volumes did much to elevate Paul's mood. The noise of the waves outside and the thrum of the engine faded until only written words remained.

That was until he saw out of the corner of his eye Sir Adrian watching him.

Paul turned the page of his book and forced his eyes to stay on the words, delaying the inevitable.

"Interesting reading?"

He forced a smile and showed Sir Adrian the cover. "*History of the Rise and Fall of the Slave Power in America* by Vice President Henry Wilson."

"I would have thought your tastes ran more toward ancient cultures." Sir Adrian looked faintly amused. "Have you taken a sudden interest in Americans?"

Paul would have laughed if his situation were different. "I've been following the other volumes. I happened to find the latest in here this morning." Paul closed his book, adopted a nonchalant posture, and waited.

Sir Adrian picked up a book from the side table and opened it. His eyes widened at the title page. It looked as if he bit back a smile.

"Something funny?"

"Not at all." Sir Adrian put his fingers against his temple and turned the page. He stifled another laugh.

Paul scowled. "I so enjoy levity. Perhaps you'd care to share?"

"Oh, no, no. I wouldn't dream of interrupting you." Sir Adrian took a satisfied breath and continued scanning the pages.

"How is Miss Marshal?"

Sir Adrian leaned back into the upholstery. "Much improved."

Paul waited for him to elaborate. He didn't. "She's feeling better then?"

"She was able to take a walk." Sir Adrian brought the book closer to his face. "We enjoyed some very pleasant conversation."

Paul focused on the golden embossed title in Sir Adrian's hands. *The History of India, as Told by Its Own Historians: The Muhammadan Period.* He ran his hand over his jaw. *A coincidence. It had to be.* "And what was the doctor's diagnosis?"

"Seasickness, no doubt, and exhaustion."

"I see." Paul tapped the edge of his book against the chair.

Sir Adrian closed his book and gazed at the wood carvings on the shelves. "All this must be very taxing for someone used to country life."

Paul narrowed his eyes. "Taxing?"

"Miss Marshal is from a different circle, you'll have to admit."

"Be careful, Sir Adrian. I'd hate to think of you as a snob."

That drew a smile from him.

A steward came by and offered them lemonade. Paul accepted a glass.

Sir Adrian lifted his glass and took a sip. "I've heard you've been to America. What's your opinion of it?"

"An interesting place. Unlike any other."

"And the women? Are all American women heady romantics like Miss Marshal?"

Paul kept his eyes on the bits of lemon clinging to his glass. "I assume American women are the same as English women in that regard."

"I have to admit that even I have not been unaffected by Miss Marshal's freshness." He sighed. "I see that so rarely in my circles. You know, I can't quite decide who is more intriguing, Miss Marshal or Mrs. Greene."

Paul stopped his glass midsip. "I think that you, above all people, understand my lack of intrigue for that woman. Shall we put pretenses aside? I know you didn't choose Madeline at random."

"Madeline?" Sir Adrian raised an eyebrow. "You speak as if you know her."

Paul lowered his voice and leaned forward. "I have heard about your social experiments amongst society. I hate to disappoint you, but I'm not going to be your laboratory rat."

Sir Adrian flipped his hand into the air. "Your life is your own. Just because I have the hobby of studying human nature doesn't mean you're under the glass. This is a pleasure tour, or did you forget?" He scooted to the edge of his chair, as if he'd just had an epiphany. "This conversation has put me in mind of something. Would you like to accompany me for a little experiment? Sleight of mind, let's say."

"I have also heard that you dabble in magic. Don't magicians prefer the term sleight of hand?"

"That is a very large misconception. For magic— and all its mystery—resides in the mind. Come. Let's go outside."

Paul followed him as they exited the library and went to the busiest place on the promenade. Two stewards stood by a cart, steadying water glasses and the pitcher as the tide rolled. Couples walked arm in arm, admiring the other ship across the way—a blur of white against the sea's horizon. Paul could just barely see the ship's flag dip in greeting. Everyone, including Sir Adrian, looked up to *Vignette's* mast to watch her flag politely dip three times in response to the strangers. Happily, the courtesy was carried through.

They passed ladies chattering amongst themselves, holding a variety of parasols to guard against the sun. Heads turned. Paul nodded and tipped his hat as they passed. Sir Adrian did the same. His silk scarf waved in the breeze, reaching toward the girls.

Feminine laughter mixed with the snap of the sails, followed by admonitions from the matrons.

Whispers came from a girl wearing a black velvet choker. She tried to hide her wandering gaze behind her parasol but was unsuccessful. "There he is." Her acute eyes widened, along with her friend's. "Sir Adrian's the richest man on the ship. And the historian—" A woman, plump and overly decorated, gave them a look that would frighten the dead.

Paul rolled his eyes.

Sir Adrian made no acknowledgment.

Trills of laughter followed—a sound akin to a tittering hyena.

"This looks promising." Sir Adrian strode to the overhanging cloth awning where there were some open deck chairs. He sat and bade Paul do the same. "Do you see those men over there?"

"The ones playing horse billiards?"

"Exactly." Sir Adrian leaned back in his chair. "A sleight of mind artist should, with due concentration, be able to ascertain certain aspects of a person's thoughts and intents, which are indiscernible to the unpracticed."

"I agree." Paul studied the three men involved in the game. One man thrust the wooden disk over the chalk diagram and landed on number five. The next miscalculated because of the reeling of the ship. He pushed the disk forward with the crutch, but it ended on a line. No point. His fellow players followed with laughter and jibes.

Sir Adrian removed a leather book and gold fountain pen from his vest pocket. He dashed something upon a single sheet of paper, folded it two times, and reached toward Paul's jacket pocket. "May I?"

"All right."

"Now." Sir Adrian held his hand aloft. "If you will continue to watch those three gentlemen."

Almost immediately the older gentleman to the left put down the crutch and bade his comrades good-bye.

Sir Adrian nodded. "Would you be so kind as to read the note in your pocket?"

Paul reached into his pocket and unfolded the paper. "'The well-dressed man to the left will be compelled to leave his companions.' But how could you have possibly known?"

Sir Adrian placed his hand on Paul's shoulder. "We are, I believe, destined to friendship, but alas, I am honor bound to an oath not to reveal my secrets, even to a friend."

Friend. The word dripped of lies. Paul looked at Sir Adrian's hand upon his shoulder until he removed it. "There is no possible way you could have exchanged that note without my having detected it. I am all astonishment."

Sir Adrian bowed his head in mock humility. "Shall we turn the mood of the experiment to a more personal nature?"

"Why not?" Paul shot him a grin. "You seem so interested in other people's affairs. I'd hate to upset your pattern."

"Splendid." Sir Adrian made no acknowledgment of the rebuke. "Now, I want you to think of something I would have absolutely no knowledge of." He studied the cloudless sky. "Without speaking the answer aloud, do you recall the last meal you had before you boarded the ship?"

"Yes."

"Then concentrate on that for a moment." He leaned forward, looked into Paul's eyes like some sort of gypsy 'round a fire, and then took out another piece of paper. He wrote with a flourish, then held the pen aloft. "If you will be so kind as to lift your right foot . . . I'll put the paper here, so you can be assured that I have no access to it." He handed Paul another piece of paper. "For future reference, write that last meal here."

Paul hid the paper behind his hand and scribbled the answer.

"Now, fold the paper and place it with my note under your right foot." Sir Adrian took out another piece of paper and wrote on it. "A childhood pet now." He studied Paul again. After Paul had written his answer, they placed both papers under Paul's left foot.

"Now, for the third and last phase." Sir Adrian leaned forward and lowered his voice. "With the exclusion of your mother, I want you to write the initials of a lady who is dear to you."

Paul stared at the blank paper, then dashed off an answer.

"Let's put that one close to your heart." Sir Adrian accented his voice with sentimental feeling, then dropped his paper in Paul's vest pocket. "Now, if you will remember, in all three instances, I wrote a prediction—no—more of a perception about some aspect of your life unbeknownst by me."

"Yes." Paul intertwined his fingers.

"In each of the three times, you wrote the truth of the matter, which you alone are privy to. These perceptions of truth, along with my answers, are safely tucked away about your person." He gestured to the hiding places of the notes. "If you're ready, we'll check the results of our experiment." Sir Adrian gestured toward Paul's right foot. "At your leisure."

Paul unfolded his paper slowly and observed the word he had written—*lamb*. He placed it upon his lap and unfolded Sir Adrian's paper. "Lamb," he spoke aloud. "But how did you know?"

Sir Adrian ignored the question. "Your left foot, if you please. We move on to the name of your childhood pet."

Paul wrinkled his brow as he unfolded the next two slips of paper. They both concurred with the same name—*Belvedere.*

Sir Adrian didn't look surprised. "There's one more remaining."

Paul moved his jacket aside and took the last two sheets of paper from his vest pocket. Unfolding his own slip first, he exposed the initials *Q. E.* He turned the paper toward Sir Adrian. "Queen Elizabeth. She is one of my favorite historical heroines."

Sir Adrian studied the initials and then looked back to Paul's face. "Such a woman does deserve admiration."

As Paul began to unfold the last slip of paper, Sir Adrian gripped Paul's arm. "Of course, you realize that experiments of this nature are seldom foolproof. I hope you'll be satisfied with two out of three."

Paul paused for a moment and then opened Sir Adrian's paper scrap. The lone letter *A* stood out.

"I'm afraid I was getting foggy by that time. Look at that—I could only come up with one initial, and that one wrong."

Paul narrowed his eyes. "Your single failure makes your previous two successes seem that much more mysterious."

"Well." Sir Adrian stood and grabbed hold of his walking stick again. "I'm afraid all this mental exercise has exhausted me. If you will excuse me."

"I do wish you were at liberty to tell me how these things were accomplished."

Sir Adrian leaned forward and whispered, "May I swear you to the same oath of secrecy which binds me to my fellow conjurors?"

Paul nodded. "I promise you my silence."

"I guessed." Sir Adrian raised an eyebrow, which seemed even redder in the bright sunshine. He left it there, cocked as if a villain had taken his body captive. He bowed and then walked away.

Sir Adrian weaved in and out of the people on deck, his scarf still as errant as a misbehaving child. He ripped it from his neck, and let it drift down to the planks. After he disappeared down the stairs, three young women dropped their parasols and ran to the strip of silk.

"I saw it first!"

"You did not, Cornelia!"

"Jane, don't be so selfish! You know I intend to catch his eye before we reach Greece!"

Paul walked to the rail, threw the scraps of paper out to sea, and watched them disappear on the rolling tide.

As she walked with Sir Adrian, Bianca kept her voice low and tried to pretend their conversation was casual. Madeline was just out of earshot on the promenade deck. "Q. E. were the initials he wrote on the paper?"

"That's right." Sir Adrian watched a porpoise jump in the waves.

Bianca's smile grew. "So, perhaps I can assume . . ."

"You can assume . . ." Sir Adrian moved his hand in the air, bidding her to continue.

"That Paul Emerson is not engaged."

"He was still a bit guarded—quite understandable—but he's smitten with you."

"He's not engaged," Bianca repeated.

"But, he may be soon."

"Sir Adrian, please!"

"You're terrified of this, aren't you?" He patted her hand. "I beg you not to faint again. He is only a man."

"He is not *just* a man." Bianca concentrated on the salt air to try to keep from experiencing the vapors. "He is perhaps my future husband."

"Ah." Sir Adrian opened his pocket watch and consulted the time. "I feel compelled to warn you, few people have shared my confidence and remained unchanged. The risks are great and the perils many."

"Nonsense. I assure you I'm a great deal stronger than you might think." Bianca studied the way the sunlight reflected off his family ring. The head of a stag was embossed in gold; its eyes were small rubies. Another name for a stag was a hart. She smiled, pleased to figure out the origin of his lofty surname. "So far I've managed to roam in your aristocratic world rather well."

"Ha! You faint at the first whiff of romance, or lack thereof." He lifted his nose into the air. "I should have chosen someone with more durability. A Scandinavian perhaps. Or, better yet, a man. Then I wouldn't be stuck in this ridiculous *affaire d'amour.*" He closed his eyes as if in pain.

"You are nothing if not dramatic," she said, repeating his earlier words back to him.

Sir Adrian gave her a genuine smile. "And you are nothing if not one of the sweetest creatures I've ever had the privilege of knowing." He took her to the rail and once again studied the sea. Then he glanced in the direction of the luncheon area. "Look who just happens to be over there—Paul Emerson—all white tie and freshly pressed suit. He has such a look of contemplation on his face, don't you think? See how the wind blows through his hair ever so often—Gad! It's enough to put me in mind of a story I read. Something about a wounded soul who never thought he'd love again, and the innocent girl who saved him. I can't quite remember the title. The whole picture has sort of a *Jane Eyre* feel, don't you think?"

Bianca smiled as everyone at the table caught her eye. She leaned in close to Sir Adrian and whispered, "You're a snake."

Sir Adrian pulled out a chair and bowed his head toward Bianca's ear. "I'm so glad you approve."

Chapter 9

Since it was a particularly fine day, the choice of taking luncheon on the deck was thrilling. The long, white tablecloths made a stunning display, thirty of them or more. The wind wafted just so, light enough to cool and bring the fresh salt air that Bianca had come to keenly enjoy. As she looked over the first-class passengers, she realized that never before had she seen so many white feathers. The ladies' hats simply brimmed with them. Certainly she had never seen so many jeweled binoculars. Someone made mention of a whale on the port side, but before she could get up, the massive beast must have slipped away because the spectators sat again.

Of course Bianca took note of all of these things for a very important reason. *He* sat beside her—Mr. Unengaged. His presence so close after the knowledge—the remembrance—of being in his arms just before she fainted was almost too much to contain. Surely her cheeks burned with it. Surely the knowledge announced itself in her eyes.

"Sir Adrian, when you and Miss Marshal sat down, you told her that you approve. Of what, pray tell?" The tips of Madeline's long black hair turned up in the wind. The red ribbons of her hat brushed her cheek.

Sir Adrian adjusted his posture and flipped out the tail of his jacket. "Why, the weather, Mrs. Greene, it is exceedingly fine."

"It's much gustier than Boston." Mr. Tabor lifted his napkin, shook it out over the floor, and swatted at the creases. "I saw a cluster of jellyfish earlier that must have been brought to the surface by a rogue current. Perhaps a storm is brewing."

Sir Adrian joined Mr. Tabor in looking at the clouds. "The ship's newspaper this morning gave no indication of a storm."

"Trust that, do you? Ha! I'd wager the captain's wife uses that toy printing press as a means to entertain herself . . . I saw more than one mention of your name there."

"Did you?" Amusement shone in Sir Adrian's eyes. "I must have overlooked that part."

A steward came and filled their glasses. Another brought soup.

Mr. Tabor craned his neck and looked back at the lifeboats. "These kinds of storms come on so suddenly. Reminds me of the time I was hunting a rare hemiptera in the swamplands of Georgia in seventy-one."

Madeline laughed. "Hunting a what?"

"Cicadas, Mrs. Greene." Mr. Tabor lowered his voice. "Red-eyed cicadas."

The creak of the ship was painfully obvious.

Bianca took a drink of water. She must not laugh. Perhaps if she thought of cross-stitching. Or rendering lard.

Sir Adrian cleared his throat. "I'm sure that was an interesting venture. I've gathered you have more than a passing interest in entomology."

"Every spare moment is devoted to the insect world." Unease buried itself in the creases around Mr. Tabor's eyes. He picked up his soup spoon, leaned over his bowl, and slurped.

Sir Adrian motioned that the others should eat.

The wind shifted, bringing with it the faintest smell of sandalwood and citrus—Mr. Emerson's shaving soap.

Bianca knew she shouldn't look at him. It would be detrimental.

Detrimental was a fickle word, completely devoid of meaning.

"How are you feeling today?" A sunbeam fell across Mr. Emerson's eyes and turned them the color of jade.

"Much better, thank you."

"You're recovered then?" The beam of sunlight shifted to his hair and played with the darker strands of brown.

"Completely."

"No lingering headaches? You were able to eat breakfast this morning?"

"Yes. Toast and lovely English tea."

He looked down at the table and smiled. "It was strong tea, I trust."

"Of course." Happiness flooded her; it flowed like the tide beneath the ship—surging, serenading things to come. He remembered their first conversation. The world faded, just how the romance novels she'd read described.

"You really had us worried," Mr. Tabor said.

"Hmmm?" Bianca tore her gaze away from Mr. Emerson.

Madeline glanced at Mr. Emerson without meeting his eyes. "I suppose if you had to faint, at least you had very capable arms at your disposal. You should have seen the way he carried you across the promenade. One would almost think he's had extensive experience with swooning females."

Sir Adrian stopped his spoon midair. "I ask you— whatever happened to a hearty stew? Do you know how tired I am of turtle soup? Some Frenchman concocts a consommé that's as thin as weasel sweat, plops a reptile in it, and it's supposed to be soup? What's next? Pickled iguana eyebrow?"

Bianca coughed into her napkin to stifle a laugh.

"Oh, that cough doesn't sound good." Madeline leaned toward her. "Perhaps this wind is too much for you."

"No—"

"We wouldn't want anything to happen to you." Madeline pouted. "You're much too important." She looked to Mr. Emerson. "Isn't she?"

"Waiter." Sir Adrian raised his hand. "Yes, you, boy. Take this pathetic excuse for soup away."

Mr. Tabor sat ramrod straight. "It's not as good as chowder, but still—"

"A sad decline in brilliance." Sir Adrian threw his napkin on the table. "I shall speak to the chef."

"I think you'd better." Mr. Tabor crossed his arms. "If this was Boston, there'd be a riot."

People at the adjoining tables stared.

Bianca searched for some diverting thing to say. "The mermaids on the plates are very pretty."

"Yes." Mr. Emerson looked like he held back a smile. "These are astonishing place settings."

"I suppose." Madeline's voice was flat. She, too, threw her napkin on the table. "Some people think the whole siren look is a little passé, although I don't know why. If it was good enough for them once, shouldn't it be good enough for them now?"

Mr. Emerson flicked his gaze toward Madeline and then turned his goblet in the light. "These glasses must be Venetian, I'm sure of it." He rubbed his fingers on the rim of his glass, causing a low hum to emanate like a parlor trick. "The way these goblets are etched remind me of a vase in the British Museum. A very old vase, full of cryptic meaning."

Madeline took a drink, leaving a smudge of pink on her glass. "I'm very fond of cryptic meanings, Mr.

Emerson. When decoded, they can bring such light to certain situations."

Sir Adrian looked at Madeline harshly. "Speaking of vases, I once met a man in Italy who made them. He fell off a cliff while I was there on holiday. Had eleven children. Left his wife without a lira."

"Poor devil." Madeline leaned back in her chair. "But he probably had horrendous secret sins and deserved it. God has a way of letting all things come out in the wash, don't you think?"

Did Mr. Emerson wince? Bianca steadied the back of her hat with her hand and wished the wind would die down. "Madeline, how can you say that without even knowing him? Think of his poor wife and all those children to feed."

Sir Adrian nodded. "The poor fool was picnicking and had the unfortunate companion of too much wine. I'd say it was the wine's fault, and not divine punishment."

"I would agree." Mr. Tabor brought his spoon to the level of his eyes and studied it with suspicion.

Mr. Emerson gazed at the flags above him, as if searching for his thoughts. "Let me see if I can remember the story about the vase . . . Something about the Apennine Mountains, a temptress, and a great deal of money."

Madeline shifted in her chair, placed her hand on her chest, and looked shocked. "A temptress? Are you sure you ought to be telling this story in front of Miss Marshal?"

Sir Adrian scowled at Madeline. "I think we could all use some diversion right about now. It might give some the opportunity to remember their place."

Bianca glanced at Madeline. What on earth had gotten into her? Why was she so peevish? And Sir Adrian had given her an outright rebuke.

Mr. Emerson lowered his goblet. "The vase was a wedding gift from a wealthy Italian merchant to his new bride, Agnese. It was made in a way that had never before been seen in the late fifteen hundreds. Two etchings are upon it—one of a lion, symbolizing the merchant's family, and the other of a ship, similar to the ones engraved upon our goblets." Mr. Emerson looked out to sea, seemingly lost in his thoughts.

Bianca saw the reflection of the waves in his eyes, and the clouds—stretching like endless taffy. They all waited for him to speak.

"I came across this story when I purchased a box of miscellaneous artifacts in Rome. Agnese's journal was at the very bottom. After I read it, I traveled three hundred miles north, where I hoped the vase to be."

"And you found it." Bianca said, amazed.

Sir Adrian looked pleased. "Of course he did."

"It wasn't easy," Mr. Emerson said. "And the story doesn't end there. The vase is not an ordinary vase. I mentioned its unique construction, but I didn't tell you that the glaze contains the ashes of Agnese's former lover."

Bianca gasped.

Mr. Tabor slapped the table. "You're making this up."

Sir Adrian leaned forward. "Go on."

"The truth is often stranger than fiction, Mr. Tabor. As history recounts, the everyday predicaments we find ourselves in are often quite . . ." He kept his gaze upon the table. "Astounding, to say the least." A line of thought formed between his brows. "Agnese's husband had her lover killed and then concocted into something that she would always view as a warning. He gave it to her as a gift on the night of their wedding."

"This is exactly the reason why I wanted you on this voyage." Sir Adrian leaned forward. "I knew when conversation lagged, you would be the one to bring us up again. Tell us more."

"Agnese broke the vase one morning. Her husband found her on the floor with bloody hands." He paused dramatically. "She had been trying to pick the small dark things out of the glass."

Mr. Tabor raised his finger and shook it. "But how do you know she cut herself on the glass? I still say you're making this up."

Mr. Emerson raised his eyebrow, accepting Tabor's challenge. "Her blood stains the last page in the journal."

Madeline adjusted the fringe on her sleeve. "My goodness, you can tell a story. You must know some wonderful stories about India. How I miss it."

"I'm afraid not." Mr. Emerson's voice was clipped. "As I said the night of the Egyptian dinner, my time in India was tedious. Perhaps the ship's library can lend you some entertainment. They're bound to have a book on Bengal tigers and their predatory nature. Perhaps information on the goddess Kali might better suit you. Isn't she the one associated with death and destruction—heart of stone and all that? The exact details slip my mind. I've always found goddesses so forgettable."

Sir Adrian guffawed. "Top notch, Emerson. We'll find no ramblings of inconsequential dates with this historian."

Bianca leaned to the side, closer to Mr. Emerson. "What about the last entry in the journal? You can't keep us in suspense."

Mr. Emerson smiled secretly. "The last page of the journal contains only one sentence—'I hope he puts me in the glass with you.'"

Bianca gasped again. She couldn't help the smile that followed.

"Very macabre," Madeline said. "I prefer happy endings—everything tied up in a pretty, neat bow."

"Wouldn't that be dull?" Sir Adrian said.

Bianca took a deep, satisfied breath. "It's better than a Gothic novel."

Mr. Tabor nodded. "Yes, now that I think about it, it's very believable. It's not the first time I've heard of an Italian doing something so dark." He raised his hands. "Has no one else heard of their treatment of the Spotted Skipper moths?"

Madeline and Sir Adrian looked at each other and cringed.

"I regret that I have not. But I beg that you excuse me." Mr. Emerson pushed back his chair. "I'm feeling a little light-headed this afternoon, and I find I'm not hungry. Perhaps it's my turn for seasickness." He walked away, the shadows of the flags stretching across the back of his coat.

"Well." Mr. Tabor pushed away from the table. "Maybe I can find a sandwich somewhere. Let's hope dinner will be more . . ." He looked poignantly at Bianca. "Up to American standards."

"And you must excuse me as well." Madeline stood. "I think I need to go lie down for a while." She placed her fingers on her temple. "My head is roaring from this heat."

"Yes. Do go and rest. I trust you'll be more yourself later." As Madeline slipped away, Sir Adrian looked at the endless ocean. Expressions passed upon his face— contradicting, subtle.

Bianca bit her bottom lip, not sure if she should ask the question burning within her. "Sir Adrian?"

"Yes?"

"I get the feeling that Mr. Emerson doesn't like Madeline."

"Do you?" He looked at her casually and then gazed back out to sea. "I hadn't noticed at all."

For Paul Emerson, various sunsets around the world held a particular memory. Morocco brought to mind the long shadows of the camels across the dunes of sand. In Corsica it was the Fortress of Bonifacio on the cliffs, flaming orange as the birds soared by. And now, as the sun slipped behind the Rock of Gibraltar, he would always think of himself in the context of standing on this ship, caught between known and unknown, familiarity and risk of everything.

He wrapped his fingers around the ship's rail and took a deep breath. He could leave when the other passengers went to Sicily—simply slip away and disappear. It wouldn't be hard. He knew his way around.

The sun dipped low, turning the sea to liquid fire. Here the Atlantic and the Mediterranean merged as one, countless tides through the ages. Spain on one side, darkest Africa on the other—The Pillars of Hercules.

Paul gave himself the liberty of thinking of Miss Marshal's perfect lips and her hazel eyes, especially the flecks of gold he saw when she didn't know he was looking. Every moment spent in her company was unlike the one before. Each one built and turned and pressed against his soul, refusing to be ignored.

He ran his hands over his face as the wind came around the ship and tore at his clothes. Words he hadn't thought about in a long time slipped back into his memory. *"My husband is away, Mr. Emerson. Come and sit by the incense. The sadhu told me it makes you forget yourself, and know the answer to your dreams..."*

"Dear Lord, I need a miracle. Please be merciful to me."

The ship's gong rang, the call for prayer in the upper cabin.

It had to end now, this torment. He had to know. Paul turned and headed up the stairs.

The sun sank lower, fading in the West, mimicking the disappearance of civilization, and all other things that must be left behind.

The easterly wind brushed across his forehead. It pushed him toward Miss Marshal, ever nearer, and everything else that was to come.

Chapter 10

As Bianca looked out from the prayer room, the sea changed from brightest sapphire to a deep, unfathomable ink. Slowly, the room acquiesced to gaslight—a soft flicker here, an amber shadow there. Before it seeped away, the last haze of sunlight lingered on the freshly painted window panes—and then it was gone.

Bianca curled her fingers around her hymnbook. "I don't see how this day could be more perfect."

The music swelled, and then the organist lightened his touch—taming the notes, slowing them—bringing tones that were both beautiful and holy.

The waves rolled, and the ship gently with it, rocked in the cradle of the deep. Bianca let her eyelids fall, feeling the music, emotions rising within her. It was joy. Pure, unbridled joy.

Something she hadn't felt in so long.

Lord, thank You that Mr. Emerson is not engaged. A smile lifted her cheeks. She bowed her head into her hymnbook so no one would see. For those kinds of smiles were the secret sort, meant for the fodder of dreams.

The music rounded back to the beginning of the hymn. Bianca opened her book, but didn't sing.

She listened.

To the hum of the people as their voices blended—young and old, believers and nonbelievers. She heard many things in those variable tones—hope, love, doubt, and fear.

Bianca listened.

To the sadness in the old man beside her—the way his voice trembled on the words. To the excitement in the little girl's voice in front of her. To the strength of the man's voice who sang behind her, boisterous and without repentance. Like he was ready to charge hell with a thimble of water.

Bianca listened through the open window to the waves lapping against the ship. They carried the tune on their lips. *Listen*, they whispered, in between stanzas. *Behold, I make all things new.*

Bianca held her songbook tighter and wanted to shout. "I hear You, Lord. I hear You in the waves, and in my heart. I believe You. You will make my life new."

The organist changed the song, and the voices around her lifted again.

"'All the way my Savior leads me; what have I to ask beside? Can I doubt His tender mercy, who through life has been my Guide? Heav'nly peace, divinest comfort, here by faith in Him to dwell! For I know, whate'er befall me, Jesus doeth all things well.'"

The door in the back opened. Bianca turned but couldn't see through the crowd. She knew Madeline still wasn't feeling well, but she thought for sure Sir Adrian would be coming. And Mr. Emerson.

"'When my spirit, clothed immortal, wings its flight to realms of day, this my song through endless ages: Jesus led me all the way . . .'"

The last note lingered tangibly in the air. The organist held his hands above the keys as if feeling the rareness of the moment.

Bianca dropped her gaze to the notes and the words on the hymnal page. Just ink, but so much more. She was afraid to close the book. Afraid the overwhelming peace she felt would fly away.

Conversation rose, dispelling the mood. The crowd filtered out, following each other like sheep.

Bianca sat, wishing they could sing again. She looked out the now dark windowpanes. The sea was the same. The room was the same. But without God's presence everything was dull. It was like He'd stepped away, gone back to His watching.

"May I sit with you?"

The tone of Mr. Emerson's voice struck her like bright light. Bianca turned and the gaslight flickered, casting shadows around his shoulders like a cloak.

"I was hoping to speak with you alone."

Lord, help me to stay composed. Calm the beating of my heart. "Of course."

He sat very still, his presence like feeling the ache and wanting of spring.

Bianca gripped the edge of her chair.

"I regret that I had to come in late." His voice took another turn; it perused valleys in her heart—found secret places that she'd long locked away. "Did you enjoy the hymn?"

"It's one of my favorites."

"Is it? We sing it often at my church." His mouth curved with something Bianca might have suspected was tenderness.

The hiss of the gaslight counted off the moments. The sun slid into the far end of the ocean and slept.

Bianca gathered a little boldness. "What church do you attend in London?"

"Metropolitan Tabernacle. Have you heard of Pastor Spurgeon?"

"Daddy once had a copy of the *Penny Pulpit*, which he'd found in Cincinnati. I enjoyed reading Pastor Spurgeon's sermons."

He smiled, and oh, what a smile it was—the softening around his lips was like sunlight upon hidden water, diamonds dancing just because. God's extravagance.

"Miss Marshal, would you forgive me if I asked you a very forward question?"

Her breath caught in her throat. "Mr. Emerson, I think you will find me the queen of forgiveness."

She could see hidden thoughts palpable upon his expression—the way he drew his eyebrows together, the slight dropping of his chin. But then, he brought his gaze back up and the green that she saw in his eyes was deeper than any mythic forest. "Since the moment I met you, a question has tormented me."

"Ask it," she whispered, barely hearing her own words.

"Is there any man in Ohio who has captured your interest?"

"Who has captured my . . ." A feeling like fever rushed over her—heat and joy, something like delirium, then fear. "No."

He took her hand in his. "I want you to know that my intentions toward you are more than friendship."

His touch was like the sun in the mist after rain, and longing—such submerged longing came. Bianca had the blind, unreasoning wish to cry.

"If we were in normal circumstances, I would ask to court you. However, you're thousands of miles away from your home. And this journey is *quite* out of the ordinary."

"You may court me, Mr. Emerson." She swept her gaze around the room. "Such as it is."

Surprise bled into his features. "I would ask your father for his permission—"

"He would approve." Bianca thought of her conversation with Daddy on the banks of the pond in Ohio. Her heart swelled at how he'd been the only one to believe in her and how right he had been. She would know her soul mate when she saw him, he had said. And now, here, she sat with Paul Emerson, a man who exceeded her dreams and called to the secret places in her heart.

"Are you certain?" Worry lined his eyes. "I have no wish to have your father think I'm taking advantage of you. I will not take advantage of you, I promise you that."

Peace flooded over her, coming in waves. Holding his hand felt like the most natural thing in the world. Right—it felt right. "Daddy trusts me." She looked deep into his eyes. "And I trust you." She tested the feel of her hand in his, afraid to hold it tighter but wanting to. "I can assure you, Mr. Emerson . . ." Her eyelids fell with her thoughts—all the prodding from Mama to settle, all the strings of eligible Portsmouth men, and all those horrid walks . . . All the Sunday dinners, and failed attempts at conversation. "I know my own mind."

"Well, then." His voice was like the first breath of spring, coaxing the apple trees into bloom.

"Well, then," she whispered.

"I think you'd better call me Paul instead of Mr. Emerson.

"I think you'd better call me Bianca."

His gaze fell upon her lips. "Bianca . . . what a lovely name."

Bianca sat in a half-lit room, waiting for the magic lantern show. *My intentions toward you are more than friendship.* Every time she thought about his words, she blushed like an infatuated, well-wooed fool.

Which she was.

Unabashedly so.

Especially since Paul sat beside her.

And now, more than ever, she had to remind herself that she wasn't one of those brainless, giggling, doe-eyed girls she'd had to put up with her entire life. Like Judith Applegate, tripping all over herself just to be near the butcher's son, or Lilith Snodgrass, laughing at every simpleminded thing her beau said.

That was definitely not her.

Bianca raised her chin. Nor would it ever be.

Paul finished talking with the man beside him and turned toward her. He pointed to Mr. Tabor sitting outside the doorway. "Is that a moth he has in his jar?"

Bianca laughed—with complete decorum, of course.

Only four people turned around and glared.

Bianca tucked her hair behind her ear and lowered her voice. "He's written something in his journal."

Paul leaned back in his chair and squinted. "Canary-shouldered Thorn moth . . . *Ennomos Alniaria.*"

Bianca raised an eyebrow. "Latin?"

Paul nodded, mirroring what she suspected was her same perplexed look. "A Boston streetcar driver who knows Latin."

"He is . . ."

"Odd." Paul supplied the word.

Just then, the photographer shut the door. Mr. Tabor was left to himself, and Bianca's thoughts of moths and streetcars vanished.

After all, not only was she sitting beside Paul, she was now in the dark with Paul.

"It'll just be a moment," the photographer said. "My matches . . ."

A small child laughed.

A muffled conversation floated through the room.

Bianca smiled in the dark. She could feel Paul's presence beside her. She dropped her gaze to the place where she thought his hand might be. She lowered her hand.

A match struck. A small flame hung suspended and then grew in the oil lamp.

Bianca pulled her hand back.

Paul quickly crossed his arms over his chest. He seemed very intent upon the pattern of the ceiling.

Beside the photographer, tendrils of smoke came from a strange metal box and curled into the air. The light grew in the room. Scene after scene flared out upon the canvas—grapevines amongst the ruins of Greece, the Bridge of Sighs in Venice, the medieval bricks in the oldest part of the Louvre.

Bianca watched with awe. On occasion, a book Daddy ordered for her would have a lithograph, but mostly she just imagined what these famous places looked like, constructing mortar out of words and palaces out of phrases in her dreams. But now it all floated before her as vibrant and full of life as Mama's hollyhocks by the crooked end of the front porch.

When it was over, Bianca clapped as if President Grant had just walked into the room. The crowd stood.

"What was your favorite part?" Paul asked.

"The sunflower fields in Tuscany."

He smiled, not bragging that he'd probably seen them in person. Another reason to love him.

A short woman pushed through the crowd with a group of her friends. "There's the historian. I'm sure he'll know. Let's ask him."

"How may I be of assistance?" Paul stepped to the side so an elderly man could pass.

"Can you tell us the history of the Bridge of Sighs? I can only remember parts, and I'm sure most of that's fantasy. I'm afraid I've read too many novels."

She's not the only one. Bianca kept her lips sealed tight.

"What have you heard?" Instantly, there was a gleam in Paul's eyes.

"Well . . ." The woman took out her fan. "What I really want to know—is it a bridge for lovers?"

"A bridge for lovers." A whimsical look altered his features. He casually placed his hands in his pockets.

The air was a pulsing, livid thing. Just that one word—*lovers*—sent Bianca's imagination, and her deepest desires, to a frenzied, unearthly height. All the novels she'd ever read, every scene she'd placed herself in, came to remembrance. Her gaze climbed Paul's waistcoat, the slight crookedness of his tie . . . Of course, Mama would say a good Christian woman would not think such thoughts, especially since he'd only just asked to court her. A tremble started, a shiver around her shoulders.

"The Ponte Dei Sospiri . . ." The words rolled off his tongue with perfection. He looked into the air, as if he could see the famous landmark materialize.

Bianca opened her fan. The sound of Italian coming from his lips sent shivers of heat along her spine.

"Built in 1602 . . . It connects the old prisons to the interrogation room in the Doge's Palace. The view from the bridge was the last view of Venice convicts saw before their imprisonment. Lord Byron gave the bridge its name when he wrote *Childe Harold's Pilgrimage*. The famous quote is, 'I stood in Venice on the Bridge of Sighs; a palace and a prison on each hand.'"

The woman fanned herself frantically. "But you're sure there's nothing to do with lovers? I could have sworn there was something involving a kiss."

A kiss.

The world halted. Its noise faded. Bianca's gaze fell upon his lips. Words from the Song of Solomon, a book her pastor never preached from, swirled at the edges of her mind. *"Let him kiss me with the kisses of his mouth: for thy love is better than wine . . ."*

"There is a local legend."

"Yes?" The woman's fan stopped midair.

Paul looked at Bianca. A smile tugged at the corner of his lips. "If lovers kiss on a gondola beneath the bridge at sunset, they will be granted everlasting love."

Bianca's breath came too quickly. She couldn't stop looking at Paul's lips. She was falling. Into very deep water.

"Lovely evening." Sir Adrian stepped into their circle and took Bianca's hand. "There's some dancing to be had and I am in need of a partner."

Paul gave her a smile that was full of later things—conversations and possibilities. The women encircled him as she walked away, all multicolored skirts and waving fans.

"Do you dance often?" Sir Adrian's voice tore her attention away. On the lantern-lit promenade deck, couples spun and stepped elaborately.

"Not as often as I would like." Bianca was thankful for the cool wind. "Do you think they'll play the Virginia reel?"

"Virginia reel?" He laughed. "Do you mean to tell me you don't know the cotillion?"

"Sorry."

"The polonaise?"

"No."

"A quadrille?"

"Sorry again."

"My dear girl, surely you can waltz." The lanterns swayed all around them, mimicking the couples.

"I hate to be the bearer of bad news, but no."

Sir Adrian stopped in the middle of the promenade and placed her hand upon his shoulder. "What do they teach ladies in Ohio?"

"We have cakewalks."

He squeezed his lips into a thin line. She assumed to keep from laughing.

"Would you like to fill in for my lack of education?"

He sighed as if they were talking about weighty matters of parliament. "Somebody has to."

A melodeon played something that reminded her of "Cradle Jane," a song that Mama sometimes played on the dulcimer. Sir Adrian turned her dramatically. "Our ballroom shall be the horizon, our canopy the stars."

"Very pretty words." Bianca looked at his perfectly combed hair, his devil-may-care expression, and his fine silk collar. In this light he was handsome—in a dangerous sort of a way—half boy, a quarter trouble, and the other quarter the means to accomplish it. "I imagine you've broken hearts over every English dance floor."

"You have no idea." He pulled her close, placing his hand upon her back. "Now be a good little American and let me do the leading."

Bianca raised her eyebrow. He, in turn, raised his. As the beat rounded back to the beginning, he took the first step.

Effortlessly, he pushed and pulled, balanced, and made her feet do the most extraordinary things. When she began to get a little off-center, he simply moved his leg the least little bit and brought her to rights again. She laughed at the feel of it—twirling, floating, doing exactly as she was commanded, led by a master.

"That's a very pleasant smile. Is there anything particular that has caused it?"

"I was only thinking that this has been the most perfect day of my life."

"That's saying quite a lot." He tilted his head and stared into her eyes. "Has Prince Charming made an offer for milady's affections?"

Bianca looked away.

"He has. Bravo." When they reached the corner by the stairs, he stopped. He led her to a darker part of the promenade. The Mediterranean wind blew through his hair and ruffled it. "I wonder if you'll invite me to your wedding?"

"He hasn't asked me that, you popinjay. He's merely asked to court me. Not everyone lives in your fast aristocratic world."

"I suppose you're right. Do you know, I've never been spoken to so plainly in my entire life. I should call you out. Cast my gauntlet right here, and see you at dawn with pistols."

Bianca giggled. "Can we at least wait until I've seen the Holy Land?"

"I've no wish to deny you the prize. No matter how sharp a tongue you have." His sleeves blew in the wind. "Have you thought about where you'll live if you marry Emerson?"

"In England, I suppose. I couldn't expect him to come back to Portsmouth. We don't even have a museum."

"So, you'd have to leave your home, your parents." He sounded like a schoolteacher, all careful dictation of facts. "Do you think London would suit you?"

Bianca smiled, full force. "I think I'd positively adore it—museums, theaters, shops, tea houses—what's not to love?"

"The thieves, the slums, the starving children, the corruption." His voice softened. "The high-minded aristocrats who do nothing to help."

"It sounds like a city of extreme contrasts."

"Yes, as the people living there—extreme contrasts. I'd take care . . ." He put his hand over hers and squeezed. "And use that head of yours in the days to come." The moonlight glinted in the facets of his ruby ring.

"If anyone has extreme contrasts, it's you."

He veiled his expression. "I am a product of my experiences. Nothing more."

"Who are you behind that mask you wear?"

A carefully placed smile, and then he grabbed her and dipped her down, almost to the floor. He held her there, aloft—between the polished planks and the intensity in his eyes. "At the moment, I'm the one preparing you to be the toast of London."

"May I cut in?" Paul's face was above her, bordered by a dusting of stars.

Sir Adrian lifted her back to standing and stepped away. "I must warn you, Emerson, if any Virginia reels are danced, we may see a side of Miss Marshal that will shock our English sensibilities."

"Indeed?" There was laughter in Paul's eyes. Beneath his gloves, she could feel the warmth of his hands. "I'm sorry I was detained. Will you forgive me?"

She was sure she would forgive him of anything. She found herself blushing again, and she hated herself for it. "You're a man that's constantly sought after for your expertise. There's no need to apologize."

He gave her a smile full of mischief and walked her to a part of the less-crowded dance floor. "Yes, I'm very handy to have around for parlor games. You never know when there might be a round of 'Who can guess how the Mongols killed their victims' or 'Why did Edward Burne-Jones bury his brown paint in the garden?'"

Bianca laughed. "Well?"

"Well, what?"

"Why did the artist bury the brown paint in his garden?"

He wrapped his arm around her and raised her left hand. "Are you sure you wish to know?"

"I wasn't born in the woods to be scared by an owl. Of course I do."

He laughed, and it was like the heavens opened. "I'm not quite sure I know what you just said to me, but regardless... Edward Burne-Jones buried his brown paint in his garden because it had mummies in it. He was so shocked at this revelation that after he gave it a proper burial, he put a daisy on top. "

"You can't be serious."

"The paint is called 'mummy brown' and it's still sold today. For hundreds of years, mummies have been crushed into a fine brown powder for the paint. In medieval times, they were ground up and put into medicine."

"Who would even think of such a thing? What in the Sam Hill is that supposed to accomplish?"

"My goodness. You're full of euphemisms tonight. Are you sure you're up to dancing with a 'sought-after historian' on a very romantic ship sailing through the Mediterranean?" Paul narrowed his eyes. "Perhaps I should take you back to your cabin before you faint again. The strain must be overwhelming . . . No doubt the combination is affecting your feeble American mind."

She opened her mouth to protest.

"You don't tease easily either, do you?" He turned her, flaring her skirt out. "I'll have to keep that in mind for future reference."

"You English cur. I thought you were serious for a moment."

"A dog, am I? That is harsh." He took on a look of a scolded boy. "Haven't you ever heard about the dry English sense of humor? Surely you must've read about it in all those novels you're so fond of."

She raised her chin a notch. "And how do you know I'm fond of novels?"

"I saw you reading one in the shadows of the ship's smokestacks earlier. And, I saw the three others you had piled up by your chair. I hate to admit it, but I was spying on you."

She looked away. "Well, I'm surprised we're having this conversation. Most men would run screaming into the night when they'd found out a woman was reading *The Mysteries of Udolpho*."

"I wasn't looking at the title."

"No? What about *Varney the Vampire*? That must have given you pause."

"It was very hard to concentrate on anything at that precise moment." He brought her closer and tightened the grip on her hand.

"And why is that?"

"Because I could do nothing but look at the way the sunlight made your hair look auburn in its light." He walked around her in a circle and stopped at her side. "And, it was very hard not to stare at the way the corner of your lips curved in a smile when you'd read something pleasing."

She breathed. In and out. Forced herself to remember this simple task. She looked up into his green eyes and then she forgot again.

"And then, you took off your hat, and you laid your book upon your lap, and you fell asleep. And there, as the waves rocked you, I had only one singular thought in my mind."

"And what was that?" The words came out raspy and weak.

He lowered his voice—all velvet and warm rain. "It's very revealing. I don't think things can ever be the same afterward if I tell you."

"Go on." They stood in line, waiting for the couple at the end to circle around.

"The only thought I had in my mind was that I was a man who was completely undone." He looked at their intertwined hands and then her eyes. "If you'd already set your sights on another gentleman, I think I would have stolen you away—taken you to Patagonia or somewhere until I could have convinced you otherwise."

In that moment, Bianca realized a very poignant thing.

One could hardly blush discreetly when one's entire body felt like molten fire.

"Ah, you're back." Madeline stood in the darkness of the cabin with her back turned. She twisted a bit of her hair.

Bianca turned up the gaslight. "Why are you in the dark? Is your headache still bothering you?"

"Thinking, that's all." She turned, her pale face as emotionless as the moon. "I came above deck earlier. I watched you dancing."

Bianca removed one of her hairpins. "Why didn't you stay? You could have danced."

Madeline laughed without smiling. "Sit down. I'll brush your hair."

"That would be nice." Bianca went to the vanity stand, sat, and handed Madeline the brush.

In the mirror, Madeline's expression was hard and cold. When she caught Bianca looking at her, she quickly smiled.

Chapter 11

*F*ive sunrises in the Mediterranean. Morning by
morning, Bianca stood at the rail and saw the
light bleed over the cradle of antiquity. A brushstroke of
orange atop a mountain. A purple blanket over the coast
of Italy, falling upon the grapevines and sunflowers like
mist. A glimmer of yellow there, over an ancient temple,
pushing through the columns where learned men had
debated things to come. And, when Bianca had risen
early on the last day, she saw hills of crumpled velvet
stretching endlessly as the ship drifted past the shore.

Now, moments before they were to sight Israel,
Bianca added two dollops of milk until her black tea was
the color of caramel. She raised the teacup and sipped
slowly, as Madeline had advised her. The crisp, malty
liquid rested upon her tongue before she swallowed.
Smooth and perfect, and obviously very fine.

Just like a certain English gentleman.

Thankfully, the other passengers didn't seem to
notice her constant, ridiculous smile, or the way she had
the propensity to daydream at the most inopportune
times.

Bianca closed her eyes, and the breath of the sea
washed over her, bringing with it words from her
memory. "'Ah me! How sweet is love itself possess'd . . .
How sweet indeed, dear Romeo . . .'"

Madeline looked up from the book she was reading.
"Did you say something?"

The bottom of Bianca's teacup scraped the saucer. "I was thinking of a line from Shakespeare. *Romeo and Juliet*. Act five, scene one."

"Ah, the balcony scene. Is it a favorite of yours?"

"Isn't it every woman's?"

Madeline dropped her gaze and smiled.

"Do you share the same ailment as I do, Madeline?"

"What would that be?"

"I'm an incurable romantic."

"I've noticed." Madeline leaned toward Bianca. "What is the world without romance? A stolen glance ... whispers in the dark ... hearing your name upon your lover's lips." She lowered her lashes. "There's nothing quite like being held by a man ... touched by a man."

Bianca jerked away. "Great Jehoshaphat's drawers!"

"Your face is quite red." Madeline's pouty lips turned upward. "Did I embarrass you?"

"There are people around." Bianca shielded the side of her face with her hand. "What if the men in our party were to happen by?"

Madeline shrugged. "What would Mr. Tabor say, do you think?"

"Say?" Bianca lifted her teacup and tried to calm herself. "Do you mean to imply that he has a vocabulary not related to insects? Or chowder?"

The shadow of a seagull danced across the linen tablecloth. Madeline turned a page. "Yesterday he did say something different. He told me he was a soldier in that horrid war between your states."

A bit of tea spewed from Bianca's mouth. She reached for a napkin. "Really?"

The wind picked up and played in the pages of Madeline's book. "I wasn't paying much attention— you know how he is—but he did say something about working in a prison camp, somewhere in Illinois."

The wind came again and stole Bianca's breath away. It couldn't be the same prison camp. She clutched the locket around her neck, wanting to open it, needing to see her brother's picture.

"Look." Madeline stood and went to the rail. The wind parted the clouds and a tower peeked through the mist. A red flag, high above an ancient fortress wall, trembled in the faltering rain.

Bianca scanned the crowd heading to the upper deck for a better view. Mr. Tabor climbed the stairs, jotting something down in his journal.

Madeline waved. "Mr. Tabor, do come here."

He closed the journal reluctantly and walked back down. "Israel, I presume? It's not as fine as Boston Harbor. It'll have to do." His blue-gray eyes shifted to Bianca. "We will bear it the best we can, won't we?"

Bianca looked back at the romantic scene unfolding across the waves—the old stone buildings, the arches and exotic roofs. "We will bear it very well."

More people came down the promenade and stood at the rail. Those going on to Egypt had brought their journals in order to draw the scene.

Mr. Tabor lifted his binoculars from around his neck. "Do you see any *Tipulidae* in the air yet?"

Madeline arched an eyebrow. "Excuse me, but I have to assume that's an insect."

"Crane flies." Mr. Tabor turned toward them, his eyes behind the glass the size of tea biscuits.

Sir Adrian rounded the corner. "We've arrived." He pushed his scarf behind him and leaned on the rail beside Bianca. "Is that the smell of orange blossoms in the air?"

Behind them, Paul pushed the library doors open and walked out. "There's a large orange grove outside the city." He nodded at Sir Adrian. "Forgive me, I was standing near the door and heard your conversations."

Heard their conversations? Bianca's heart slammed into her throat.

Madeline smiled like a cat who'd eaten too much cream.

Paul walked to stand at Bianca's other side. His gaze was on the city and the waves. He lowered his voice. "Good morning."

"Good morning." Bianca pulled her shawl tighter. "We missed you at breakfast."

"That's very kind." Paul turned to her, giving her a look that was just for her—locking eyes with her like he never meant to look away.

Her grip on the shawl relaxed; it slipped from her shoulders.

Sir Adrian picked it up. "I wasn't at breakfast. Did you miss me?"

Bianca smiled. "I did miss you. There was such an overwhelming quiet that I hardly knew how to get on."

"Is that how it is? I'm cut to the core." Sir Adrian's smile said otherwise. "Tell me, Emerson, what did you learn about Jaffa in the library?

Paul angled his body toward the group and spoke like he would at one of his lectures. "The timbers used in the construction of Solomon's Temple were floated here on rafts. We should still be able to see the narrow opening in the reef where they passed them to shore." He pointed to a shadowy place just beyond the waves. "There."

"Excellent." Sir Adrian leaned on his walking stick; this time it was the head of a falcon. "Two gentlemen said earlier that Jonah sailed from here when he ran from God. Perhaps we passed the very place where he was swallowed by the whale."

Paul nodded. "According to the Bible, he was on his way to Tarshish, thought to be the end of the world at that time. It's in Spain, before the Strait of Gibraltar."

"Fascinating." Sir Adrian tapped his walking stick again. "Do you think God is like that, Mrs. Greene?"

"Like what?" The black feathers on her hat blew against her forehead.

"Does God go to great measures to chase us down until we do what He wants?"

"Religion's not my expertise." Her gaze deviated to Paul. "Perhaps you should ask Mr. Emerson. I've heard he takes great pleasure in such trifles."

A shadow crossed Paul's expression. "Look there by the lighthouse. That's Simon the Tanner's house where God gave Peter the vision of the beasts let down in a sheet."

Madeline wrinkled her forehead. "Let down in a what?"

"A sheet." Paul voice was cold. "Are you not familiar with the Book of Acts? Oh, I beg your pardon; you did say the things of God were not your forte." He turned back to the sea, his gaze lost on an indeterminate point on the horizon.

Bianca leaned toward him. "Are you all right?"

"I'm fine." His knuckles shone white on the rail.

Sir Adrian seemed unnaturally fascinated with watching the boats casting off from shore. His face was stoic, like a cemetery angel.

The light rain stopped and the clouds parted. "What a lovely day it's turning out to be." Madeline removed her hatpin and untied the bow beneath her chin. A splinter of sunlight fell across Madeline's face.

"Enjoying the exotic air?" Bianca asked.

Madeline closed her eyes. "Perhaps I'm praying."

Sir Adrian nodded like something weighty had been said. "Perhaps we should all be praying for our pilgrimage—praying that the scenes hallowed by our Savior's life will bring the dross and mire out of our own."

The beam of light brightened, bringing out the deeper streaks of cinnamon in Madeline's black tresses. "This reminds me of the sunshine in India. If I imagine hard enough, I can almost smell the fragrance of orchids." She took a cleansing breath. "I used to grow them and wear them in my hair." She opened her eyes abruptly, a shimmer of tears lacing the brown. "But all that's gone now—that part of my life stolen."

Paul slid his hand from the rail and walked away without a word.

Madeline put her hat back on, her expression bland. "I wonder what's wrong with him."

Paul disappeared behind the staircase, a scowl on his face that matched the brooding of the sea.

Sir Adrian surveyed the scene in front of them and then pushed away from the rail. "We should be on those boats within the hour."

"I think I just saw an *Apamea lithoxlaea*." Mr. Tabor ran down the promenade, his binoculars bouncing against his chest.

"Let's go see about the luggage, shall we?" Madeline laced her arm through Bianca's. "The adventure begins." She smiled. "I do so hope you're ready."

Paul slammed his cabin door. The bed was a blur, the washstand inconsequential. Of course she'd remember that. Of course she'd flaunt it.

India. Two years ago. The Elephant's Eye—a diamond conveniently loose from the temple idol of Ganesha—over a thousand years old. The merchant who'd stolen it and made the proposition to the British Museum . . .

The hellish voyage to Benares. Wandering through the streets with the monkeys and the cows. The holy men begging under the shadows of the ancient towers. The sweat running down his back and clinging to the scratchy fibers of his linen shirt.

The old stairs leading down to the Ganges River—a sea of animated rags—sleeping, singing, washing. A group of four carrying a body to the river, plunging it down, and then placing it upon a funeral pyre—so aloof when they'd set it to flames, so disconnected when the smoke rose and peeled the dead man's flesh away.

And, while the half-naked men chanted, he'd turned and seen her—Madeline, his point of contact from the merchant, wearing a white orchid woven into her long, black hair.

She'd stood at the river with her eyes closed, the sun falling upon her face like a shroud.

His footfalls made no noise against the dilapidated stone. He smelled the orchid in her hair as he slipped behind her.

"Did you have trouble finding our little paradise?" Her voice was soft and low.

"No trouble," he'd answered. "I stopped to see a few sights on the way. From what I see of this place, I'm not quite sure you should be here alone."

"Shouldn't I?" A slow smile spread upon her face as she turned. She was pale English skin amongst a plethora of brown. "Am I in danger of getting freckles from the sun? Or do you speak of something more alarming?"

"You don't seem like a woman who'd be easily alarmed." He'd studied the gentle curve of her neck, her cheek, her lips. "And as far as the sun goes, you mustn't blame it if it freckled you; it would only be trying to kiss perfection."

Her smile deepened. "You must be very tired after your journey."

An old man wailed as he washed in the river. Red flower petals floated around him as abundantly as the flies. He held his hands up, full of water, and prayed to the sun.

"I'm not as tired as I was," he'd said. *"May I escort you back to the English colony? Someone must be very worried about you."*

Her brown eyes had reflected the descent of the sun. "Yes, someone should be, shouldn't they?"

And he'd taken her hand. In it was the diamond, wrapped in a ripped piece of a sari.

The ship's engine stopped. There was a sudden silence, broken only by the sound of the sea.

Paul leaned over the washstand, his breath coming too hard. "I wasn't going to do this. My wanton days are over. With God, it's all forgotten. It's forgiven."

Noises came from above—the ship's bell, shouting.

The memories came again—scene after scene, word after word, vividly picturesque.

Sweat. Sweat like India. The smell of cardamom mixed with rain . . .

Paul clutched his chest and the feeling there that felt like poison. "God, You know I wish I could take it back. If only . . ."

It's forgotten. It's forgiven. This time, the words didn't seem true.

"Vengeance is mine; I will repay, saith the Lord" . . . God will judge.

"Bianca . . ." Paul looked toward the sunlight streaming in from his cabin window. "I don't deserve you. I never did."

Chapter 12

Clouds hung low over the water, gripping the waves and swirling them with their hands. The little boat rose and fell, like a child's toy in a bathtub.

Bianca gripped the side of the boat to avoid poking Sir Adrian in the eye with her parasol. The Turkish boatman kept rowing, plowing through the waves. He didn't seem to care when a wave soaked his back, or when foam spilled in and soaked all their shoes. Just back and forth, back and forth. Taking travelers to shore coming from places he would never see.

"Tell me, does this constitute a luxury tour?" Madeline stomped, sending water up to their knees. Seaweed wrapped tighter around her ankle.

"How long are we to be on this dinghy?" Mr. Tabor opened his pocket watch and nearly lost it to the next wave.

"Courage. I see sand ahead." Sir Adrian held his hat down upon his head. Beads of water ran down his face.

Paul stared out to sea, his arms crossed as if he was being led to an execution.

Mr. Tabor squinted toward the beach. "Those people look positively oriental with all those turbans." His hat tumbled from his head and landed in the waves.

Madeline scowled. "How did you expect them to look? Bowler hats and sack suits?"

Paul kept his eyes upon the water. "Perhaps Mr. Tabor is only saying that seeing them for the first time is a surprise."

"Take in every scene from this moment on." Sir Adrian tapped his walking stick against the bottom of the boat, splashing water upon his soaked trousers. "Your minds will be replaying these moments back to you when you're old and gray."

Madeline closed her eyes and looked ill. "That's what I'm afraid of."

The boat thudded against something hard, then slid onto the sand.

Sir Adrian dropped a piece of paper and some coins into the Turkish man's hand. The man climbed out of the boat and ran toward a palm leaf shelter where a richly dressed foreigner waited in the shade.

Sir Adrian stepped onto the sand and offered Madeline assistance. "Emerson, feel at liberty to comment at any time."

Paul stepped out of the boat and then held out his hand toward Bianca. Standing on the sand, he shoved his hands in his pockets and looked down the coastline. "Jaffa rose into early importance as the chief harbor of Judea. I must warn you all, like most Eastern cities, the interior of Jaffa may disappoint you. The narrow streets are said to be soggy in the winter and choked with dust in the summer."

"An interesting, howbeit brief, assessment." Sir Adrian walked toward him, his walking stick making holes in the sand. "I say, you don't quite seem yourself today."

Paul adjusted his tie, which was completely soaked. "Forgive me, I'm usually full of stories, aren't I? Let's see . . ." His drenched vest clung to him, as well as his fine white shirt. He moved his hands to his sides and water dripped from his sleeves onto the sand. "A Greek, Latin, and Armenian convent make up the majority of the people in Jaffa . . ." He took off his hat and ran a hand through his hair. The mahogany strands flared out in the wind, giving him the look of a poet. "There's a mission school here, started by an American friend of Florence Nightingale."

Madeline smiled at him and twirled the handle of her parasol. "Do you think she taught the heathens any proper manners?"

"I imagine that was a problem." Paul looked at her and scowled. "People tend to do the most alarming things abroad. Don't you agree?"

Madeline raised her thick eyelashes and laughed. "Why, Mr. Emerson, you are rather peevish today."

The boat containing their luggage came to shore. The Turkish boatman ran back, holding a small trunk and a note. He handed them to Sir Adrian.

Mr. Tabor's eyes narrowed. "About these heathens— how will we keep from being accosted?"

"We will not be accosted." Sir Adrian took off his soaked gloves and flung them out to sea. "Our plans have changed." He looked down at the note. "My friend, Samuel Owenburke, has been detained. I'm sending our luggage on to Jerusalem without us."

Madeline's pout was in full regalia. "But what if it gets stolen?"

"We'll be much safer in Jaffa without dragging our finery through the streets." Sir Adrian opened the little trunk and began to pull out robes, veils, and turbans. "Samuel sent these so we can blend in. If we don't take these measures, every beggar, thief, and peddler will be attacking our heels. Once we're on the carriage road, we shouldn't have any problems." He pulled out two black cloths. "Emerson, Tabor, put these on around your head and drape them like so." He lifted two thin veils out of the trunk. "Ladies, I've no wish to fend off some Arab who wants to trade a herd of camels for you."

Madeline draped the veil over her arm. "Wouldn't it be much safer just to go around the city?"

"Where's the adventure in that?" Sir Adrian removed his coat. "Take off your hats. And put away those parasols. As for your ... posterior region, would you ... it would be much easier. . ." He looked to the clouds for some sort of inspiration.

Bianca took a purple and yellow robe from his hand. "Do you want us to go behind those ruins and take our bustles off?" She snickered, a mental picture coming to her. "It would look odd having something stick out under our robes like a caboose."

Mr. Tabor stopped winding the turban around his head. Sir Adrian blew out pent-up breath. Paul put his hand on his side and coughed.

"What?" Bianca held up her hands. "Can't you see the impracticability of English bustles? My bustles in Ohio are half the size."

Madeline dangled her robe from her fingers like she suspected it to be full of vermin. "Let's go discuss that."

Mr. Tabor's voice faded to a whine as they disappeared behind the rocks.

Sir Adrian's voice rose. "Dash it all, man, where's your spirit of adventure?"

Shock laced Madeline's features. "What were you thinking, saying those things? A lady should never speak of her undergarments."

"You're going to lecture me about etiquette? After what you said on the ship?"

Madeline's mouth gaped. "What on earth do they teach young ladies in Ohio?"

"Just about the same things they teach English girls—to sit in a corner and look pretty." Bianca stepped hard in the sand and then turned. "What is going on between you and Mr. Emerson?"

Madeline stopped fidgeting with her robe. "Going on? I don't know what you mean."

"Don't you?"

"Here, turn around. I'll untie your bustle."

Bianca rested her forehead against a tall, crumbling wall.

"Men can be so trying, especially their moods. Mr. Emerson doesn't like me, that's all." Madeline's fingers slowed on the knot.

"I've seen the animosity between you."

"Well, I can only take so much. How long should I let him glare at me before I retaliate?"

The bustle dropped to the sand. "Why wouldn't he like you?"

Madeline smiled, slow and sure. "Perhaps it's only that he wants you all to himself and I'm in the way. I am your chaperone, after all. It can hardly be denied that he has feelings for you. From what I've seen on the voyage, I can guess that you return the sentiment."

Bianca opened her mouth but no words came.

"I thought so."

Relief flooded Bianca. She'd wanted to tell Madeline so many times, but never felt at liberty. "You've been married. I'm sure you could offer some insight."

"If only I could save you from the mistakes I made."

"It can't be that bad. Everyone makes mistakes."

Madeline wiped wet strands of hair away from Bianca's face. "You're so young."

"Not that much younger than you."

"A lot can happen in five years." Madeline turned toward the sea, her face stoic. "Do you think Sir Adrian expects us to wear these robes over our dresses? We'll collapse under the heat."

Madeline's sudden change of subject was not lost upon her. "What do you suggest?"

"If we don't take off our dresses, our collars are bound to show. It would give us away immediately."

"I think you're right." Bianca touched the lace at her throat. "But I've always worn a collar. I don't want to be immodest. "

"Look, the robe neckline is no lower than a ball gown. You have worn a ball gown, haven't you?"

"Portsmouth doesn't have a ballroom. When we dance, I just wear a nice dress."

"I see."

Bianca bit the corner of her lip. "We do have a train station. And a post office."

"Well, that makes all the difference. What do you do for fun?"

"Long walks, church socials, reading."

Madeline removed the pins from her hair. Each section fell loose and whipped around her face like a dark willow tree vine. "Have you ever been to the opera?"

"No, but I would love to." Saying the words made Bianca feel worse. "The only time I've ever been out of Portsmouth is this trip."

"It must be awful for you hearing about all the places I've been."

Bianca frowned. Lately Madeline had acted so arrogant. Since she'd had that headache, it was like she was a different person. "You did mention that you've traveled a lot. Your husband was a merchant, wasn't he?"

"Yes . . . I had three servants at my beck and call." Madeline looked past the stone ruins like she could see the days she spoke of. "Every morning I tended my orchids and watched the elephants play."

"It must have been very hard for you to leave when your husband died."

"It was hard to leave India, but I had to." Her voice faded and was replaced by the lapping of the waves. "Bianca, I haven't been entirely truthful with you."

Panic gripped her. Surely it was about Paul.

Madeline dropped her gaze to the sand. "I didn't think you'd be my friend if you knew."

"If I knew what?"

"My husband didn't die." Her pale cheeks flushed. "He divorced me."

"He divorced you?" Bianca repeated it slowly.

"And now I work to support myself, alone." Tears formed in her eyes. "Sometimes it's so hard. I'm so grateful that I won this contest. With the prize money, I'll finally be able to do more than survive." She pushed her wrists into the sleeves of the robe and dabbed her eyes.

Bianca wrapped her arms around Madeline. She looked down at the cracks in the rocks and their footprints in the sand. Her eyes came back to the horizon. Their ship turned and pushed away, back into the deep. "I don't know what to say."

Madeline pulled back and gave her a weak smile. "Will you forgive me for not telling you?"

"Of course."

"It was another woman. His affections went on the spree."

"Your husband left you?" Bianca ran her hand along Madeline's arm.

"They smile at you one day and curse you the next." Madeline patted Bianca's hand. "You want my advice about Mr. Emerson? Take this—just when you think you can trust a man, that's when it hits."

Bianca leaned closer, afraid that the wind might carry their voices. "What hits?"

"His eyes wander. It's not long before his heart follows."

"But Daddy's been married to my mama for thirty years. He's never strayed, and he doesn't even like her."

"He's never strayed that you *know* of."

"I . . ." Madeline's thought jarred her.

"Be careful with Mr. Emerson. I've seen the way you look at him . . ." She sighed as if it were a sad story told too many times. "And the way he looks at you." Madeline gripped Bianca's shoulders. "You can't trust him. Not any man. Especially one who's as good-looking as he is. Think about it—why isn't he married yet?"

"He hasn't found the right woman, I suppose." Her voice sounded weak to her ears.

Madeline narrowed her eyes. "You're smarter than that. He makes good money and has a smile that would make the Queen beg for more. Do you think you're the only woman who's noticed? Why hasn't some English girl snatched him up by now?"

"I . . . don't know."

"I'll tell you why; because there is a reason. Men always have secrets."

Chapter *13*

Mrs. Greene," Sir Adrian's voice dragged out. "Miss Marshal? Excuse me, ladies, but we are on a schedule."

"One moment, if you please." Madeline's eyes were cold and dark, a contrast to the openness she'd displayed moments ago. She fidgeted with attaching her veil to her hat.

Just beyond the ruins, Sir Adrian's shadow paced back and forth. "I have an appointment with a horse dealer in London next month. Do you think I'll be able to attend? Or will I still be waiting to enter Jaffa? I'm just asking out of curiosity."

Bianca captured Madeline's hand and squeezed it. "I won't say anything." She nodded, hoping that gave her comfort. "I promise."

Sir Adrian made an exasperated sound. "It's quite something to feel the moments of your life ebbing away, don't you gentlemen agree?"

Madeline rolled her eyes. "I've never known any man who was patient."

Bianca thought of Daddy and the way he pretended to listen to Mama's conversations. *You can't trust them.* The words pressed on her mind, over and over again, no matter how fiercely she willed them away.

Why wasn't Paul married yet? Was she naive to think he'd been waiting for her?

They walked around the rocks and then she saw him, bathed in sunshine, wearing a turban and robe that made him look like an Arabian prince.

She must stop. She must not be the brainless, lovesick fool.

"You look quite the part." Paul's voice was quiet. "You'd do any novelist justice." As the wind blew her veil to the side, he reached and put his hand in the air, just barely touching it. "You're a perfect heroine, ready for an adventure."

Bianca searched his face, and the enigmatic expression that it held. *Don't have secrets. You're too perfect to be marred.*

As if he'd heard her thoughts, he furrowed his brow. "Is something pressing on your mind?"

"I'm just a little nervous, I think."

Sir Adrian turned to them. "As appealing as standing about all day is to me, I think we'd best get on with it." He pointed toward the city gate. "At your leisure, of course." He walked quickly toward the Jaffa gate, contradicting his words. "I'll advise you all not to speak once we're inside the city."

Mr. Tabor nodded and wiped sweat from his forehead. "You won't hear a thing from me."

"Good." Sir Adrian turned to Madeline.

Madeline smiled. "Don't worry about us, Sir Adrian. What harm could two women, a streetcar driver, and a historian possibly do in this remote corner of the world?"

He seemed to find something amusing. "You'd be surprised. If only they could see us back home. What would they say?"

Madeline fell into step with him. "They'd say you ought to have found a softer fabric for these robes." She took his arm. "There is our comfort to be considered, after all."

"I can assure you, Mrs. Greene, your comfort is ever before my mind." He removed her hand from his arm. "Now, if you would be so kind as to stop walking like you're strolling through Regent's Park, you'd do us all an invaluable service."

"What's wrong with the way I'm walking?"

"You're looking decidedly English. Do try to blend in. Observe the local women."

"Yes," Mr. Tabor said. "All the local women seem to be walking behind the men. I rather like that. Shows respect."

Paul scanned the crowd. "I assume you're saying that because you've studied their culture, not because you're prone to agree with medieval thinking."

They passed through Jaffa's enormous front gate. People pressed in tightly, every face olive or brown.

A man pushing a cart forced Bianca closer to Paul. She tripped on a loose cobblestone and fell against him. The sleeve of his robe flipped up as he righted her, exposing the cuff of his white English shirt.

"I'm sorry—"

"Don't speak." Paul's voice was dangerously low.

Robes were in every color, holding faces that were unreadable, wrapping people who thought differently, lived differently.

Paul pulled Bianca closer and bent to her ear. "Keep your eyes down."

She nodded, but couldn't pull her eyes away from his. The thought that all men have secrets … surely Madeline was wrong. Surely she knew him.

The look Paul gave her chilled her to the core. "Do as I say. Now."

Bianca snapped her head down and anchored her eyes to the back of Mr. Tabor's shoes. How could his eyes look like that? How could the green turn flat and gray in an instant?

Peddlers shouted. Children pushed between them and laughed as they ran away. More people pressed in, the smell of their skin foul but mixed with strong, strange spices.

Light-headed, Bianca tried to focus on Madeline's rose perfume.

The wind gusted and stirred up dust. Canvases used for shade slapped against wooden poles. Tiny bits of sand pelted her face. Bianca pulled her veil tighter and tried to shield her eyes.

Sir Adrian consulted his map, then nodded toward an alley.

They huddled together, not speaking, their hands firmly pressed against the narrow walls. Stairs appeared to the left. The noise from the crowd dimmed as they descended.

"That was quite an experience," Madeline said, too loud.

Mr. Tabor wiped his forehead with his robe sleeve. "Yes, and not one that I hope to be repeating."

"Do shut up," Sir Adrian whispered without looking up. "May I remind you both that we're not yet to the carriage road?"

Above them, rugs hanging from windows flapped like spirits from the dawn of time. She was a world away—an ancient world—right in the maze of antiquity. Bianca ran her hand along the cool, smooth stones—older than anything in Ohio, or even America.

A sunbeam fell between the buildings, illuminating the dirt alley, pushing away the shade. Two beggars sat with their heads down. Open sores oozed upon their legs and drew the attention of the flies.

"*Baksheesh*," a faint voice said. A small boy with his knees deformed backward hobbled toward her and held out his hand. His eyes were pools of chocolate, drowning in sorrow, and miserable to behold.

"Oh, my," Bianca whispered. The world seemed to stop—the noise from before, the smell of this place, the urgency to go on. She locked eyes with him—pitiful child, little lost one, alone in the world. "Oh, my," she said again when she saw the dirt caked upon his fingers. "Let me help you." She mouthed the words, but the sound didn't come.

The boy held out his hand. "*Baksheesh*."

She reached inside her sleeve to the little purse she'd pinned there.

"Don't." Paul took hold of her hand with ferocity and pulled her away.

"I have a coin."

"Trust me." He looked beyond her to somewhere in the shadows. His body was tense, his eyes filled with apprehension.

"I don't understand." The boy still held out his small, empty hand.

"Bianca—"

A man stepped from the shadows and tossed aside a strange-looking pipe attached to a hose. He blew a stream of smoke through parched lips. Two men appeared by his side. The three blocked their path.

Sir Adrian turned. He nodded to Paul, and Paul nodded back.

The men came closer.

"What's going on?" Mr. Tabor said.

Madeline grabbed onto his sleeve and stepped behind him. "We're being accosted, you idiot! Can't you tell?"

"Accosted?" Mr. Tabor held up his finger. "Sir Adrian, a moment, if you please."

The foreigners laughed. They came closer.

"Ameerikan." The dirty-haired man circled them. He leaned toward Bianca, so close she could smell the rot on his breath. "*Ta'alay*," he whispered.

Paul put his hand on Bianca's waist and pushed her behind him.

"*Ta'alay,*" the man said again. Paul stepped back, his body shielding her.

Bianca clutched the back of his robe. Her hands shook and her entire body felt like wispy air.

Paul raised his chin. "*A'ed men fadlek, kalb.*"

Surprise bled onto the Arab's face.

Sir Adrian pulled something from his boot and stepped toward the other two men. He flipped open a knife and held it aloft, letting the sun dance upon the blade. "Quite. Is this what you ruffians had in mind? You see, I'm trying to keep to a schedule."

In one fluid motion, Paul removed a knife from his sleeve and held it against the foreigner's throat.

"Good gravy." Mr. Tabor held on to Madeline. "Why didn't I think to bring a knife?"

"Shut up." Madeline gripped his robe so tightly the neckline hung from his shoulder.

"*Ana Asif.*" The leader waved his hands in the air and backed away. "*La taqlaq.*"

The other men parroted the same words and bowed as they moved toward the shadows.

The small boy was gone.

They all ran down alleys until their breaths came ragged and forced from their throats. At last, they stumbled upon a courtyard. Peddlers shouted their wares from every direction. After a gate, they filtered out upon a dirt road.

Mr. Tabor put his hands on his knees and wheezed. "I think I could have done without that hubbub. Never had to deal with that in Boston."

"Capital experience," Madeline said through breaths. "Sir Adrian, you were correct earlier. I will be reliving those moments when I'm old and gray. Bianca, dear, are you all right?"

"Yes." Bianca looked back at the gate. "We're all fine now." She locked eyes with Paul. "Thank you."

"Again, Sir Adrian, quite the luxury trip." Madeline put her hands on her hips, her breathing starting to slow down.

Sir Adrian hiked up his robe and took his pocket watch from his vest pocket. He flipped it open and wound it as if it were the most important thing to do in the world. He let his pace fall back in step with Paul's. "I had no idea you spoke Arabic. What did you say to them?"

"Saying that I speak Arabic might not be a proper assumption."

"No? Then what was that?"

"I'm currently learning Arabic." Paul shrugged his shoulders. "That was from page ten of an Arabic phrase book. It's in my office at the museum. I believe it means something like 'Can you repeat that again?' I'm not quite sure. I do know that the man wanted Bianca to come with him. *Ta'alay* means 'come with me.'"

Sir Adrian stopped winding his watch. "So, you mean to tell me that you saved our lives with something you happen to remember from the first ten pages of a phrase book?"

"That's about the straight of it. But the knives did help."

"So they did. Spot on."

"It's all about intimidation. You, above all others, should know that. Setting the scene is imperative."

"Oh, yes, scene is very important." Sir Adrian looked pleased. "Almost as important as the characters."

Paul adjusted his sleeve. "And, making characters do things is rather thrilling, I would think."

Sir Adrian was quiet for a moment. "One can never really make another person do something, you know. There's that little matter of free will. Even with our ruffian friends back there, it could have gone either way."

"It could have," Paul said. "But it didn't. I'd say God was watching out for us."

"You know, on this occasion, you might be right."

Bianca could faintly hear the ocean and the seagulls they'd left behind. Sheep grazed beside them on the hill.

"Look there." Sir Adrian pointed to a dusty carriage waiting on the side of the road.

A man bowed, placed his hand upon his heart. "I bid you welcome." He spoke in perfect English.

"Thank you, Raheed." Sir Adrian returned the man's bow. "Unfortunately our walk through Jaffa was not as pleasant as expected. The map you drew was a bit skewed. We ended up in an unsavory quarter of the city. Have you anything to say?"

If it were possible for brown skin to turn ashen, Bianca witnessed it.

Raheed lowered his head. "A thousand pardons, Sir."

"You may need a thousand when I'm done with you." Sir Adrian turned and offered Madeline his hand. He helped her into the open carriage.

Bianca wondered at the transformation on Sir Adrian's face. It was hard, a formidable rock not to be trifled with—the face of an aristocrat, from a long line of aristocrats.

Sir Adrian settled into the seat next to Madeline, causing the carriage to sway. Raheed took the driver's seat and stared straight ahead. The horse pawed at the ground.

"My mouth's as dry as this landscape." Mr. Tabor climbed in opposite Sir Adrian. His face was pale and his turban balanced precariously.

"I couldn't agree more." Paul placed his hand on the small of Bianca's back as she climbed. He settled into the seat beside her. "Sir Adrian, will your friend—

this Owenburke fellow—have any tea worth an Englishman's trouble?"

Sir Adrian sat back and took off his turban. He looked back at the outline of Jaffa as Raheed snapped the reins and the carriage lurched forward. "Samuel has tea aplenty and much more. I think you'll all be pleasantly surprised."

As her heart slowed down to its normal rhythm, Bianca caught Sir Adrian's eye. Blue eyes locked with hazel, just like that night at the Egyptian dinner when she'd first met him. Blue eyes fathomless, compelling, and sometimes, far more aloof than she suspected him to be.

"I see now why you had us in disguises," Mr. Tabor said. "I can only imagine how it would have been if we'd been in usual clothing."

Madeline reclined. "It might have been fine if you'd taken the trouble to keep your mouth closed, Sir. The one time you decide to open it and we're surrounded by brigands."

Sir Adrian leaned forward. Again, his expression took on another mask. "Must you always be so outspoken?" He took a deep breath. "Madame, I have a headache. We've all been through a difficult ordeal. Laying the blame at anyone's door right now won't make the situation better. I suggest you close your eyes and take a nap—dream about whatever it is you dream of."

The rebuke hung in the air like a solid weight.

"How dare you speak to me in such a manner." Madeline placed her hand upon her chest and sniffled. "To think of all I've endured."

Sir Adrian looked at Paul and held his hands in the air. "Actresses. What can I say?"

Bianca looked at Madeline. "You're an actress?"

"Yes," Madeline said matter-of-factly. "I am."

Chapter 14

*T*he sun was unbearable, the dust was abundant, and if Madeline's leg knocked against hers again, Bianca was going to scream. Mr. Tabor breathed through his nose like a rhinoceros with a cold, and a metal piece of the carriage seat had come through the leather and was biting into her side.

Surely it wasn't much farther. If she only had something to put between her and the consarned spring.

Paul's head sagged toward his shoulder, his turban sliding. It dropped into his lap and she snatched it away, wadding it behind her back.

The rocky landscape faded. Through half lids, Bianca saw the gentle impression of the telegraph lines above them, following the road.

At least Paul was asleep. Bianca hated to think of him looking at her now. She must resemble a border ruffian, or a prairie girl who'd been too long on the wagon train.

Bianca's head fell forward and she jerked awake. A headache came full force and pounded in sync with her heart. She pressed her hands against her temples and tried to dull the pain.

"The landscape that time forgot," Sir Adrian said, but it sounded like an amplified roar. "Are you all right?" His hair resembled a red bird that was molting.

"A slight headache." Bianca tried to smile, but pain shot behind her eyes.

"Are you sure?" He ran his hand over his hair, disheveling even more of his vagabond style.

She would have thought it funny, had her brain not been in a meat grinder. "How much longer, do you think?"

He consulted his map. "Just a few more miles." He looked at Madeline and Paul. "Perhaps we should wake them."

Mr. Tabor rested against the carriage wall and stared at the sky.

"No, don't. I'm sure they need the rest."

Sir Adrian leaned forward. "You don't look well. How bad is your headache?"

Bianca paused until a wave of pain took another course. "On a scale of what?"

"On a scale of one being a 'tra la la' and ten being a Romanian impalement."

Again, she tried to smile, but the gesture worked against her. If red-hot lava were being poured over her skull, this headache might have a point of comparison. "Nine. I'll say a nine."

"A nine simply won't do." Sir Adrian made a tsking sound. "Give me your hand."

His face was a hazy silhouette of ghostly proportions. Colors came in waves, spiking like nails. "Excuse me?"

"Give me your hand," he repeated, a little impatiently.

"All right, but I don't see what—"

"Very good." He grasped her palm. "You follow directions as well as any trained monkey."

Bianca cringed. "What are you doing?"

He pressed the place between her thumb and forefinger and rubbed. "Acupressure. I spent some time in China a few years ago. Do you know much about the Chinese?"

"Nothing at all." He pushed harder and the pain spiked. She focused on his thumb and breathed.

"The Chinese have a magnificent history, especially medically speaking. What I'm doing to your hand right now is part of their healing art. I'm applying pressure to the part of your hand that corresponds to your head. This pressure will send a signal to your brain that recommends your body heal itself."

"Recommends my body—" Bianca stared at his bare hand upon hers. "I've never heard of such a thing. Have you had much success with this procedure?"

"It's very popular with certain ladies of my acquaintance."

"I'm sure it is." She wasn't going to give him the satisfaction of pursuing that line of thought.

"Any better yet?" Sir Adrian stopped moving his thumb.

"I don't know for sure. Perhaps."

"You must have a very severe case." He scanned the faces of the others, who were still asleep. "Would you mind if I held your foot?"

Bianca widened her eyes, causing her head to split apart again. "Did you say my foot?"

"Yes." Sir Adrian held out his hand as innocently as if he'd asked to hold her hat.

She hesitated. "For more acupressure?"

He rolled his eyes. "I can assure you, if I wanted to hold your foot as an overture to romance, I most certainly would not be asking to do it in the middle of a crowded carriage. Do you want to get rid of the headache or not?"

Bianca gripped the back of her neck and pressed. Waves of pain crawled and spread. "All right." She lifted her foot.

Suddenly, she remembered a newspaper article and the scandal it had caused back home. "Cincinnati Actress Appears as Arabian Dancing Girl: Was Not

Ashamed to Show Her Feet or Her Ankles. Local Woman Says Husband Hasn't Been the Same."

"I think I'm feeling better now." She attempted to pull her foot away.

"The shadows under your eyes say differently." He looked like he was trying not to laugh. "Now this might pain you, prepare yourself."

"What are you going to do?"

"I'm going to take off your boot." His blue eyes danced with amusement. "Courage." He untied her bootlaces and slipped the boot off. He peeled her sock away.

Bianca sat ramrod straight. "Is that necessary? I'm rather fond of socks."

His hand stilled. "Am I scaring you?"

"No." She swallowed and glanced at the others. Sir Adrian touched the bare bottom of her foot. She leaned forward and whispered, "Are you sure this is how the Chinese administer healing?"

"Absolutely." He ran his thumb along the bottom of her foot in lines. "Now, tell me when I touch a place that hurts . . . What's that look for?"

"Did I give you a look? Why should I give you a look when you're holding my foot in the middle of a carriage ride in a foreign country?"

"You did give me a look. It was a look that said I've either got horse dung smeared all over my face or . . ." He shifted his gaze to Paul and grinned. "You've decided to abandon the historian and make a play for me."

"You're a cad." She lowered her voice. "Does your mischievous streak ever end?" Again she tried to pull her foot away.

"I'm afraid not." He tightened his grasp. "Be still, and answer my question. Where does it hurt the most?" At just that moment, he put pressure beneath the ball of her foot.

"There," she hissed through clenched teeth.

"Good. We've found it. Now try to relax. I'm going to push harder."

"Harder?"

"I'm afraid it's necessary, but you'll thank me in a minute." He pushed harder.

Everything within her begged to pull away.

"Concentrate. Listen to my voice. What was your earlier look about?"

"I . . . was thinking about your hair earlier. Perhaps the look had something to do with that. I can't remember now."

"Breathe. What about my hair?"

"I was thinking you look nothing like yourself. You look more like a vagabond, a beggar, a hooligan."

"As charming as that?" His cheeky smile tipped up a notch. "I'm flattered."

"I'm sorry, but that's what came to mind." She felt a slight change in her headache. "It feels a little better, I think."

"Excellent. I'll let it rest for ten seconds and then do it again. Back to your comparison. If I look nothing like myself right now, what do I normally look like?"

Bianca relaxed her shoulders. "You're not fishing for compliments, are you?"

"I merely wish to know how I appear to the outside world."

"Outside London, you mean?"

"Yes, Portsmouth in particular. What would ladies say if I blew into town like an impetuous storm?"

The mental picture made her want to laugh. "They'd swoon, no doubt. Those who could speak would utter such things as 'Oh, my socks and garters!' and 'Great day in the morning!' Then they would all beg you to marry them."

"Really?" He seemed fascinated. "But you didn't do that when we first met. I wonder why?"

Paul roused awake and turned to them.

She inched her foot away, hoping Paul wouldn't notice.

His gaze was stuck somewhere around the region of her ankle. "Well, that's something I didn't expect. But, then again, after the day I'm having . . ." His eyes measured them both, darting back and forth, searching their faces.

Bianca curled her toes under. "I had a headache and Sir Adrian . . ." She held out her hand toward him, as if the gesture were somehow explanation enough.

Sir Adrian held her boot and sock aloft. "I was administering acupressure."

"Were you?" Paul glared at him. "How convenient."

Madeline opened her eyes. "What did I miss?"

"Not much," Paul said, as if the entire conversation were beneath his dignity. "Sir Adrian managed to disrobe Bianca's foot, and he was fishing for compliments. Of the romantic sort."

"Well," Madeline said. "What could I possibly add to that? Carry on."

Paul's green eyes darkened as he held Sir Adrian's gaze. "There was also something about abandoning the historian, but I suppose that part is inconsequential since they didn't know I heard it. This is, after all, supposed to be a pleasure tour. Thoughts along those lines would just dampen the mood. Severely."

"Excuse me." Mr. Tabor clutched his stomach. "Are we almost there?"

"What's the matter, man?" Sir Adrian leaned over and put his hand on his shoulder. "Are you ill?"

"Yes." His breathing was too quick. "Not feeling well. Haven't been this entire time."

"Why didn't you say something earlier?" Paul asked.

Mr. Tabor's expression was steeped in pain. "I thought it would pass."

"When did the pain start?" Sir Adrian lowered his head to look him in the eyes.

"A while ago." Mr. Tabor's voice was strained. He doubled over.

Bianca leaned closer. His hairline was drenched with sweat and held traces of white powder.

"Do you need us to stop?" Paul asked. "It could be the movement of the carriage—and the boat earlier."

He clutched his midsection tighter. "My stomach . . ."

"I hope he hasn't caught some foreign disease." Madeline frowned. "He looks positively morbid."

Paul glanced at her quickly. "Your ability to state the obvious is uncanny."

"Does anyone have a tea cracker?" Bianca searched her purse. "Perhaps if he ate something."

"It's all in the luggage." Sir Adrian ran his fingers through his hair. "But, look, the city is just there."

Mr. Tabor moaned again.

Sir Adrian cringed. "My friend will know of a doctor."

Madeline rolled her eyes. "A doctor in this corner of the world? Someone who births sheep perhaps."

"Really, Madeline, you're not helping." Bianca took off her hat and fanned Mr. Tabor. "Almost there, Mr. Tabor. I can see the gate."

"Jerusalem . . ." His voice trailed off.

Sir Adrian pressed a handkerchief into Mr. Tabor's hand. Mr. Tabor pushed it against his mouth. Beads of sweat ran down his cheeks.

A group of palm trees passed in a blur.

Sir Adrian turned. "Raheed, you have to hurry. Tabor is ill."

"I'm dying." Mr. Tabor squeezed his eyes shut.

"You're not dying," Sir Adrian said. "I forbid it. You only need a doctor."

Bianca took Mr. Tabor's hand. "Just a little farther."

Mr. Tabor fell forward onto Madeline and groaned.

"What if he's contagious?" Madeline turned her face away. "Get him off."

Sir Adrian pulled on his arm, but the man resembled hot jelly in the sun. Paul took his other arm and helped lie him down. Bianca knelt upon the floor.

"He salivated all over my robe." Madeline searched their faces in awestruck horror.

Paul's look to her was as dark as murder.

The carriage passed through the stone arched gate. The horses' hooves echoed like cannons upon the stone.

The driver pulled back hard on the reins as a group of beggars ran toward them. "What the deuce?" Sir Adrian stood and reached for the horse crop. "Get back!" The people pressed in, some reaching to step into the carriage.

The carriage lurched forward, knocking Sir Adrian off balance. He slammed into Madeline's shoulder.

A shot cracked through the air, echoing off the stone walls, causing the horse to bolt into a full gallop. Raheed fell backward and into the open carriage, losing his hat to the cobblestones. The reins dangled over the rigging and slid against the road.

Paul reached for Bianca and pinned her against the seat.

Raheed crawled back over the seat but couldn't right himself. He fought to hold on to the footboard as the carriage swayed precariously.

"This is intolerable!" Madeline tumbled, her long hair falling against Bianca's face.

"Devil take it!" Sir Adrian fought his way toward sitting upright.

Paul gripped the side of the carriage. "Raheed, grab the reins."

Sir Adrian stretched his arm toward Paul. "Take my hand. Try to reach Raheed."

The horse swerved around a corner. Sir Adrian's shoulder slammed against the door, flinging it open.

Paul grabbed Sir Adrian's hand and climbed over the seat. He grasped Raheed's arm. "Lower yourself down. You have to try!"

The man looked to the dangling strips of leather and then to the horse. "I cannot."

"Do it." Paul locked eyes with Raheed. "I won't let you fall."

Raheed disappeared from view. Sir Adrian wrapped his arm around Paul's ankle and held it anchored against the seat.

The horse tore down an alley. People screamed. Something crashed.

"We're going to die!" Madeline clutched Bianca's arm.

Mr. Tabor's head rolled against the seat. His body slid toward the open door.

"Help me, Madeline. He's passed out." Bianca put her bare foot against the inner wall and dug her knee into the floor, throwing her body against him.

"I can't." Tears streamed down Madeline's face. She gripped the edge of the seat.

"You can." Bianca reached for her arm and pulled her down. "Just hold on." Bianca's hands went numb. Her knuckles were white.

The carriage hit a pothole. Mr. Tabor's body slid. His arm dangled out the door.

"He's going to fall." Madeline wrapped her arms tighter around his leg and sobbed.

Paul voice sounded distant over the noise. "Raheed has the reins."

Bianca's foot began to slip. "Hold on, Madeline. With all that is within you, hold on."

Chapter 15

*I*ncense hung in the air, thick and tangible. Bianca stood at the bottom of the iron staircase and stared at the balcony above.

"Bianca, either sit down or go and see what's keeping the men. That worried look on your face is exhausting me." Madeline reached for her teacup. It shook against the saucer.

Bianca laid her hand upon the railing. "The doctor's been in there so long. That can't be a good sign."

"You could at least go and change. You have dust from the road all over you. What will Mr. Owenburke think?"

"I'd think he'd understand, given the circumstances."

Madeline spoke slowly. "A lady should always be mindful of her appearance, in every circumstance. The first thing I did when we got here was make myself more presentable." She walked over to Bianca. "Come on."

"Where are we going?"

"To get you out of those hideous clothes." She took Bianca's hand and pulled her up the staircase. The carved cedar door at the end groaned open, telling its age.

Bianca walked inside and had the undeniable feeling of slipping into *Arabian Nights.* Persian rugs lay upon a floor of octagonal-shaped stones. Oil lamps hung between tall windows framed in silk. Shutters were closed halfway, casting the low bed in a mysterious light. The draped canopy around the four wooden posters billowed and shifted in the breeze.

"And that's not all." Madeline pushed against a shutter.

Bianca squinted as light flooded the room. When the glare of the sun faded, she saw the courtyard below, framed in weathered columns. Vines and flowers blew gently in the wind. Beyond the tile roof, people walked the narrow alleyways. In the distance, the golden dome of the Mosque of Omar rose like a scene from a mystic's dream.

"Your trunk is there, see?" Madeline pointed back inside to a shady corner.

"So it is." Bianca walked across the room and knelt. She pushed the lid open and fished out a nightdress. She brought the cloth to her nose and closed her eyes. "It smells like home—like Mama's washing soap and the lilac bush where we hang the laundry."

"May I?" Madeline took the garment, brought it to her nose, and closed her eyes. She smiled and gave it back to her. "Did you do the embroidery yourself?"

"Yes." Bianca ran her finger over the blue thread. "And I hated every minute of it."

"Why?"

"All I could think about was how much I'd rather be doing other things." Bianca took out a few skirts, then found a simple dress made of cotton. She stood and went behind the dressing screen. "When I think about all those hours I spent sewing . . . Imagine all the books I could have read."

"If you're fortunate to marry a husband who's well off, you could hire twenty maids to do your sewing."

"Wouldn't that be something?" Bianca considered the possibility for the first time. "You make it sound like life gets more interesting after marriage. I hope so."

"You have no idea. Perhaps *interesting* isn't quite the right word."

Bianca peeked around the dressing screen. "Is there a better word to sum up marriage?"

Madeline sat upon the bed and idly played with the blanket fringe. "Quite a few. Although I don't think your ears are ready for them."

"No?" Bianca gave an exasperated sigh and continued changing. "What shall we talk about then? The thickness of Mr. Owenburke's walls? They do a very good job of keeping the house cool, don't you think?"

"Yes." Madeline laughed like she knew Bianca was annoyed. "The house is obviously very old and well thought out. Perhaps our time here will not be as uncomfortable as I'd originally thought. Up until now, I've only heard about barbarians in this part of the world—decrepit ruins and diseases."

Bianca draped her socks over the edge of the screen. "I don't think all the rumors are true. Why would people come here if they were?"

"We'll find out tomorrow, I suppose. Did you see Sir Adrian's face when he held that crop?" Madeline pshawed. "I'll never get that picture out of my mind."

"He did look rather fierce, didn't he?"

"And the way Mr. Emerson took charge . . . I can almost see why you're so fond of him. Almost."

Bianca gathered her clothes and stepped out from behind the screen.

"Perhaps I'll stumble upon a lonely duke one day and become a duchess. Do you think I'd fit the part?" Madeline went over to a basin and poured water into the bowl. She dipped a rag into the water and twirled it around by its corner. "

"I don't know." Bianca smiled. "You might find the weight of the excessive jewels a hardship."

"Perhaps I should aim a little lower. Do you think Mr. Owenburke's available? From what I've seen of this house, he seems to be a wealthy sort."

"I hardly know. I saw him for ten seconds when we barged through the door." Bianca took the rag that

Madeline offered. "Money won't make you happy, you know."

"You're the expert, are you?"

"It's true. But if you're bent on that, you could try for Sir Adrian. I think he has more money than he could spend. He probably uses it to stoke the fires at Hartwith House." Bianca washed her face with the rag.

"The man is positively immune to me. Perhaps if I could get him alone and someone found us in a compromising situation, then he'd have to marry me." She smiled like a Jezebel reborn.

"Madeline!" Bianca slapped her arm with the wet rag. "I can't believe you just said that."

"Shocked you, did I?"

"I know you have been married but Great Jehosha-phat!"

"Poor Bianca." She smoothed a wayward curl from Bianca's forehead. "And you don't even know me that well. Imagine if you did, the things I could tell you."

Bianca draped the washcloth over the basin. "Sometimes I don't understand you."

"Trust me, Bianca, someday you will."

Paul leaned into the corner and observed Samuel Owenburke—crossed arms, unmovable posture, and a commanding air that would rival any sultan's. In fact, he did rather resemble a sultan in those silk robes and pointed shoes. If it weren't for the shock of blond hair sticking out from underneath his turban, one would think Samuel Owenburke was born into the role.

Doctor Avram removed his hand from Mr. Tabor's brow and packed away his medical instruments. He left a brown bottle on the side table near the bed. "I've given him laudanum to help him sleep. Is your manservant, Jaharre, about?"

Mr. Owenburke barely raised a finger and a man came through the doorway to stand at his side. The man's skin was black and his expression stern. He was dressed similarly, but lacking the gold embroidery on his cuffs.

Doctor Avram lowered his spectacles. "Jaharre. This man has had a seizure. His symptoms are not the most severe I've seen, but he'd better be watched through the night. Give him a dram of laudanum in four hours and another in six."

"Yes, Doctor." Jaharre's voice was cultured, but decidedly foreign and heavy with accent. He went to the glass-covered bookcase and turned the latch. After choosing a thick volume, he sat in the chair beside the bed.

Mr. Owenburke motioned for them all to step out of the room. "You'll check back in the morning?"

"Yes." The traces of white powder in his hair concern me. There's no telling what it could be."

Sir Adrian twisted his walking stick. "A shampoo paste, perhaps?"

"I have some suspicions, but I must consult my books."

Mr. Owenburke nodded. "We'll know more tomorrow then."

"I sincerely hope so." Doctor Avram walked away as quickly as he'd come—a flurry of black cloth, cornered beard, and serious expression.

Mr. Owenburke slid his turban off. "How do you think the ladies are faring? I feel positively medieval for not giving them a proper welcome."

Sir Adrian put his hand on the man's shoulder. "We didn't give you much time for introductions, barging in like we did."

Mr. Owenburke waved the comment away. "I had dinner sent to their room."

"I'm sure they're fine then." Sir Adrian nodded. "They're probably comparing notes on corsets. Or men."

Paul rubbed the nape of his neck. "About that tea you mentioned earlier, Sir Adrian. My apologies, it's just that this day has quite taken it out of me."

"Don't give it another thought," Mr. Owenburke said. "This way. I thought we'd go to a more private place. One of my sanctuaries."

As they neared the end of the hall, Mr. Owenburke stopped. He put his finger to his lips and leaned close to the door. Feminine laughter wafted through the cracks. He smiled. "They're definitely not talking about the weather."

Paul ignored the urge to burst open the door. The thought of Madeline filling Bianca's imagination with God knows what did nothing to alleviate the weariness he felt to his bones. This was one of those days you ended by drowning it in a bottle of cognac. Paul breathed deeply. But that was another life ago.

"Are you coming?" Sir Adrian asked.

Paul hadn't noticed that he'd stopped at the bottom of the stairs. "I was just thinking." As if he could think himself out of this predicament or concoct a plan to win Bianca once Madeline had her way. The things she could say . . . He put his hand upon the railing and climbed. A disgusted sound escaped him.

The two men looked back.

Paul plastered on a fake smile until they turned forward again.

It was an awfully cruel joke. Having the perfect wife dangled in front of him like the finest, rarest thing . . . His punishment, he supposed. He rounded the corner on the spiral staircase. *That's what you get when you bed a whore, cause her divorce, and steal a diamond.* He clenched his jaw and felt his teeth grinding. "God, I'm a sorry excuse for a man."

Mr. Owenburke went through the doorway, but Sir Adrian stopped. "Did you say something, Emerson?"

"What did I do to cause you to hate me so much?"

Something flickered in Sir Adrian's eyes. "I don't hate you."

"Really?" Paul stepped closer. "Then send the she-devil home. Tomorrow. Whatever game you're playing. End this now."

Sir Adrian worked the muscles at his jaw. "I can't do that."

"You can do anything you please. You pour your derision on me like syrup—every step of this journey you've planned with care, with purpose."

Sir Adrian kept his eyes locked to Paul's. "It's very important to me that Madeline stays."

Mr. Owenburke called to them. "Are you two gentlemen coming?"

"I can't begin to fathom what's going around in that sick aristocratic head of yours, but I do know this—you know what's at stake." Paul searched his expression for confirmation.

Sir Adrian gave none.

"You know Bianca will be heartbroken when she finds out." Paul nodded, the permanence of the idea settling in. "She's so innocent . . ." His voice failed him.

Sir Adrian looked away, to the carvings on the stairs, and the smooth boards upon the wall. "Sometimes the end justifies the means."

"Does it really?" A sick sound escaped him. "I thought so once. And now do you see how I am tortured? Did you know that I have to see that hellish diamond every day in the museum? I walk past it every morning at precisely seven thirty-five."

Sir Adrian's expression gave way, a small crack in the facade.

"You do know that." The knowledge sickened Paul.

"What I do know," Sir Adrian began, "is that you're tired. It's been a long day. We've all been through a great deal."

"I really thought winning the contest would give me a chance to escape it all—just rest, just be." He shook his head in disbelief. "What will you tell Bianca when she finds out that the man she loves is . . ." He gripped the handrail until his knuckles turned white.

Sir Adrian was as still as a stone.

"But that won't bother you, will it? The end justifies the means." Paul let go and stuck his hands in his pockets. "Do you know what the worst part is?"

"What?" Sir Adrian said, barely audible.

Paul felt himself sinking inside. He didn't want to say it, but then he did. It happened so abruptly, breathed into the air like a vaporous poison. "When Bianca's married to another man, and I'm wanting her for the rest of my life, I'll think about the way you're looking at me now. And how you could have stopped it."

Chapter 16

S ir Adrian Hartwith stood at the threshold.

He saw his longtime friend, Samuel Owenburke, just inside. He saw a man who knew him better than anyone else and yet didn't know him at all. He glanced back at the long, winding stairs where Paul had disappeared.

Masks were a troublesome business.

Samuel struck a match, and one by one, he touched the flame to bundles of incense lining an outcropping of stone. Smoke curled up like outstretched fingers and reached for the jeweled rings he wore.

Sir Adrian walked around an inlaid chest, an old statue, a broken frieze of a lamb. "Paul's not coming."

Samuel nodded, continued to light the incense, and hummed. The tune was strange and mystic, just like the shadows yawning and stretching in the twilight. He blew out the match and cupped his hands over the smoke, bringing it over his face. "He seemed very interested in a hot drink. What brought about his change of mind?" Samuel looked at him sideways, a shadow of a smile tugging at his lips.

"He's too tired to be social." Sir Adrian picked up a bundle of incense and turned it beneath his nose. He coughed. "What is this?"

"Ketoret. It's the same incense that was offered in the Jewish temple here, as stated in the Book of Exodus. It's a mixture of stacte, onycha, galbanum, and frankincense."

"Well that clears it up, doesn't it?" Sir Adrian contorted his face in disgust. "It smells like a camel's backside."

Samuel laughed and flipped out the cuffs of his robe. "I'll admit it takes a little getting used to. I wonder if Moses thought the same thing. It's what he would have smelled when he walked past the animal-skin Tabernacle in the wilderness, when he went to the mountain to see the face of God." He waved his hand toward the low chairs in the middle of the room. A silver coffeepot and cups were laid out on a tray. "Shall we?"

"Please. I've had quite a day, I can assure you." Sir Adrian sat.

The hanging lamps swayed from the breeze of the open balcony. A painted Byzantine ceiling stretched out between rafters of inlaid cedar. An empty birdcage hung in the corner.

Samuel poured the coffee. It was dark and thick, more Turkish than Israeli, the foam on top absolute perfection.

Sir Adrian sipped slowly. "Your man, Raheed, has a serious problem with direction. He might be better suited as a scullery maid than a guide."

Samuel grinned, tight-mouthed. "Is that a fact?"

"His map led us down an impossible alley in which we were set upon by miscreants."

"You survived, I see." The light blue of Samuel's eyes caught the waning light. He rested his hand against the side of his face.

"Barely. I think those scum wanted to put Bianca and Madeline in a harem. Not that it would be much of a change for Madeline, but still, it's the principle of the thing." He leaned back and looked at the ceiling. "Do you know what it's like orchestrating a pleasure tour with two Americans, a spoiled castoff, and a historian too smart for his own good?"

"No, but I'm sure you're going to tell me."

"It's a dog and pony show, that's what—cocker spaniels and those bloody little circus things." Sir Adrian rolled his eyes. "I swear if I'd known of Madeline's lack of tact I would have reconsidered . . . This tower room is very well thought out."

Samuel raised an eyebrow. "Not nearly as well thought out as your schemes, Adrian." He poured more coffee and reached for a piece of cinnamon cantaloupe. "So, which one of the women is in love with Paul?"

Adrian swallowed his bite of cantaloupe, almost choking on it. "Why do you say that?"

"Because there's only one reason why you would have an essay contest, come halfway 'round the world, and bring two women with you. You, my friend, are scheming."

"*Scheming* is an awfully harsh word."

"Is it?"

Sir Adrian grinned. "It's just a little experiment, that's all."

"A little experiment?" Samuel raised his eyebrows. "I remember the last time you used the word *little* around me."

"Was it that time at university when I set up the tryst between you and the dean's daughter?"

"No, but that was amusing. I'd forgotten all about that. How is Samantha?"

"Still pining for you, the last I heard."

"Unlikely." Samuel tapped his cup. "We didn't exactly part on good terms."

"Would you like me to fix that? I imagine she'd change her mind if she knew of your growing fortune." Sir Adrian looked around the room again. "She might even think of setting up house in Jerusalem."

It was Samuel's turn to choke. He spit his coffee back into his cup. "Wouldn't that be pleasant? I doubt I could keep her in bonbons in this far corner of the world. If my dealings with you have taught me anything, it's to not let you meddle in my dealings." He lowered his cup and rang a bell. A servant stepped from behind a loose-hanging tapestry and brought another cup. "If only I'd listened to my intuition more where you were concerned, I might be a different man."

"Intuition is for women. Adventure and gain are for men like us." Sir Adrian placed his hand on his chest. "I'm deeply hurt. When I think of all those times I helped you—Gad! You didn't have a problem when our excursion to China brought you fifty thousand pounds in tea profit."

"True, but I didn't exactly appreciate the silk worms stashed below the tea. And neither did the owners. You could have at least alluded to the fact that you were using my ship to smuggle out a national treasure."

"I thought it best to keep that fact incognito. After all, I didn't want you to be responsible for such information. And the owners were paid, dearly. It's only a pity for me that the worms died before they reached England. Do you know how much money I could have made?"

Samuel shrugged. "Do you know what it's like to be chased by a nine-ring broadsword, a chicken sickle, and an iron fan?"

Sir Adrian put the back of his hand over his lips and stifled a smile. "Exhilarating, I'd wager. But I'd hardly know since I was occupied with three geishas at the time."

"In Japan, were you? How convenient to take a little trip whilst I was waiting for you in Canton. For three days."

"I thought so," Sir Adrian said, tongue in cheek. "It would've been a shame to miss out on Japanese culture when I was so close. Would you like to hear about it? They have the most interesting festivals, and the music—"

"Another time, perhaps." Samuel obscured his face as he tipped up his cup. "At least I can say that I've never been bored when you're around."

Sir Adrian held his cup up in mock toast. "To not being bored then."

"Hear, hear. Anything but boredom."

The last traces of the sun disappeared behind the rooftops. The night started to come in colors that were blue and black and misty. The hanging lamps swayed as another breeze shifted through the room.

The wind danced like a maiden here, in this old city of Jerusalem. It lingered to put its fingers through the chimes; it lifted the fringe on the carpet as if to inspect it; it leafed through the book of maps left open on the floor.

"You know I'm dying to know the details." Samuel's voice brought him back from the reverie.

"The details?"

"Your experiment, of course."

Sir Adrian looked out onto the rooftops once again. The last color of the day disappeared like a thought not worth remembering. "It's all about transformation, Samuel."

"Transformation?"

"Yes. Although the transformation of whom is the part that remains to be seen."

From the hallway, Bianca tried to pull the bedroom door shut without a sound. Slowly. Inch by excruciating inch. The old iron hinges groaned like a half-dead man. Through the crack, and into the room, Madeline stirred. "Stay asleep," Bianca whispered.

Madeline pulled the blanket over her shoulder, sleep-sighed, and turned toward the wall.

One last pull and the door met the cedar wood frame. A deep silence breathed throughout the house, as if it were a living entity, a great old thing in a land as old as the sky.

A grandfather clock kept meter with the darkness. Odd in a Jerusalem house.

Bianca looked into the dark and the landing below. Only the moonlight stirred. It shifted across the windows with the movements of the clouds. She was finally alone. Away from Madeline.

She would go to the courtyard garden. It would be safe. No one would see her and the air would clear her thoughts.

Shadows hung like curtains upon the stairs. Bianca looked behind her, thinking of where Paul slept and then stepped down.

She looked down at her nightgown. She should have dressed. "No, love is wild, not a tamed thing. And I won't be tamed, at least on this night." She turned the back door handle. It was a magical world, a secret garden, and all for her.

The trees swayed, keeping watch over their secrets. She held the corner of the door and slid down to reach a rock. She wedged it in the doorway and let the door fall.

She pulled the pins from her hair; it fell about her shoulders and tumbled down her back. She took off her slippers and placed them by a lion statue crumbling with age.

Bianca walked in and out of the columns, in and out of the moonlight, touching flowers as she passed.

Footsteps sounded on the gravel outside the gate. Bianca sat up, her heart racing. She could run for the door, but she wouldn't make it.

The footsteps stopped. The bar on the gate lifted. The gate creaked open.

A shadow of a man stood in the gaping black.

She was going to be murdered. And never married.

"Bianca?" The clouds shifted and blessed moonlight rained down. Paul stood like an apparition, his hand upon the latch. His hair was blown askew by the wind. His shirt was open at his throat. In his other hand, he held his tie.

"It's you." She looked toward her slippers by the door and pulled her shawl tighter. "I couldn't sleep . . ." She searched for the right words, certain she must sound like a wanton fool. "I wasn't expecting anyone. I apologize for . . ." She looked down at her nightgown and bare feet.

He pushed the gate until it latched. "The first time I saw you, you were twirling in the King's Library. Do you remember?" He spoke in an odd, but gentle tone. "You looked like a little girl in a toy shop. So euphoric. But then I saw your face and my opinion changed."

He stepped around the fountain, looked first to her hair and then to the hem of her nightgown. "And now I find you alone in a garden in Jerusalem."

Something about the way he held his posture made her look away. Heat played in her cheeks, spreading like a blanket. "It's late. I should be going in."

His gaze lingered on the edge of her shawl, which had fallen from her shoulder. "That would probably be wise."

"Goodnight." She took a few steps toward the door.

"Goodnight." His voice was strained and sad somehow. "Sleep well."

Bianca looked back. "Were you walking in the city just now?"

He draped his jacket over a stone bench. "Yes. I've been walking for hours."

"I thought you were with the men all this time."

He looked down at the pathway stones. "They're old friends. I didn't want to interfere."

She looked toward the door, a sudden chill grasping at the back of her neck. The wind picked up again, blowing a few stray leaves across the patio. Something lingered in his expression. There were shadows underneath his eyes.

"What is it?"

She looked away. "It's nothing."

"Your expression says otherwise. Your face is a bit transparent you know. Especially your eyes."

She hadn't realized she'd been holding her breath. "That's horrible."

"No, it's endearing. Most women do nothing but play games with men." He looked into the rippling water of the fountain. "You're not like that. It's refreshing."

She stepped closer. "I was only thinking that it probably wasn't safe for you to be walking all alone out there."

The corner of his lips turned up. "You're worried about my safety?"

"Yes. Anything could happen in a foreign country. What if you were accosted?"

He shrugged and half-laughed. "Law of improbability. Being accosted is like lightning; once you experience it you've pretty much paid your dues for the day. And if the alley in Jaffa didn't count, the carriage incident pretty much secured it."

She searched for something clever to say, remembering how he'd dangled by the carriage rigging, the back hooves of horses, and the front wheel. "Technically, it's not the same day. You could be lying dead in the street and none of us would be the wiser."

"As you can see, I'm not lying dead in the street." He gestured toward the gate and the streets beyond. "I'm here having a wonderful conversation with you at three o'clock in the morning when you should be in bed. Not standing in a garden alone. Talking with me. In your nightgown."

"You're absolutely right." She nodded and turned. "I'm glad you're not dead, because I have to tell you, I would have been very upset to find out that information in the morning. Goodnight."

"Pleasant dreams."

She made her way down the stone path and knelt by her slippers. She turned her head just so, making it possible for her to spy on him. He sat on the wide edge of the fountain with his back toward her. She collected her hairpins and slid on her slippers.

Paul held his face in his hands. The moonlight reflected off his white shirt and made it opalescent blue. He mumbled something and then combed his fingers through his hair.

Bianca let the door fall back onto the wedge of rock. She crept back and stood on his opposite side. "Are you all right?"

He jerked and sat up straight. "I thought you went inside."

"You looked a bit . . . something. So I came back."

"I looked a bit something?" He laughed under his breath. "I just have a lot to sort through, that's all."

Bianca eased herself down beside him and arranged the fringe on her shawl. "Is any of this sorting anything I can help you with?"

He made a fist and leaned his cheek against it. "I'm just dealing with a lot right now."

"'A lot.' Well, that gives me so much to go on. Very helpful, thank you."

"Are you always this persistent? Or is it just the unusual hour that brings it out in you?"

"Strange things do happen in the early morning."

"Yes, they do." He gave her a sideways glance. "Which is why you should probably go inside."

"You're right. I probably should." She nodded but didn't attempt to stand. "That sounds like the reasonable thing to do."

"You don't seem to be very reasonable at present." Paul sighed and slid his hand across the fountain stone. He intertwined his pinkie finger with hers. He looked off to the other side of the garden, where the rose bushes were.

"Sometimes being reasonable is overrated." She looked down at their intertwined fingers. She was afraid to move, afraid that somehow moving would make him pull his hand away.

A dog barked in the distance. The wind died down and sent a hush upon the land. The palm trees shuttered and fell asleep.

Paul noticed it too. Even the clouds stopped, just over the moon, and darkened the light.

"I'm glad you're here. You're a great comfort to me." He looked sad again, like something deeper weighed him down.

"I'm glad too. At least I'm good at something."

"You are quite superior at many somethings, my dear. But I don't think I'm going to name them right now." He gave her a sideways look again and kneaded his eyebrows together.

"And why is that?"

He tilted his head. "Because it wouldn't end well. Actually, it would end very well . . ." His gazed raked over her body. He shook his head and looked away. "But I've already got a lot to sort through, remember? Help a man out. Please."

She laughed. "I have absolutely no idea what you're talking about."

"Good." He pulled his hand away. "Let's keep it that way."

"All right. But at least tell me something that I can understand."

He leaned forward, put his elbows on his knees, and clasped his hands together. "Tonight I've been thinking a lot about your family."

"Have you? What about?" The green of his eyes again enchanted her. She felt dizzy sitting so near him, like leaning backward upon a swing and watching the sky fall away.

"I was thinking about your father specifically. From what you've told me, I think you're the apple of his eye. You must miss him very much."

"Not so much. My mind has been on other things."

He furrowed his brow and looked at his shoes. They were covered in dust from the road. "Your father must have very high expectations for you . . . and the man you marry. From what you've said, your father seems like an honorable man."

"We often talk well into the night about everything. He's the real reason I'm here. He brought me Sir Adrian's advertisement. And he encouraged me to enter when I didn't think I'd win."

"I'm a bit envious, you know. As a rule, English fathers are not so doting. My father was hardly home. And when he was, we definitely did not have conversations."

"I'm sorry," she said, and she truly was. "And your mother?"

"Always away." He didn't explain, but speaking the words made a shadow cross his face.

Bianca's heart ached. Somehow it made her relationship with her mother seem comfortable. Was that possible? At least Mama talked to her. If one can call the manipulating Mama did talking.

He must have noticed a change in her demeanor because he added, "There's a rampant misconception in England that children are to been seen and not heard."

"In America too," she said softly, trying somehow to make the situation better. There was so much of him that she didn't know. Years to be uncovered. "Would you be a doting father?" As soon as the words were out she regretted them.

He pressed his palms into the hard, cold stone of the fountain and hardened his jaw. "If I were afforded that blessing." Once again a shadow crossed his face, a sadness that she couldn't explain. He looked off into the darkest place of the portico. "Bianca, I need to tell you something."

"Of course. You can tell me anything."

"Can I?" He closed his eyes for a moment.

She laid her hand upon his arm. "What is it?"

"I don't really know how to phrase this. Or where to begin." He rubbed his hand over his forehead and stood.

"The best place to begin is at the beginning. At least that's what Daddy always says."

"You know that I went to India two years ago?"

"Yes, I've heard you say that."

He walked to the stone bench and then back again. "Two years ago, in India, I was a very different person." He jiggled some change in his pocket and shifted his weight onto the other foot. "I don't think you would have liked me back then."

She stood, feeling the importance of what he was trying to say. "But I didn't know you back then."

"Yes, well, if you had known me . . . Bianca, there are a lot of things in my past that I'm not proud of."

She stepped closer, alarmed that something in the air had changed. "I can say that too. Everybody's done things they're not proud of."

"Perhaps I phrased it wrong." He looked past her to the outside balconies. "Every day I regret . . . I regret it more now that I know your goodness."

"My goodness? Perhaps I should tell you about how I like to go frog gigging with Daddy in the Bottoms. That's not exactly a very good thing for a lady to do. And, I like to eavesdrop on occasion, you can find out the most interesting things. Strawberries are a definite weakness of mine. I can eat four quarts on my own. Would you like to know more of my flaws?"

"I might not be able to take the shock." Paul tucked a tendril of hair behind her ear. "I think you're trying to change the subject." He again seemed to be measuring his words. "So, let me get this right—you adore strawberries, some would say to the point of gluttony, and you enjoy eavesdropping. When you put it that way, my past does seem inconsequential." He tried to smile, but it died upon his lips. "What the devil is frog gigging?"

Bianca laughed. His English accent made the word "gigging" sound like a disease. "I think I'd rather show you than tell you." Images flooded her imagination— his fine linen shirt covered with mud, a picnic by lantern light, a kiss.

"Does it involve killing amphibians in some torturous way?"

"Sadly, yes, but it's great fun. You might not be able to handle it, though. There is a rumor in America that the English are rather . . . stodgy."

"Stodgy?" He raised an eyebrow. "That's severe."

"Yes, and some people even say that Englishmen are trite—all that overuse of 'dash it all' and 'jolly good.'"

"Well, bee's knees, Bianca, you are a cheeky sort." He stepped closer. "Blimey."

"I was just teasing. I . . ." The word died on her lips. His gaze was as soft as a caress. "I love the way you talk. I adore your voice. It's one of the most beautiful things that I've ever heard."

"Really? You think my voice is beautiful?"

She lowered her eyes to his chest and watched the way the wind played with the edge of his collar. "Yes."

The wind rustled in the leaves of the palm trees and weaved throughout the courtyard, in and out of the portico columns. It brushed through her hair and pushed it toward Paul; the edges spread across his shirt like a dark veil.

He caught a bit of it in his hand and threaded it in and out of his fingers. "You have beautiful hair. I've always admired it. Ever since that night at the museum."

She considered not telling him what was deepest in her heart. The look he gave her brought such longing that the words came tumbling out. "I've kept this list for ten years—my heart's desire for a . . ." She couldn't say the word *husband*. "I burnt the list on the ship when I thought you were engaged—but that list was your description."

He still stared at her hair. He rubbed his thumb over the ends of it. "Are you just saying that to make me feel better?"

"No, I am not." She felt the telltale blush enflame her cheeks.

"Hmmm. So you thought I was engaged?"

"Yes."

"Who was the lucky lady? Was she as pretty as you?"

Bianca's lips parted. Paul Emerson thought she was pretty. She wanted to laugh and cry at the same time. "A blonde. At the Rembrandt exhibition. She said her name was Amelia."

"A blonde Amelia. Something Sir Adrian did on the ship now makes perfect sense to me. Almost. He did this magic trick and asked me to think of the name of a woman who was dear to me. On his paper he'd written an *A*."

"Really?" She pretended to be occupied with adjusting the fringe on her shawl. If her expressions really were as transparent as he said, he'd know in an instant that she and Sir Adrian had been in leagues to find out the information. She closed her eyes for a moment. The feel of his fingers combing through her hair was beyond distracting. "You'll let me know if you figure Sir Adrian out, won't you? Just when I think I have, he does something completely out of the ordinary."

"Like Chinese methods of pain relief?" He glanced down at her bare feet.

She curled her toes under his inspection. "Amongst other things."

"I heard about him scaring you with that monkey on the ship. I'm not very fond of those creatures. They're resourceful little thieves. They run wild in the streets of India." He grew serious again and dropped his hand to his side. "I'm not sure how much you should trust Sir Adrian. I have reason to believe that he's brought us all together for strange reasons."

"He's eccentric, but I don't think he means to harm any of us. He wears a well-kept facade, but I think there's goodness behind it."

Paul sighed and sounded exhausted. He reached out for her cheek, and cupped it with his hand. "You're far too sweet for your own good. Do you know that?"

His touch melted her instantly. Her voice came as a whisper. "Is that a compliment?"

He leaned into her, closed his eyes, and put his forehead against hers. "It's not very hard to compliment you."

The world stopped and everything in it. Bianca closed her eyes. *Kiss me. Ask me to marry you. I am yours.*

He radiated a vitality that was like the sun. At noon. In the Kalahari Desert. His breath was soft against her lips.

"You couldn't be more perfect." His voice was velvet and silk, the gentle lap of the water, and the warmness of rain.

She put her hand upon his chest and felt his heart beating there.

His hand moved to the back of her neck. "You really need to go inside now."

"I don't want to go inside."

"You're torturing me." He turned his face away, walked a few steps, and leaned against a tree. He filtered half smiles through the moments. "You do realize that in English society, you're only supposed to show your hair unbound like this to your husband."

"Yes. I know that."

His eyes were dark, obscured in the shadow light. "You always were perceptive." He pushed away from the tree, walked to her, and took her hand.

"Where are we going?" Bianca whispered.

"Shhh." He stopped in front of a large stone urn filled with flowers. He picked some and continued to lead her. When they reached the door of the house, he moved the stone wedge with his foot. He walked before her, up the stairs.

They crept like thieves, in and out of the shadows made by the moonlight. He brought her back to her bedroom door and stopped before it.

Paul pushed back her hair and tucked the flower stem behind her ear. Its petals caressed her temple. She heard a faint chime from somewhere in the house.

"Paul, I—"

He put his finger upon her lips and leaned down close to her ear. "Goodnight, Bianca. And don't follow me. Promise?"

"Promise." As he walked away, and disappeared into the shadows, she thought of all the other promises she hoped to make.

Chapter 17

Madeline's voice jarred her from dreams. "Did you make the pilgrimage to Jerusalem to sleep?"

Bianca sighed and threw off the blanket. "It was a tiring day yesterday, that's all." She ran her fingers through her hair and started untying the rag strips. Her gaze went to Paul's flower.

"I don't remember that being here last night."

Bianca snapped her gaze back to Madeline. "What?"

"That."

"My bobby pins?" Bianca raised an eyebrow.

"No." The bite in Madeline's voice was obvious. "Good try, though."

"My Bible? Isn't it pretty?" Bianca reached over and picked it up off the stand. Her fingers brushed the cup that held Paul's flower. "I bought it in New York before I boarded the ship. It's just the right size for traveling." She bit back a smile.

Madeline put her hand on her hip and scowled.

"The Bible I brought from Ohio was far too big. Daddy took it back with him after he waved good-bye." Bianca waved her hand in mock reverie.

"How nice."

"Yes, it was." Bianca turned the Bible over as if she were examining it for the first time. She tapped her finger on the seven seals of the spine. "Today I'll get to compare things I've read in here with the things I see. Can you imagine?"

Madeline eased down on her bed, careful that the folds of her skirt fell in all the right places. "Seems like it might be a good day for you." She took the Bible from Bianca and tossed it on the pillow. "But that's not as interesting to me as the small pink flower just there."

Bianca folded her hands and waited.

"When I went to bed, that flower wasn't in this room. That leads me to believe two things—one, you're a sleepwalker. You must have had a fit in the middle of the night, and I was too sound asleep to help you. Yet you somehow made it down to the garden and picked this flower."

Bianca grinned. "Sounds logical."

"But not my first choice."

"Do tell." Bianca put her hand on Madeline's arm for emphasis. "I hate delayed conjecture."

Madeline pried Bianca's fingers away like they held the plague. "There's a certain man in this house who fancies you. I think he gave it to you."

Bianca rose and went to the water basin. "You're better at conjecture than I thought." She poured the water and splashed her face.

Madeline crossed the room. "When did this occur?"

"Last night." The memories wrapped around Bianca like fine silk. "Around three o'clock in the morning."

Madeline's mouth made a silent O. "I hardly know what to say."

"Then don't say anything." She knelt down to her trunk and threw it open.

Madeline paced. "I'm grasping here . . ."

Bianca lifted a blouse from the trunk, then decided against it.

"I'm trying to think the best of you." Madeline stopped. "My mind is going in so many directions, I hardly know how to respond."

Bianca rummaged deeper in her trunk. "The Baedeker-Cook travel guide said it's best not to wear anything too American, English, or European."

"I need to sit down. The worst has happened. I can't breathe." Madeline used both hands to fan her face.

"What's the matter?"

"I just need a moment." She ran her fingers down her throat and made a strange sound, like nervous humming.

"Should I call Sir Adrian? Do you need a doctor?" When Madeline didn't answer, Bianca went to the nightstand and poured a glass of water. "Here. Drink this."

Madeline gulped the water, then coughed. "Better now. Yes, I can see the end in sight." She turned her head toward the flower.

"You're not making any sense. You're having an attack because Mr. Emerson gave me a flower?"

"A flower?" Madeline's lips parted in surprise. "You don't know what that is, do you?"

"It's a pretty pink flower. I've never seen one like it before."

"Didn't they teach you anything in finishing school? How to flirt with a fan? The language of flowers?"

"I know a little."

"Silly me, I forgot. You didn't even go to finishing school, did you?"

"Finishing schools aren't exactly in abundance where I live."

"What a shame." Madeline walked to the flower and picked it up. "You'd really enjoy the secret meaning." She opened her fingers and the flower dropped. It ricocheted out of the cup, landing on its side. Madeline walked toward the door.

Bianca put the flower back in the cup. "Where are you going?"

"Downstairs. I have things to attend to."

Bianca tripped on the rug. "What things?"

"Things that don't concern girls who sneak out of their rooms to have secret liaisons."

Bianca's eyes widened. "Is that what you think? You think that Mr. Emerson . . . you think that we . . ."

"Didn't you?

"No! How could you think that? I couldn't sleep last night. I went to the garden alone. Mr. Emerson had been walking in the city but I didn't know it. He came through the gate about three o'clock in the morning and we talked."

"You talked?"

"Yes. That's all. He gave me the flower just before he escorted me to that door."

"Did he kiss you?"

"No."

"Did you kiss him?"

"No, Madeline, I didn't!"

Madeline's features began to soften.

Bianca took a deep breath. "Tell me what the flower means."

"Why don't you ask Mr. Emerson?"

"Because he'll think I'm an idiot, that's why."

"You've got that right." Madeline fiddled with the ribbon on her sleeve. "The language of flowers is one of the first things covered in finishing school." She raised her eyes heavenward, as if entreating divine help. "The flower's Ambrosia, Bianca. It's a symbol for returned love."

"What did you say?"

Madeline looked at her like she was a child. "Apparently Paul Emerson's more than smitten with you. And you didn't even know it until now. What a shame."

Bianca grabbed Madeline's hand. "Are you sure about its meaning?"

"Are you saying I'm a liar?"

"No." At Madeline's hurt look Bianca stepped back. "I didn't mean anything by it." Bianca walked back to her trunk and chose a light gray skirt. "You must know how these things are—how delicate such things are."

"Yes, that I do know."

"I plan to marry him if he'll have me." She whispered the words, not quite sure if Madeline should hear them.

"Do you?" Madeline said softly. "Therein lies the rub, darling."

"Excuse me?"

Madeline reached for the door handle. "Men are so unpredictable. Sometimes the combination of two little letters can mean all the difference in the world."

Bianca closed the lid on her trunk. "I don't understand."

"You said it yourself, you plan to marry him if he'll have you . . . If." She winked just before the door thudded against the frame.

Bianca made her way downstairs. No one was in the room below, but there, just beyond the lattice divider— Paul. Standing by the window, bathed in colors from the glass lanterns above. He sipped something from a porcelain cup.

Her stomach clenched. Did he really love her? Perhaps in the language of flowers, but . . . She should have studied British etiquette more. It would have been as easy as ordering a book. But in what catalogue? *The Portsmouth Druthers?*

Clouds passed by the gray, soggy sky. Palm tree shadows reached for his cheek, his shoulder, the paper he held in his hand. The shutter outside swung wildly, squeaking as it spun on old hinges.

The sky was growing darker so quickly, the blues and purples changing into blacks. A brewing storm. The thought unnerved her.

Lord, help me. You've brought me this far. You can see what's ahead. I hate this feeling of dread. The hem of her dress swept behind her, a silent afterthought. She crossed the rug, went past the ancient cabinet, the low chairs. "Good morning."

"Bianca." Paul's head jerked up. Tea slopped on the cuff of his sleeve. He crumpled the paper and shoved it in his pocket. "You surprised me." The cup clinked against the saucer as he set it upon the table. He shook out his handkerchief. "You're awfully good at sneaking." He scrubbed at the tea stain like he was going to war.

"I'm sorry." She bit her lower lip. "I suppose it's a talent I acquired during those times I was . . ."

"Eavesdropping?"

"I'm afraid so."

He offered her a forgiving smile but it didn't last.

"Is something wrong?"

Paul folded the handkerchief and placed it back in his vest pocket. "I was just lost in thought, mostly about the past." He leaned on the window frame and looked out.

The crooked street gave way to wandering beggars, peddlers, and bedraggled dogs. The star and crescent of the Muslim flag billowed in the distance, its dark red a strange contrast to the gloomy sky. A blue dome farther on rose above cramped, whitewashed houses.

"Do you believe that God can forget?" Paul's body stilled. She could plainly see an alteration in his eyes.

"No, I . . ." Just then a light rain splattered against the window pane. "That sounds like a very deep question."

His eyes burned with urgency. Everything about him quieted.

"No, I don't think that's possible."

"A lot of people share that opinion. Especially the idea that He takes pleasure in punishing the wicked."

Bianca nodded, absorbing the weight of his words. "You didn't let me finish. I don't think it's possible for God to forget, at least in the way that we as humans forget."

"Go on." Something savage shone through his usual flawless deportment.

"God might be able to forget on occasion." Dotted shadows moved on the floor from the rain.

He was so close to her that she could smell the mint tea on his sleeve.

"What occasions?"

"Like when He casts our sins behind His back when we ask Him to. Surely God knows the sins are there, but I think He chooses not to look at them. He chooses to forget."

"Like selective memory?" Paul half sneered. "I wish I could employ it."

"But why would you want to? Your memory is one of your best qualities. How else could you be the brilliant historian that you are?"

"There's a price for being able to remember so much. Especially when it comes to your own life." He watched the Muslim flag absentmindedly. Hardness magnified in his eyes. "I never escape. Not even in my own mind."

Bianca sat upon the windowsill. "I don't know what you want me to say. Something's obviously bothering you."

"Something is bothering me—my past. And the sins I committed across another ocean."

Without thinking, she placed her hand upon his arm. "Paul, if we ask Him, God puts our sins as far as the East is from the West. You did that when you accepted His free gift of salvation. He redeemed you then and the payment was made. He plunges our sins down into the depths of the sea and then He covers them—the covered deep of His perfect forgiveness." She lowered her lashes to the buttons on his shirt. "When you love someone, and you know about something that hurts them, you purposely don't bring it up. You choose to forget."

He put his fingers under her chin and made her look him in the eyes. "But even if sins have been forgiven, there is a natural law of consequences. Some things can't be avoided." He lowered his voice to an aching whisper. "Some ships always come in."

Bianca curled her fingers around his hand. "What are you saying to me?"

Paul gave her a look of such regret that she wanted to cry. "I'm saying that God cannot deny Himself. He is the true judge, and He never forgets. "

And then she knew. She knew by the way he said things and didn't say them. She knew by the way his bright, deep soul seemed to withdraw and fold in on itself. She knew by all the looks he'd ever given her that said he could love her and yet, said in the same glance, that he couldn't.

This was about India. And Madeline was right. Men always had secrets.

She jerked when another torrent of rain hit the window. "You're talking about yourself, aren't you?"

"Yes."

With that one word, she felt herself slipping. "But what about mercy, Paul? And long-suffering? And grace? Those are traits of God also."

He sighed and looked back out, his gaze as cold and indifferent as the rain. "Bianca, you're a lot smarter than you're pretending to be right now. Look at me." He spoke in a suffocated whisper. "In just a few words I can shatter all your hopes."

Bianca froze. Fear, stark and vivid, shone in his eyes. "Don't." The rain was louder, overlapping the pain that came in waves, sucking ebbs and sharp, contaminating flows.

"I can shatter your idea of me." The way he nodded was cruel; it sent dread through every pore of her body.

Tears stung her eyes in a primal dance that was too familiar. Her throat ached with defeat. "Do it then."

Chapter 18

*P*aul's emerald eyes turned passionless. "Remember when I told you last night that you wouldn't have liked me if you knew me two years ago?"

"Yes." Bianca pushed her back harder against the window, the cold from the glass seeping into her bones.

"That's because I was the opposite of everything that you are. Everything that you stand for." His voice was dangerously low.

Her mind was languid, lost in a nameless sea.

"I took things that weren't mine to take. In India I stole a diamond from a temple. I was paid well." He brought himself to his full height, his shoulders braced.

He stole a diamond. The words sunk in, and she let them ruminate. "So, you're a thief?"

"Yes. I'm a thief." The rain still pelted the window, running down in snaking streams.

She knitted her brows together. "I read a story about a thief once."

"I beg your pardon?"

"It happened not far from where we sit." She flipped her hand toward the window. "Somewhere out there. You might recall it—the thief on the cross. Luke chapter twenty-three, I believe."

"I know the story." His gaze shifted to the polished tiles upon the floor.

"Evidently you've forgotten that he asked for forgiveness. And that Jesus forgave him. Do you think you're unforgivable? Is that what this is all about?"

Anger flashed in his eyes. "I can't live under the weight of this anymore. I can't lie to you anymore."

"You haven't been lying to me. I never asked you, not even when you started to tell me last night. How can you lie if no one asks you a question?"

He closed his eyes and exhaled with effort. "You're missing the point entirely. If you'd just listen—"

"I am listening, but the words you're saying aren't making any sense." She stood, her body rising next to his, inches away. "If you're sorry, and you've tried to make restitution, what else is there? You're torturing yourself. You'd be surprised what sort of things I've heard of. I don't think you could shock me."

He laughed, hollow and devoid of feeling.

"If you've changed your mind about me, just say so." She laid her hand upon his arm without thinking. "If you don't want me—"

"I never said I didn't want you." He spoke through clenched teeth. "That's one of the problems here." He stepped backward, breaking free of her hand. "Do you have any idea the amount of restraint I have to put forth when I'm around you?"

It was her turn for silence. He stepped away and circled her, like a star set upon a course that would not be altered. He stopped when he was behind her. He was so close that she could feel his body's warmth. "Since words don't seem to be working, I think I'll try something else. Shall I enlighten you?"

Her heart became a wild thing, pounding against a cage. She couldn't answer.

"You've all but given yourself to me a hundred times. Every time you look at me, I see an invitation . . ." His breath was hot and cold at the same time against her neck.

She shivered.

"You've no idea how many times I've wanted to kiss you." He laid his hand upon the back of her head and traced the curve of her skull. "I know there's a question you want me to ask you . . ." His fingers skimmed the back of her neck; they moved to trace the indent of her shoulder. "But there's something I need you to understand." His palm pressed against her spine and inched lower. He leaned into her body and put his cheek against her. "I'm going to say this only once, and I'm going to say it in the cruelest way possible so I can make you feel the weight of it."

"Why?" She tried to free herself—turn so she could see his eyes.

Paul wrapped his arm around her waist and held her still. "Because it's the way it has to be." His voice held the weight of the entire world.

"I don't understand." Her chest rose and fell in a cadence all its own.

"I'm going to make you understand, darling." His hand slid slowly up her back; he buried it in her hair. "You're not the first woman I've touched like this. The last one was in India and she was married. I didn't care."

His lips were so close to her ear. This time the words were poison. Silent tears dropped from Bianca's eyes.

"I caused her divorce." He choked out the words. "That is who I am. That is what I live with. That is the man you think you love."

How long she stood there, she didn't know. The patterns of the rain changed, but still, stayed the same. Colors passed before the window—different robes and faces—different thoughts and different scenes.

Still, she felt his arms around her.

Still, she heard his voice in her ear, whispering horrible things.

Her Paul—whispering horrible things.

A door slammed from a distant place in the house. Voices rose and fell.

"There you are." Mr. Owenburke came from a door behind a tapestry, his robes flaring out behind him. "I was beginning to despair that I might never meet you." He took her hand. "It's an absolute pleasure."

"How . . . how do you do, Mr. Owenburke?" She had no idea how she'd managed to construe syllables into a thought.

"We're all waiting for the doctor's report on Mr. Tabor before we go anywhere. Sir Adrian is with him. Mrs. Greene's in the garden. I saw Mr. Emerson earlier, but I couldn't find him just now. Do you know where he is?"

"No, I don't. How is Mr. Tabor? Has there been any improvement?"

"Very little. His fever is lower, though. That can only be a good sign. Would you come with me? I'd like to offer you some refreshment. And have the chance to get to know you better." He led her out of the room and up a narrow set of stairs.

The stairs gave way to an outside balcony, another oasis in a city that was half shambles. The rain had stopped, and only drips—plunking afterthoughts— were left behind. The sun parted the clouds. Beams of light reached down, like thrown spears—touching the houses, the old temple Wailing Wall, the streets.

"One of my favorite spots. You can see most of the Old City from here." He pulled his chair closer to her and sat. "You weren't at breakfast. Have you eaten?"

"No." Her gaze dipped to old ruined columns and the churches scattered here and there.

"Well, that simply won't do. I can't have you not eating. You have to keep up your strength when you're traveling." Mr. Owenburke consulted the heavy gold watch hidden in the folds of his robe. "It's more like luncheon now. Will that be all right?"

Bianca nodded, hardly knowing what he'd said.

He rang a bell and a servant appeared. "Yes, Halim, we'll take our refreshment now."

The tall servant bowed and disappeared.

"You should have found me earlier. I can't imagine what you've been doing while you've not been eating." He bent his head low and looked into her eyes. "You've simply not lived until you've tasted Holy Land food. I'd wager what you're about to eat was eaten in Bible times. That's part of the charm of this place."

She looked into his kind, light blue eyes and then away. "I didn't feel much like eating. I'm sorry." She was sorry for so many things.

There was hesitation in his eyes. "Is there anything you need?"

It was too much. She didn't need kindness from another man. She wanted to cry until she couldn't breathe anymore. She wanted to find Paul and shake him, or slap his face. "I'm fine."

"I'm not quite sure I believe you. But no matter. Just know that I understand what you're going through. That friend of mine has a way of taxing a person—in ways that affect both the body and the mind. I've traveled with Sir Adrian many times before. Be thankful you're only going to be in his company for a month." He patted her hand. "Once, I spent six months with him and I almost had to have my right foot amputated. But that's a different story—look." He rested his forearm over the balcony rail and pointed to the Western Wall. "The last remnants of King Solomon's Temple. See the men dressed in black? The ones bowing to the wall? They're praying for the restoration of Israel."

The scene surfaced though a rush of wetness in her eyes.

"You just missed Tisha B'Av, the great fast which commemorates five calamities. The Jews sit on the ground there, reciting the Book of Lamentations, liturgical dirges called kinot, and the Book of Job. The first calamity has to do with the twelve spies that Moses sent to see the Land of Canaan. The Jews today lament their ancestors' lack of faith at the report."

Bianca curled her fingers around the arms of the chair and squeezed. Why would Paul be so cruel? He didn't have to put his hands on her as he said the words.

"The second calamity was when the First Temple built by King Solomon was destroyed by the Babylonians . . ."

Bianca barely heard Mr. Owenburke's words. Paul's voice rang in her mind, and that awful tone—devoid of hope.

"The third calamity was when the Romans destroyed the second temple in 70 AD . . ."

What did Paul think he was doing, running off? Did he think he wouldn't have to face her? Did he now expect a formal letter expressing her regret that she could no longer accept his attentions? *Dear Sir, you are a cad. Of the worst sort . . .*

Mr. Owenburke's voice filtered back in. "The historian Josephus wrote that over a million people were killed during the destruction of 70 AD. I found out earlier that Josephus is Mr. Emerson's favorite historian. I suppose he looks up to him as a pioneer in the field. A very old pioneer. First century." He smiled again at Bianca. "Josephus mentioned Jesus, you know. He called him the Christ and he spoke of the resurrection. He also mentioned James, the brother of Jesus."

Shock coursed through her body at hearing Paul's name. "Of course Mr. Emerson must like him."

"Ah, look, here's the luncheon."

Halim eased the tray down beside her.

Mr. Owenburke tipped the teapot and let the amber liquid drain. The smell of cinnamon mixed with cloves.

Bianca took the cup he offered and just held it, not even its warmth comforting. Paul was an adulterer. He knew the woman was married and he didn't care.

"Drink, Miss Marshal. Please. Otherwise I'll be forced to tell you the last calamity and bore you beyond your kind indulgence. I don't get many visitors, as you can probably tell."

"I'm sorry if I don't seem interested. I'm just overwhelmed." She sipped the tea to prove something, she didn't know what. "Yesterday in Jaffa we were set upon by street urchins. And then Mr. Tabor grew ill in the runaway carriage." She lowered her teacup. It shook against the saucer and sounded like rattling bones. More tears came to her eyes.

He withdrew a handkerchief from the folds of his robe. "Put your mind at ease. You are safe here. Shall I go and find Mrs. Greene?"

"No." The word came out louder than she wanted. She didn't need Madeline gloating that she'd been right about men and their secrets.

"All right." He set his teacup aside. "Perhaps you could tell me what's bothering you. I know we just met, but please believe that I have your best interests at heart." He reached for a plate and filled it with fruit and fish. He slipped a spoon into the hummus and handed her the plate. "Eat. It's the first step in healing a broken heart."

Bianca's hand froze in midair. "But . . . how did you know?"

"After spending these past weeks in perfectly orchestrated romantic situations, how could you not fall in love?"

He was right. Everything had been perfect, just like a fairy tale—even the first night when she'd met Paul. "I find that I'm in dire need of some wisdom, Mr. Owenburke."

He sat back, took his teacup, and smiled. There was something entirely different in his expression. The wind blew through his thick, blond hair and the sunlight gleamed off his jeweled-studded fingers. "Well, then, Miss Marshal, I find that I am inclined to give it."

Chapter 19

*O*ut of the corner of her eye, Bianca saw red hair.

"So, this is where you're both hiding." Sir Adrian stepped forward, as silently as he'd approached. "This house is like a tomb, as quiet as a tax collector's prayers." In one fluid movement, he took Mr. Owenburke's teacup from his hand. "Everyone's scattered like rats. I wonder why?" He went to the balcony and turned the teacup over. The amber liquid fell in a straight line until the wind blew it to the side.

A Hebrew voice yelled from below. "*Oi! Kacha HaChayim!*"

Sir Adrian looked over the railing. "So sorry, my good man."

The man mumbled something else and then slammed a door below.

"I do believe that was my gardener, Hartwith." Mr. Owenburke raised his eyebrows and sat back like a spoiled rajah at court.

"Was it?" Sir Adrian poured new tea in the cup and drained it in one gulp. "This tea's gone cold, Samuel. Didn't your upbringing in England teach you anything?" He tilted the cup and inspected the dregs in the bottom. "What must Miss Marshal think of you, allowing good tea to go insipid?"

"It's all right, Sir Adrian." Bianca set down her teacup. "The tea's also good cold. We drink it cold all the time in Ohio."

Sir Adrian cringed. "Yes, I've heard of your Southern punch teas. So sickening sweet one feels like shaving his tongue afterward." He turned to look into the hallway. "Where's your man, Samuel? I haven't seen any of the servants since breakfast. What the deuce is going on around here?"

Mr. Owenburke's light blue eyes grew openly amused. "Calm down, Hartwith. I'll get you some fresh, hot tea." He reached into the folds of his robe, withdrew a small golden bell, and set it upon the table. "I wouldn't want you to have an apoplexy. It's best we take precautions to see to his absolute comfort. Don't you agree, Miss Marshal?" He searched another pocket of his robe and came up empty. "I know it's here somewhere . . . Ah, yes." He withdrew a small, silver bell and put it next to the golden one on the table.

Sir Adrian raised his eyebrow in a perfect arc. "Please don't tell me you have a different bell for each one of your servants."

"Of course not." He held the bottom of his robe and reached into a deep embroidered pocket. "But I do have a gong for Omar, and he happens to be close-by."

"A gong?" Sir Adrian rolled his eyes. "I'm all astonishment."

The metal disc swayed as Mr. Owenburke placed it next to the other bells. "Now for the mallet." He fished in another pocket and withdrew it.

Sir Adrian leaned toward Bianca. "And he calls me eccentric." He held his hand aloft. "Why don't you just install a rope and pulley system?"

"Because it's too modern, that's why." Mr. Owenburke's voice drawled out with distinct mockery. "And I don't much care for modern things. Colossal factories and constant noise, belching black smoke inventions." He hit the mallet against the gong. "That world kills romance."

"I see." Sir Adrian made a pyramid with his hands. "And a robe with forty-two pockets is more romantic." He looked heavenward. "Why be clothed in Paris silk when you can be a self-inflicted pack mule, clanking with every step?"

Mr. Owenburke struck the gong again. "I don't have forty-two pockets, you coxcomb. There are only twelve."

"Twelve, of course." Sir Adrian grinned and stroked his chin. "The number of governmental perfection, the tribes of Israel, the apostles, the foundations in the heavenly Jerusalem, the gates of pearl. The combination of the heavenly three and the earthly four. The twelve precious stones on the Jewish priests' ephods. Have I forgotten anything?"

"Quite a bit." Mr. Owenburke returned Sir Adrian's smile.

Bianca felt like she was watching some sort of play unfold. Both men were perfect in their cues; so quick-witted they didn't miss anything.

When the gong sound faded, Sir Adrian bent down and struck it again. "Perhaps I should bring this back to London. My butler would enjoy calling the housekeeper this way. And the look on her face might be worth hearing it."

If things had been different, Bianca would have smiled thinking about a gong in his London situation. Would he ring it for his bath? Would his servants carry in a succession of towels and soaps and oils?

Footsteps echoed in the hallway and a servant appeared. He was larger than any man she'd ever seen. His skin was light brown and his eyes were a subservient gray.

"Another pot of tea, Omar."

"Yes, Sir." The man bowed and disappeared.

Mr. Owenburke stood and joined Sir Adrian at the edge of the balcony. "Did you have a purpose for coming up here? Or was it to simply steal my tea, dump it on my gardener, and interrupt my conversation with Miss Marshal?"

"I do everything with purpose, Samuel. You, above all people, should know that."

"Yes, I do know that." Mr. Owenburke fell into an animated silence, adjusting the cuff of his robe and twisting the ring on his first finger.

The two men were an interesting contrast standing side by side—both fascinating in their own ways. Both opulently dressed, old world next to modern, sky blue eyes next to dark, unfathomable sea.

"Well then?" Mr. Owenburke asked. "Your purpose?"

Sir Adrian reached into his vest pocket. "We found this in Tabor's things." He held out a brown bottle the size of his palm. "It matches the white residue he had in his hair."

Bianca took the bottle, held it in the light, and read the label. "The Traveler's Best Friend. What is it?"

"Whatever it is, it has a very high level of arsenic. The doctor came to that conclusion an hour ago."

"Arsenic?" Bianca tilted the bottle until the powder slid down the interior wall like sand. "But arsenic is in paint and wallpaper glue. Also some ladies' complexion crèmes. How harmful can it be?"

Sir Adrian and Mr. Owenburke locked eyes with one another.

Mr. Owenburke cleared his throat. "Some think it caused George the Third's madness. In the eighth century, an Arab alchemist named Jabir became the first to prepare arsenic trioxide, an odorless and tasteless powder. It became a favorite murder weapon in the Middle Ages, especially amongst the ruling classes in Italy."

"Its other name is Inheritance Powder." Sir Adrian looked poignantly at one of Mr. Owenburke's rings. "It has long been a favorite poison to those of dubious intent."

Mr. Owenburke pulled his hand behind him. "But, very convenient for those who need a solution in difficult times." His mouth thinned with displeasure. "A man never knows when he might find himself in a Muslim prison."

Bianca's mind raced to all the Gothic novels she'd read about poisoning. "What are you saying exactly?"

Sir Adrian waved his hand toward the Dome of the Rock. "Samuel has sympathies with Jews. But don't worry. He's a very careful man."

"Are you in danger?" In the short time she'd known Mr. Owenburke, she'd grown fond of him. He was clever and kind, and he did seem only to have her best interests at heart.

"There is always danger abroad." Mr. Owenburke's voice was soft. "But, Sir Adrian is right. I am careful— careful not to jeopardize those who are being treated as second-class citizens in their own country."

The wind blew the hair sticking out from beneath his turban. The blond locks moved against his well-tanned temples. "The Jews can't even ride a camel within the city limits. Or have evidence given by them recognized in court."

"That's deplorable," Sir Adrian said. "As I have told you before—For the love of England! Where's Omar? Picking leaves off the *Camellia sinensis* plant to boil? Is he letting the tea leaves oxidize in the sun?"

"He'll be here in a moment." Mr. Owenburke looked like nothing Sir Adrian could say would ever bother him. He gazed at the Wailing Wall. "You should hear the Jews cry at the wall, Miss Marshal. They beg God for forgiveness. There's nothing worse than hearing a people who've been forsaken by their God."

Bianca hardly knew what to say. This place, this Jerusalem, this Holy Land... How many people had died here? How much blood soaked the streets? How many battles were yet to come?

"This country has long been a place of strife. And redemption." Bianca gripped the arsenic bottle. It felt colder in her hands.

Mr. Owenburke looked past the city walls to the uncultivated wilderness. "There is little justice in this corner of the world."

Sir Adrian rested his hand on Mr. Owenburke's shoulder. "Perhaps that will change soon."

The lines around Mr. Owenburke's eyes softened. "Perhaps."

Sir Adrian took a deep breath. "Look at us all. If someone stumbled upon us, they'd think the Apocalypse was imminent." He took the little brown bottle from Bianca. "It says here to sprinkle the powder in your hair every night and in your bed. I suppose the severity of Mr. Tabor's ailment depends on how much of this he used. And for how long."

"What's the doctor doing about it?" Mr. Owenburke asked.

Sir Adrian pocketed the bottle. "He's giving him sulfur and charcoal. If it's arsenic poisoning, that's the best course of action."

Mr. Owenburke nodded. "So, I suppose now we wait."

"Now we wait," Sir Adrian echoed. He looked at Bianca. "And we pray."

Mr. Owenburke stood and held out his hand to her. "I've never been one for being idle. Shall we go to the church?"

Bianca took his hand and stood. "Which church would that be?"

He laughed and looked at Sir Adrian in disbelief. "Is she serious?"

Sir Adrian grinned and adjusted his scarf. "Apparently."

Mr. Owenburke put her hand in the crook of his arm and pulled her toward the hall. "I'm talking about the Church of the Holy Sepulchre. It's the first place pilgrims go when they come."

"Yes, of course." Bianca couldn't believe she'd forgotten about it.

Mr. Owenburke was saying something. ". . . servants shall keep an eye on Mr. Tabor. We'll only be a short walk away. Shall we find Mrs. Greene?"

"She'll want to see it." Sir Adrian turned to Bianca. "Do you know where Emerson is?"

"I don't know where he's gone." Bianca hoped the tremor in her voice didn't sound as severe as she thought.

"Perhaps he went for a walk," Mr. Owenburke offered. "The air in the house can sometimes be stifling."

"I hear he walks a lot," Sir Adrian said. "In fact, he walked outside the Old City walls last night. Imagine that, walking around fourteen thousand souls in the middle of the night, with the wind blowing through the trees, and the moonlight pushing him on." He laughed and it sounded like a reverie. "He must have a great deal on his mind."

Bianca saw Sir Adrian out of the corner of her eye— the fine suit, the silk scarf, the ebony cane.

And the expression in his eyes that said he knew too much.

The crowd outside the church was massive. Bianca searched every face for him, every corner of the courtyard. Nothing. Paul was like a wish upon the wind. Her heart twisted to think she might never see him again. Fear swirled in her stomach like brine.

The eyes of beggars implored Bianca—tight, drawn, hopeless faces—faces that would haunt her until the day she died. The wind began again, pulling at her hair and licking her cheeks, a wild, cold thing.

The poor shivered and pulled their scraps of robes tighter.

Sir Adrian leaned close to her ear. "Don't look at them. It's easier that way."

"You could give them some money." The wind came around the corner and stole her voice away, for not even it would give mercy.

"It shouldn't be much longer." Mr. Owenburke stared at a group of men leaning on the wall. They wore turbans, as he did. One man caught his gaze and raised his chin in acknowledgment.

Madeline rubbed her arms. "Seems like a godforsaken place, doesn't it?"

An Arab, heavily robed and smelling of sweet spices, walked between them. He strode up to the door holding a ring of keys and then plunged one into the lock.

"No one but a Muslim can open the doors," Mr. Owenburke whispered. "The sects within would have an all-out war if only one were allowed to hold the keys. Six denominations share this roof." He spread his hand out and touched his fingers as he counted. "Greek Orthodox, Syrian Orthodox, Ethiopian Orthodox, Armenian Apostolic, Roman Catholic, and Coptic. They each have a chapel." He inclined his head toward the corner where a group of uniformed men stood. "The Turkish guards there try to keep them all from killing each other."

The Arab man turned the large key and swung open the door. The incense wafted out, so strong Bianca shielded her nose.

A ghost of a smile tugged at Sir Adrian's mouth. "What a shame Emerson's disappeared. I'd like to hear what he'd have to say about all this." He crossed the threshold, his boots echoing against the stone floor. "Maybe he'll turn up. I can hardly see him staying away from this place, can you?"

"He would want to see it." Bianca's voice caught.

Someone shut the doors and most of the light disappeared. The people whispered.

Madeline pulled her shawl tighter and made her way across the multicolored tiles. "Let's see what's to see and go. I don't like this place. It's too dismal." A couple of dark-hooded figures passed by, their candles flickering in the gloom.

People filtered down every hallway, every staircase. They walked around their small group like an exodus from the bitter wind outside.

"What's this?" Madeline circled around a rectangular, roughhewn stone upon the floor. It was surrounded by a border of polished tan marble. White lanterns hung above it, held in place by gold chains in the shape of crosses.

Mr. Owenburke stepped behind the lanterns, their glow of orange, yellow, and red softening the patterns on his robe. "The Stone of Unction. Believed to be the place where the Lord's body was anointed after His death."

A woman dressed in black bent and kissed the stone, then spoke something indiscernible. She withdrew a small shoe from her pocket and left it. Tears were in her eyes.

Sir Adrian bent down and laid his hand upon the light rose stone. The lanterns above him flickered as the wind breathed. "The place where the Son of God lay broken, His body drained of blood, His heart not beating."

Mr. Owenburke walked on the checkerboard of black marble on the floor. "If not here, somewhere near, at least. This is Jerusalem, after all."

"What do you think, ladies?" Sir Adrian kept his eyes down. "Are we to look at this place as sacred, as these people do?"

Bianca's skirt fanned out upon the floor as she bent. It all seemed surreal, so cold. Was this really the place where they laid Him? She reached for the stone but stopped her hand an inch away. She wished she could read the foreign words carved there.

Paul would know what they said.

She gazed up at the high ceiling, her senses spinning—the smells and sounds overwhelming, the day like a bad dream. How can she not be profoundly affected? Her heart felt lifeless. And this was the one place where it should be full of fire.

Sir Adrian traced a crack in the stone. When he pulled back his hand, the tip of his glove was black. "I read that this stone was laid down in 1810 after a fire. What a shame we can't see the real one."

"Shall we move on?" Mr. Owenburke's gaze lingered on Sir Adrian, as if he could feel the disappointment within his friend. "There's much to see."

Sir Adrian stood. "How convenient for us that St. Helena was able to find so many sacred places and put them all beneath one roof." His voice was flat. "I wasn't much in the mood for extensive walking." Where he normally would have placed a smile, his face was too still.

They walked around the corner and entered a great hall. Paintings lined the stone walls. Two thrones stood facing one another at the end, velvet carpets leading up to them. High above, a golden dome shone in the light of the many windows.

A mosaic depicted Jesus in the center, holding a book. And, Bianca assumed, four of the disciples in the triangular corners, most likely Matthew, Mark, Luke, and John. The golds, violets, and blues melded in the sunshine, giving an effect so serene, Bianca's heart caught for a moment, but then it faded.

"This is the Catholicon," Mr. Owenburke said. "Large masses are held here and this is where the patriarchs of Jerusalem are chosen." He walked deeper into the room and over a tiled floor of pink and black marble, circular shapes within a rectangle, like a permanent Oriental rug. "Here marks the center of the world, according to ancient map makers." He gestured to a chalice-shaped stone in the center.

Madeline circled it, looking bored.

Mr. Owenburke studied the stone for a moment longer. "Shall we go to the tomb? It's just through there."

"Yes, let's," Sir Adrian said. "That should be worth something."

They passed through a stone archway and entered a massive rotunda. Wide columns surrounded the circular room. Three levels of archways reached to the dome above. A sunburst flared out from the hole in the ceiling. A solid beam of circular light plunged down, highlighting the worn stones upon the floor. People moved to and fro, holding conversations and pointing to the relics all around. A tall, stone building was in the center of the rotunda—a building within a building. Candlesticks taller than Bianca framed the red door. A tapestry hung from the roof, a picture of the crucifixion woven in faded thread.

Mr. Owenburke gestured toward the door. "I find that it's a very personal experience. I will leave you to inspect the tomb yourselves." He smiled and then strolled away, walking in and out of the columns with his hands clasped behind his back, seemingly deep in thought.

Sir Adrian took a deep breath and then entered the building.

Bianca followed him into the antechamber of the tomb. The entire room was elaborate white marble, and gold lamps hung from the ceiling in abundance.

"It's freezing in here." Madeline inspected a part of the marble that looked like a falling curtain. "I don't know how you can be so interested in all this, Bianca. All these symbols, and incense, and chanting." Madeline glanced back at the door from which they had come. "Go on with Sir Adrian. I'd like to get some fresh air."

"I don't think that's wise. You never know what sort of people you might run into."

"I won't be long." Madeline's smile didn't reach her eyes. Her skirt fanned out like a gypsy's as she turned and disappeared.

Sir Adrian pinched the bridge of his nose. "You can never please women who are given to the stage." He held out his arm to Bianca. "I learned that the hard way, I can assure you. She'll join us when she's ready."

"Are you sure?"

"She'll be fine." Sir Adrian scanned Bianca's face and drew his eyebrows together. "What's wrong? Don't you want to see the tomb of Jesus? I would think—"

"Of course." Bianca glanced behind her, an unsettling feeling creeping into her bones. Why would Madeline go off alone? "The tomb and Calvary are in this same church?"

"So they say. The church also has the pillar of flagellation, the prison room where Jesus was held, and the Chapel of Adam—a place that holds Adam's skull and the very dust he was made from. And look, here, this must be the Angel's Stone."

Directly before them was a stone encased within a stone. Glass lay over the top. Carvings of draped fabric lined it all around. Two lit candles coming out of the box cast an otherworldly glow.

"Tradition says that this is a fragment of the stone that the angel rolled away, Samuel told me as much. But what do we say? What shall our verdict be?"

"I hardly know." Bianca drew closer to him and wished for all the world that she could talk to Paul. It *was* cold in the little room, and the look in Sir Adrian's eyes chilled her even more.

They stooped to go into the tomb. The space was even smaller, the air more dense. Golden candlesticks surrounded the slab.

"The tomb of Jesus." Sir Adrian's voice was a whisper. "So here we are, after all these months of waiting."

"Here we are," she echoed, feeling the same malaise that was in his expression.

He worked a muscle at his jaw. "It is a shame that most of the church has been rebuilt. I would have liked to see it as it was in the beginning. You know, I read it was leveled to the ground in the eleventh century. The foundations were hacked down to bedrock. Some caliph trying to purge the land . . ." His face darkened. He turned and led her back out into the rotunda. The beam of light slanted at a different angle, flooding the pathway before them. He raised his gloved hand to shield his eyes.

Mr. Owenburke sat off to the side, watching the crowd. A priest approached him, his golden robe and red sash tight around him. His beard was black and closely trimmed. He slipped something into Mr. Owenburke's hand.

Sir Adrian turned Bianca away, putting his hand at her back. "It's a funny thing, truth. Some seek truth in the way their fathers sought it—believing everything, unconditionally. Others invent truth, making it into what they want to see."

"And which one are you?"

"I search for truth endlessly, Bianca." It was the first time he'd ever called her by her first name. Those dark blue eyes locked upon her and somehow she knew that he realized it too. Conflict passed upon his face—something like fondness and regret. The veil he so casually wore fell into place again and he looked away from her. "I always find the truth, regardless of the cost." His voice, like a ghost that haunted just beyond reach, fell like the last bit of hope in her heart.

Paul followed Bianca's every movement, studying every nuance. Wearing a tan robe and an Arabic scarf, he blended with the multitudes. Why didn't she touch the Stone of Unction? When she'd passed the Crusader graffiti on the wall—hundreds of crosses etched in the stones—she hadn't even noticed. There had been tears in her eyes.

"Forgive me, if you can." He whispered the words and knew they didn't count for anything.

He walked to the Seven Arches of the Virgin, eleventh-century remains. He leaned against the wall and watched the tall candles upon the floor, their thin flames barely shedding any light.

He stuck his hand in his pocket and crumpled the note from Madeline again.

Monks weaved in and out of the room, their faces hidden, their dark cloaks swallowed by the blackness all around. As they chanted, their breath moved the flames of the small candles they held.

"*Attende Domine, et miserere quia peccavimus tibi . . .*"

Paul whispered the translation: "O Lord, listen and have mercy because we have sinned against You—"

"Hello, Paul." Madeline's false, honeyed voice was beside him. The feeling of revulsion came, just like it had every time since the Egyptian dinner. He could taste her perfume in the air—too thick, too sweet.

"Tell me what you want."

She walked in front of him, the fabric of her skirt rustling. He could feel her eyes upon him. They were the eyes of Jezebel—the eyes of Potifar's wife, only unlike Joseph, he hadn't had the sense to run.

The bottom of her dress cast long shadows upon his shoes. "Come now, Paul, I hardly think that's the proper way to start our conversation."

"The proper way for us to start a conversation would have been if we hadn't."

She tsked his comment away. "You're angry. You have every right to be."

"Why is that?" He brought his gaze up to her and wished he hadn't. He hated the feigned innocence that he saw.

"You've obviously been put in a very awkward position." A look of sympathy passed across her face. "But I can't say I'm not glad that fate has brought us together again."

Paul stepped away and looked over the balcony. "And in this case, fate has a name, and an aristocratic title. How much is Sir Adrian paying you to be my antagonist?"

She backed up against the archway and looked at him with doleful eyes. "Do you think I'm for sale?"

He clenched his jaw. Syllables came out in a growl. "How can you pretend to be serious? I'm tired of your games. What do you want?"

She put her hands behind her back and held on to the column. "Just to be near you."

A hollow laugh escaped his lips. A draft blew through the hall and extinguished a candle. "The note you sent me says differently, and you're lying. Do you think I'll ever trust you again after you almost had me killed in that alley?"

"I don't know what you're talking about."

"Don't you? It just so happens that when I left your husband's house that cursed day, two men were waiting for me. Two men with clubs, Madeline. Two men I'd seen you with earlier that day."

"You know how India is, there's vermin everywhere, especially in human form. I had nothing to do with it." A slow smile spread. "Since you're standing before me now, I assume you beat them off. You've always been so adventurous and brave." She laid her hand upon his arm.

Repulsion raked along his skin. "Don't touch me." He stepped back. "And don't pretend you didn't want the diamond." Groups of Armenian priests gathered below, their black robes a stark contrast to the jeweled hats they wore. "Don't pretend you didn't have it all planned perfectly. As you and Sir Adrian have things planned now."

"The years have jaded you, Paul. I'm sorry for that."

He closed his eyes and bit the inside of his cheek. "According to the note I have in my pocket, you have a demand, and it says I shall never be free unless you get it."

"Words, Paul, that's all. Words to get you here so we could talk."

He stepped closer to the candlelight. He thought about Bianca and the candle path in the museum where he'd first seen her. "You may congratulate yourself. I have been tortured daily for what I did in India. Do you want to talk about that?"

"I've been tortured too."

He knew she was lying; she always was. "I'll ask you again. What do you want from me?"

"Not much." Her voice was a whisper in the darkness. "Just a small payment for leaving your tie in my house that day, and for being the instrument that brought about my social destruction."

"I'm listening." He knew he deserved this.

"I want you to look at me the way you look at Bianca."

His gaze froze upon her. "It's not going to happen. It's never going to happen again."

"I could change your mind, if you'd let me." She reached out and gripped his tie. "You must be so tired of all this. It's been weeks and we haven't been able to talk." She licked the gloss on her lips. "You've been alone since you left me in India. That must count for something."

Yes, it meant something. It meant he was so traumatized from the experience he'd buried his nose in books for two years. It meant he'd rather study the history of chamber pots than have another experience with her. But it meant even more than that. Since India, his life had changed. Starting with Moody's revival service and the first steps he'd taken down that aisle. "How do you know that I've been alone since India? Sir Adrian, I suppose."

She nodded, a little too quickly. "He thinks you're brilliant, as I do. He chose you because you'd entertain him with your stories about history."

"He could have just brought along a tour book. It would have been a lot cheaper." He ran his fingers through his hair to keep from choking her. "And I suppose you just happened to be chosen randomly out of all the contestants."

"Of course not." She had the audacity to smile. "I didn't win the essay contest, you know that. Sir Adrian found me in the theater and asked me to come."

"For what purpose?"

"I already told you. Because we belong together. Because Sir Adrian knows our history." Her brown eyes looked black in the low light. The perfect paleness of her cheek made her look like marble.

"Have you ever told the truth?" He grabbed her arm and almost threw her behind a column. "I curse the day I took that diamond from you. How I wish I'd never gone to India."

"You don't mean that. I think about you constantly." She dropped her gaze. "I remember."

"Be quiet."

"I remember the way you held me, Paul. My husband never held me like that."

"If you say another word . . ." He made a fist at his side and counted off the seconds. How easy it would be just to bash her head against the column and be done with her forever . . . "I'll leave."

"I've dreamed of you for two years—"

"I've been punished for two years. I've hated myself since then." He tightened his grip on her arm. "Do you want money? Are you trying to blackmail me? Do you want me to pay you not to tell Bianca?"

"No, I don't want your money. Besides, how could you give me any when you bought that large house immediately after you'd returned?"

"How do you know that?"

"I know a lot of things. I know it's a very impressive house. I saw it before the Egyptian dinner." She tugged at his sleeve. "I came to London to find you because I couldn't forget."

He looked down at her hand upon his arm. "You came to London to make a living, doing what you do best—the oldest profession in the world, some would call it." He pried her fingers away. "Also to make a disaster of my life, but who's counting?"

Tears welled in her eyes. Bona fide actress tears. "That's very harsh."

"Be prepared, then, because it's about to get a lot harsher."

Chapter 20

$\mathcal{H}$ ome. Bianca wanted to go home. Away from this pain. Away from this foreign soil. Away from whatever Sir Adrian had planned.

She wanted to talk to Daddy. She wanted to feel his arm around her shoulder, and she wanted to cry—great soul-cleansing tears. Daddy wouldn't ask her what was wrong at first, he never did. He'd take her to their hillside and they'd sit, looking at the valley like they were seeing it all over again.

The tall grass would be blowing like God had swept it to the side, just to feel its softness against His hand. And farther on, there'd be smell of the fresh moss against the ground. The aspen leaves would quiver by the stream.

Bianca rubbed her arms and wished she'd brought her shawl. The monks still chanted. Sad, sad, chanting. She put her hands over her ears.

Dark was everywhere in this place, around every corner, every staircase, upon every stretch of floor.

Bianca turned her face to the wall. "Daddy, I need you. I wish you were here."

A priest held a candle. It illuminated his hard, wrinkled face, like a ghost in the dark, haunting Sir Adrian beside him. He spoke broken English and handed Sir Adrian a folded paper. More secrets. More things she wasn't supposed to know.

Bianca thought of home—her garden; Mama's biscuits; and sweet, white corn. But she'd hate it again ten minutes after she arrived. Mama would say how wrong she'd been to look for a husband.

"What are you doing over here, alone in the dark?" Sir Adrian's voice reached behind her.

Bianca's heart sped up. Above all else, Sir Adrian must not know. "Just wandering. I should have stayed with you."

"Yes, you should have." He came between her and the altar.

"I'm sorry. I don't know what I was thinking." She took his arm even though she didn't want to.

He was staring at her. She could feel it.

"Are you all right?"

"I'm fine."

"Are you certain? You can tell me if something's wrong."

Anger radiated through her, but anger was good. Anger was a strong soldier against tears.

"Bianca, you seem a bit off today. Perhaps we should go back."

She hated the sympathy in his voice. "I said I'm fine." She broke free of his hand and walked ahead, out underneath the rotunda. "I'm quite capable of touring a church without becoming overwhelmed."

"More than one Arab has looked your way today." He looked to the side, to something that Bianca couldn't see. "I won't have you disappearing."

She ran her hand along a column and walked around it. "You didn't care when Madeline left. Why? Is it because she's older than I am? Am I so naive that I have to be watched like a child?"

"You're being ridiculous—would you stop spinning?"

"I'm not spinning." She held onto the marble and leaned out. "I'm walking around."

"Has someone said something to you?" His dark blue eyes bore into her until she couldn't stand it.

"No one's said anything." She walked down the hall.

Sir Adrian followed. "Are you lying to me?"

Bianca looked past his dark red hair to the painted angels above. "I always tell the truth. Why wouldn't I?"

"People lie for many reasons."

"I remember you telling me that once, on the ship— Look at that mural, up there on that dome. I've never seen so much gold in all my life."

He glanced at it.

"But, you know that. Silly me. You know I've never seen real gold before. You know so much about all of us. I imagine all this is rather passé to you."

He stepped closer again, tapping his walking stick upon the floor. "What do you mean?"

"I'm just saying this church must bore you." She could see her reflection on his shoes. "You're surrounded by wealth every day."

"You might be surprised." He checked the heavy gold watch dangling from his side. "Samuel should have joined us by now."

A crowd mingled in and out of the passageways.

"Let's go on to Calvary." An easy smile lifted the right side of his cheek. "Just this way, I think. It's the highlight of this trip, after all. Too bad Paul's not here."

"Yes, too bad." The words caught in her throat. She was so cold. Nothing felt stable. She left him standing there.

"Gad, wait!"

His words from earlier reverberated throughout her mind—*I search for truth endlessly and I always find it, regardless of the cost.*" She wanted to scream. Right here in the church. What truth? What cost?

"Odd's teeth, woman!" His walking stick beat upon the floor as he came.

"Poor Sir Adrian. I feel sorry for you."

"What is that supposed to mean?"

She rounded the corner and went up a set of spiral stairs. On the walls, hundreds of painted angels looked toward a golden altar. Hundreds of stars spread also on the walls, and painted open books—books of judgment, no doubt. God's judgment. Judgment on those who forgot His laws. Men who caused divorces.

A bell rang. And then another. Bells calling for the mass of the death of the Lord. Reenacted every day, never forgotten in this place.

Pain gripped Bianca's heart. There was another woman somewhere in the world with a broken heart. And Paul didn't care. Bianca squeezed her eyes shut. She could feel Sir Adrian behind her. She could smell the chicory on his breath.

"I hardly think you should feel sorry for me. I have everything I've ever wanted."

"Pity," she said, her voice choked with emotion. "A little want might have taught you something." Like not pairing her up with an adulterer, knowing that she'd love him instantly—knowing he was everything she desired. She turned and faced him.

The skin wrinkled around his eyes, a subtle gesture. Realization dawned. Sir Adrian had studied her. The questions on the essay had been his compass. Paul had tried to warn her in the garden, but she'd been too blind.

He made a sound that only a haughty aristocrat could muster. "You're majoring in being peevish today, aren't you?"

"Am I?" What about Paul's essay answers? Had Sir Adrian seen a perfect opportunity for entertainment?

"Yes, blast it. You are. Why are you looking at me like that?"

Bianca breathed deep, pushing her ribs against her corset until it hurt. Sir Adrian knew what Paul did in India—the diamond, the divorce. And he had to know how she'd feel about that. He also knew she'd fall in love with Paul, pathetic, incurably romantic creature that she was.

"Are you going to tell me what's the matter with you?"

Bianca took a step closer, fury so real she could taste it.

"What's happened?" His eyes pleaded with her, but she didn't care. "All right then, Bianca. Since you're bent on silence, let's follow your line of thought—you say a little want might have taught me something."

The sound of her heartbeat was in her ears.

"Let me think . . . how could want have improved my self-absorbed life? Oh, yes, I could have learned how to make do with potatoes." He walked behind her. "Want might have taught me perseverance. It often works out that way for the common man, does it not? I hardly know about those kinds of things. As you're indicating, I'm only a cold aristocrat." He stood in front of her, waiting. "Your father knows a bit about want, doesn't he? He wastes his life in a factory, making shoelaces for gentlemen like me."

Her eyes locked onto him, dared him to say anything further. "Don't—"

"Ah, a reaction." He leaned in closer. "Very good." His voice fell to a whisper. "What shouldn't I do?"

"Don't talk about my daddy."

"It's true, isn't it? All those hours he stands tending bobbins like a woman. How fortunate that I took pity on—"

Bianca slapped him hard and recoiled. She tripped on the altar.

He grabbed her wrist and caught her. His jaw clenched. Rage clouded his eyes.

"Let go." A tremble went through her body.

His grip was iron. "When did you learn how to bite?" The impression of her fingers rose up on his cheek; it was a ghost's hand on a perfectly shaved jaw.

She jerked her wrist out of his grasp. Hot tears finally came to her eyes, along with shame. "I learned it from you."

"Bravo." His fingers wrapped around the handle of his walking stick, so tightly that Bianca could hear his leather glove moving against the wood. "I was wondering when you'd start acting like the women in London."

"I'll never act—"

"I'm going to forget that you just slapped me. It never happened."

Tears spilled onto her cheeks. He was a blurry apparition of a gray cashmere suit. "Why should you do that?"

"Because I deserved it." He walked to the altar and lit a candle.

The room felt small. She wished there was some sunlight. "I don't believe you anymore ... I don't know what to believe anymore."

His entire body was still. "Don't tell me you've lost your faith. And here of all places."

"I ... haven't."

"I expected more from you."

She looked at the crack in the rock below the altar— the crack they said was caused by the earthquake after Jesus died. How could she have slapped him here?

His eyes held nothing and yet too much. "You're stronger than this. You'll see."

Mr. Owenburke wandered into the room. "Sorry it took me so long. Are we—Miss Marshal? Are you crying?"

Sir Adrian placed her hand securely into the crook of his arm. "She's overwhelmed by this place,

Samuel. If I'm not mistaken, you were too when you came here the first time."

Bianca tried to pull away.

Sir Adrian clamped his other hand over hers, a subtle warning.

"I remember." Mr. Owenburke narrowed his eyes at Sir Adrian.

"I trust, Samuel, that everything is as it should be."

"Everything's fine . . . Except Miss Marshal here. What did you do to her?" He moved to Bianca's left side and took her other hand, placing it into the corner of his arm. They all walked down the stairs. "Where's Madeline?"

"She'll be along momentarily. Would you let go of Miss Marshal? I'm quite capable—"

"I'm not so sure about that, Hartwith. Every time I leave you alone with a woman she ends up crying."

"Every time?" He rolled his eyes. "Are you still not over the heiress?"

Mr. Owenburke's expression clouded. "I wasn't thinking of my heiress just now, but since you reminded me . . ."

"Oh, in that case . . ." Sir Adrian looked off to the right. "It's about time for supper, don't you think?"

Mr. Owenburke's body stiffened. "Look, you end-less diatribe, if you had something to do with the way Josette refused my letters that entire last month in England, you'd better tell me. Now."

Bianca tried to pry her hands from them. She needed a handkerchief. Desperately.

Sir Adrian pulled his arm, and hers, closer to his side.

"Well?" Mr. Owenburke stopped on the staircase.

"Were you involved with Josette that last month? For some reason I thought—"

"What? That I'd bought that ring because I liked the color?"

"All right." Sir Adrian stepped in front of her, twisting her body. "I'll admit it. Your mother thought she was all wrong for you."

"When did my mother's opinion ever matter?" Mr. Owenburke stood at Sir Adrian's toe, dragging her into their twisted triangle.

"It would have mattered when she cut off your inheritance."

"My inheritance! I can't believe—"

"Ugh!" Bianca ripped her hands free of them. "Would you both just cease?" She jerked open Sir Adrian's coat, plunged her hand into his pocket, and reached for his handkerchief.

"Gad!" He stepped backward.

She blew her nose hard, not caring at all.

The four monks around them stopped chanting.

Bianca folded the handkerchief and blew her nose again.

Mr. Owenburke reached into his sleeve and withdrew a silk handkerchief. "Take this. At least one of us knows how to treat a lady."

"I'm not sure I like your attitude." Sir Adrian glared at him.

"Good." Mr. Owenburke took Bianca's hand, walked across the tile, and threw open the doors. "Because I'm not entirely sure I like yours."

"Madeline." Bianca stopped short outside the church doors. "What are you doing out here?"

"Taking some air." She fidgeted with the cuffs of her sleeve. "If I never smell incense again it will be too soon."

Mr. Owenburke looked at the position of the sun and the shadows made by the rooftops. "We should go and check on Mr. Tabor."

Sir Adrian closed the door behind him. "Yes, why don't you? And take Miss Marshal with you. She's tired."

"Tired people normally don't cry. But if you say so, Hartwith."

"I do say so. I thought I'd show Mrs. Greene the Pool of Bethesda." He put on his hat. "What do you say? Are you up for it?"

Madeline's eyes brightened. "I'd love to see it. You don't mind, do you, Bianca?"

"Of course not." Bianca turned her back on them.

Mr. Owenburke took one last look at Sir Adrian. "I'd say we both could use the reprieve."

Sir Adrian watched the sunlight change the coal black of Madeline's hair to umber brown. In every light, she was beautiful. Her skin was the perfect blend of cream and seduction. Her eyes did things to a man that made him want to forget. But underneath . . . a heart of ash and poison. "What did you say to Bianca?"

She tilted her chin and sent her hair cascading over her shoulder. "No questions after my welfare? No pleasantries?" She slid her hand under his arm, and a little too close to his side. "All business and no play makes Jack a dull boy."

"I've never been much of the playing sort." He pulled his hat lower against the sun. "Not unless I'm the one calling the shots."

"So I've noticed." She opened her parasol. The lingering smile said things that her words didn't. The ribbons in her hair blew in the wind.

"Are you going to answer the question? Or shall I answer it for you?"

"Now, that sounds like fun." Her full lips curved. "Do tell. What did I say to Little Miss Country Mouse that has you scowling at me?"

Sir Adrian locked eyes with her. "You told her about you and Paul in India."

Her hand moved higher on the parasol handle. "I didn't." She looked offended. "Do you think I'd break our agreement that easily?"

There'd always been that risk.

"I'm not an idiot." She raised an eyebrow at him. "I understood your instructions. I understood them when you found me. I understood them on the docks as I boarded the ship. I think I've got it."

He nodded. "Don't forget. Don't let it slip at any time. Bianca must not hear it from you." He led her past a vendor selling dirty rugs. He waited until they were out of view before continuing. "If you do ever tell her, you won't get the thousand pounds. And I'll make sure you pay me back for your traveling expenses, amongst other things."

"What's the matter?" She pouted at him. "Feeling insecure? Are you afraid your carefully laid house of cards is going to fall?"

He squeezed the handle of his walking stick. "You just keep to the plan. You only plant doubts with Bianca, that is all. You gave her the first inkling about Tabor?"

"Yes. On the ship."

"Good. And as for Paul, you're only meant to be a test for him—to reveal his true character."

Madeline laughed. The sound mingled with foreign voices and barking dogs. "I could save you the trouble and tell you right now. He's a fool." She squinted against the sun. "A lucky fool, but a fool nonetheless."

Sir Adrian looked down at the pebbles along the pathway. The way he saw it, Paul was a man who fell to a moment of weakness, and Madeline almost killed him for his pains. "If only things had worked out better for you in India. You'd have that diamond now."

"All water under the bridge." Her expression was the exact opposite of her words. "Retribution will be made, I can assure you."

The sun dipped near the roves of the primitive houses. "I do wonder how you can hate Paul as much as you do. We both know he wasn't the real reason for your divorce. You were holding on to your marriage by a thread because of your past actions."

"He was *a* reason, and that's good enough for me." She snapped her parasol shut. "I had very carefully laid plans until he altered them. Don't pretend to be so virtuous, Sir Adrian. Because if there's anything we both know, it's that you're not."

"Touché, Madame." He moved a rock out of his way with his walking stick. His heart clenched. No. He must see it through to the end. He must play the part. "Did Paul meet you in the church?"

"He was there."

"Tell me what he said. Tell me how he looked—everything."

Madeline took a long breath, as if drawing in her thoughts. "He looked tortured, as he always does—tortured with his fascination for her."

"How fastidious you've been to endure it all." He raised his chin for effect. "One can only take so much of Paul and Bianca making eyes at one another."

Madeline twisted her mouth. "It's taken a great deal of restraint—especially on the ship. I hope you know that."

"Of course I know it." He reached into his pocket. "Your fortitude speaks volumes." He handed her a small pouch. "Here. Since I know, once again, that I can trust you—a token for your pains."

She nodded and slipped the money away.

"Now, what did you say to Paul?" He led her down a quiet, but safe looking alley.

"I offered myself to him." She said it as though she was talking about the weather. "I used every lure imaginable, but it didn't work."

"Are you sure you tried everything?"

"Of course I did." Anger flared in her eyes. "I'm at a loss. I hardly had to try two years ago."

"Yes, well . . ." Maybe Paul had changed. Was it really possible?

"He wanted to know if I was blackmailing him."

"And what did you say?" He led her around something vile looking on the street.

"I told him all the standard things men like to hear."

"Well, at least you know your business."

His comment was lost on her. She didn't even flinch. "As much as I like seeing Paul writhe, I don't know how much more he's going to put up with. There's retaliation in his eyes."

"Good." He reached in his vest. "The next thing I want you to do is detailed in this letter. Don't read it where anyone can see you. Destroy it when you're done."

"I understand. I will be your instrument."

He nodded, not really hearing her. He still felt the sting of Bianca's hand on his cheek. "He loves her, you know. And she loves him." The words slipped out. He hadn't meant to say them.

Madeline laughed. "You can't be serious."

"No, I suppose not." The loneliness crept back in. The emptiness was even worse.

"Let's pretend that's true. Even if they did get married, she wouldn't last a month in London."

"There would be difficulties." He made his smile look indifferent. Inside, he knew Bianca would find a way.

"Can you imagine her trying to run his household? Can you see her giving a dinner party for the museum donors?"

"What would she serve? Fried chicken and collard greens?" His sneer ended abruptly.

Madeline dabbed her eyes as she stopped laughing. "And her accent! Laud! Have you ever met anyone so uncultured? So innocent? So naive?"

"No." He spoke with quiet emphasis.

"She's pathetic. Can you imagine the dread Paul would have after he figured that out? Can you see him coming home to her after his fascination wore off?"

He pictured it, and he could clearly see her in Paul Emerson's home. There'd always be love in her eyes.

"But that won't happen, thanks to us." Madeline took a deep breath and looked at the ancient horizon.

"Yes. Thanks to us." He took a grassy path off the beaten road. The word *traitor* rummaged through his mind.

"Maybe we should let him marry her. That might be the worst punishment of all."

Sir Adrian made himself smile again—the one that was easiest, the one that was false. "Perhaps."

They came to a Crusader church and walked around the eastern wall. A cavern in the ground was scattered with ruins, five porches, wells, and grassy knolls.

Madeline walked to the edge, her boots kicking pebbles over the side; they fell like tiny drops of rain, scattering down the deep walls below.

His heart clenched. "Do you know what this is?"

"More meaningless stones from a book of fairy tales?" She walked off to the side and leaned upon a railing, boredom in her dark brown eyes.

He gazed down at the Pool of Bethesda. The place where the angel stirred the waters in the Gospel of John—where the first person in those waters was healed instantly, made whole of whatever disease they had.

The sun was a warm hand on his back. It stretched his shadow to the depths of the pit. All the water was gone now, and the angel too. Nothing stirred this place anymore. Nothing but vicious wind.

"You should see yourself," Madeline called. "Staring at rocks like they could talk to you." She twirled her parasol and cast lace shadows upon the grass. "Holy Land, indeed."

Sir Adrian gazed back down to the crumbled porch that held on by fragments. His mind removed the centuries and he saw it crowded, everyone rushing to be the first in the water. There—by the portico— perhaps that was where Jesus healed the man who had lain there for thirty-eight years. Perhaps that's where Jesus told the man to take up his bed and walk.

Thirty-eight years.

His age.

But men like him didn't get healed. Especially after everything he had done.

And was going to do.

Chapter 21

*H*er face was chapped. Her back hurt. An angry foreboding licked at her shoulders like demon voices in the wind. When they finally reached Mr. Owenburke's house, Bianca was ready to collapse. She needed a place to sleep. Anywhere would do.

She'd told Mr. Owenburke everything, and now, as he held her up as much as she held onto him, she didn't know why she'd done it. A moment of weakness. Someone to listen to her so she wouldn't feel so alone.

All the reasons sounded weak to her now, considering Mr. Owenburke would probably tell Sir Adrian everything when he came home. And then everything would go exactly how Sir Adrian had planned.

Tears ran down her cheeks again, and she didn't care. She'd failed. She couldn't marry Paul. Or any other man.

Papers, mingled with dirt, flew around the garden wall. Bits of dust flew into her eyes. She held her breath against another gust of wind.

Mr. Owenburke opened the gate. It flew back and ripped itself free of his hand. "Blasted, torturous devil-wind!" He claimed the gate again and pulled hard, slamming it shut. He took her hand without any reservations. "Let's get you something warm to drink, and perhaps you'd like to change." Regret shone in the depths of his light blue eyes. "There's dirt all over you."

"Is there?" Her boots scuffed against the garden stones. She looked to the tree where she'd stood with Paul in the middle of the night.

It was an ugly tree. And it was a stupid garden. A garden of lies.

They crossed the path and reached the door. When they were inside, Mr. Owenburke jerked the door against the frame. Instantly, the noise of the wind was deafened. Only the tick of the clock she'd never seen remained.

"Thank you." Her words were numb. "I'll just go rest now."

"Rest will do you good. I'll go and check on Mr. Tabor."

"You'll tell me if he's improved?"

"Yes, I'll tell you." He walked a few steps and then turned back. "Don't worry about anything." He nodded, almost like he was trying to convince himself. Then he was gone.

Bianca took off her hat and dragged it by the ribbon— across the Persian tile, the polished oak floor, the rug in the main hall. She thought it strange how that morning she'd been so full of hope.

And then, there by the window, Paul had told her the truth.

And everything had changed.

She walked over the faded lattice shadows and stumbled toward the stairs.

A creak sounded.

Paul sat in the corner, a sliver of light across his features. "Hello."

Her breath disappeared. Heat raced to her face.

"Is there anything I can do for you?"

Her bitter laugh ended in a sob.

The light fell on his sleeves, which were rolled up to his elbows. His lips parted before he spoke. "I will do anything you ask."

Bianca let herself look at him.

"Say something. Please."

She looked into his eyes, so green. "Where did you go? Why did you leave me here?"

He stood and walked to her. "Bianca, I'm so sorry."

She wiped her eyes with her hands. Dirt smeared over her palm.

He reached in his pocket for his handkerchief.

"Keep it."

"But—"

"I don't want it." She slapped his hand away. "I've had enough of men and handkerchiefs today, thank you very much."

The *E* disappeared on his handkerchief as he gathered it in his hand. "I don't know what to say."

"Obviously." She sneered. "Why else would you have disappeared at the most important moment in our conversation?" She hated that she could smell his shaving soap. She hated the way his hair looked perfect, even messed by the wind. "How convenient for you."

"I thought you needed time."

"Does it look like time did much for me?"

"I had to tell you."

She hated the tones in his voice—velvet mixed with pain.

A pin fell out of her hair.

He reached for it. Just like the first night at the museum.

He stepped forward to hand her the pin. Without thinking, she reached. Their fingers almost touched.

"Don't touch me!" She threw her hat at him.

He caught it. Feathers spread out over his shirt. "I'm sorry. I'm—"

"Sorry. Yes, I heard that." She turned and strode up the stairs.

"Where are you going?"

"Why? Do you care?"

"Of course I care." He followed her onto the staircase. "Wait, please." He slipped his fingers around her wrist.

"I said—" She lost her footing and slammed into his chest. "Paul Emerson!"

He gripped the rail to keep from hurling them backward.

"Let me go." She pushed against his shoulder, hot tears spilling onto her cheeks.

"I . . . of course." He stepped back and gazed down at her crumpled hat. He pushed parts of it out, trying to right it again. "A feather is broken . . . I'm s—"

"Sorry." She wrenched the hat from his grasp and threw it over the staircase. "Yes, I know." Her breath came in raged bursts.

Paul's eyes widened. His forehead was fixed in concentration.

Bianca put her hand on her hip. "Is there anything else you'd like to say just now?"

He worked the muscles at his jaw. "I'll be leaving tonight."

"Leaving?" She narrowed her eyes. "Where will you go this time?"

"I'm going back to Jaffa. The doctor needs more supplies." He paused and looked her in the eye. "Tabor's dying."

"He is?" She put her hand on her forehead. "Are you sure?" The world tilted again. "Is there anything I can do?"

Again, he offered her his handkerchief. "You could sit with him tonight. I'm sure he'd find your presence very comforting."

"Of course I'll sit with him." She took the handkerchief and wiped her eyes.

"The doctor has enough supplies to get him through the night." He looked up to Mr. Tabor's door. "But that's all."

She glanced out the window and furrowed her brow. "It's almost dark. Perhaps you should wait for Sir Adrian to come back. Perhaps one of the servants could go."

"I'm not afraid of the dark." He gave her a shadow of a smile. "If I ride fast I can be there in forty-five minutes."

"But you don't speak the language, Paul. You only knew bits and phrases when we were attacked in that alley. What if—"

"I can speak nine languages, Bianca. I only told Sir Adrian that I don't know Arabic because I don't trust him." He put his hands deep in his pockets and looked out the window. "The less he knows about me, the better."

"Well, then." She should say something meaningful. Because she might not ever see him again. She already had so many regrets. And those regrets were mirrored in his deep green eyes. Perhaps she could tell him that she could try to forgive.

Bianca gripped the railing and tore her gaze away. "You'd best be going."

Chapter 22

The thin morning light shifted through the gauzy curtain. The faint beams moved over Mr. Tabor's blanket and stopped by his pale hand. Bianca squeezed his fingers tighter, willing some of her strength into him, knowing it would make no difference.

"I imagine Paul is getting very close now."

Mr. Tabor moaned again, and it brought back the memory of her brother's letters—his description of the sound of horses dying on the battlefield, his loneliness, the wasted lives, and his regret that he'd crossed the Ohio River and joined the Southern cause. And the worst memory of all—opening that last letter on the porch that had given news that he'd been captured by their own side.

Chills gripped her neck. She pushed back the hair clinging to her face. She felt the necklace he'd given her before he went to war—her thirteenth-birthday present. What would her brother think of her now? What would he think of Paul and Sir Adrian?

He doeth all things well. She ran her thumb over the engraving on the back of the silver locket. It was much easier to believe before, when her heart wasn't split and conflicted.

"Hush, Mr. Tabor. Be still." She reached for another cloth and wiped his forehead. "How could you have poisoned yourself with bed bug repellant? Insects are all you talk about."

He turned on his side and ripped the blanket from the bed. "Help me."

"I'm here." She leaned her forehead against the top of his hand and closed her eyes. "God of miracles, God who walked this land, don't let him die. Let him see Boston again."

She glanced at the clock—4:15. The laudanum would last until five. She tucked the blanket tighter around him. Her gaze wandered to the window. Jerusalem was sleeping. The houses were dark as tombs. Nothing moved. Not even the trees.

Mr. Tabor's fever was turning the cold cloth warm. Bianca plunged it into the water again and wrung it out. "Just a little longer. One of them will come."

Mr. Tabor opened his eyes, shards of pain evident. "Water."

Bianca poured it quickly, her hands shaking.

He took a few drops then coughed up the rest. "I want to die." Each breath caught, and tormented him again. "Don't give me any more . . . garlic."

"The doctor said it has sulfur in it. The sulfur may leech the poison from your body. It's your best hope until someone returns."

"I don't have any hope, you stupid cow!" He made a fist and held it to his stomach. "Give me the rest of the laudanum." He dove for the bottle next to the bed.

"No!" She pushed his hand away. The bottles clanged together and fell.

"Look what you've done!" He fell back against the pillow and grabbed the iron bed rail. "You evil witch!"

Bianca fell to her knees and righted the laudanum bottle. The fluid seeped between her fingers and snaked through the floorboards. She ran for another cloth and tried to sop up the medicine. "You can't drink it all. Do you understand me?" She squeezed the cloth.

Only a few drops of laudanum dripped back down into the bottle.

Mr. Tabor glared at her, his eyes pinpoints of fire. "You have to go to sleep sometime, Delilah."

Bianca put her hands on his cheeks and held his face still. "You will be strong. Someone will return with the supplies. If you choose to die after the treatment, so be it. But I will not let you kill yourself."

"Paul's been gone too long. He's probably dead."

Bianca's heart twisted. It wasn't true. She had to believe. "Then Sir Adrian will come. Mr. Owenburke will find something."

"I pity Paul if he wants to marry you." He coughed. "You're an unfeeling harpy." He coughed again. Blood spattered over his lips. "There's no mercy in you at all."

She ripped another towel out of a drawer. She wiped his lips, sat on the bed, and wrapped her arms around him. "Just rest. Please, just rest."

He closed his eyes. Silent tears ran down his skin. "Worse than the prison camp . . ." He swallowed hard. "The men were just skin over bones. Lying in their own excrement." His raspy voice rose, stretching into the small space. "I took their clothes and gave them sacks. Cut out holes for their head and arms . . ." His chest expanded. His lungs struggled, as if rebelling against the air. "Stripped . . . the men down . . . in the snow." A chill ripped over his body. His teeth rattled. At the same time, sweat poured down his face, drenching his beard.

Bianca held him tighter. "Don't die. Please, God . . ."

The clock ticked. Three seconds. Five. Eleven.

"And the roaches crawling . . ." He snapped his eyes open and swatted at his legs. "Eating into their flesh! Crawling over me when I hauled the bodies!"

Bianca jerked back. Tears rolled down her cheeks. Is that how her brother had died? Dressed in a sack?

"You demon!" He picked up the water basin and threw it against the wall. The ceramic shattered. Water ran down the wall like rain.

Bianca held herself. "It's almost five. You can have a little more laudanum now."

He laughed; it came out in a raspy wheeze.

She poured the last few drops of liquid onto the spoon. Her hand shook.

He opened his mouth like a newborn bird, then swallowed. "More. Give me more."

She corked the useless bottle and took it across the room. "I'm going to open the window now."

Over the ancient city, more light filtered, pushing through the wide curtain of the night. A sound, mournful and distant, came over the houses. The sound was a man singing, from the direction of the mosque.

"The Muslims," Mr. Tabor said, coughing. More sweat ran into his dark hair.

Footsteps were upon the stairs.

Bianca went to the bedroom door and opened it. "Doctor Avram. Thank God."

He held his hat, rushed to the window, and slammed it shut. "Five times a day. Every day." His thick accent plunged deep. "Always praying to that moon god!" His gaze shifted around the room and stopped on the bloody towels. "How much of the garlic did you get down him?"

"Half, I think. I tried every fifteen minutes after you left, just like you said."

"Half is not good." His long white beard shook as he opened his bag. He took out an ear trumpet and placed it against Mr. Tabor's chest. "That's it, breathe." He closed his eyes as he listened. He stood up slowly and put the trumpet back in his bag. He snapped the latch shut.

Bianca heard the clock ticking again. "Did you find any supplies?"

"I checked every connection. No sulfur." Sadness laced his eyes.

"Perhaps there's sulfur at the Dead Sea. Mr. Owenburke left two hours ago, but . . ." Even as she said the words she knew he couldn't make it back in time.

The doctor took off his glasses. His understanding nod was barely discernable. "And Sir Adrian?"

"He went with him." Bianca adjusted Mr. Tabor's blanket. "Madeline is still here." But what did that matter? Madeline acted like she didn't care if Mr. Tabor lived or died. "She's sleeping."

Mr. Tabor doubled over and groaned.

The doctor grabbed the pan just in time. The stench of garlic and acid filled the room. Black charcoal skimmed the filth like fat on stew.

Bianca pushed the window open so hard that the frame bounced against the stone.

The foreign voice was there again, wailing as the black night sky turned to ocean deep blue.

More tears stung Bianca's eyes as the stench wafted behind her. Mr. Tabor retched again. She gripped the windowsill. "Lord, God, tear down any obstacle. Save this man's life. Send Paul." She pushed away, jerked the dresser drawer open, and found another cloth. She poured more water. She wiped Mr. Tabor's face.

"Thank you, Miss Marshal." The doctor took the cloth and wiped Mr. Tabor's mouth. "She makes a very good nurse, doesn't she, old man?"

Mr. Tabor's eyes were flat and full of pain. He focused on something in the corner. "I hate her, and I hate you. Give me more laudanum."

"It's the pain," the doctor explained. "Don't pay any attention—"

Horses' hooves echoed on the pavement outside, coming closer.

Bianca looked up and locked eyes with the doctor.

"That horse is at a full run." The doctor rose up in disbelief. "One of them did it."

She leaned out the window and smiled. "He did it."

A door slammed below. Hard footsteps sounded upon the stairs. The door flung open.

The doctor ran to him. "Thanks be to Jehovah! Emerson!"

"It's . . . all there." Paul was out of breath. He handed the doctor a bag. "Everything . . . you asked for."

"All of it?"

"All of it." Paul massaged his hands like they were numb.

The doctor dumped the contents on the bed—bottles, brown packages, a small box. "But how? This is the end of the world. Shipments only come into Jaffa once a month. And never on the same day." He pulled his glasses down and looked at the pills in disbelief.

Paul went to Mr. Tabor and helped him sit up. "Apparently that was yesterday."

"Praise Jehovah." The doctor unwrapped a package and started making a paste with some water.

Paul put his hand on his side and took a few breaths. "Is there anything else I can do?"

The doctor pulled the blanket off and applied the paste to Mr. Tabor's feet. Excitement danced in the crinkles at his eyes and the quick movements of his hands. "I'll know more in about four hours but I think he has a very good chance now. Do you hear that, Mr. Tabor?"

"I'll be dead in four hours."

The doctor smiled. "Fight is good." He looked up. "Go. Rest. You too, Miss Marshal. There's nothing more you can do."

Paul nodded. "I'll come back later, Tabor."

Bianca walked to the bed and leaned down. "I told you he'd come."

Mr. Tabor's blue-gray eyes locked with hers.

Bianca shut the door behind her. She squinted at the harsh light on the landing above the main hall. All the emotions of the day came to her in waves. She wiped her eyes, thoughts turning into nothing.

Paul walked to the window on the landing and picked up a water pitcher. His hand was dirty, remnants of sand and earth were scattered across his arm. He swallowed the entire glass of water and then wiped his lips with the back of his hand. "You must be tired."

"Probably not as tired as you." She forced her eyes away from him, but then looked back.

His expression stilled. He turned the glass and the sunlight caught it, sending triangles of sparkling light against his mud-splattered shirt. "I'm not that tired."

"Neither am I." Her hair fell across her forehead. She crossed the long rug. "I'm glad you're back."

He gave her a devastating grin. "I'm glad to be back. Here. With you."

The light from the window was hot against her cheek. She took a step forward to stand in the purest part of it—white and yellow glow.

"Bianca." He put the glass back on the table. It barely made a sound. "Do you trust me to show you something?"

Bianca exhaled hard.

"Do you trust me with your safety or don't you?"

"I know you won't hurt me." She was surprised at the words and knew she should contradict them. He had hurt her.

"Who else is in the house?"

"Only Madeline."

"Is she still sleeping?"

"I think so."

"Can you meet me in the garden in twenty minutes?"

The sky was periwinkle and powder—crisp, cool breeze with the promise of later warmth. Someone walked outside the gate, accompanied by the sound of a horse. The latch turned and the gate swung slowly open, creaking on the hinges.

Paul's smile was hesitant. "Ready?" He held a fine, white Arabian that had hints of dapple-gray. He climbed into the stirrups and held out his hand.

Bianca looked back to the house, took a steadying breath, then reached for Paul's arm. He leaned over and pulled her up behind him.

Being so near him was a sudden kind of pain, a shock she wasn't prepared for. The wind blew through the green vines attached to the alley wall. That vine clung for security, faltering in places—a branch dislodged here, a twisted new vine cast loose there. That was the way it felt being near Paul Emerson. Things in her heart clung even though there was no use. The force against them was too strong.

Bianca reached behind her to the back of the saddle. She would not touch him. That was the small dignity she had left.

Paul clicked his tongue and urged the horse forward. It walked leisurely, dragging its hooves in the dust. "Bianca, I'm sorry I ruined Jerusalem for you."

"This entire trip was doomed when Sir Adrian chose me."

Paul took a long breath. "I saw your face in the Church of the Holy Sepulchre."

"You were there?"

"Yes."

Bianca looked down at his polished boot.

He turned the horse down a long alley of stone. The old high walls blocked out the sun. "If you'll let me, I'm going to give it back to you."

"What's that?" She searched the shadows on the wall. "My heart? My hope?"

"The magic of this place—the mystery, the legends, the truth. The reasons why you entered the contest. I owe you that much."

Bianca took a deep breath and tried to push away the heaviness in her chest. She supposed they owed it to each other. Being as how they were both pawns in Sir Adrian's game.

They turned the corner, and after a few moments, they were traveling alongside the Temple Mount. The golden dome loomed above them like some lofty sun, hung by the clouds.

"This is the beginning of the Sorrowful Way, also known as the Way of Grief, the Via Dolorosa. The Antonia Fortress was thought to stand here, built by Herod the Great. This is probably where the mock trial was held for Jesus."

She stared at the road, numbness coursing through her mind.

"What are you thinking?"

The horse swatted its tail and flicked Bianca on the leg. "I remember sitting at the Egyptian dinner, talking about this with you. And now we're here."

"Does it seem like a long time ago?"

"Yes and no." The long cobblestones were smooth and shiny in the morning sun. Rugs hanging on clotheslines above blew in the breeze. "It seems like a long time since I was in Ohio. That I do know."

"A lot can happen in just a few weeks." Paul twisted the reins tighter around his hand. "This is the Ecce Homo Arch. Traditionally the window where Pilate's wife told him to have nothing to do with Jesus because she'd suffered many things in a dream. It's in a remarkable state of preservation, don't you think?"

"It looks fairly modern."

"This city has been destroyed so many times. I only wish we could have some good archaeology here and discover the truth exactly. But, if you will permit me, I'll tell you the tradition as we go."

Bianca surveyed the rugged walls and overhanging palm leaves. "I'd love to hear it, that's part of the mystery of this place. There's always a little truth masked in tradition."

He turned his head to the side and glanced back at her. "Always seeking, always looking beyond the obvious. Are you sure you weren't educated at Oxford?"

"A one-room schoolhouse on Lick Run."

"Lick Run," he pronounced slowly.

"You can laugh if you want, I won't be offended."

"If your mind was shaped at Lick Run, then I say half of London ought to go there."

Bianca leaned to the right to see his face. "I hardly know what to think when you compliment me."

He looked up at an archway. "Why is that?"

"Most people back home think I'm too different." She drew her eyebrows together. "And my ideas too lofty."

Paul stopped the horse and turned in the saddle. His leg brushed against hers. "I won't ever lie to you. That's why I told you what I did yesterday."

She felt her skin color. All of it.

"You can ask me anything and I'll tell you the truth. Honesty is extremely important to me."

"Anything?" She looked away from the intensity in his eyes. "Are you sure?"

"Anything."

Bianca wanted to reach up and put her hand over his. She wanted just to forget the weighty things that pressed in on her mind. "I do have something to ask you, but not now." She looked down at her hands. "It's far too warm for gloves, don't you think?"

He smiled and it brought an easiness to his expression. "Take them off. You can hardly go exploring looking like a proper city lady."

"You're right." She peeled the kid gloves from her fingers. "And since Madeline isn't here to laugh at me, I'm taking this hat off too."

"Let's not talk about her or Sir Adrian." The pleading in his eyes unnerved her. "Without gloves, I suppose I'll get to see what you're like in Ohio. That is, if frog gigging doesn't require hat and gloves. You'll have to forgive me, as I have no point of reference."

"You're forgiven." The words were out before she realized the weight of them.

The look in Paul's eyes said he felt their significance too.

Chapter 23

*T*hey came to a narrow street with five arches above. A bay window protruded from the stone wall. The slats in the shutters were broken.

"See that broken column?" Paul pointed. "It's where they believe Jesus fell under the weight of the cross. The cross gave this column such a blow that it immediately broke in two, as you see here."

"Really?" Bianca looked at the column and wondered how it had managed to get through so many destructions, sieges, and crusades.

"Tradition. This is the residence of St. Veronica. When the Savior passed this place they say she came out and wiped His perspiration with her handkerchief. The print of His face remains upon the handkerchief until this day. There are four handkerchiefs in the world at present. There is one in Spain, one in Paris, and two in Italy. In Milan it costs five francs to see it. In St. Peter's at Rome, it is almost impossible to see it at any price."

The information only added to her despair. Was everything an imitation? Even love?

"There are countless duplicates of relics scattered throughout Europe. In France two rival monasteries each have a skull. One is John the Baptist when he was a child and the other is John when he was a man."

"That can't be true."

"I'm sorry to say that it is." They turned another corner. "Everyone wants a piece of this place and the stories. Everyone wants a bit of divinity."

"I can see why there are so many skeptics in the world then." She really hadn't considered it before. There was one church in her town, and she went to it. People in Portsmouth didn't think about relics or Jerusalem or columns that may or may not be true. She thought of Sir Adrian and felt as if a sharp lance plunged into her soul. "I've never really seen a cathedral. I know they must be beautiful, though, from what I've read."

"They are beautiful." A man and his donkey, burdened with goods, passed them on the street. "You can't tell a cathedral's beauty by an instant glance, though, much like a woman. One only finds out how beautiful a woman truly is by considerable acquaintance with her."

Her breath caught. She didn't want him to say such things. "You're making me blush."

"You seem to do that a lot when I'm around."

"Ah, once again you noticed."

"I notice a lot more about you than you probably know. You've been my favorite subject for some weeks now. Even more fascinating to me than history."

The devil was a gentleman. That's what Mama always said. And he was charming and probably had green eyes.

"You're awfully quiet back there. Are you all right?"

"I'm fine." Did he talk to the married woman like that? Is that how he made her a fallen woman?

"Mark Twain said that quote, by the way. About a beautiful woman."

"Mark Twain?" Bianca closed her eyes. Of course he read Mark Twain. Pain ripped through her again. The Mark Twain point was the last requirement on her list.

"He was talking about the Mosque of Omar's wonderful beauty, exquisite grace, and perfect symmetry, and then he compared that to the beauty of a woman."

"In which book did he say that?" The words came out like broken promises—shallow and pleading all at the same time.

"*The Innocents Abroad*, his book about his journeys here. You haven't read it?"

"No." How could Sir Adrian know about the Mark Twain requirement? She had never showed him the list and had burned it on the ship.

"I have a copy, but it's in my home in London."

"Maybe I can buy it in New York."

"I'd love to give it to you. When we get back to London, you could come—"

"What's this indentation from?" She couldn't breathe, couldn't think.

"Ah, the rock. Tradition says that was made by the Savior's elbow as He fell." Paul looked at her from the corner of his eye. "There's another quote I like in *The Innocents Abroad*."

"Yes?"

"'The night shall be filled with music, and the cares that infest the day shall fold their tents like the Arabs, and as silently steal away.'"

Bianca knew he was thinking of himself. And everything that was between them.

"Let's stop here."

A wonderful smell came from the house. Smoke wafted over the roof and down onto the street.

Paul threw his leg over the horse's neck and jumped down. He held his arms out for her. Just like a medieval knight. He lowered her down, put his hand upon her back, and led her toward the door.

The small room held a few empty tables. Herbs hung from the ceiling. Incense burned somewhere; the light smell was all around.

"I'll be right back." Paul pulled a chair out for her and went to an old woman in the corner. Hebrew words flowed effortlessly from his tongue.

Bianca leaned on the table and put her cheek in her hand. He spoke Hebrew like a native, and of course, it sounded beautiful.

Paul looked back to her and smiled. He said something to the woman that made her laugh. The woman put her hand over her heart and then kissed him on both cheeks. Like he was her son.

He walked back to the table. "She'll bring us some food."

"What did you say to her?"

He picked up a carafe and poured something into her cup. "Nothing."

"That didn't sound like nothing."

He looked down at a crack on the table and traced it with his finger. "I told her that the price of cotton has gone up in Georgia."

"That's not what you said."

"Perhaps I was discussing the import of sheep herding in Jericho. My Hebrew's a little rusty, I can't be certain. We'll be lucky if she brings us food. She probably has no idea what I was asking." A small smile curved his lips.

"Are you always this mischievous?"

His voice was low. "Only with those I'm most comfortable with." He pulled his chair closer to the table. "I told her that you were from America. And that you're very special to me."

The woman walked over and put flatbread and tea upon the table. She asked Paul a question.

He looked down and smiled. He said something that seemed hard for him.

The woman spoke in elevated tones, becoming more and more excited.

Bianca leaned forward. "What is she saying?"

His face grew serious. He said something else and the woman grew somber also.

"She's bringing us lamb." His smile was weak. "And lentils."

She knew he was only telling her half.

"Bianca, would you pray with me before the food comes?"

She hesitated. Praying with someone was intimate, a gift.

"When in Rome?" He stretched his hands toward her. "Please."

She gave him her hands. Instantly, his touch felt right.

Paul closed his eyes and leaned over the table. "*Barukh Attah Adonai Eloheinu Melekh ha'Olam, Shehakol Niheyah Bidvaro, Shehakol Bara Likhvodo, Shetamid Zokheir B'rito, Shekhocho Malei Ha'Olam, B'Shem u'VaDam Yeshua Meshicheinu . . .*"

She peeked at him. His lips moved but no sound came. And then he spoke again. She caught bits and phrases here and there—words that sounded important, words that he laced with feeling. The tones pulled at her heart.

"Bianca . . . *Ve-ishto . . . yitboShashu. Selah.*" A fire crackled somewhere. He ran his thumbs over her hands and then drew back. He looked shy for the first time since she'd met him. He poured their tea.

Bianca wrapped her fingers around the warm clay cup. "I don't suppose you'd tell me what you just prayed."

"Not yet. But someday I hope to."

The old woman in the corner smiled.

The meal was perfect. Paul had gone to every length to be kind. He'd not mentioned serious things, only asked her questions about Ohio, her favorite books, and her childhood dreams.

He was still courting her, even stronger than before. For him, it seemed that yesterday never happened. But it did happen.

"You enjoyed the food then?" Paul studied her every move, every glance. There were unspoken things in his eyes.

"Yes, thank you." Bianca looked down, preferring the cobblestones to questioning green.

"I'm so glad." He mounted the horse. "Ready? You're not too tired?"

"You've asked me that three times today. Do I look tired?"

"No. I didn't mean—"

"Lead on, Mr. Emerson." She took his hand.

"Mister? I see I've fallen quite far." He turned the horse around. "Change of plans then. I have a question for you, *Miss* Marshal."

"Say on."

"Before this day, have you ever ridden an Arabian?"

"Never." She'd only ridden workhorses when she'd been pretending to be riding to marry a man like him. "What does the Arabian have to do with our change of plans?"

"Quite a lot." A mischievous smile reached the corners of his eyes. "Hold onto me."

Bianca hesitated. Her breathing quickened. Her palms skimmed the buttons of his shirt. She leaned into his back. Maybe just for this moment she could pretend.

"Yah!" Paul's voice boomed between the stone walls.

The horse leapt, and then it flew. The horseshoes sounded like a battle charge, echoing off the walls. Street after street passed by. The Golden Dome became a blur. They passed through the gate and into the open. The old wall fell behind them, stone after stone.

He turned the horse to the right, followed a road, and plunged into a valley of ancient stone.

Bianca turned her face into his linen shirt. Her smile had a will of its own, curling up higher. The pins fell from her hair. Her curls came loose.

"This is the Kidron Valley, where David first founded Jerusalem."

Old ruins dotted the hillside, a sea of granite passing.

Paul spurred the horse on. "I'm glad you're here."

The wind in her ears roared; it forced tears from her eyes.

"Are you still with me?"

"Yes!" If only for the moment. "Go faster!"

"Are you certain?"

She held him tighter. "Do it."

Paul slapped the reins on the horse's neck. It whinnied, increased its speed, and thundered across the dirt road.

Bianca closed her eyes and felt their bodies as one. She laid her cheek against his back.

It was reckless.

It was hopeless.

Just like love.

Paul's voice rose above with the wind and the horse's hooves. "Are you always this brave?"

Bianca tightened her grip around him. "You caught me on a good day."

The landscape sped by in colors of green, white, and brown.

Paul loosened the reins and gave the horse its head. A low place in the road held water. The horse plowed in. The light caught the droplets and threw them down as diamonds.

"You're crazy!" Bianca's wet hair clung to her face. Her blouse clung to her arms.

"Yes, I am!" They climbed the hill. When they reached the top, the horse snorted. Paul pulled the reins back. The horse reared and whinnied, pawing at the air like a storybook steed. "We've taken the hill." He laughed, a carefree, boyish sound. The horse came down, stamped at the ground, and turned in circles.

Bianca laughed, waves and waves of laughter. The horse stopped, and she fell against Paul's back.

All of Jerusalem lay below them in the valley. The sun broke through the clouds, seeping pink and orange as far as she could see.

"How beautiful." But Paul was looking at her instead of the sky. His cheeks were full of color; he looked fully alive. He pushed her wet hair away from her face. "Thank you for coming with me."

"I'll never forget this as long as I live." Before she knew what she was doing she covered his hand with hers.

His green eyes darkened.

Bianca pulled away and slid down from the saddle. She ran her hands through the horse's mane and leaned into its neck. The sweet smell of hay mingled with water and earth. She stroked the horse's nose and the velvet of its mouth.

The leather saddle groaned as Paul dismounted. "He likes you."

"Of course he does." She kissed his white nose.

He looked down into the valley, still smiling. "They say there's a first time for everything."

"What do you mean?" Bianca scratched the horse under his bridle and he nudged her arm.

"I just can't believe I'm jealous of a horse."

Fire seeped into her cheeks. She looked away to the massive trees and pathways lined with pebbles. She would die if he tried to kiss her. "Where are we?"

"The Garden of Gethsemane." Paul put his hand under her chin and tipped it up. "Don't worry, I promise not to kiss you."

How could he read her that well? "I wasn't . . ."

"You can trust me, remember?" Paul wrapped the reins around his hand. "Come on." He gave her a tight-lipped smile and stepped away, leading the horse to a patch of grass.

The wind blew through the thin leaves of the olive trees.

It was beautiful. He was beautiful. And, despite herself, she was still drawn to him. She loathed herself for it. *Lord, I need You. Help me to be strong.*

"Many of these trees are more than two thousand years old." He tied the horse to a tree. "Would you like to walk?"

The trees muted the sunlight, making the entire garden seem timeless. Up ahead, monks weeded around the trees. A hush came over the place, a deep breath before a sigh—a mother's kiss on a sleeping child.

"Where do you think Jesus prayed?" Being in Gethsemane seemed surreal, like falling into a dream.

"Let's find it—the exact spot where they prayed." Paul held out his hand.

Bianca took it without hesitation.

They weaved in and out of the sunlight and trees.

"Perhaps here."

"Or here." Paul stopped by an ancient knarred tree.

"It looks like a likely place." Bianca laid her hand upon the tree and leaned into it. *Lord, I love him. I can't help it.*

"I've always wondered if I would have fallen asleep." Paul crossed his arms. "It's the nature of man, I suppose. But even the disciples—those who loved Him best—couldn't watch with Him for an hour."

Bianca looked back to Jerusalem and thought of the Roman soldiers climbing the hill to take Jesus captive. And He knew they were coming.

She noticed the worry lines around Paul's eyes for the first time. She stared at his left hand and the bare ring finger. *What about forgiveness?* Her own words from yesterday rang in her mind. *What about mercy and grace? Those are traits of God also.*

"What is it?" His smile made the pain worse.

"Nothing." She rubbed her arms through the wet cotton of her blouse, trying to chase a sudden chill.

"You can tell me whatever it is you're thinking."

She'd told him that same thing in Mr. Owenburke's garden. She'd lied to him. She'd told him his past didn't matter. But it did. "That's very kind of you." She unbuttoned her sleeves and let them flap open.

"Is the water on your sleeves making you cold?"

"No. I'm fine." She was anything but fine. She put her back against the tree. "I do want to ask you a question."

"Ask me."

"Do you and that woman . . ." Her eyes shifted to his hands, and the way he laced them tighter. "Is there a child?"

Chapter 24

*B*ianca held her breath, afraid to breathe, afraid of what his answer might be.

"Is there a child?" he repeated. He turned his eyes down toward Jerusalem. "No. That never happened."

"You're certain?" The words escaped her lips before she thought. She felt the red hot betrayal of flame in her cheeks.

"Do you think I would lie to you?"

She rubbed the olive leaf between her fingers. The side of it ripped, tearing along the vein. "No."

"You don't sound so sure." The tones in his voice dropped, just like his expression.

"How can I be?" She straightened her back, willing herself to stay calm. "I've only known you for a short time."

Varied expressions crossed his face, like the morning light that was changing before them—so subtle, yet so different all the same. "Fair enough." He sat down on a rock and held perfectly still—too still.

Bianca sat down beside him but as far away as she could manage. "I'm just trying to be honest."

"Of course." His eyes betrayed his light tone. "As you should be. You'd be very foolish not to have reservations about my past." He put his palms against the rock. "I'm just trying to figure out how best to overcome them."

Bianca ignored his statement, just like she ignored the few inches that now separated their hands. "How long were you in India?"

"Seven days."

She nodded, hating his closeness, his honesty, and the way he pleaded with her with his eyes. "Seven days." Her heart hammered in her chest. "One hundred and sixty-eight hours ill spent."

"If you're counting." Paul let his breath escape like slowly leaking air. He spread his fingers out over his freshly shaven jaw—the jaw that just hours before had been dark with stubble as he rode back from Jaffa. "While you're at it, you might as well add the time I spent selling the diamond in Amsterdam, and then having a fake one made for the museum." He gave her a sideways look. "And I suppose you might want to add all the thoughts of ill intent that led me up to that moment. Let me see . . . January. You can start there."

Shame spread within her until she couldn't breathe. She looked at the dampness in his hair instead of his eyes. "That was cruel of me."

"Yes. It was." His expression softened.

"I'm sorry." The words came out in a whisper. She wanted to walk away, far away, and never have to see that look on his face again.

"I know you're angry." He threw his gaze to the pink in the sky. "You have every right to be. I want you to know that you're not on a time limit to make any sort of decision. I will wait."

All the loneliness from so many years slid around her, clutching at her heart like a kitten with claws newly sharp.

Paul laid his hand on her back. "What is it? Just ask me."

"Did you ever see her again?"

He took a deep breath. "Yes." The wind pushed his hair forward and then dropped the locks, like something had scared it away.

Panic rose within her—unseen fears. She stood and went to the tree across the path. "Yes?"

"It wasn't my choice that I met her again."

"Then it was hers." She stepped back and pushed her fingers into the deep, moist bark. "And yet you remain unmarried. How is that possible?"

"You think I should have married her."

"That's the normal course of action, at least where I'm from."

"There's much you don't know about her." Fear crossed his face and lodged in his eyes. "She cares only for herself. She'd rip out my heart if I'd let her."

"Perhaps you should have thought of that before." She searched his dark eyes for something familiar. "Perhaps you should have told me up front before I—" She couldn't say the words. She couldn't tell him that she'd fallen in love with him.

"And how would that have gone?" he said with heavy irony. He stood. "Right after I took your hand in the King's Library, I could have made it the first topic of conversation." He circled her, looking up at the olive leaves. "How do you do, Miss Marshal? Can I tell you about the time I disregarded the sanctity of marriage?" He stopped beside her and lowered his gaze. "Would that have made this easier?"

Bianca pushed away from the tree. "Don't be stupid, Sir."

"*Stupid* normally isn't a word people use to describe me."

"Perhaps I'll be the first." Her throat ached with unshed tears. "Wait . . . You casually gave that privilege to another." She lowered her voice. "Maybe I should go and find a man who hasn't."

He noticeably swayed. "You could." The fire in his eyes all but melted her. "But you wouldn't look at him the way you look at me."

"What am I to you?" She choked the words out. "A plaything to torment?"

"No." His face darkened, and he struggled for words. "There is only one thing I desire you to be."

Wife. The word hung in the air between them; it rode on the sunlight as it passed through the trees. It skipped upon the shadows on the ground.

"I don't believe you. You don't know what you want."

He mumbled something and looked heavenward. "Do you honestly think I act like this on a normal basis? Give out ambrosia? Dance on ships under lanterns and starlight?" He laid his hand on her cheek and raised her face to look at him. "Pray that the woman I adore can forgive my past?"

Her voice shook as she pulled away. "I wouldn't know what your normal is like."

"If I'm lucky, I fall asleep in my own bed and not at my desk. That's if I'm not combing through archives all night, in the British Museum or one of hundreds around the world. Most often I go back to London accompanied with a nice fever or a lingering stomach illness."

"You're obviously a very busy man—one who finds time for adultery and stealing."

He laughed, and it held no humor. "When I am at home, I have to constantly meet with donors to give them the assurance that their money is being well spent. If I can't placate their egos, they withdraw their donations and my salary is docked. I travel so frequently that it's hard for me to remember where I've been—which university, which country."

"You're right, that does sound terrible." Bianca circled him this time, pulling down more olive leaves as she went. "Poor Paul, all those people hanging on your every word. All those students idolizing you for being an expert in your field. What an inconvenience." She threw the handful of olive leaves at his chest. They fluttered down like confetti. "Perhaps I'll get the chance to hear one of your lectures before I go home."

"The point is . . ." He raked his hand through his hair. "I don't normally do this. I don't have time for romance. You're different to me. Don't you understand?"

Different. Not beloved. "If you don't have time for romance, I hardly think a woman would want to marry you." Bianca gave him her sweetest smile, met his gaze, and held it there. "What a dull existence that would be."

"My wife would not have any complaints. Especially not in that area." His steady gaze bore into her and pushed her heart into frantic racing.

"Do you know what Daddy would say if he knew what you'd done?"

"Would he tell me I couldn't have you?"

Bianca closed her eyes. He stood far too close. And his voice was doing that silky, velvety thing again. Daddy would spit in his face for what he did to the woman in India. For what he did to her. "Did you have any remorse when her husband cast her out?"

"Of course I felt remorse." He lowered his voice. "If you would have . . . known her . . . you wouldn't be saying these things."

"Make me understand." Her voice trembled and then fell. "I don't."

He stepped closer. "Understand this—I am a man who sinned grievously two years ago. I can't change that. With God's help, I won't ever do anything like that again."

"God would have helped you back then. That's not much consolation, though. Especially since you don't sound so sure you wouldn't ever do that again."

"I am sure." He gritted his teeth and looked like he brought himself under measured control. "Our lives are filled with choices. I won't ever make that choice again. And my wife will never fear it."

She'd always fear it. She'd always wonder. "I can't pretend you don't scare me."

He closed his eyes for a moment, took a breath, and then opened them. "I know. Your complete trust is something I intend to earn. If you'll let me."

Bianca raised her chin. "What's the woman's name?"

He looked at her with such conflict that she wanted to cry. "It's better to not know everything sometimes."

"You want me to forgive you, but you want to control how much I'm to know. You're just like every other man besides Daddy."

"That isn't true."

"It is true. On the surface, you're everything I've ever wanted." She thought of her list again, and it stabbed at her heart. "You're beyond intelligent, kind, noble, the perfect gentleman. You escort me through an ancient city and woo me with Hebrew. You put me on a horse and I wrap my arms around you, and you make me feel free . . . But then you cage me again. You cage me with your secrets."

"Do you really want to know her name?" Paul said it so softly she could barely hear. "Do you really think that would make it better for you, because I don't."

Moment after moment passed. The sun broke through the trees but then faded, like it wasn't willing to intrude.

Bianca's lips trembled. "Do you understand so little of a woman's heart? She must love you." She nodded, hating the word.

"She doesn't." He said it quickly and then scowled. "Absolutely not."

"You know this because you've asked her?"

"No. It was never that way." He looked past her shoulder and his eyes searched for something they didn't seem to find. "It wasn't love, Bianca. It was lust. There is a difference."

Somehow, his confession made it worse. To think of him in such a way . . . At least before she thought maybe he loved the woman. "I wouldn't know," she whispered, horrified.

"I think you do. Maybe on both accounts." His eyes turned the color of the greenest sea, and she was lost in them—drowning in the waves, feeling herself being pulled deeper. The current was warm, and it lulled her far too easily.

"How dare you imply . . ." The words died upon themselves because they were true. She lowered her lashes and watched the way the wind tore at his vest. She couldn't let him kiss her. He would do to her what he'd done to the woman in India.

The wind on the hillside was music, written by the ancients; sung by tongues licking flame. She felt her resolve dissipating, like dew in the affection of the sun.

"What am I going to do with you?" Paul took her hand and turned it over. "You'll be the death of me." He brought her palm to his lips and held it there.

The leaves above shivered and then stood still. Moments turned into phrases, none of which she could understand. "I thought you promised you wouldn't kiss me."

Paul lowered her hand and took a deep breath. "That wasn't a real kiss." He pulled her toward the horse. "Perhaps I'll show you the difference one day."

He was an arrogant, too handsome, devil of a fool. "Your lips were on me. How was that not real?"

He looked over his shoulder at her. "Could we please stop talking about this?"

"Why?"

"Because you're making me anxious."

She tried to pull her hand away from him. His grip was iron. "Where are we going?"

"Back to the house."

"What if I don't want to go?"

He stopped at the horse so abruptly she almost ran into him. "I'll take you anyway."

Fury boiled within her. How dare he treat her like a child? "Perhaps I'd rather see what your real kiss is like." She snapped her mouth shut, horrified she'd said it.

"Sorry." He checked the saddle belt frantically. "Not today."

"Why not?" She was taunting him, and torturing him, she knew that. She didn't care.

"Because. I won't kiss you until I can't see any more doubt in your eyes." He grabbed her chin and turned her face toward him. "It would be far too easy for me to mold your affections, you silly woman." He lowered his voice. "I won't do it. You deserve more than that."

"It's my fault, then?"

"If you come to me, it will be willingly. If you forgive my past . . ." His face was a mask, hard and unreadable. "I won't have her always in your mind. And I won't have you hating me thirty years from now for something I did to manipulate your feelings."

"All you do is confuse me." Bianca wanted to crawl in a dark place and sleep until she couldn't remember. "Why should I believe anything you say?"

"Exactly, Bianca, why should you?" He put his hands on her waist and lifted her into the saddle. "I think it's time you figure that out."

The ride back was one of the most horrendous experiences of his entire life, including the dysentery in Bolivia. And the scorpions in the Copan Ruins. And almost being sold into slavery at Aswan.

Paul held his arms away from Bianca's body, as best he could while holding the reins. It was a brilliant plan, really, putting her in front of him on the horse so he'd have to hold her. Definitely made things easier.

His arm brushed Bianca's side. She scooted forward and gripped the pommel like her life depended on it.

"Is there a problem?"

"As a matter of fact, yes. I'm trapped in this saddle with you."

He took a deep, controlled breath. "I could walk, but you might not fare so well with the Arabian by yourself. These horses require a great deal of strength to control them." And presence of mind, which he certainly didn't have at this precise moment.

Bianca turned and met him with an ice-cold stare. "I'm strong enough to knock you on your blessed assurance, and I'm tempted to do it."

He clamped his lips together to keep from laughing. "That might be interesting. I wonder how you would accomplish that."

"Keep smirking at me and you'll find out."

A laugh started deep in his throat but he stifled it. "Sorry . . . I, ah, saw something funny."

"Really?" Her cheeks flushed, but he wagered it was not from embarrassment. "I adore good humor. Care to elaborate?"

He turned up his smile a notch. "Not at the momen—"

Her eyes turned to fire. She slapped him.

His cheek felt like lava. The horse pranced to the side. Its back hoof skidded across a rock.

"Easy." Paul pulled back the reins. "Pray tell me, what was that for?"

"You just looked like you needed it." Her smile was beyond the realm of friendly.

"I won't tell you what you need." She needed to be kissed until all that temper went out of her—or spanked. He squeezed his fingers on the reins. "You weren't scolded often as a child, were you?"

"What does that have to do with anything?"

"Thought so." He gave the command to canter.

"Why is that?" She was forced to lean against him. She twisted her hair and held it away from him.

He leaned close to her ear. "Because, Bianca, if you weren't such a spoiled daddy's girl, you wouldn't be begging to be kissed and slapping me all within the space of half an hour."

"That's the meanest thing you've ever said to me." She let go of her hair. It flew all around him, enveloping him in the smell of honeysuckle.

"Yes, it was. And that was the first time you've slapped me." He hoped it was the last. He led the horse around rocks and his arm touched her waist. She moved forward as if he'd burnt her. "For heaven's sake, I'm not going to hurt you."

"That's a matter of opinion."

The horse kicked up sand and pebbles as it cantered alongside the ancient wall. They passed under the city archway and onto the main street.

He slowed the horse. The sun brought out the auburn in her hair and made it shine like garnet.

Garnet—*garantus* in Latin, referencing the pomegranate. In Greek mythology, the gift of love, passionate devotion, stability, intimacy. Thought to heal the broken bond for lovers. That's the ring he'd give her if she said yes.

She turned in the saddle again. "Is there a reason you have the horse going slower than molasses?"

"Not in particular." The red tones in her hair made the hazel in her eyes look gold. "Just thinking."

"Maybe that's your problem." She pointed her finger at his face. "You think too much. And two years ago, you didn't think at all."

"Would you get your finger out of my face, please?"

"When you get your . . ." She pointed at his arms and his chest and his legs. "Everything off of me!"

He bit back a smile. "Am I making you nervous?"

"Of course not." Her expression said otherwise. She raised her chin a notch. "Your nearness doesn't affect me at all."

"That's good to know," he said in a mock tone. "Because your nearness does nothing for me whatsoever." Except drive him witless and turn him into a simpering romantic fool. "I might as well have Rumpelstilzchen sitting in my lap. That's just how much I am affected."

Her mouth dropped. "I think I just might hate you at this precise moment."

"Be careful." His smile widened. "There's a fine line between hate and that other word."

"I'm going to walk." She moved to get out of the saddle.

He put his arm around her waist and jerked the reins accidentally. The horse misinterpreted his command and danced to the side, capsizing a cart of olives. The handle of the cart hit a shabby brown dog on its backside.

Bianca fell to the left and grabbed the pommel. "Let me go!"

The dog growled and advanced.

The horse flared its nostrils and whinnied.

"Stop it, Bianca." He pressed his knee against the horse's side to steady it. The beast's muscles twitched beneath him. "Easy . . ."

The dog hunched down and growled.

Bianca stilled.

Paul clicked his tongue but the horse stood frozen.

The dog growled and inched closer.

"What's the matter? Why aren't you going?"

"Quiet." The dog bared its yellow, half-rotted teeth. Drool dripped upon the broken cobblestones and sand.

"Go, Paul. Get us out of here."

"Shhh. I'm trying." He pushed his boot into the horse's side again. "Look at the horse."

Bianca turned and saw what he saw—its ears were pinned against its head and its eyes were wild. It dug ruts in the sand with its hooves.

She reached forward and put her hand on its neck.

The horse took a step forward, and then one back, throwing its head from side to side.

Another dog skulked from the alley and circled. Its fur was matted and missing in places.

"Hold on," he whispered. "This might not go well."

"What do you mean?" Bianca held the pommel tighter.

Paul reached for the crop.

The dogs jumped.

Teeth met flesh.

The horse cried out and reared.

Bianca slammed against his chest.

The leather reins slipped from Paul's hand.

His back hit the pavement.

He heard frantic barking and the horse running away. He tasted sand and blood and . . . honeysuckle.

He opened his eyes and saw nothing but Bianca's hair and blue sky. "Are you—" He coughed and took her hair out of his mouth. "All right?"

She was lying across him, shaking, her back jerking in spasms against his side.

"What hurts?" He tried to sit but failed. His shoulder screamed. He almost did. He rolled onto the other elbow. "Tell me what hurts."

A noise came from her that started like a low moan. "I'm not ... crying." The sound grew until it became deep, bellyaching laughter. Tears rolled off her cheeks.

"You're not hurt?"

She sat up and turned around. "Not at all." Her laughter stopped, then exploded again.

"What's so funny?" He tried to push himself up farther. The pain in his shoulder took his breath away.

She held her stomach as her shoulders rocked. "You look normal for the first time since I've met you."

He pushed himself up between shredding, knifing pains. "I look normal?" He wiped blood from his mouth and felt throbbing in his tongue.

"Oh, yes. Not perfect, like usual. Your hair really is charming. Perhaps you should consider that style for London." She tried to suppress another grin but failed. "You could call it ... Jerusalem Street at the Backside of a Horse."

"That's lovely, Bianca. I won't mention what your hair looks like at this precise moment." It was soft and beautiful. As always. And he still wanted to have it in his hands.

"Why not?" She pouted. "Still playing the stodgy Englishman?"

He stood and went behind the cart to spit blood and sand. "One day I'll show you how unstodgy I can be." He looked back at her, sitting in the middle of the street with her skirts spread out like a dervish. "But not today."

She frowned, and it wasn't even a real frown. "Pity. But I suppose you're right." She sighed. "As I'm so used to your stodginess, my poor heart might not be able to take it."

He held out his hand. "Let's go, people are staring. And I'm about to completely lose my sanity."

"Of course. We wouldn't want to be a spectacle. Not like two people falling off a horse in the middle of Jerusalem is anything like that." She took his hand and pulled herself up.

Pain lanced his shoulder again. "You're incorrigible." Blood pooled in his mouth again.

"Thank you. And you make a very nice break to a fall." She walked like she knew exactly where she was going.

He followed her. "I'm glad I could be of assistance. Anything for a lady of your particular bent of mischief." He spit more blood behind her. "If I knew all I had to do to get you to smile was fall off a horse, I would've done it sooner."

She stopped at the fork in the road and waited for him. A look of concern came over her face as he neared. "You're hurt, aren't you?"

"I just bit my tongue." From the feel of it, he'd probably broken his shoulder. "Nothing serious."

"Are you sure? Your shoulder doesn't look right." She reached to touch it, but he pulled away.

"I'm fine." He made a fist to keep his mind off the pain. "Let's go."

"At least let me help you." Bianca withdrew a handkerchief. "You can't show up at the house looking like that." She wiped his cheek and his bottom lip. She hesitated, then combed her fingers through his hair. Her eyes turned liquid again. "However do you manage by yourself all over the world?"

He couldn't breathe with her hands on him. People in rags gathered all around, but for the life of him, he didn't care. "I've never had problems until now."

"You must get yourself in all sorts of trouble." A shadow of something crossed her beautiful, innocent features.

She was thinking of India again. His heart sank. She was going to find out about Madeline, he could feel it. She'd leave him forever. He didn't even have her now.

"You've cut your hand." She wrapped the handkerchief around it. "Does anything else hurt?"

"No," he lied. "I'll be fine." He'd be fine if she could forgive him, but what slim chance was that? He held out his left arm to her, hoping she'd take it. She did. Each step made his right shoulder feel like it was submerged in fire.

"Maybe you should see the doctor when we get back."

"Perhaps I should." He looked at her sideways. "All that excessive weight you carry may have fractured my ribs."

She smacked him on his left arm. "I'm almost half your size."

He cringed and held his breath again. "Yes, darling, I know. I've held you in my arms before. Remember? When you fainted on the ship?"

She blushed like a girl at a coming-out party who'd just seen someone's knickers. He smiled, despite the pain. He loved that making her blush was so maddeningly easy.

"I didn't faint on the ship." She drew herself up to her full height, which wasn't much. "It was just far too hot that day."

"Hmmm. How fortunate for you that I happened to catch you then . . . when you became overheated."

"It was." The corners of her lips turned up. "Sometimes you're a very useful gentleman to have around.

When you're not frustrating me beyond all measure." She turned her face away and whispered, "And if you'd just kiss me."

"What was that?" He suppressed a smile. "I couldn't quite hear you."

"It doesn't matter."

"Yes it does," he said but didn't explain. If she ever did forgive him, she'd see why.

Chapter 25

O mar stood at the door when they arrived. "You seem to be missing the horse, Mr. Emerson. Were there difficulties?"

"Yes. If you would be so good as to show Miss Marshal to her room and get me another horse, I'll go and find the Arabian."

"No need, Sir. He always comes home." Omar stifled a smile.

"Brilliant." Paul fought the urge to shake the man. It was physically impossible anyway. His shoulder felt like it was being crushed by the second. "You're saying the horse goes on the spree often?"

"It depends upon your definition of *often*, Sir. Were there, by chance, any dogs involved?"

"Two dogs," Bianca said. "Very vicious."

"Well." The glint in Omar's eye told Paul all he needed to know. "I'd best be getting back to my duties."

"You do that, Omar." Paul hoped sweat wasn't running down his face like he suspected.

Bianca went to the staircase. "Thank you for an interesting morning. Perhaps I'll go and try to sleep."

"All right." He could feel himself slipping into unconsciousness. He took a breath. "Sleep well. Lock the door . . ." He leaned on the banister with his left arm to keep himself upright. "I'll be about the house somewhere when you wake up."

"I wonder when Sir Adrian—"

"Don't worry about him. Everything will be fine."

She gave him a shadow of a smile. "Are you sure you're all right? You look pale."

He leaned harder on the banister. "I'm feeling . . . a little tired. Maybe last night finally caught up with me." He gave her what he hoped was a convincing smile.

She hesitated but went up the stairs.

Paul focused on the hem of her skirt as she took an eternity to ascend. She disappeared around the corner. He waited until he heard her door latch click. He gripped the staircase railing, focused on Mr. Tabor's door, and climbed.

When he opened the door, the doctor looked up from wiping Mr. Tabor's forehead. "Mr. Emerson, how good—what happened to you?"

"Went base over apex . . . Fell off the horse." He took another breath. "How's Tabor?"

"Much better. Sleeping soundly for the first time, as you see."

"Thank God." Paul felt some measure of relief wash over him. Some.

"Come with me." The doctor grabbed his medical bag and led him into the next empty room. "Let me look at you." He motioned that Paul should sit on the bed.

"I probably just pulled a muscle." Paul focused on the shutters outside the window. A worse pain came when the doctor touched him. "Sweet . . ." The doctor lowered his spectacles. "Belt of Orion," Paul said through clenched teeth.

"Yes, indeed." The doctor bent to undo Paul's vest buttons. "You're not hurt at all, are you?"

Paul moved to push the doctor's hand away. "I can do that."

"And damage yourself more in the process?" The doctor slid Paul's vest off and then his shirt. He hesitated. "When was the last time you were seen by a physician?"

He'd obviously seen the scars on his back from his trip to Aswan, Egypt. "I don't know." Paul sucked in a breath as a sharp pain tore through him. "University?"

"I thought so." The doctor came around and took Paul's arm, checking his elbow. "You adventurous, besotted-in-love types are always like that."

"Besotted?"

"I noticed the first time I saw you and Miss Marshal in the same room." The doctor lowered Paul's arm and then lifted it again, moving it in circles. "Both trying not to look at one another."

"Do you have to do that? It feels like you're ripping me apart."

"Yes, I do." He went to his bag and opened it. He took out a long sling and laid it on the bed. "Your shoulder is dislocated. It's going to hurt a lot more before I'm through. Lie down."

Paul laid back and cringed as his shoulder hit the mattress. He scowled at the tiles on the ceiling. "I've never had a dislocated anything. Not even when I fell down a rock face in Scandinavia looking for some Viking—"

"I just need to wrap this sling around your ribcage and tie it to the bed." He tied it in the direction opposite Paul's hurt shoulder.

Paul squeezed his eyes shut. "Will this take long?"

"Young people." The doctor shook his head as he came around the bed. His long, white beard moved from side to side. "Always impatient." He lifted Paul's arm. "Now comes the fun part." He moved Paul's arm up, bit by bit. "When are you going to marry Miss Marshal?"

"It's not as simple . . . as . . . that." Paul spat the words out between ripping pains.

The doctor put his steady hand beneath Paul's armpit. "No, why not?"

"She's not entirely . . . persuaded."

"Then persuade her." He pulled Paul's arm toward him. "Marry her in Jerusalem. I know a rabbi who could accommodate you."

Paul gripped the side of the bed. The pain was a hot, sharp lance. "I'm from England . . . She's from Ohio . . . I haven't even met her father or asked . . ." He closed his eyes and swallowed a scream.

Something popped. The room spun, and then the pain faded. Paul let go of the side of the bed.

"All over now." The doctor pushed his glasses back up his nose and nodded. "Seems the adventurous, besotted-in-love types howl just as loudly as the other ones."

Paul laughed, but it came out like a cry. He put his hands on his chest, sweat falling into his eyes. "You would have never wanted for an occupation during the Inquisition."

Paul made his way down the long hall to his bedroom. He passed a window and saw Madeline sitting in the garden, reading something. He twisted his mouth in disgust and walked farther.

"Great merciful God, have mercy on me." The prayer escaped his lips as he turned his door handle. "Please, don't give me what I deserve. Turn Bianca's heart toward me. Teach her to love me, and not just her idea of who I am." He picked up a mirror and surveyed the damage—the cut on his tongue, the matted blood in his hair, the sand lodged in his ear. He collapsed on the bed and groaned. "Lord, let me be the man she needs. I never want to make her cry again."

He covered his eyes with his arm. "I love her more than I've ever loved anything."

That's why he hadn't kissed her.

Because she was so innocent she'd think that feeling was true love. She'd force her forgiveness. Because she'd melt into his arms and he might not be able to stop. Because if she didn't choose him, she wouldn't be tainted. She'd still be pure for another man.

"Good God. Show Your goodness to me." He looked at the bottle of pain-killer the doctor had given him but didn't reach for it. He had to be alert, just in case.

Sir Adrian and Madeline were planning.

Something was coming. It had to be.

He sat up and went to the bedroom window. He pushed the shutter open, just a fraction. Madeline's black hair blew around her like a witch casting a spell. Her perfectly pale hand came into view as she turned another page in her book. Shadows from the noon sun spread across her like dark lace.

He closed the shutter again and checked his pocket watch. It could be hours before Sir Adrian was back. Maybe he should sleep. What would fifteen minutes hurt? Twenty?

He sank back into the bed and closed his eyes. He heard the tick of his pocket watch and the gusts of wind outside. He let his mind soften and saw Bianca in a white dress, holding orange blossoms. No guilt in his heart. No uncertainty in her eyes. They could marry in early October, with the changing leaves all around.

Pastor Spurgeon could marry them at The Metropolitan Tabernacle. Or they could be married at the little church Bianca attended in Ohio. Quaint and simple, probably painted white with tall windows. There'd be an abundance of light. Her friends and family would see her off. A breakfast afterward, and then . . .

He could take her to the Blue Ridge Mountains. Or the Crystalline Appalachians in New England. A cabin. A fireplace. And no one but them for miles around . . .

He ran his hand over his face. He needed to get his mind on something else. His journal—he could finish the speech for the torture exhibit at the Tower when he returned.

Paul stood and went to his steamer trunk. He undid the leather belts and took his key out of his pocket. "Start with an overview of torture 'round the world—the East—Chinese water torture. First described in sixteenth-century Italy as Hippolytus de Marsiliis." He flipped open the latches and pushed open the lid. "Tension builds up as the victim tries to predict when the drop of water will fall. When the drop finally does fall, a sense of shock mixed with relief follows." He removed his hatbox. "Relief is replaced with more tension about the next drop." He lifted the coin box and laid it on the floor. "The victim is psychologically prevented from mentally withdrawing inside himself."

He looked down to where the journal should be. He ran his hand along the bottom of the trunk. No journal. Panic welled. "It was here." He flung his trousers onto the bed. "I put it here last night." He threw his extra boots on the floor. He checked the document compartment. Pens. Paper. Extra money. He laid his Bible on the bed. He threw the *History of Civilization* by Henry Buckle, *Roughing It* by Twain, *The History of the Jews*.

He looked up at the window. "She couldn't have. I had the key."

His mind raced over the contents of his journal—notes from the archives in Rome, newspaper clippings from the Napoleonic wars, notes for his unpublished book.

He opened the shutter and looked at Madeline. "I wrote about India."

Madeline turned another page.

He ran his hand over the back of his neck. He'd written about Bianca and all his feelings toward her.

Madeline shut the book. The cover was faded brown leather.

Leather he'd had bound in Belgium on a whim.

Chapter 26

*P*aul opened the door to the garden, his chest rising too fast with each breath, his fists clenched at his sides. His every thought was laid open for her. Every day recorded down with precision.

Madeline leaned over the journal and whispered something he couldn't hear. The wind carried it like fears in the night, lengthy shadows upon his soul.

"Be sure your sin will find you out." The verse tore at his conscience. *"He that covereth his sins shall not prosper . . ."*

"But whoso confesseth and forsaketh them shall have mercy." He mouthed the words as he passed across the pathway stones. "Lord God, let me be free of this."

The air flowed, carrying Madeline's fragrance with it, that scent he despised.

His shadow grew over her like a cape; it bled onto the pages of his journal. He twisted the book out of her hands.

Her fingers hung like claws, midair. Madeline glared at him, her eyes as dark as a raven's.

"Come with me." He clenched her upper arm and pulled her toward the garden gate.

"Where are you taking me?" The sunlight passed over her like judgment, flooding her eyes.

"Somewhere we can talk."

"Where's your beloved?" Madeline looked over her shoulder at the house. "I'm sure she'd like to hear what you have to say."

The gate slammed against the fence. "Trust me, what I have to say to you shouldn't be said to a lady."

"I doubt you have the stomach for it." Madeline's smirked. "Your sort rarely does."

He squeezed his journal until his fingers turned white. "How would you know what sort—" He stopped the words. An old man looked up from his prayer book. His face was worn like burlap. His eyes were too full of questions. Paul leaned down to Madeline's ear and led her to the alley. "Every day you and Hartwith have pushed me."

She kept her eyes on the dusty street.

"Exploited me. Cornered me." He pushed her into the wedge of the wall and lowered his voice to a deadly whisper. "How am I supposed to react when I finally have you all to myself? Tell me that."

"I'll scream."

"Not for long."

"Please." She flattened her back against the stones.

"Please?" He raised his eyebrows, mocking her. "That's a word I never thought I'd hear you say."

"Let me go." The tears were gone, just like that. Her devil-eyes grew hard.

Inwardly, he postured his soul. "Then let me go, Madeline. Let the past go. There is a better way—"

She pushed away from the wall like a viper and spit in his face.

Her hot saliva ran down his cheek. It smelled of figs and wine.

"I won't leave until I've told Bianca every detail. When I'm finished she won't even look at you anymore."

"You could have told her a hundred times already. You're a puppet on Hartwith's string."

The faltering in her eyes told him that he was right.

"Your master has given you a set of rules not to break or you won't be paid." Paul nodded as a thought occurred to him. "Perhaps you'll never tell her. Are you even allowed?"

The brown of her eyes bore into him, like dead leaves showing through snow. "I can tell her anytime I want to."

"Perhaps you're only meant to be pressure. A test."

"You think that if it comforts you."

"I saw Hartwith bring you to heel more than once on the ship. How does it feel to escape your husband only to play devil's handmaid to a meddling aristocrat?"

"My husband was dull, but at least he took care of me. All that ended with you."

"And would you have shared the diamond with the captain if you'd succeeded in killing me?"

Madeline leaned back, looking like a queen ready to pass sentence. "You're boring me, Paul. If your defense is only to talk me to death, my job is going to be a lot easier. Especially since you've succeeded in making Bianca love you. Poor, foolish girl."

"This road leads out of the city. I'll give you the rest of the diamond money if you leave now."

Her mouth twisted. For a moment, she seemed to consider.

He opened his journal and ripped out the small numbers written on the back page. "This is what you'll need. Take it. Forget all this. Just walk away." He held the paper aloft and it fluttered, like his hope.

The wind tore around the corner of the stones. It lifted Madeline's sleeves and pushed them out like wings. "How much?"

"Two of your lifetimes. Much more than Hartwith is paying you."

She laughed and stared at the page. "No woman should have to hear the words my husband said to me."

He cringed. That was true. "You must decide. What do you want more, money or revenge?"

"Both." She reached for the paper.

He snatched it away. "Choose one."

"You took away my choices."

"I wasn't your first diversion from the captain." Her look of righteous indignation was almost comical. Almost. "I know all about your services to the British regiment before I came."

"What are you imply—"

"You see, like your paid thugs who almost killed me in that alley, I have friends in India too."

"How clever," she said, not even making the pretense of denying it. "Just like the way you were with me that day."

He closed his eyes as his blood soared with unbidden memories—the feel of the diamond in his hand, her silk sari against his skin. He pushed the images away. "Shut your mouth." He stepped away from the wall.

"Is that what you plan to do with Bianca?" Her voice carried over the noise of the carts. "You with your moonlit trysts and gifts of ambrosia."

"No. I'm finally going to do what's right." He backed away from her. "This is the last time I'm offering you another way out. This will not end well. It will not end as you hope."

The wind lifted her hair. The look on her face sickened him to his bones. He turned his back to her and began walking.

"Where are you going? Answer me!"

He looked up at the darkening clouds and prayed. *If You don't give me an answer, I'll convince an Arab to take her for his harem. I'll gag her and throw her into the sea. You must fix this, God. Please. Show me the way.*

She followed him, buzzing around him like a fly. "Years from now you'll remember me. And this moment—the calm before the storm."

"I won't remember you at all." He walked away, step by step, his shoulders rising and falling like the fading Jerusalem sky.

"You won't forget me," she yelled behind him. "Not even if, by some miracle, Bianca does marry you."

Verses came to his mind. *I have blotted out, as a thick cloud, thy transgressions, and, as a cloud, thy sins: return unto me; for I have redeemed thee.* Paul closed his eyes and breathed fresh Jerusalem air. *Yes, Lord. You washed me with Your blood two years ago. You bought me. You have forgiven me. This body is Yours. I am redeemed.* Red seeped across the vault of heaven, like a brushstroke. It stretched beyond the alley and the crumbling stones; it dipped below the spires in the distance.

"Your mind will wander in the quiet moments." Her voice rose and fell, like she was grasping at straws. "Even then you won't be free."

"You're wrong." He turned to her. "My chains, as heavy as they are, will always be lighter than yours."

The only sound within Owenburke's house was the grandfather clock, its ticking relentless, oblivious to the turmoil around. Paul walked toward the stairs.

And he considered.

He could take Bianca away. They could travel up the coastline to Cyprus. He could teach her to blend in. They could disappear. Sir Adrian would never find them.

Until England.

"Most High, be with me now. Strengthen me." The pressure in his chest tightened. "Help me to be the man Bianca needs me to be."

The wind breathed, scraping tree branches against the window. Paul looked out to Jerusalem, the City of

David. "The king who stayed home instead of going to war. The king who saw beautiful naked Bathsheba from his rooftop." Paul's eyes dipped along the horizon, the roofs of the houses, the streets. "The king who bedded her and sent her husband to be killed on the frontlines. The king who took what wasn't his and tried to cover his sin."

Truth. Just a word, plain and simple. Paul heard it deep within.

The leaves turned over, like pulling a blanket tighter in the morning.

"The truth shall set you free." He whispered it to the window. He turned away and walked toward Bianca's room. "Though he slay me, yet will I trust in him."

There was no other way.

No more hiding.

He had to be the one to crush her. Not them.

He had to break Bianca's heart.

The ancient hills were covered with clouds, black with silent intention. Cool air fell like a worn-out blanket— thin in places, and in others, as thick as freshly shaven wool. Thunder rolled up to Jerusalem's walls, like a battering ram, relentless and careful for nothing.

Sir Adrian reached for his scarf as the wind clawed at it. "Do you ever have good weather here?"

Samuel's robe flared out like he would fly. "The day you arrived was the first time we'd seen rain in months. Our normality is dry and hot, mixed with blood and rubble—an endless stirring of the centuries. Seems this special show is just for you and your fortunate companions."

Lightning shredded the purple in the sky, turning it to lavender-thin crepe.

"Fortunate?" Sir Adrian licked his dry lips and wished he hadn't. The wind chaffed them immediately. "There's something in your voice I don't quite like. What's the matter? Don't you approve of my quaint little entourage?"

Samuel's eyes flashed. "You've never cared much for my approval—or lack of it."

"On the contrary. You've always been most helpful."

"Helpful." Samuel parroted the word and twisted his mouth. "So helpful that there's probably a dead man from Boston in my house. So helpful as to give you a playing board for your charade." He wiped black grime from his face and mock bowed. "I'm glad I could be of service to you once again."

Sir Adrian straightened his back. "I could never have foreseen that Tabor would poison himself. We tried, Samuel."

"*We* didn't do anything, Hartwith. It's always been you, the grand orchestrator, meddling in people's lives." The wind grabbed at the horse's tail, flaring it out like loose strings. "One day your careful plans will crack. I think that day is upon you."

Sir Adrian pulled his horse to the wider space in the road. "I hope you're not thinking of taking the place of my mother." His lip curled. "I can assure you, I'm not the one that needs mentoring."

Samuel gripped the pommel of the saddle like he would crush it. "Three days ago, you brought evil to my house. I would never have allowed you to come if I'd known what your plans really were."

Thunder broke through the distance again. The Damascus Gate cast jagged shadows on their horses. Stragglers, here and there, ran into houses—clutching their turbans, closing shutters, shouting to those still upon the street.

"May I remind you that if I'd not come, you'd not have the weapons you needed for your revolt against the Muslims? Do you know how hard it was for me to smuggle those guns onto the ship?" He leaned to the side, waiting for an answer. "How many letters did you write me, asking me to bring you aid?"

Samuel took his turban off and ignored the question. His light blond hair flared out as if electrified by the storm.

"I did what you asked without question, Samuel. Despite the expense, and the risk, I came."

Samuel's horse faltered with another clash of thunder. It threw its head up and sidestepped in the darkness. "After knowing Bianca for only a short time, she feels like a sister to me. And you've traveled with her, watched her every day. How can you do this to her?"

Sir Adrian hesitated. "What exactly has she said to you?"

"Enough," Samuel spat out. "She truly loves Paul. I don't know how you matched them so perfectly, but you did. Had you ended there, you'd have been a much better man."

"You've gone soft." Sir Adrian flinched as the virgin rain pelted him. "It's not like you."

"You've no right!" Samuel yelled over the storm. "You've no right to risk her innocent heart. You've no right to pry into Paul's life like you've done."

"How else am I to know if his faith is genuine?" Sir Adrian's collar flared out with the wind. The silk felt cold against the road dust caked at his throat. "If I ask him the questions I really want to, he could easily lie."

Samuel ran his hand through his hair. "So, you do things backward again. Tell me, how long did it take you to dream this up?"

"Long enough." Sir Adrian pointed at him as they turned the corner. "Everything has been carefully thought out. Don't you dare ruin this for me. Don't you dare get some kind of false chivalry now."

They both spurred their horses. The beast's hooves slid on the cobblestones and threw sand onto the narrow houses as they passed.

Samuel's hair blew against his forehead. "I won't watch as you bring this lamb to slaughter. I won't let you do this to her."

Sir Adrian shuddered as cold lodged in his back. "I want you to trust me as you always have done."

Samuel laughed and the sound disappeared in the rain. "You've brought Paul's worst moment back to haunt him. I would have killed you by now, but he's smiled, eaten meals with you, and done nothing."

"He hasn't done anything *yet*."

"You practically have one man's death on your hands and still you push and plan and torment." Samuel squeezed the reins. "When Bianca finds out that the woman she's been traveling with was Paul's whore, it will destroy her."

Sir Adrian looked into the gathering darkness upon the street in front of them. Remorse clawed at his heart. Once again he pushed it away. "That has always been a possibility."

"A cruel possibility. One I wouldn't take." Samuel brought his horse closer. "Let Paul's demons stay buried in the past. Send Madeline away. Make any excuse."

"Excuses are never very amusing." Sir Adrian led his horse underneath an awning and stopped. The rain came down in unapologetic sheets. "Paul Emerson is the most perplexing man I've ever come across. I will play this to the end. And you won't stop me."

"That's for me to decide." Samuel's gaze grew hard. The thunder was a barrier between them and the whispers in the rain.

Sir Adrian took off his ruined gloves and threw them into the street. "Well then, at least you're good enough to inform me before you turn into Judas."

As each second passed, the air grew colder. The vapor of Samuel's breath assaulted the rain.

"I didn't tell you about the first time I saw Paul." Sir Adrian hated the weakness in his voice. He hated the way his hands shook. "It was at Her Majesty's Opera House in London. I went on a whim two years ago to hear the famous American preacher, D. L. Moody. All of good society disapproved of him, even the Queen."

"Your curiosity has never served me well." Samuel didn't look at him. "It doesn't serve you well this time."

Sir Adrian felt the change in Samuel. He felt it tangibly in the air. He smiled falsely, one last grasp of happier days gone by. "I thought everything that preacher said was complete rubbish. Until I noticed Paul Emerson walking down the aisle, tears running down his face like a child." He laughed. "Paul Emerson, prominent historian. He'd just come back from India, you know."

Samuel looked at him with disgust.

"That preacher talked about salvation in a way I'd never heard before." Sir Adrian paused, remembering the relief on Paul's face when he'd got up from the altar, the look of total absolution. "That preacher had the audacity to tell us that all our good works counted for nothing. Can you imagine? He said that Christianity was a choice, not our inheritance as Englishmen."

Samuel brought his eyebrows together. His horse pranced again, nervous in the dark.

Sir Adrian pursed his lips, no longer feeling them from the cold. "I assume that amongst other things, Paul asked God for forgiveness for what he'd done with Madeline."

Samuel's voice was quiet. "I assume you found out about Madeline after a great deal of digging—what you do best."

"It took awhile. And a great deal of money. But day after day, I couldn't get Paul out of my mind."

"So you studied him, had him followed, no doubt."

"He changed over the next six months. In so many ways. He took himself away from every temptation. He was like a new man."

"So he found religion. You should have left him alone."

"He didn't find religion. That's what I'm trying to tell you. It was something much more than that, something deeper—a peace I've never had."

"Men like us aren't allowed peace." Samuel sneered. "You invented the Holy Land contest knowing he wanted to come here. So you could study him, test him, see if you could crack him."

"Yes," Sir Adrian said without emotion.

"You dredged up Madeline like filth from the bottom of the Thames."

"That part was harder."

"And you chose Bianca because?"

"Because she's everything he's ever wanted in a woman. It took me a full year before I pieced that together. It was destiny that she entered the contest. Paul was an expert swindler before D. L. Moody. He could charm the Queen out of her knickers and she'd thank him for it. I wanted to see if he'd use that talent on her. Also, she shares his faith. I wanted to see how strong it was when tested."

Samuel looked like he wanted to say something but held back.

"It would really be helpful if you'd tell me everything Bianca's said to you."

"Sorry," Samuel replied. "Then I'd be her Judas. I'd rather be yours."

The words hung in the air, and he knew that their friendship was over.

"Indulge me one last time," Samuel said. "Tell me why you chose Tabor."

"He . . ." Sir Adrian paused at the words. If he told him that, Samuel would certainly cast him off. He wouldn't be able to handle the depths of his cruelty. Half-truths were always better. "Tabor is—was—a Darwin man, fully given over to the new theory of evolution. I thought it'd make for some interesting banter between him and Paul. You know how I hate to have lags in conversation. Unfortunately, the man is—or was—not very vocal. Very disappointing."

"Yes." A full look of contempt spread upon Samuel's face. "One can't expect all the details to work out perfectly. Otherwise you'd be God." He dug his heel into his horse's side and took off into the rain.

Chapter 27

*B*ianca put on her shoes and pulled back the curtain. Rain fell on the street in waves, splattering white on the ancient stones, reflecting in the neighbor's lantern glow. "I forgive him. I choose to love him."

She washed her face and smiled at her reflection, pale in the dim light. She could do this. She could trust Paul with her heart.

She turned the doorknob, stepped into the hall, and almost fell on her face.

Paul caught her and knocked over the chair he'd been sitting in. "Careful. I haven't been sitting here for the past hour just to have you fall over the railing."

"I'm sorry." Bianca held on to his arms, feeling only the cold linen instead of his usual warmth. "I shouldn't have slept so long." The lantern light played in his eyes, making the green seem nonexistent.

"I'm glad you rested." Paul let her go and picked up the chair. "I just thought I'd sit here for a while and wait for you."

His face looked too pinched. It was an expression she'd never seen before. "You look so tired. Why didn't you sleep?"

"I am tired." He leaned back against the wall and stared down into the darkness.

Bianca stepped toward him and tried to catch his gaze. "You haven't slept in two days. Maybe you should go—"

"You don't have to worry about me."

"I know the trip to Jaffa wasn't easy on you. You've taken very good care of me, but what about yourself?"

"I haven't taken good care of you." He looked as if he'd lost something precious. "And I'm not a noble man. Please don't make me out to be."

"What are you talking about?"

"I wouldn't have let you get so close to me if I'd been noble."

She took a step forward. "I want you to know that I've forgiven you. India doesn't matter anymore." The words dropped from her tongue like prayers, sad and earnest, hopeful and full of expectation.

Paul looked out the black window, seeing nothing.

"Do you think tormenting yourself any longer would be a good thing?"

He brought his gaze back to her. "Bianca, I don't deserve you. I just don't."

"Let me decide," she said, hating this change in him. "I already have." She walked the short distance and leaned into him, hugging him spontaneously for the first time.

Paul's back stiffened. He pushed himself against the wall. "You've made your decision on things I've done to sway you."

"You really are like a brooding hero in a penny dreadful novel, do you realize that?" She smiled against the buttons on his shirt. "I'm not easily swayed. If you could talk to my family, they would tell you as much."

"I think your father would tell me a great deal more than that." His words were too fast and his heartbeat frantic. "Bianca, I'm sorry about the way I told you about India. It was vulgar and base. There's no excuse for it. I suppose I was trying to chase you away—let you know what you'd gotten yourself into."

She lifted her cheek from his chest. "Well, you can stop that. I know exactly what I've gotten myself into."

He cleared his throat. "Would you step away from me, please?"

"Why?"

"Because you're tempting me to do wicked things. I find it very hard to concentrate when you're this near to me."

She stepped backward and crossed her arms. Flames spread across her face. "I need some water or tea or ... olives or something."

"Olives, hmmm?" He looked up to the ceiling absentmindedly. "You left the olives on your plate at breakfast. I didn't think you liked them."

"Do you notice everything?" She turned and looked down into the empty foyer.

"It's what I'm paid to do—write down everything, make sense of details."

A sudden streak of mischievousness coursed through her. "What color was the dress I wore to the Egyptian dinner?"

"Emerald green," he said without thought. "With velvet on the sleeves and cream silk around your neckline."

She put her hand to her neck and her blush deepened. "What was the first thing we talked about on the ship?"

"The untouched beauty of the sea."

And he had quoted poetry to her. She smiled, secretly, her back still turned to him. But perhaps he only remembered things about her. "What color was Madeline's robe in Jaffa?"

Silence stretched behind her. She turned around. "There. You don't remember everything."

"Red and white," he said, tiredness woven throughout his tone.

"I can't believe she never told me she was an actress. She's so . . . I hate to say this, but I really don't like her at all."

"Neither do I." He pushed away from the wall. "Allow me to get you something to eat." He put his hand on her back and led her down the stairs. "Omar's probably lurking around somewhere. If not, we'll find the kitchen ourselves." A terrible quiet settled around him; it was in the way he moved and how his eyes stayed upon the floor.

No lanterns were lit in the corridor. They walked in silence, the rain outside once again their voiceless song.

Bianca didn't care about India anymore. Paul wasn't that person anymore. She knew who he was and what he had done, and she accepted it. God had brought them together. Across the miles, and despite Sir Adrian's plans, he was meant to be her husband. She slid her hand into his.

Paul flinched.

"I'm sorry."

He tightened his grip. "No, it's not you . . ." He dropped the sentence and whatever he had meant it to be was lost upon the stillness in the room.

They wove in and out of the rooms, saying nothing. When they came into the kitchen, a window was open. Cool air pushed the curtains toward them. Splatters of rain were on the floor.

"Mr. Owenburke would not be pleased." Bianca felt like a fool saying the words. She closed the window and twisted the latch. She felt Paul behind her, watching.

A cabinet door opened and then closed. He appeared beside her, holding a plate of fruit.

"Thank you." She reached for it but kept her gaze upon his face.

Silence breathed between them until it became unbearable, like a living thing.

Paul stared down at the plate. "Aren't you going to eat?"

She twisted off a grape. "If only . . ." She wanted to tell him that she wished she could take his guilt away. "If only we could stay a month instead of a week. There's so much we won't get to see."

He gave her a shadow of a smile. "And what would we see if you were the tour guide?"

"Petra," she answered quickly. "We'd ride there on the back of a camel."

"Like a caravan of Nabateans, the people who built it." An unusual sheen was in his eyes.

"We could have a picnic on the stairs of the treasury room. Underneath the columns."

"Where else would we go if things were different?"

Different. The word wrapped around her like ghost's fingers. "Nazareth. The Sea of Galilee. Bethlehem."

Paul looked out the window to the moon and the slacking rain. "You can see Bethlehem from a high place in Jerusalem. I should have pointed it out to you when we were on the Mount of Olives. It's only nine kilometers away."

"We should go then."

He gave her a sideways glance and nodded, like he was indulging a fantasy.

"We should go now."

"Now? In the dark?"

"Why not?" Excitement coursed through her—and something else. Freedom. The chance to get away from Sir Adrian. And Madeline. The chance to help Paul rid himself of his guilt.

"What would Sir Adrian say when he found you gone?"

"It doesn't matter. You're right about him. He has brought us all together for some purpose. I know it in my heart."

A door slammed deep within the house. Paul stepped into the doorway and peered at the balcony. "Did something happen with Sir Adrian while I was away? Did he say something to you?"

Bianca could still feel Sir Adrian's iron grip on her wrist.

"Bianca? What did he say?"

She met his gaze and the lanterns flickered in his eyes. "I think he knows about India. And we're all just a game to him somehow. I don't trust him anymore."

"How smart you are."

She might have taken it as a compliment, but the tones woven throughout his words were too strange. "He has planned everything carefully, just to study us all. Mainly me, I think."

A door slammed again.

Bianca looked over her shoulder at the phantom that wasn't there. "Let's be done with it all. Mr. Tabor is well taken care of. I'll leave a note for Mr. Owenburke."

"I won't deny that I have wanted to take you away." He drew his eyebrows together. "What would your father say?"

"He'd tell me to get away from them. I trust you. You'd never do anything to harm me."

Madeline's voice was muted through the corridors—too high, too fast. The doctor's voice followed, muddled and primitive.

"Bianca, when I told you that I wasn't noble—"

"Stop." She placed her hand on his mouth. The ceiling boards groaned. Someone walked above them. Bianca lowered her voice and leaned in, her eyes pleading. "You are a noble man."

He eased her hand away. "I won't take you. You'll hate me tomorrow if I do."

Bianca curled her fingers, still feeling his warm lips. "Why?"

The rain paused against the window, as if even it wanted to hear.

When she looked back up, there was another alteration in his eyes.

Bianca reached for him and he stepped away.

Horses' hooves sounded outside.

The kitchen door flung open. Mr. Owenburke stood there, drenched with rain. "Paul . . ." He held out his hand like a plea. "Take Bianca away from here."

"Why?" Bianca stepped toward him.

"Sir Adrian's coming." Mr. Owenburke's eyes were full of pity.

Paul's eyes indicated that he understood the weight of those three little words.

Chapter 28

*P*aul's face was blank and emotionless. The rain slanted from the black heaven above—diving, assaulting. Bianca closed her eyes, and it ran down her cheeks like tears.

"Hold on to me." The water spiked his eyelashes. "This isn't going to be easy."

Bianca wrapped her arms around him, and she felt the full weight of his words. Behind them, Jerusalem faded away, along with the last bit of sureness that she felt.

Pressing her cheek into Paul's back, she felt deep sadness churning within her. She'd come to him and forgiven him. And he didn't even want to take her away. It took Mr. Owenburke's warning to sway him.

The clouds towed their shadows over the rain-soaked hills. Their blackness dipped into valleys and then out again, following the call of the moon, slipping like thoughts in a dream.

And still, Paul was silent—even when the moon took off the clouds and blushed, chasing away the rain with its glow.

But then the rain started again, even harder than before. And when the dark, walled city of Bethlehem finally came into view, Bianca couldn't think of anything else besides the cold, or the way her back clenched every time she shivered.

They wandered in and out of alleys, the beat of the rain like clubs. Finally, Paul dismounted and held out his hand.

Bianca sat still, her hair clinging to her face, her clothes weighing her down.

"We're here." Thunder growled in the distance. "Come on."

The rain was so thick she could barely see him. "Why? So I can vex you more?"

"You haven't vexed me." He wiped his face but it didn't help. "Get off the horse."

She blinked in the rain, her arms stiff, her body rigid.

Paul jerked her out of the saddle like a disobedient child and held her.

"Let go of me." She pushed against his chest. The cloth of his shirt sopped in the rain.

"Forgive me for not allowing you the privilege of taking in the weather."

She wrapped her hand around the back of his neck. His skin was freezing. "You moody, impossible man! Why won't you talk to me?" A pool of water formed on her stomach between their bodies.

"It's complicated." He walked to a large door and pounded. "Like this day." When he looked down, rain dripped from his chin onto her cheek. "I needed time to think."

"Are you normally so distant when you're thinking?"

"Only when my thoughts are not pleasant." He beat on the door again, violently.

A voice yelled from within. Paul yelled back in Hebrew.

The door creaked on ancient hinges. An old man peered into the night holding a lantern. He looked up at the rain, said something that must have been unpleasant, and waved them in.

Paul set her down just inside the door.

"Where are we?" A water puddle formed around her on the floor.

"An inn in Bethlehem." Paul spoke again to the innkeeper. "This man is a friend of Owenburke. We'll be safe here."

"And tomorrow?"

Paul ran his hands through his hair and flung off the rain. "Tomorrow will take care of itself."

Bianca heard the rest of the verse in her mind. *"Sufficient unto the day is the evil thereof."*

The innkeeper bowed and pointed to a door. Paul returned the bow, water still dripping onto the floor. The old man and his light disappeared up the stairs. The timeworn wood creaked with the weight of him.

Paul walked down the hall and opened the door. "You'll stay in here."

Bianca stepped into the room, then turned back to face him. "Could you stay awhile?"

"You need to get dry." He leaned against the doorframe. "The innkeeper's wife will bring you some clothes."

"Thank you. That was very kind of you to arrange that." She hugged herself and rubbed her freezing arms. She should say goodnight, she knew that. Out of all the times to use propriety, this one was key. But she was lonely. And she had so many questions. "Would you come back and talk to me when you're dry?"

Paul hardened his jaw. His eyes strayed to the bed.

"Don't leave me alone. Please?"

"I'm very tired. I'd much rather talk in the morning."

Bianca nodded, sudden tears coming to her eyes.

"All right." Paul held up his hand. "Don't cry. I'll come back." He backed into the hall. "I promise."

Bianca smoothed down the rough fabric of the robe as she sat by the fire. She ran her fingers through her hair and wrapped the damp ends around her fingers. Her gaze went to the door. Again. For the hundredth time.

"Lord, help me. Be in our conversation. Help me rid him of his guilt. And whatever he has to tell me, don't let it be as bad as I fear."

His knock was so soft she hardly heard it.

"Come in." She looked at her clothes hanging by the fire. She should have braided her hair. And, she most certainly should have kept her socks on.

Paul opened the door. When he turned around to shut it, he left it cracked. Blackness from the hall lingered just outside like a lecher. "Better now?" He was dry and wearing his own clothes. He looked at the small rug, the cracks in the wall, the faded picture of Mary and Joseph.

"Yes. Thank you for coming back."

He nodded and straightened the water pitcher on the stand.

"Would you like to sit down?"

"Perhaps I should stand."

"Please." She scooted over on the couch. "Sit beside me."

He ignored her request. "I hope these accommodations are suitable."

"They're fine. We're not in the rain anymore, and there's a fire. You've taken very good care of me." She gave him a smile but he didn't notice. "Paul, I would be happier if you sat down."

He paused as if she'd said something weighty. Then he walked, every step a hesitation. He sat, pushed himself into the corner of the couch, and crossed his arms.

A log in the fire fell, sending sparks above. "I'm very sorry you've had such a horrible day."

His expression softened. "Not all of it can be lumped into that category. We had a very pleasant breakfast."

"Yes, we did." Bianca thought of the old woman who had cooked for them. And the way Paul had seemed so at ease and made her laugh. "I wish I spoke Hebrew."

His gaze flicked to her. "You could learn it if you wanted to. I could easily teach you. You're very quick-witted."

"Thank you. That means a great deal to me."

"You're welcome." He laced his fingers together and leaned against the couch arm.

She needed something to make him feel comfortable. Some subject that was familiar to him. "Hebrew sounds so beautiful when you speak it."

"I sincerely doubt if anything I do is beautiful."

"Well, I think so." The firelight shone on his hair and made it glow deep mahogany. "And I've only heard three of the nine languages that you speak." She smiled mischievously. "If you were to speak the other six, well, I might just think I'd died and gone to Glory."

Something like a laugh came out of his mouth. "So, instead of courting you and making a complete fool out of myself, I should've just spoken random languages?"

"Absolutely." She laughed, then quieted as a thought occurred to her. "Since something is obviously bothering you, perhaps you should tell me in another language first. If you want to."

Sadness was in his eyes. "If you want me to."

"Do you speak French?"

"Mon cœur était perdue pour vous depuis le premier instant que je t'ai vu." He reached for her face and touched her cheek. "My heart was lost to you from the first moment I saw you."

Bianca swallowed. Her throat was dry and the room—entirely too hot. "Italian?"

"Desidero che avevo incontrato voi prima che ho viaggiato in India." He threaded his hand into her hair. "I wish I had met you before I traveled to India." His fingers passed over the tip of her ear.

Bianca closed her eyes. She was lost to him, and with each inflection of his words, she felt herself falling deeper. "Our experiences make us who we are." She remembered Sir Adrian saying that to her. She opened her eyes. "Don't be sorry anymore."

His cheeks were heated with a flame not from the fire. *"Mi vergüenza se magnifica cuando te miro a los ojos.* Spanish. My shame is magnified when I look into your eyes."

Bianca reached for his hand. "Forgive yourself. Sometimes that's the hardest part."

"Wenn ich mit Ihnen betete bat ich Gott, dass Scham nehmen. German." He lowered his voice to a whisper. "When I prayed with you, I asked God to take that shame away."

Bianca looked down at their hands. *Take it, God. Do whatever You have to. Take this pain from him.* She scooted closer. The nearness of him was like warm velvet wrapping around her, sliding against her skin. The room seemed smaller, and the only thing that mattered was the feeling of his hand against hers.

"Turkish. *Her şeyi vermek istiyorum.* I want to give you everything."

Everything. The word was wrapped in hope.

"Greek." He closed the space between them and laid his cheek against the side of her forehead. *"Phobamai spasei tēn kardia sas.* I'm afraid of breaking your heart."

She turned her face into his neck and felt his heart beat. "It's forgiven. Don't think about India tonight." The smell of his skin was the purest, deepest thing.

"Not thinking about it won't change anything." He smoothed his hand over her hair. "There's one thing I haven't told you. You asked me to tell you this morning. Do you remember?"

Bianca held onto him tighter. "Is that what's been bothering you?"

"Yes. It's bothered me for weeks." His heartbeat quickened against her cheek.

"I think you were right." She pulled away from him so she could see his eyes. "It's better if I don't know."

"That's not true." He took a deep breath. "Her—"

"Stop." She put her other hand on his shoulder. "I know this is going to be hard to hear. I can see it in your eyes. Why do you want to put this in my mind?"

"Because you have to know. And I have to be the one to tell you." He pulled his hand away. "It's the honorable thing to do."

"Who else would tell me?"

"Sir Adrian."

"I suspected he might know about the diamond, but—"

"This is the reason he brought us all together." Paul's eyes fixed upon her, watching her every movement. "If I hadn't been interested in you, I would never have come. If I hadn't fallen in love with you, I wouldn't have stayed."

Tears came to her eyes. Tears mixed with joy and fear and longing. "You love me?"

Surprise crossed his features. "Of course I love you."

"I love you too." She made herself look at him. "So much."

Paul closed his eyes, like the words were a balm to him. "I know you do. And that's why you have to know." He brought her hand to rest over his heart. "I'm so sorry."

"I'm sorry too," she said, although she didn't know why.

"I will completely understand if after you know, you want to go home."

"I will still love you after I know."

He brushed her hair away from her face. Everything in his eyes told her he didn't believe it was true.

"Would you do something for me?" The words were out before she could weigh them. She swallowed, not believing she'd allowed herself the liberty.

"I'll do anything for you."

"I would like . . ."

"Yes?"

She considered not asking. But this was everything that she had wanted—this love, this man. Only one more thing would make it perfect. "I would like it very much if you would kiss me. Kiss me when I don't have her name in my mind. Kiss me in Bethlehem."

"That's asking quite a lot." His eyes strayed to the door. "I told you I wouldn't kiss you until I couldn't see any more doubt in your eyes."

"I don't have doubt in my eyes."

"You will again." He moved like he would stand.

Bianca held him still. "Please. Do this for me."

"Bianca . . ." He looked at the bed. He looked at the floor.

"Please." She brought her face closer to his. "Please." Her breath mingled with his. And the faintest smell of sandalwood and other things she couldn't quite name.

The smoldering fire she saw in his eyes terrified her and lured her all at the same time. "You're asking too much." His hand slid around her back despite his words.

She spread her fingers into his soft, thick hair.

Paul closed his eyes. "God help me." He gathered the back of her robe in his hands.

Bianca arched her back against his touch. The only thing she wanted was for her fear to go away, for him to wrap her in his arms and make her forget. To be kissed, truly and properly kissed—like all the heroines she'd been reading about for years.

His breath was on her neck, deep and shallow.

She pulled him closer.

He pinned her other hand to the couch. "Bianca." The tones were soft and strained, like music stumbled upon from far away.

"Kiss me, Paul." She lowered her eyes to his lips.

He locked his fingers with hers and held on. "I need . . ."

She melted into the green of his eyes. The way that he held her—it was urgent and aching, and all of the things she'd ever dreamed.

She let her eyelids fall.

And then there was the sound of his voice again.

"Her name is Madeline."

Chapter 29

*B*ianca's hand stilled in his hair. A wave of nausea swept through her body. *Madeline.*

Paul's breath on her lips was fast, frantic.

One last bit of storm crept through the window and pulled at the fire; it fainted and collapsed, then swelled the flames.

"Did you hear me?" His chest rose and fell, like the light from the fire, like the shadows in the room.

"I heard you." Deep shaking took hold.

Paul waited, his familiar eyes leery, his entire body leery.

A log fell in the fire and further quenched the light. The shadows crawled over him like hell's fingers— reaching, stretching, stopping at the corners of his eyes. He reached for her cheek and anchored his hand there. "Madeline Greene."

Pain, hot and magnified, coursed through her body. Bianca ripped herself away and fell onto the floor. She couldn't speak. The way Madeline had always looked at him. The look of panic in his eyes at the Egyptian dinner . . .

Paul went to his knees beside her. "I wanted to tell you a thousand times—on the ship, in the garden, at the window."

"Then why didn't you?" She clawed at the threadbare rug, scooting away. Tears bordered her eyes, blurring the regret upon his face.

"I was afraid of what I see in your eyes right now."

Bianca's back slammed against the wall. She stood, her shoulders heaving. "You're a coward, then." She closed her eyes and thought of Madeline's words. *"There's nothing quite like being held by a man... touched by a man."*

Sobs came in spasms, rocking her body against her will.

"I have been a coward." Paul's voice was passionless and far too resigned.

"You've kissed her. And worse." Waves of anguish washed over her. The naked consent upon his face shattered her into a thousand pieces.

"Just tell me what you want me to do. I'll do anything you ask of me."

"Wouldn't that be a turn of events?" She thought of all the times she'd silently begged him to kiss her, and the moment just before, when she'd actually asked. She thought of how she'd asked him to stay longer that morning in Jerusalem. She thought of the agony she'd had just hoping he would like her early on.

Bianca stood and reached for the crude vase upon the mantel. She gripped its narrow neck and squeezed. She pulled it, inch by inch toward her. Her eyes met his and dared him to look away.

Paul raised his chin. "What are you doing with that?"

The fire trembled below her, dying down, lessening the heat upon her legs, as if it sensed the shift within her.

"I think you'd better leave."

"Bianca, put that down." He held up his hand like he was scolding her. "There's no need—"

"Don't tell me what there's a need for!" She flung the vase at his feet. It shattered. Like all her expectations.

Paul jumped up, shock on his features.

Bianca pointed at him. "Do you have any idea how long I've waited for you?"

He stared at the shards of ceramic. And then her face.

"All my life." She stepped over the rubble.

"You'll cut your feet."

"Night after night I prayed for you. Begging God to bring us together."

Paul wiped his hand over his jaw. "You're bleeding."

Bianca ignored him and the wetness between her toes. "You couldn't even have the decency to tell me that the woman I've been traveling with is *the* woman!"

"Darling, calm—"

"Did you think I wouldn't find out? All this time, Sir Adrian . . ." Another wave of nausea hit her. Footsteps were on the stairs.

The innkeeper shouted.

Paul said something in Hebrew, his voice panicked. He shut the door.

"How could you?" She grabbed her dress from the line and threw it at him. "You let me sleep in the same room with her."

He tripped over the rug, but righted himself. "What was I supposed to do?"

"Every day you talked to her like nothing was between you."

"It was necessary." Paul backed into a table. The water pitcher tumbled to the floor and shattered. "Sir Adrian had me cornered, Bianca. It was the only way I could get close to you."

She stopped just before she reached him. "I didn't make that very hard for you, did I?" All the times she'd fawned over him replayed in her mind. "Do you know what she said to me at the Egyptian dinner? She said you were handsome, and she asked me if I agreed. She toyed with me from that day on and you let her."

"She's cruel. She only wants Sir Adrian's money. But she wasn't allowed to tell you. I figured that out today when I spoke to—" He abruptly cut off the words.

Bianca's eyes widened. "You spoke to her while I was sleeping?"

"She stole my journal. She was leafing through it in the garden when I passed the window. I went to her and—"

"What else did you do with her while I was sleeping?"

Shock crossed his features. "Bianca!"

"What's the matter? Are you offended?" She stepped forward until her toes almost touched his shoes. "Are you as offended as me?"

"I would never do that to you."

The innkeeper pounded on the door, shaking it against the frame.

Paul yelled something in Hebrew, splattering English words throughout. He lowered his voice when he turned back to Bianca. "I talked with her. That's all." "That's all?"

He flinched. "I offered her money to go away."

Bianca's mouth fell open. "You weren't going to tell me any of this, were you?"

The innkeeper beat on the door again. Other voices came from the hall.

"I hoped somehow a solution would present itself. I tried to make her just go away. I thought—"

"What? That I'd be too stupid to figure it out?"

"No. That I could think my way out of a hard situation."

"This is much more than a hard situation." She made a fist and aimed for his face.

He caught her wrist and turned her into his embrace. His arms were iron, wrapped around her stomach and holding her still. "I've always known what we'd have to overcome just to have a chance. And now you know. But on my life, I didn't want to put you through this."

Anger and horror coursed through her, over and over again. She struggled against his grasp. Mama was right. She should never have come. She should never have tried to find a husband. "You were right." The words tore and clenched in her throat. "What you told me earlier . . . You aren't a noble man." Tears rolled off her cheeks and coursed down her neck, hot reminders of every way she'd failed.

"I tried to warn you." His breath beat upon her neck like fallen angels' wings. "At the window." He held her tighter, as if she would vanish in his arms.

The innkeeper shouted again. The door flung open and ricocheted off the wall. The picture of Joseph and Mary shattered on the floor.

Paul spoke Hebrew so quickly the words slurred.

Bianca had no idea what he said, and she didn't care. She didn't care that the innkeeper looked like he was about to pitch them out. She sank into Paul's arms, the syllables fading. The conversation seeped into her soul like poison. She only heard one thing, over and over.

The woman's name.

Paul's lover.

Madeline.

Paul's voice was in the hall, the Hebrew phrases flowing fast and hard like gorge water. Bianca closed her eyes against the sound, against him, against this place.

She stumbled to the window, marking the floor with crimson half-moons. She pushed open the shutters and leaned into the Bethlehem night. Stars dusted the arc of heaven. The air was a monstrous thing, cold and brutal, knifelike in its sincerity. "God, kill me. This is too much to bear."

The door opened behind her. Tears dripped onto her hands. Black night blurred. The stars trembled.

Hesitant footsteps sounded. She didn't have to turn. She could always feel him, and now it was no different. Now, when he'd shattered her soul.

"I've brought you something. Some gauze for your feet." His voice was the same—beautiful and velvet. But, oh, how tones lie. Every beautiful thing held secrets below. That was the one thing Madeline had taught her. In that one way she'd been true. "Leave me alone."

"Please sit down for a moment."

Bianca ground her fist into her forehead and squeezed her eyes as if that would dull the pain. "I was thinking more along the lines of dying. Go away."

Without a word, he came to her. His arms came around her and he lifted her. "Sorry. You're not allowed to die."

His touch was like fire coursing through her body—raking, pulling, enflaming her rage.

He placed her upon the couch.

Bianca fell back against the cushions and glared at him. "I hate you."

"I know." He pulled the water bowl from the stand and set it beside him on the floor. He reached for her foot.

Bianca jerked it away.

Paul grabbed her heel. "Be still. This will be cold." He removed his handkerchief and dipped it into water.

"What are you doing?" Blood ran down his hand and seeped into his sleeve.

Paul ran the cloth over her foot and then plunged it back in the water. "You've got a rather nasty cut here."

Bianca drew her breath in as a hiss. "Stop that!"

"You have a piece of the vase in your foot." He pressed gauze over the wound and then reached under his vest and withdrew his knife.

"What are you going to do?" Bianca pushed herself into the back of the couch.

He plunged the knife into the fire and held it in the flames. "I'm going to make it so you can walk in the morning." He looked at her poignantly. "Just in case there's anywhere you plan to go."

Bianca clenched the arm of the couch. Blood quickly seeped into the gauze, trickled over his thumb, and disappeared in the hollow of his hand.

"It's quite deep." He raised her foot, spilling her blood down his arm. "Ready?"

Bianca dug her fingers into the couch and nodded.

Paul locked eyes with her and then hardness bled into his eyes. He drew his eyebrows together, brought her foot closer, and plunged in the blade.

Searing hot pain shot through her foot. The room tilted. A scream fled over her lips.

The firelight glowed around him, casting his body in a silhouette of flame.

"There." Pressure replaced the pain. He showed her a bloody piece of ceramic and then threw it into the fire.

Bianca stared at the ceiling. His fingers worked against her foot—tying and tucking a bandage. "You can go now."

His hand stilled on her ankle. "If I go, will you be here in the morning?"

Bianca laughed through tears. "Where would I go? I can't speak the language. I'm limited, you see. Too many dreams . . . thrust into a very hard situation."

The room ebbed like the sea drawing away sand. She felt him rise and walk past. Then there was the gentle click of the door.

Firelight lapped over her, soothing hands of orange and yellow—hands that tried, but just weren't enough.

Sir Adrian had manipulated her life. His friendship was false. He had betrayed her. Madeline had lied and laughed secretly. And Paul... Handsome, imperfect Paul was just a man in the end. A man like the millions before him—selfish, self-preserving, and cruel. He'd become more important than God to her—everything. And that brought the deepest kind of shame.

"Nothing about this journey has been right. Forgive me, Lord."

Through the cracked shutter, the searing light of sunrise hit her full in the face. Slowly, it began to warm her.

Chapter 30

*B*ianca opened the bedroom door. Paul sat upon the stairs, his head bent over his hands. He looked up, anxiety firmly etched in his eyes.

Her gaze roamed over him, memorizing. A ripping pain—hard and deep—coursed through her. She waited for him to speak, but only faint sounds from the back of the inn wafted through the air. "I have a little money. I don't think it's enough to pay for what I did last night to the vase. And, all the trouble—"

"I took care of it." His eyebrows pulled together and the lines around his eyes deepened. "It was my fault."

"But—"

"I take full responsibility for everything." The early morning light caressed him, falling over his shoulder like a shroud. "May I ask you something?"

She nodded.

"You have every right to want to go home, but you may never come back to Israel. Spend one more day. I'll show you Bethlehem and more." The question in his eyes was primal, as fragile as a child.

Bianca's heart caught at the sight of him—the boy within the man—that part that he so rarely showed. Here was no man who had the ear of intellectual London; this man was only a man, begging with his eyes, trying not fidget with the hem of his jacket.

"One day." She dropped her eyes to his shoes. "My last day with you."

They wandered through the narrow streets of Bethlehem. Paul told her stories, bringing to life every crumbling stone and every hill that surrounded them. Where there should have been worry on his face, Bianca saw only passion for the ages. He pretended nothing was wrong, and she hated him for it. He walked amongst the people like he belonged, and more keenly Bianca understood that she didn't.

She tried to concentrate on what he was saying— the Chapel of the Innocents, where the bones of the children that Herod murdered still lay; the prophecies that were fulfilled on the night that Jesus was born; the Tomb of Rachel, Jacob's greatest love . . . how she died in childbirth and the Jews say that she wept as she saw her people pass her tomb on the way to the Babylonian captivity. And King David, how he grew up and was crowned in Bethlehem.

Now Bianca stood before the well that David longed for when he'd hid from Saul in the Cave of Adullam.

Paul knelt on sandy patches of grass intertwined with ancient stone. "David's three best warriors shed Philistine blood just to come here for one cup of water for their King. They fought their way through, just for this."

Bianca stared into the water, not surprised that she looked like all those ghosts from the past—her eyes hollow, the spark gone.

Paul dipped his canteen in the water and scattered the image. "I'm sure you remember that when the men returned, David poured out the water on the ground saying that he wasn't worthy. He used it instead as an offering to the Lord."

"I remember." Bianca stared at the drops that fell like tears from his hand.

Paul offered her the canteen. "You must be thirsty."

"I . . ." If David had refused, how could she drink it? She above all people. Bianca Marshal, the wanton fool who threw herself at a man. Bianca Marshal, who traveled thousands of miles just to be kissed. "No."

"It is the only water here. It's very important that you drink in a climate like this. Please."

Bianca took the canteen and raised it to her mouth, careful not to touch the edge where his lips had been.

Paul noticed, of course, as he noticed everything, and remembered all. Displeasure shone in his eye. Like the master he was, he tucked the expression away and hid it with a smile. "Two more places and then we'll be off."

Bianca tore her gaze away, bitterness reaching to her bones.

The Casanova laid his hand upon her back.

Bianca stepped away. "The sooner this day is over, the better."

They turned into a smooth plaza where a massive structure stood. A bell tower rose up to the right.

"Can you guess what this is?" His eyes lit up as he scanned the stones.

She was in no mood for guessing games. "A fortress?"

"True." He walked toward a small open doorway on the farthest side. "This is the Church of the Nativity." Paul looked into the gaping black of the open door. "This is the Door of Humility, put in by the Crusaders. Most likely, the door was partially walled up to prevent carts being driven in by looters. Shall we go in?"

"Why not?" The sarcasm in her voice was evident.

The church was simpler than the Church of the Holy Sepulchre, but beautiful in a timeless way. Brown and tan marble columns reached to exposed wooden beams.

Paul walked in and out of the columns and paused by the stairs. "Downstairs should be the Grotto of the Nativity, an ancient cave."

Bianca descended the stairs without a word. A few lanterns hung from the ceiling, casting a trembling light upon the smooth stone walls.

"The Chapel of the Manger," Paul whispered. A monk sat beneath a tent-like awning over a marble square upon the floor. "And this must be the traditional birthplace." Two red and gold curtains were pulled to the side. Below them, underneath a smaller white curtain, light emanated, soft and serene.

Paul knelt, his eyebrows drawn together. He stared at the inlaid silver star.

Bianca fell to her knees, wishing she could concentrate. Paul's scent and everything that he was enveloped her in the small space.

"In AD 160, Justin Martyr wrote that this spot was the birthplace of Christ." Paul's voice was hushed, like love whispers. The tones wrapped around her as did the incense. Dizziness stole her breath away. "In 326, the Emperor Constantine ordered this church to be built. In 530 Justinian rebuilt it. The Crusaders later redecorated . . ." His voice trailed off as he placed his hand on top of the star.

The lanterns above the star swung, pushed by some unfelt breeze. Chanting began somewhere far away in the church, probably a song for the dead. Or perhaps it was a song for the living—a song for people whose dreams never came to pass.

Bianca lowered her hand upon the marble, just beside Paul's. She thought of that night, almost nineteen hundred years ago—the shepherds, the angels—God in the flesh. The Savior of the world.

She spread her fingers out toward Paul's and closed her eyes. Her heart swayed toward him, momentarily; it was deceitful, and traitorous, and full of illogical romantic notions. She made a fist and pulled it away.

He stood watching her when she opened her eyes. "As you probably noticed, most of the marble's been stolen."

"What?" She felt like she'd been caught bathing naked in the spring back home.

"The original marble," he said slowly. "It's gone. Are you all right, darling?"

"Don't call me that." Bianca stood. "Don't say things like that."

Paul looked down and flipped open his pocket watch. "Are you ready, then? We still have much to see."

Bianca stared at the hard planes of his back. Why did she feel so guilty when he was the one to blame?

Shadow and light flashed upon them as they entered the cloister. They walked out onto a sun-drenched street that led into the main part of the city.

"Let's get the horse."

"Fine." Bianca wanted to cry. Their conversation had deteriorated into phrases; passionless, meaningless phrases—just like her life.

Paul stopped abruptly and turned down an alley. Shrouded by the roofs above, it made a quiet oasis from the sun.

"Look." His voice was strained. "Those men there, at the end of the alley. I think they're carving mother of pearl. Let's go and see."

"If you want to."

"Franciscan friars from Damascus introduced this art to Bethlehem in the fourteenth century."

Bianca wanted to scream. Was there anything he didn't know? Mr. Knowledgeable About Everything. Except how not to lie to a woman whom he pretended he wanted to marry.

Five men sat in the sand, tools and baskets all around. Their faces were as weathered as the wall behind them. The caps upon their heads were plain white.

Paul smiled at the man in the middle and spoke to him in Hebrew.

The aged man held out a basket and spoke, every word laced with excitement.

"I like this one." Paul picked up a little carved star and turned it in the light. It shone with iridescent colors. "What do you think?"

"It's fine," she offered, knowing her voice was flat.

"Hmmm." Paul put it back down and chose another. "This one is slightly different. See the different colors around the edges, when the light hits it just so."

"Beautiful." Disdain seeped through the word.

Paul gently replaced the star and said something else to the man. The man looked sympathetically to Bianca.

Of course she had no idea what Paul had said, but she was sure he left out the part about being an adulterer who traveled with the very woman in question while courting another.

The old man clasped his hands together, then spoke for what seemed like an eternity. He disappeared inside a small doorway then returned with something wrapped in soft black cloth.

The start of a smile began on Paul's lips. "He's wondering if you might like this."

Bianca looked into the man's eyes—a light, understanding brown. His eyes reminded her of Daddy's eyes. The man smiled at her, and somehow, it brought her comfort.

The man unwrapped the cloth slowly, revealing the most beautiful—almost unearthly—masterfully carved star. Bianca's hand went to her chest. The little thing, just the size of the middle of her palm, threatened to take her breath away.

Paul gave her a sideways glance. "He says the star's two hundred years old. Should we believe him?"

Bianca wanted to touch it, hold it, stare at it for hours. The sheen was not just a sheen, but a deep, calling thing. Finally, she found her voice. "You're the historian."

"So I am." He drew out the words like spun silk and then held the star. "The craftsmanship is undeniable. Can you imagine what was going on here when this was carved?" He brought the star fully into the light, furrowed his brow, and turned it over in his hand. "The oyster came from the Red Sea, no doubt."

Bianca stepped closer, despite herself. An oyster from the very sea that Moses parted, that would be a treasure for always.

Paul ran his finger along the delicate leaf pattern around the star. "To see such a fine example as this . . . It's weathered the ages." Paul reached into his pocket and withdrew a very large amount of money.

"What are you doing? You're not buying it, are you?"

"Of course I am." Paul handed the money to the man and bowed. "I'm buying it for you." He handed it to her as they walked away.

"You gave him a fortune." Bianca was afraid to hold it too tight. "What if he lied to you?"

"I am the historian. I didn't gain employment at the British Museum by having dull judgment."

"No, of course not, but . . . Why would you spend that much money on me?"

"Because I love you. And even long after the sun rises tomorrow, that won't ever change."

The horse swayed beneath them, a quiet cadence over the hills—back and forth—into the wild and almost uncharted countryside. Bianca held the carved star in her hand and still couldn't believe he'd bought it for her.

She wrapped the star back into the cloth and tucked it into her purse. "Are you going to tell me where we're going?"

"I thought you liked surprises."

"I'm afraid I can't afford any more." Bianca frowned. "Just tell me."

"The Jordan River is just ahead, where Jesus was baptized. I've always wanted to see it. I hope you share that desire."

She had no more desires. He'd killed them all. Bianca cringed, knowing that wasn't true. She did want to see the Jordan. She'd wanted to see it all her life.

The landscape faded into bulrushes and ancient trees. The sound of water over rocks increased.

Paul led the horse between the thick brush and stopped on the bank. "Are you hungry? I have some food and a blanket in the saddlebag. We could have a picnic here if you like."

She was dying inside. She still loved him. But how could she when he'd sinned with Madeline? Madeline, who had the heart of Medusa. Madeline, who was prettier than she. "You may continue on."

"As you wish." He didn't try to veil his disappointment. He nudged the horse down the bank. Its front hoof slipped on the mud.

Bianca slammed into Paul's back. She gritted her teeth and cursed the smell of sandalwood. And English accents. And exotic adventures. And all men in general.

The water was at the horse's knees, the stirrups, and finally, the bottoms of Paul's feet. "You might want to hold your feet up." The horse took another step. The water flowed over Paul's ankles. He pulled back on the reins and stroked the horse's neck. He was saying something, but over the noise of the river, Bianca couldn't make out any of the words.

She waited. One minute. Two. "Is it your intention to have the horse stand in the water all day?" When Paul didn't answer, Bianca leaned to the side to look at his face. His eyes were closed and his lips were moving.

She sighed and looked down at the cedar leaves gathering around the hem of her skirt. They were in the middle of the Jordan River. His feet were soaked. The horse was up to its chest in water. And suddenly, he felt the need to pray.

The water changed course and her reflection shifted in the water. Just as quickly, a bird flew overhead. Bianca saw the shadow of its wings.

The landscape rolled by and the sunlight faded. Just a little longer, and she'd set him free. He'd go back to London and marry some proper English girl.

Someone not like her.

Paul stopped the horse at the base of a hill and dismounted. "We're here."

"Where exactly is here?" She ignored his out-stretched hand and slid down.

"You'll see." Calmness surrounded him—it played in his easy smile and lingered at the corners of his eyes. "Take my hand and I'll help you climb the hill."

"I'll be fine."

"I'm not going to trick you."

But he already had. In the worst way. She laughed, ignored his outstretched hand, and walked past. Yellow flowers grew just ahead, between the rocks and the grass. The blue crispness of the sky was fading, smearing into something indiscernible.

The pain she felt was different now; it was building—stronger than at the window when he'd first told her about India, tearing like it had last night, but worse.

Paul stopped at the crest of the hill, just before she could see the other side. He looked into the sky and must have noticed the change, the moments slipping. "Bianca, this day has meant a great deal to me."

The wind blew suddenly; it pushed Bianca toward him, just a step. He put his hand on her arm. "Careful."

She dropped her eyes to the flowers swaying. They danced as if there was something to celebrate—as if some unheard melody played on the wind.

Bianca smelled water, earth, and fish. She widened her eyes when she saw it—the most beautiful lake, full of diamonds, scattered in the last grip of the dying sun.

Purple hills embraced the water as far as she could see. The entire field was lush with yellow flowers, bending toward the water with the wind. "It's so beautiful."

"This is the Sea of Galilee. Where Jesus walked on the water and calmed the storm. A great deal of His ministry happened on these shores."

Bianca nodded, almost in a trance. "He called three of the disciples here while they were fishing. And the Sermon on the Mount . . ."

"Could have happened right here." Paul finished her thought.

Bianca walked and stretched out her hand against the flowers. *"Blessed are they that mourn: for they shall be comforted."* The sunlight shone through the tall grass beyond and turned it gold. "Jesus, comfort me," she whispered.

At the coast, Paul tied the horse to a tree. He took off the saddlebag and threw it over his shoulder. "Do you know how to fish?"

The lighthearted look that he gave her threw her completely off guard. "Yes. Do you?"

"Of course I do." His twisted his face like his ego was shattered. "I spent my childhood in the Lake District. Have you heard of that region of England?"

"I don't think so." The Lake District sounded like the country, which was strange considering she'd always thought him a city man. She followed him down to the water. The water lapped upon the shore, moving the silt below the surface.

"In all the places I've been, it's still one of the most beautiful. It's wild and untouched. I used to walk there for hours." He dropped the saddlebag on the sand and knelt to rummage through it. "I stumbled upon the stone circle at Castlerigg when I was very young. That's where my love of history first began. I don't think I told you that yet, did I?"

"No." She wished they would have known each other then, when sin and regret didn't exist.

"I suppose it would take a long time to tell you about all the places I've been." The tone in his voice told her that he wished that he could.

And, if things were different, she'd love to listen. "I just assumed you always lived in London."

"No. God forbid." Paul scowled. "I only came to London to work at the British Museum... Here it is." He pulled out a bit of wire and the knife. "I'll just be a moment." He searched and finally picked up a stick. He broke off a small piece and whittled it.

Bianca focused on his hands and the fluid way that he worked. Against the backdrop of the water, he was perfectly at ease. The sun spread its rays in abandon, turning the purple clouds to pink. "What are you doing?"

"I'm making us a pair of excellent hooks. Combined with this wire, the Queen herself couldn't ask for anything better."

He knew how to make fishing hooks? He'd teased her about frog gigging like he'd never set foot in the country.

"I see some small branches on that tree. Would you get them?" He handed her his knife and knelt to rummage in the saddlebag again.

Bianca's boots sunk into the wet sand as she went. She picked through a few young branches and then cut two.

He'd taken his shoes off, and his trousers were rolled up to his knees. He walked toward her. The sun was at his back, casting his shadow into the water. "Almost ready over there?"

Her heart caught at the sight of him. The wind blew again, combing its fingers through her hair and jerking it loose from the pins. "How about these?"

"Excellent." His smile was disarming. And unnerving. And everything it always had been. But more now—more in this isolation, this beauty—this place that held so many miracles. He rigged up the poles as they walked. He took off the leather satchel slung over his shoulder and dropped it onto the ground. "There's a jetty of rocks just down the way. I thought perhaps you could sit there."

They walked in silence, urged on by the wind and the waves.

Bianca tucked her wayward hair behind her ear. Her shadow on the sand intertwined with his, as if her soul couldn't help but want to be near him, just to touch him.

Bianca took a step to the side and ripped her shadow away.

Chapter 31

Sir Adrian Hartwith fell against the wall and wished for the impossible. Like a taste of the currant drops his sister used to sneak to him after his father had flogged him with the birch rod. He could never bring himself to eat a currant drop after she died, but now—*now*—he could almost feel the sugar dissolving on his tongue and the lingering tartness near his teeth.

He wished for foolish things, like the afternoon in Hyde Park when he'd fed the duck with the broken wing. And no one had asked anything of him for that short time. Nobody smiled just because of his money. Nobody was false.

Sweat ran down his face, pasting his hair like clumps of dead autumn leaves. He took a step. At least he thought he did. And then he fell against the grime-covered bricks again. He'd been here too long, he knew that. He shouldn't have come in the first place, he knew that too. But what bothered him more at this precise moment was the fact that he couldn't find the door.

He always found the door.

He closed his eyes, hoping some of the nausea would pass; it came in waves that forced and clenched, just like the conviction of God. He fell against the wall again, his gaze rising to the sagging ceiling. He vaguely remembered walking underneath it shortly after Samuel had thrown his steamer trunk onto the street. And told him to take his lies and manipulation elsewhere. "After all I've bloody done for him. The upstart!"

A door opened somewhere. Stale air crawled toward him, smelling of alcohol and sweat, and things taken that didn't belong. He closed his eyes and put his hand out to steady himself.

If only he could take back all the sins he had committed when he was bored. He took a breath, then doubled over. More than that he wished he could take back all the sins he'd committed when he was lonely. Violent waves shook his body. Whatever he'd eaten splattered on the floor and slid against the baseboard. The sight of it made him retch all over again.

Feminine laughter wafted through the dim hall; it chilled the back of his neck like fingers stroking him, telling him to be still. He heard the voice of the honey-skinned beauty he'd been with and he cursed her—because she'd given him too much wine and God knew what else. Because she couldn't take the emptiness away.

He pushed away from the brick wall and heard his boots upon the wooden floor, dragging as if a corpse wore them. It certainly wasn't the walk of a nobleman. The decades thinned, and his father's words clawed in the dark. *"You are above common people."* "Yes, common." He wiped his mouth on his sleeve. "Common like Bianca and Paul."

He stumbled into the main room, the one with the single shaft of light coming from the hole in the roof. His silk coat slid from his arm. Papers spilled from its pockets and landed like staggered cards in a gaming hell. Words ... he couldn't read any of them now. He squinted. They should be important. He waved his hand against them. "Just smoke and mirrors ... Illusions ..."

But it seemed like more. It has something to do with testing ... Paul. He took a breath and tried to remember. The three tests ...

There was a lantern just ahead, in a crevice in the wall. He reached for it, but fell short. He got his fingers around the thing and pulled it low, down to the warped floorboards, over the ink on the perfectly folded parchment. *The three tests—the lust of the flesh, the lust of the eyes, and the pride of life.*

"Oh, yes, I remember." Sir Adrian threw his arms wide like wings. "The world." He moved toward the women's voices. "The flesh. And the devil—the three things a true Christian should be able to fight. The three things Paul had to pass to prove to me that he'd changed."

"Over now." He felt his expression fall. "Samuel made sure of that." He had so much more to try, to test him with . . . But Paul took Bianca . . . probably married her. Another wave of nausea hit. He leaned against the back of a half-broken chair.

A dark-haired woman slid from behind a curtain like a ghost. "What are you doing? You the Englishman?"

Her voice was spice and despair. She was the one he'd passed by earlier because her brown eyes had reminded him of Madeline's. "Your servant, Madame." He bowed to her. "You look like someone I know who's incompetent." He walked toward her, his chin raised like his father had taught him. "Madeline couldn't even steal Paul's journal. Even after I had his trunk key copied on the ship." He looked up, toward the shaft of light. "It ought to have been easy."

Madeline's look-alike said something in another language and then added in English, "You crazy!"

Women came from behind curtains and down the stairs. They gathered around him and laughed.

"Madeline took it to Samuel's garden!" he yelled to silence them. "Read it like a novel and Paul caught her there."

Their laughter magnified. The curtains blew toward the center of the room.

Sir Adrian bowed his head. He should see what time it was. But the numbers didn't make sense on his gold pocket watch. He walked to the tallest woman, her eyes so heavily lined with kohl he didn't know what color they were. "Here, maybe you can read it." He took her cold hand and closed it over his watch. "My father gave this to me, on the day that he first introduced me to his gentlemen's club."

The tall woman's eyes widened. They were blue. Just like his. Tired, worn-out blue. "I'm supposed to give this watch to my firstborn son—my heir. But that's quite impossible." He inched closer to her and bent to whisper in her ear. "Because I'll never marry. They all just want me for my money." He reached out and ran his finger down her weathered cheek. "Just like you do."

The women pressed in close. They all stared at the engraving of the deer on the watch. "This is what I'll do . . . You'll all like this." He reached into his vest pocket and pulled out a roll of bank notes.

The women shouted and pushed each other when they saw the money.

"I'll do what I've been taught all my life." He handed a bundle of notes to the nearest woman. "I wasn't a very good man today." He tipped her chin up. "No, don't try to convince me otherwise." He handed another woman some money. "I was quite the sinner, so now I must pay." He walked down the line of them, their faces all hopeful and laced with greed. "When we sin, we have to do something to make it right—ten prayers, thirty prayers, shed the blood of an animal like the Jews out there." He reached into his pocket again and his voice rose. "Build a hospital, walk on glass, wash in a river. Pick a tradition—pick whichever one you think might work."

He leaned close to a woman with a scar across her lips. "But not Paul, he went to God directly, the audacity." He took her face in his hands. "He repented and asked Jesus to wash him clean. And that was it." He walked into the shaft of light and let its brightness blind him. "Sins gone forever." His voice faded. "Covered in the deepest sea."

A small voice made him open his eyes. A little girl stood beside him. What was she doing here? She was much too young. He put his hands on his knees. "What do you think? Do you think that the blood of Christ, God's Son, cleanses us from all sin, and only that?"

The girl was silent. In his mind he saw her in ten years and disgust washed over him. "Paul believes what happened out there almost two thousand years ago. Can you imagine? God in the flesh, shedding His own blood for our sins, and then rising from the dead. How can that be the only payment God will accept?" His hand dropped, and the rest of the money fell to the floor.

The women fell before him, like subjects before a king. They shoved and scrambled for what they could grab.

Sir Adrian held his head in his hands, blocking them out. "Jesus who walked these streets of Jerusalem . . . He said, 'Ye must be born again.' He was either right or He was a liar. Truly God incarnate or insane." He stepped around the bodies kneeling on the floor.

"That American preacher said that if any man be in Christ he is a new creature . . . old things are passed away . . . all things are become new. That's all I wanted to know. Because if Paul could resist the flesh, the world, and me, the devil . . . If he could be forgiven, maybe—" Maybe he could too. But now he'd never know.

Light flooded the room. Sir Adrian covered his eyes with his arm then lowered it. A man wearing a turban stood in the doorway. "So there's the door." He walked toward it and passed the man. Just before the door closed, he glanced back. The man was near the hall picking up the papers and Sir Adrian's silk coat. But he could have them. He wouldn't need them where he was going.

The Muslims' call to prayer echoed off the high, stone walls. The light was too bright, pain ripped at his eyes, tore at his throat, settled in his head. He pushed through the sea of robes and headed toward Potter's Field.

And the tree where Judas hanged himself.

Bianca sat on the rocks, oblivious to the fishing line in the water. The sunlight, although it had taken her breath away earlier, now only skimmed the water like tainted gold. And the rock she sat upon, it was worn by the waves of this sea. It had weathered countless storms here, maybe even the one that Jesus calmed.

Bianca wrapped her arms around her knees and dropped her forehead into the cradle of her body. The air pulsed around her. She closed her eyes and she wished. For the light not to be fading. For the things which had been, not to be. For time to reverse. For the shore to be nineteen centuries removed. Most of all, to be here with Him—that blessed One who walked here in the flesh. Her Creator. Her Redeemer. The Unchangeable. The only One faithful and true. She'd lay her head upon His chest as John did, and she'd listen to the heartbeat of God. She'd beg Him to take her love for Paul away.

Paul walked toward her, his footsteps soft in the sand. Dark water stains were on the bottom of his trousers. "I've caught some fish and made a fire. Are you hungry?"

"I don't know." The sun spread its arms and surrendered, mourning in colors that tried to hold on, but couldn't—orange, coral, apricot.

"The wind has grown. It'll be cold in a while." He dug his foot into the sand and took it out. "Would you come and sit by the fire?"

Bianca slid down the rock and walked toward the glow of the fire behind the trees. The sunlight disappeared, as if God had blown out His candle. The tall grass beside her whipped in the dark, reaching as the black water reached—stretching, pining, receding.

Paul knelt, close to the heat of the flame. "It'll just take a few minutes to cook the fish."

She should start by saying something nice. "Thank you for showing me Bethlehem and the Jordan River. And this place."

"You're welcome." He drew his eyebrows together and looked like he might say more. He gave her a piece of fish instead.

She tried again to speak, but couldn't. This was the end to everything she'd hoped for.

Paul threw more driftwood into the fire, then stared at the dark water down below.

He doeth all things well . . . Bianca pulled her locket from underneath her collar. She rubbed the inscription on the back, like she always did.

"I've always meant to ask you about your necklace. I've noticed that you've worn it every day. Even that night when I first met you."

Bianca's hand froze on the silver. She didn't want to think of that night in the King's Library. "I never take it off." She took a breath and let the air, already colder but mixed with the intention of the fire, fill her lungs. She put her fingernail between the latch and opened it.

Paul studied the picture, then looked at her face. "He has your eyes."

Bianca snapped the locket shut, not willing to see. "My brother, Ashabel. We don't say his name at home. Mama won't let us." She widened her eyes, realizing how strange that must sound. "Not since we received the letter that he was killed in the war."

He looked sad and stared into the flames. "I'm so sorry. Truly I am. I'm sure he loved you very much."

"I loved him." She tucked the locket beneath her collar again. "I still do."

"I'm sorry I can't know him . . . at least this side of heaven." Paul blew out pent-up breath. "But I suspect he wouldn't think much of me."

"He'd probably kill you."

Paul shifted his gaze toward her and looked like he didn't doubt it. "Yes, well . . . I have a brother, Rupert. He's much more sensible than I am." He poked at the fire with a stick. "He's a barrister, and he doesn't care a wit about artifacts or travel. But we're very fond of each other. As fond as we can be, I suppose."

The sea trembled, blown by the desire of the wind. Bianca reached for the grass and ripped it. She should just tell him. She couldn't be his wife. She had to go home. "Is your brother older or younger?"

"Older." Paul looked relieved somehow, like he knew she'd meant to say something else. "He has a lovely wife, and a little girl, Pippa." The half smile that turned up his lips tore at her. There was a fondness on his face that told of hours and conversations she would never know of. "I brought Pippa back a doll from Vienna once. You should have seen her face."

Bianca smiled, despite herself. Then the smile faltered. The thought of him buying dolls, and having a brother who loved him, this other part of his life that she was desperately drawn to . . . She couldn't think of it. Because she would want to stay. Because it would make her love him more.

She stood. What was wrong with her? It should be easy to hate him. "I'm going to take a walk."

"I'll go with you." Paul started to stand.

"No." She put out her hand and the wind made her sleeve flap like a bird's wing.

He sat back down, reluctantly. "There are all sorts of dangers out there. You could fall into the water and drown in this darkness. I wouldn't be able to see you, or hear you if you'd gone too far."

"I'll stay close by." She pointed toward the last bit of visible hillside. "Just down there." Bianca closed her eyes and let her voice fall. "Where I can think."

"Take the blanket in the saddlebag." His voice washed over her, as the sound of the sea washed over her. "I wouldn't want you to get cold."

How could his voice still affect her after what he'd done? He probably stole that blanket at the inn. He was good at stealing. Especially hearts. "Give it to me then." She stared at the same distant point in the darkness and didn't watch him go.

When he came back, he held the blanket out to her. "I suppose you've guessed we'll have to sleep here tonight. We're very far from a decent town."

The edge of the blanket stirred in the wind. "How convenient for you." Bianca snatched the blanket away. "I'm sure you planned this, bringing me up here all alone. What were you going to do? Seduce me, like you seduced Madeline? Did you think that then you could keep me?"

"No." His hand shot out into the space between them. "I only thought you'd want to see the sea. As far as keeping you, I never had you in the first place. You're not something to be possessed . . . I only meant to love you honestly, Bianca. Honestly, before God, as I've tried to walk since I became a Christian. And honestly as a man who wants to take away this pain I've so cruelly inflicted."

Bianca lowered her hand and the blanket unfurled, fluttering above the sand, skidding to the boundaries of the firelight, pulling her toward the unknown. "Pain is a funny thing, Paul. Even after it's gone, its memory remains." She looked one last time into the deep green eyes of the man who had ruined her forever. "Only God can perfectly forget. And although, because of Calvary, your sins with Madeline are cast into that sea of God's forgiveness—covered by the deep—I can still see them." She slipped into the darkness. "I always will."

Sir Adrian Hartwith sat on a hillside with the dead. He wondered if Judas was buried here somewhere. Or had they let him rot on the ground after his body had fallen from the tree?

The betrayer of Christ. That one who was evil from the beginning. Secret motives. Selfish agendas. Just like him.

The way he saw it, he only had two choices—Find some work to do to absolve his sins, just like always, some tradition of man. Then hope it worked, never knowing for sure. Or kill himself and go and see if Paul and Bianca's Christ was real.

Because they were gone. Because he couldn't test them anymore. It was the only way.

He pulled his knife from his boot and went to the largest tree—a gnarled, looming demon in the dark. Within minutes he would know. There'd be an end to his two-year obsession.

His last great experiment, here in the Field of Blood.

He thought of how he'd embezzled Grandview's money. And then Grandview had shot himself. And the look on the man's feeble face still haunted him. But then he had donated a large portion of that money to help the factory workers who'd been in that fire . . .

He thought of the opium he'd made Samuel smuggle to China, unbeknownst. He thought of the peoples' lives he'd ruined there, just to increase his wealth. But then he'd built that orphanage in the East End of London.

It never felt like enough. And that didn't even begin to cover all the sins he'd committed in Scotland. And Gavina Sheighly, Bianca's made-up chaperone, had been alongside him for them all.

He thumbed the knife's blade. It was warm from being in his boot.

Did his good works outweigh his bad works? Is that what it took?

Sir Adrian stared at the kiss of the moon on the knife's cold, thirsty blade. This whole place was thirsty—this barren, rocky wilderness, this place of betrayal.

He could do this.

It would be easy.

He pressed the knife hard against his neck and gazed up at the sky. "Jesus said, 'I am the way, the truth and the life, no man cometh to the Father but by me.'" He closed his eyes. "I think He lied."

Chapter 32

Bianca looked back at the fire, which was close to dying. If anyone would have told her that in the course of mere weeks she'd fall in love, be willing to marry on the spot, and then find out her life was an experiment to a cruel aristocrat—her emotions and actions judged the entire way—she wouldn't have believed them. But, then, to be so close to having that love, only to have it ripped away by a strange and unlikely courier—honesty, something she'd placed above most things—that truly was tragic.

The wind ripped the blanket from Bianca's hands and tossed it into the water. But it didn't matter. Paul should be asleep by now. She walked toward him. It was possible he didn't sleep at all at the inn. She hadn't. Neither had he slept the night before he'd gone to Jaffa.

She crawled through the tall grass as quietly as she could. She saw his boot and the glow of the fire on his trousers. His face was hidden behind a tree stump. He was lying down. Surely asleep. She could hear the horse to the left, but it was too dark to see. He'd taken off the saddle, and it lay next to him, just a few feet away from his hand.

Bianca lowered her head onto the ground. Why did he have to be so responsible and take off the saddle? She took a breath, snapped her head up, and looked through the weeds. It didn't matter. She could get it. She crept, bit by bit, only when the wind blew, to cover up her sound.

She reached for the saddle. She knew she shouldn't look at his face. But then the wind blew its fiercest, and the sound of rustling pages drew her gaze.

Paul's eyes were closed. His chest rose and fell steadily. His journal was open beside him. A pencil was in his hand. The wind's fingers played in his hair, as if to show her how important he was, how dear. As if it wanted to remind her again how lonely her days afterward would be.

She should leave and not linger. But she couldn't pull her eyes away. The soft orange from the fire glowed upon his cheek. She'd never had the courage to even kiss his cheek. She dropped her gaze to his hands. Hands so strong and kind. Hands that would never hold their children. Some other woman's perhaps, but not theirs.

Another woman would love him better than she could. Another woman wouldn't have to forgive.

Bianca allowed her last indulgence—she looked at his lips. She thought of the balcony at Mr. Owenburke's when he'd whispered goodnight in her ear, so close to kissing her.

The wind flipped the pages of his journal impatiently, urgently, exposing the faded ink on the inside cover. *Paul Emerson, 147 Providence Street, London.*

Providence. Bianca would have laughed if things had been different. Of course he'd buy a house on Providence Street. Once she'd believed that God's providence had brought them together. Not anymore.

Bianca tore her gaze away and lifted the saddle as carefully as she could. She moved when the wind moved. She snuck through the field of flowers, the stems tangling around her ankles, trying to anchor her to earth. Bianca ripped their beauty out of the ground, and trudged on.

"We will trust each other," she whispered to the velvet-nosed horse. "We'll follow the river. How hard can it be?"

Sir Adrian wasn't afraid. He leaned against the tree, took a deep breath, and then another. When the silver cloud passed the moon, he'd do it. He increased the pressure on the knife. The blade cut into his flesh and a hot trickle of blood rolled down his neck.

Almost there.

The wind pushed, like a kind, benevolent friend; urging that cloud on, hastening the beat of his heart, the rise of his chest, and the two tears that dropped from his eyes as they widened.

No one would see. Here, on the brink of heaven or hell, no one would see. He would cross this valley alone.

Alone, as he always had been.

The silver cord around the clouds broke. Sir Adrian choked a laugh, and more tears fell. "White muse... sickle of a moon... show yourself to me."

The wind blew again, like a trembling note suspended; it whipped around the tree trunks and the rocks. It clawed at his trousers and his sleeves. An ill wind from the different direction. The silver cloud dangled near the moon.

"Slide on!" he yelled into the echo of the wind.

But the cloud stood still.

His vest flapped in the wind, and then something danced in the darkness; fluttering in front of him. A paper.

But it didn't matter. He didn't care about a paper from his pocket. "By God, move!"

The silver cloud stood still.

The paper fluttered, caught against a rock.

It didn't matter. He didn't need a cloud. Sir Adrian squeezed the knife handle and turned his head.

The paper fluttered.

He cursed. His hand shook. He dug the edge of the knife into his flesh and screamed.

The paper fluttered.

He cursed again, louder. "Move the blade, you coward!"

The wind blew again. And the paper fluttered.

He thrust away the knife and walked to the paper. He snatched it up, like a wild thing in his hand. He marched back to the tree and wrapped his fingers tighter around the knife. "I will do this!"

Moonlight shone on the paper. *"Don't do this…"* Three words were exposed. It was Bianca's handwriting—her essay—the reason why he'd chosen her. "Bianca." His eyes widened. The only one who ever tried to like him for himself.

Sir Adrian dropped the knife and fell against the tree. He opened the paper and held the side of his neck smeared with blood. And he cried.

> *… If I don't do this I'll never forgive myself. I've been sitting here for three hours, staring at your advertisement. I'm afraid of this journey. I'm afraid of changing, although I want to—although I hear God whispering courage to me every day… I haven't answered your question. You said to write about a regret from my past, here it is: I had the opportunity to visit my brother a week before he died and I didn't do it. The journey was too far. A mere fifty miles.*

So, you see, I have to go beyond those
fifty miles to prove to myself that I can do it. I
will trust you to bring me to England, if I am
chosen. And then to the Holy Land. I tremble
at the thought of being in the place where
Jesus showed His love to the world.

I want to open up my heart for whatever
God has for me. I want to trust Him, as I've
never trusted Him, and cross the vast ocean,
and come and meet you, and the other
people you choose. Everything happens for
a reason. Not even a sparrow falls without
the Lord's notice. Whomever you choose will
be exactly who's meant to be there. I hope
that whomever is me.

Moonlight shifted on the paper. The silver cloud slipped away silently, revealing a raw, smiling moon. He crumpled the paper and slid down the tree to the ground. He was cold. He was ready to kill himself two minutes ago and now he found that he was cold.

He laughed, but it was choked with sobs. "Where the devil is my coat?" He looked around on the ground. "Where—" He'd left it in the brothel on the floor. And the Muslim had picked it up. Fear gripped him. "Samuel's plans were in my pocket." His entire body shook as he stood. "Samuel's plans for the revolt." He ran, as fast as he could.

They'd kill Samuel if they found those plans.
They'd kill his only friend.
Or worse . . . they could do worse.
Dear God, what had he done?

It was hard. Terrifyingly hard. Worse than all the parting scenes she'd ever read in all those stupid Gothic novels. The wind still blew, but fiercely now, like a force wanted to thwart the horse's every step. The wind was a different thing altogether, not gentle like when she'd left Paul sleeping on the grass, all alone. Not gentle like in Mr. Owenburke's garden, when Paul had held her hair in his hands and told her how beautiful she was. And, had she married him, the wind would have been gentle on that day also.

Her plans . . . they'd seemed sensible at the time. Follow the Jordan River south. And once the river spilled into Bethlehem, she could get to Jerusalem. She'd find Mr. Owenburke. He'll help her. He'd get her home.

But now, nothing seemed sensible. There was only darkness, fear, and regret. It was too late to turn back. She was beyond lost. She and the horse had long ago lost sight of the river. All because of those clouds shrouding the moon like a silver cloth.

Bianca held on to the horse, petting its neck, trying to ease her own fears. She couldn't even smell the river. She gripped the reins too tight. The horse jerked and whinnied, its voice echoing off the high cliff walls in the wilderness—the scattered rocks. "God, bring some good from this. Even if I die tonight—"

"Having trouble?" A silhouette of a man stood out against the sky, high on the rocks above. His voice was thick with an Arabic accent.

Time froze. Bianca's heart slammed in her chest.

"It is dark for sightseeing. And you're a long way from home, I expect."

Bianca kicked the horse's side. It wouldn't budge.

"Let me have a look at you." The man scrambled down the rocks, sending debris as he came.

"Move on!" She slapped the horse with the reins. Still, it wouldn't move. Bianca jumped and ran.

The man yelled behind her. "You'll only kill yourself that way. There's a cliff up ahead."

A black void opened its mouth before her. Bianca skidded to a stop and fell, ripping her skirt. Her head slammed into a rock. Blood soaked her hands. The silver cloud above blurred. She thought it moved. And then the moon was naked and bright. So this is how she would die. Murdered by a Bedouin in the wilderness.

His wrinkled face loomed above her, blocking out the pure, white moon.

"Make it quick." She took a deep breath and then his turban blurred, a crimson cloth that looked black. She closed her eyes. "Oh, Lord, take care of Daddy. And Paul."

"Make what quick?" The man pulled her up to sitting.

"Killing me." Bianca held her head.

Disgust washed over the man's face. "You're crazy."

"Probably." She locked eyes with him. "So you're not going to kill me?"

He rolled his eyes and said something in another language. He stood and walked back toward the rocks.

"Wait. I'm lost." Bianca tried to stand but swayed. "Can you help me?"

The man turned back and walked to her, his robe billowing. "That's depends. You have money? Akeem does nothing for free."

"I . . ." What little money she'd had, she'd spent at Bethlehem. The rest of the money was in her trunk at Mr. Owenburke's. "I can get you money."

"I've heard that before. Good-bye, strange one."

"Please!" Bianca grabbed the sleeve of his robe. "I need to get to Jerusalem. There's a man there who will pay you."

Akeem narrowed his eyes. "What are you running away from? Maybe you're the murderer. Maybe you kill your husband and leave him in the desert, eh?"

"I . . . haven't left anybody . . . I'm a tourist who's lost. I need to get back to Jerusalem. Please."

"You lie very poorly. No matter . . ." He studied her face and then his eyes went to her neck. "It is silver?"

Bianca put her hand over her locket. "It's not negotiable. Take me to Jerusalem, and I'll pay you well. The money is there."

"The necklace." His gaze was hard. "The necklace or I leave you now."

Paul felt her absence before he opened his eyes. His heart caught as if someone hit him. When he sat, he saw only blackness, cruel and hollow. The voice of the wind echoed, over and over again, like the distant calls of a missed ship.

"Lord God, no."

One cloud, shrouding the moon, laughed as it stared down, a silver demon in disguise.

Sir Adrian burst through Samuel's door and almost knocked over Madeline. "Where's Samuel?" He grabbed her by the shoulder. "Where is he?"

"Laud, is that any way to greet a woman?" Her pout was in full force. She widened her eyes in mock offense.

"Samuel!" He ran down the hall and then back.

"He's not here. I don't know where he is." Madeline put her hand on her hip. "But, now that you're here, perhaps you'd like to give me my money."

Sir Adrian pushed past her and ran up the stairs. He heard shouting from behind Mr. Tabor's door.

It was the doctor's voice. "You must take the medicine. If you won't let me bring the rabbi."

"I don't need your God." The word died, choked in phlegm. "He let this happen to me." Something smashed in the room.

Sir Adrian opened the door.

"Ah, the very devil!" Sweat caked Tabor's hair to his forehead. The stench was unbelievable, like fruit mixed with decay. "Come to see me off, have you?"

Tabor really was dying. And he had been from the start of it. "Do you know where Samuel is?"

Dark circles rimed the doctor's old eyes. He stood and removed his spectacles. "What happened to your neck?"

"Never mind. I must find Samuel." Tabor's eyes, full of pain and blame, bore into him.

The doctor reached for Sir Adrian's neck but stopped his hand midair. His face went pasty as he studied the cut. "He went to see a man about something. Is there anything I can do for you?"

There wasn't any time. "Did he say when he'd be back?"

"No, I'm sorry." The doctor put his hand on Sir Adrian's arm. "Let's go into the other room and talk."

"I can't." Sir Adrian backed out of the room. He tripped running down the stairs. He should go back to the brothel. He could find out who the Muslim was.

Madeline grabbed his arm on the stairs. "About my money."

Rage filled him. He ripped her hand away.

"I intend to collect what you owe me."

"Your contract is broken!" Sir Adrian strode toward the door. "And you're the most incompetent woman I've ever met. Go to the devil." He put his hand on the doorknob. "I hope I never see you again."

Madeline pushed the door closed and threw her back against it. "I did what you said." Her voice was the hiss of a viper. "I tried to seduce Paul but he wouldn't have it. How was I supposed to do it when he always kept his door locked? I planted the doubts in Bianca's mind . . ."

"Get out of my way." Sir Adrian put his hands on either side of her neck. "Or I'll crush your throat. Then I'll never have to hear your voice again."

Madeline winced. "I did it. I cut out the pages."

"What?" The word came out between clenched teeth.

"Paul's journal. I cut out the pages so he wouldn't know they were gone. Before he took it back."

"Little good that does me now. Since you let them leave."

She gripped his wrists. "How was I supposed to stop them? It's your friend's fault. And that doctor locked me in the room with Mr. Tabor. Blame him."

He threw her as hard as he could. She skid across the floor, a flood of red satin. "I curse the day I ever set eyes upon you." The lamplight pulled at her wide eyes. "And I'm sorry for tormenting Paul. I'm sorry he had to look at you day after day." He reached for the door handle again.

"Paul has to go back to London."

His hand stopped on the brass.

"He has to go home eventually, even if he has married Bianca. You could finish your experiment there. You could blackmail him in London for the pages. See if he would steal again."

Her words swirled about him. And he considered it.

Glass broke. Fire turned the night to day. Arabic voices mixed with screaming.

Chapter 33

*A*keem disappeared with her necklace. He slipped away, just like that, behind the Jerusalem gate.

Bianca fought tears as she walked. But tears didn't matter anymore. There'd be plenty of time for that later. She'd go in the back way to the house. Use the alley. She'd try to get Omar's attention and he'd get Mr. Owenburke.

The alleys were strange without Paul; so were the Crusader ruins and the closed up market. It was a town for phantoms and broken dreams. When she passed the woman's house where Paul had taken her to eat, Bianca thought her heart would shatter. But she willed her feet to walk. Just a little farther, and it would be done.

The ink black of the sky was changing to blue.

"This too shall pass. One day this pain will fade . . ."

Smoke billowed in the sky. The wind blew it closer. Bianca ran until she heard men yelling in Arabic. And then she saw them, faces black with hatred, throwing fire bottles through the windows of Mr. Owenburke's house.

Sir Adrian felt glass cascade off his body. He pushed himself up and saw Madeline screaming through the flames.

"Help!" The doctor screamed from the landing. "Help me get Mr. Tabor out of here!"

Sir Adrian gazed through the flames. "Samuel . . ."

A crash came from the back of the house and then Muslims were all around, running up the stairs, running through the hallways, circling Madeline.

Something crashed upstairs. More glass broke. They'd found the guns. They found them behind the clock.

The heat of the fire grew. Sir Adrian looked at his leg, covered in blood. He heard Samuel's voice and saw him through the open door.

He crawled toward the door. The Muslims had Samuel. They stripped off his robe and hit him with broken bottles and clubs. His friend . . . They hit him over the head. He slumped. "Samuel!" Sir Adrian reached out, so close to the door. "Samuel!"

They dragged his friend away.

Bianca heard Mr. Tabor's screams when she came through the garden gate. She pushed open the back door. There was only the roar of fire and smoke. She ran up the back stairs.

"Miss Marshal!" The doctor was on the landing, his forehead seeping blood. He held Mr. Tabor limp by his side.

Bianca ran to him and took the rest of Mr. Tabor's weight. His moan was drowned in the roar of flames. "Where are the others?"

"I don't know." The doctor's voice was weak.

They stumbled down the stairs and into the street.

The flames raged on, a black and orange rebellion against the night sky. Wood crashed. Glass broke.

In the alley, Bianca helped the doctor lay Mr. Tabor down. "What can we do?"

The doctor didn't answer. The old man's eyes were fixed upon the flames. "They had guns . . . it happened so fast."

Madeline's scream came from the alleyway behind them.

"It's Mrs. Greene." The doctor took a step and then crumpled on the ground.

"Doctor!" Bianca bent over him.

Madeline screamed again.

Bianca's head snapped up. And she didn't think. She just ran.

Sir Adrian woke in a pool of his own blood. The Mosque of Omar loomed over him.

He deserved this. Now death would come.

A foreign voice was behind him and then a kick, sudden and swift. His ribs splintered.

Before he blacked out again, Sir Adrian heard Samuel scream.

Bianca followed their shadows, moving through the alleys. When the man stopped to hit Madeline, Bianca hid. Shaking came fierce and she felt as if she might fall. Her heart was near exploding.

She deserves it. Let him take her. She took your happiness from you.

The Muslim call to prayer came as the sun started to rise. The tones chilled Bianca's soul, stealing her breath away.

Madeline screamed again.

The sunlight filtered across the roofs.

The Muslim call wailed again, echoing over Bianca's breath. Louder than the beat of her heart. Louder than her fear.

The man threw Madeline down. He ripped her dress and exposed her shoulder.

Sunlight crossed the alley. It peered into the corner where Bianca hid.

Madeline's scream turned into a sob.

Bianca inched away from the wall. The sunlight was full on the man—his hands cruel.

Madeline's blood was on the ground.

"Oh, God, help me." Bianca's heartbeat was in her ears. "What do I do?"

A barrel was at the corner. A barrel with a rusty fitting. A spike.

Madeline screamed like the damned.

"Lord, hide me. Jesus hide me."

The sunlight fell upon the barrel.

Take it. Use it as a knife. The impression was there. Bianca clearly heard it.

She reached for the spike.

The man yelled in Arabic. He tore more of Madeline's dress.

Bianca wrapped the end of the spike in her handkerchief and pulled it loose.

She walked toward the man.

And raised the spike over her head.

Sir Adrian rolled when they threw him from the cart. A cliff loomed over him. A skull. The holes in the cliff looked like eyes . . . a nose. Sir Adrian's gaze fixed on the mouth. Calvary . . . Golgotha. The place of the skull.

Pain flooded his body. Like thick darkness. Like sharp light. His eyelids drooped. And then the pain didn't matter anymore.

"Bianca, I'm talking to you."

Bianca stared at the blood on her hands.

"I wanted to say thank you."

Bianca closed her eyes against Madeline. Paul was in the wildness. Mr. Owenburke was gone . . .

"Did you hear me?"

"What . . . happened to Sir Adrian?" She had to wash the blood from her hands.

"Are you listening to me?"

Bianca looked out of the window at the doctor's house. The street thrummed with people. And none of them seemed to care that she'd just killed a man. None of them knew what she'd done to Paul just that morning. None of them cared what happened at the house. "How is any of this good, God? I wish I'd never come."

Madeline shook her.

"Don't touch me!" Bianca ripped herself away.

Madeline's lip curled. "I just wanted to say thank you."

Bianca stared at her—the woman who ruined Paul. She looked at Madeline's hands. Hands that held Paul. She looked at her lips. Lips that kissed him.

"I am grateful," Madeline said, and it looked like it pained her. Her eyes rimmed with tears and when they fell, they streaked lines through the soot on her cheeks.

Bianca turned and looked at Mr. Tabor. He was finally sleeping.

"He might live if he can take the shock." The doctor's voice faded to a wheeze.

Bianca knelt by the doctor's bed and smoothed the old man's hair away from his forehead. "Are you feeling any better?"

He wrapped his hand around hers and attempted a smile. His eyes went to Madeline. "Paul told me about her," he whispered. "I know."

Bianca nodded, then turned back to Madeline, who walked toward the door. "I didn't do it for you."

"What?" Madeline said.

"I did it for me." Tears fell from Bianca's eyes. "To prove to myself that I'm not like you."

"You won't see me again. That's my gift to you." Madeline's brown eyes turned hard. "But if you see Paul again, tell him something." She cracked the door open. "Tell him that I won't ever forget India . . . and the afternoon we spent together." A knowing look spread upon Madeline's face. "Think about that; you're a smart girl."

"And you're cruel." Bianca locked eyes with her. "Just like Paul told me you were."

The doctor squeezed Bianca's hand.

Madeline looked surprised, but the expression passed. "Well, there you have it." She took a breath and looked into the crowded street. "Apparently Paul Emerson is an extremely honest man."

Madeline slipped into the sunlight. And then she was gone.

As Jerusalem's gates fled away, Bianca tried not to think. She could only feel, and the pain came in waves—each moment worse than the one before. The old doctor still held her hand like a father. And, for the past six hours, that's what he'd become.

Mr. Tabor leaned against the carriage door, saying nothing. His lips were cracked. Soot caked his cheeks and beard. A fly landed on his face, but he didn't move to shoo it away. He looked like a phantom who'd seen too much of the world, but one who was forced to linger in between. A resignation had settled in his blue-gray eyes—a resignation that begged for release.

Bianca remembered his words from the day when the ship had docked in Jaffa. She repeated them, not knowing what else to say. "We will bear this the best we can, Mr. Tabor."

"I don't want to bear this anymore." His voice was weak, but he scraped out a laugh. The sound was out of place, adding to all of their despair.

"We can wait if you want to." The doctor looked at her kindly from above his broken spectacles. "There's no rule that says we have to go to Jaffa today."

Bianca's whole body ached with defeat.

The horse clipped off the steps and took them farther away.

"I have to go. I need to close this chapter. Besides, Mr. Tabor needs to rest upon a ship bound for home."

The doctor turned his head and studied the landscape slipping away. The Garden of Gethsemane was above them, the city wall behind. "I think I know someone who wouldn't want you to close this chapter. I'm sure he's looking for you now." Sadness was written upon his face. "Wherever he is."

Bianca listened to the horse's hooves and the wheels of the carriage. "He won't look forever." She turned her face away. "And then he'll forget about me."

"Do you think so?"

She hoped not. "I believe it."

He looked like he might say more. After a few moments he patted her hand. "You think that if it gives you comfort."

Bianca looked up, to the top of the hill that was just ahead. "That looks like—"

"It's Sir Adrian." The doctor leaned toward the driver. "Stop the carriage."

The doctor moved to get down.

Bianca placed her hand upon the lapel of his rumpled coat. "No. You should rest. I'll go." She stepped down and climbed, over rocks and tangled undergrowth, casting pebbles down the hill. Her body shook as she found the path. The wind bit hard, ripping across her body and throwing her skirt against her legs. Finally, she crested the hill.

"Ah, Bianca." Sir Adrian's hair blew in the wind, more black now than red, so much soot and blood was caked into it. "What a sad state of affairs I find myself in." He coughed. His eyes were heavy with tears.

"I . . . you're alive."

He laughed, and it sounded like a dead man laughing. Tears rolled down his swollen skin. "Seems I can't die . . . no matter how hard I try."

She should hate him. This pain that she felt had so much to do with him. "Do you know where Mr. Owenburke is?"

He nodded slowly. "They took Samuel."

Her heart sank. "The Muslims took him?"

"They'll torture him and worse." He searched the horizon endlessly. "And it's all my fault. It should have been me."

Bianca covered her mouth. Her breath caught in her throat. "God, protect him."

"But he has the poison ring. Do you remember?"

The ring. He'd kill himself. He said that he would. "I remember."

"It shouldn't take long." He smiled a strange smile. It chilled her to her soul. "Maybe he's already done it." Sir

Adrian closed his eyes and a tear fell. "This is where it happened, you know."

Grief pressed in, like a crushing vice. "What are you saying?" She locked eyes with him, hazel to ice blue.

"The crucifixion . . . here, outside the city." He looked at her but couldn't meet her eyes. "On a hill that looks like a skull. Or didn't you notice?"

"Here?" She looked at the ground and saw the blood from Sir Adrian's leg seeping into the dirt. Dizziness swirled around her. She started to walk away. "I have to go."

"Bianca, now you can go and have your happily ever after."

She turned back. Their gazes locked. "It doesn't exist." The shaking was stronger. "Paul told me about India and Madeline."

Surprise spread upon Sir Adrian's face. He lowered his hands. "He told you? But why would he do that? That jeopardizes everything he wanted."

Why? She wondered that herself now. Paul said he told her because he loved her. She took Sir Adrian's face in her hands and she stared into his eyes—eyes that could have been her friend's. "I suppose you'll have to ask Paul that someday. He could have easily said nothing. Considering how you used us, he wanted to protect me." She thought of Paul's kindness, and all the ways he'd treated her like a queen. "He's not the same man as he was in India. God changed him." She felt Sir Adrian's face tremble beneath her palms.

"Ah, yes, the Christian thing." His gaze drifted to the carriage below. A miscarried thought worked its way through his pain laced expression. "Tabor's down there." He wiped his face with his hand, smearing blood across his chin. "The old boy made it." His laugh was a painful scrape, dredging up deep things from the bottom of her soul. "Did you ever wonder why I chose him?"

"I don't care." She turned to leave, her mind just a fragment. The hot wind blew like hell's fingers, taunting her with its triumph.

"He killed your brother."

The words plunged deep, ripping the last hope she had left. Bianca opened her mouth to speak, but realized there was nothing there. Of course Mr. Tabor killed her brother. It all fell into place—Sir Adrian's twisted experiment. Madeline as a test for Paul and Mr. Tabor for her.

"He was a guard in Douglas Prison Camp. He purposely withheld rations. Your brother would have survived if it wasn't for him." The lines in his face grew deeper. "I needed to know if you could forgive him." His sapphire eyes, full of things never meant to be, embraced hers one last time. "You will."

The words fell like thistles among thorns.

Somewhere in her soul they mattered.

Somewhere, but not a place she could reach.

Numbness set in, wrapping its arms around her.

She left him there.

Staring at his blood dripping on Calvary.

Chapter 34

*T*he city of London passed by the coach window like a dream. Houses. Parks... Was she here so little time ago? Bianca leaned into the window.

Two hours until the ship left for America. She let the coach rock her. She dozed and thought of Mama's biscuits, and Daddy's laugh...

"Cor blimey!" The coach lurched and Bianca almost fell into the floor.

"What's goin' on?" The woman beside her swatted at her husband.

"Why have we stopped?" The man who hadn't spoken the entire trip now looked ready to implode. His neck was red and he beat his cane upon the ceiling. "I demand to know why we've stopped!"

The door opened. "'Orse threw a shoe, 'e did. You gentlemen and ladies 'old tight. We'll get all things to rights."

"I need to take some air." The woman fanned herself. "You, girl, come with me."

Bianca tried to manage a smile. "I'd rather stay here, thank you."

"Nonsense." The woman grabbed her hand. "I feel quite responsible for you. You look like you'd blow away in a strong wind. And you're too pale." Bianca let the woman lead her onto the sidewalk. "I doubt you've had much experience with men, poor thing."

"Excuse me?" Bianca pulled her hand away.

"Those men there ... they've been making eyes at you for the past half hour."

"Please, Madame ..."

"You poor thing. What were your parents thinking letting you go so far from home?"

Bianca tried her best not to scowl. "I'm sure I have no idea. It's lucky I'm even alive."

"Exactly. It's so dangerous in the world these days. I'm sure you have no idea how men can be."

"Not at all," Bianca said dryly.

"And don't I know it." The woman patted her on the hand. "The moment I set eyes upon you, I marked you for a good, pure girl. Never a wrong thought in her head, I said to myself."

"Never." Only asking Paul to come into her room at the inn. And wanting to kiss him. And wanting to kill Madeline. And then really killing a man. "Not much enters this head of mine, I can assure you."

"Good girl." The woman patted Bianca's cheek.

Bianca feigned coughing and turned, just to get away from the woman's hand. "Excuse me ... there must be something in the ..." Her gaze fell on the sign across the way—Providence Street. "Something in the air ..."

"Plenty in the air in London, I can assure you. All these factories clogging things up. And then there's the coal. Oh, look, we're ready to leave. The driver fixed ..."

But what she said after, Bianca didn't hear.

Bianca stood in front of the most beautiful house she'd ever seen, not because it was grand—although it was grand in its age and character—no, because every inch of it spoke of Paul.

147 Providence Street.

Bianca peeked at it from underneath the rim of her hat, then looked down at the grass. She shouldn't be here. What if somebody saw her and told him later on?

Yellow roses tipped with orange climbed up the side of the stone like they'd been scattered by their own whim. How could he have her favorite roses?

She laid her hand upon the wrought-iron gate, but then drew it back again. Paul's hand had been there, just a few short weeks ago.

What did it matter if she lingered just for a moment? After all she'd been through. She raised her chin and looked down the quiet street. No servants were about. Bianca bit her bottom lip, and stared at the gate latch. Slowly, she took off her glove. She laid her bare hand upon it.

She closed her eyes. "I'm so sorry I left you at the Sea of Galilee." Saying it didn't make her feel any better. She thought of how he must have felt when he'd woken.

Tears came, but she pushed them away. Her gaze lifted to the front door. Even if he managed to take the ship after her, he still wouldn't be in London for a few days. What harm would it do if she just looked in the window?

She looked at her watch. Since she was leaving in a few short hours . . .

Since she'd never return.

She pushed open the gate, walked up the wide stairs, and passed through the lattice wrapped in vines. She was standing on Paul Emerson's porch. She let the thought sink in. It was so quiet here, not like the rest of London. It was hidden from the world.

Bianca walked in the shadow of the vines and went to the window. She saw his desk in the corner. Deep longing washed over her, so much so that she thought she might die. She took her hat off, and lowered her forehead against the cool glass. "He sits there . . . and he writes and studies for his lectures." A fountain pen was uncapped. "And that's a map of Israel. He must have forgotten it on the day that we left on the ship . . . the day that he knew Madeline was onboard. But he went anyway . . . he went for me."

She looked down at the porch slats. She didn't even deserve to hold his affection, even for a little while. Although he sinned, she was the haughty one. "I thought I was better, and above him. Pure. But I was worse. I was a Pharisee."

Bianca opened her carpetbag and took out the Bethlehem star. "I don't deserve this either." She pressed the mother of pearl to her lips. She laid it on the windowsill.

And there she left it.

London, Six Months Later

Paul Emerson hated snow. He couldn't stand it. He detested it in the morning when he took the crowded coach to the museum and saw nothing but sludge on the streets. He abhorred the snow's presumption as it pushed itself through the crack in his office window near the back of the building. And as he sat there, day after day—scribbling useless words, reading useless words—the snow just kept falling, churning out of heaven like damaged cotton. Good for nothing. A waste.

And, late in the evening, when he finally did come home, the magnified silence was worse because of that snow. And how great was that silence, in the foyer, in the hallways, all throughout the parlor, and in his bedroom—especially there, but he didn't sleep there anymore. He reckoned that the sofa was just more comfortable. And it was warmer in the library anyway. So, really, he was just being practical. That's the way he saw it. And it'd been that way for a while.

And now, here he sat, sprawled out on the same place where he'd slept. He stared out the window to the porch. And he watched the snow.

It never quit.

It was constant.

Unlike a woman's love.

He heard a noise and craned his neck. Rupert was at the front gate, bursting his way through. Paul ran his hand over his day-old beard and stifled an oath.

Rupert pounded against the door with his palm. "I know you're in there."

Paul put his head in his hands. Then he forced himself up, walked to the door, and opened it. Snow swirled in, reaching for every thin place in his house coat. "This had better be important, brother. I was quite busy."

Rupert gave him a black look and pushed past him. He threw his hat and gloves upon the hall table. "You do realize that Mother's tea was an hour ago?"

Paul pushed the door shut. "That was today, was it?" He rubbed the back of his neck and headed toward the library. "Would you like something warm to drink? It's too blasted cold."

"Yes it is." Rupert followed him like a shadow. "And Aunt Hester came out in this cold specifically so you could meet her ward today. Miss Hawkins very much wanted to meet you." Rupert looked him up and down. "Although I can't imagine why."

Paul collapsed back onto the sofa and looked out the window again. "What color were her eyes?"

"Her eyes? I was too busy apologizing for your absence to notice." He shoved his hands into his pockets. "Blue, I think."

"Blue, you think." Paul reached for the book nearest him. "It wouldn't have worked ... poor Miss Hawkins and her blue eyes." He opened *Empedocles on Etna, and Other Poems* to the creased corner. *"Come to me in my dreams, and then ... By day I shall be well again. For so the night will more than pay ... The hopeless longing of the day ..."* He looked up. "You and mother ought to listen to me when I tell you I'm too distracted with work." He slammed the cover of the book shut and tossed it onto the floor. "Then nobody would be disappointed. Everybody would be perfectly happy."

Rupert looked at the book and then sat down beside him. "Everybody's worried about you, Paul. You haven't been the same since the Holy Land."

Paul made a fist and leaned his cheek against it. "It was an especially tiring trip, I've told you that. You know how it is when I come home. It just takes awhile to get used to London again."

"It's been six months, you liar."

Paul looked away from the green eyes that so closely mirrored his own.

"What happened, man? Why won't you tell me?"

Paul slid the Bethlehem star from the side table and ran his thumb over it, like he always did. He didn't have to look at it, he knew every curve, every crevice by heart. "I have been brought very low, Rupert. I don't think I shall ever recover." He half smiled, more from embarrassment than anything else. "I'm sorry, old chap. But there it is."

"Don't you think I haven't known that for months?" Rupert's gaze scanned the room. "Look at this place. Your papers are spread all over ... half empty teacups all around ... Where the devil is your butler? And your housekeeper?"

"They needed a holiday." Paul sat up and fidgeted with a teacup. He drained it. The tea was cold. "And I was tired of them hovering over me every second." And asking questions. And giving him sympathetic looks. "I paid them for the winter and told them to come back in the spring when it's warmer. They're both getting on in age and this climate isn't good for their bones."

There was an uncomfortable silence.

"Please tell me that the cook is still here."

"What do I need a cook for?" Paul's voice rose. "What do you think I do when I'm stuck in some godforsaken jungle? Wait for mutton stew?" He closed his eyes. Because he had a headache. And it was growing.

"All right, then, Captain Cook, what did you eat today?"

"Water crackers. They were quite delicious."

Rupert made a disgusted sound, stood, and paced the room. He stopped in front of the bookcase. "Your statue is broken. The one you brought back from Italy on your first research trip."

"Yes." Paul looked at it briefly, then turned his face toward the wall. "Quite the misfortune, that." He couldn't tell him he'd smashed it against the wall because it reminded him of Bianca. "I dropped it one night. Take it if you want it. Maybe someone on Bond Street can glue it back together for you."

"I don't want your blasted statue." Rupert leaned against the bookcase and tapped his fingers methodically. Then his expression softened. "Charlotte wants you to come for dinner on Thursday."

"Tell her I'm busy . . . I have a lecture at Cambridge."

"You used that excuse last time, brother."

Paul ran his thumb around the edges of the star again. Why couldn't Bianca accept the simple gift from him? But he knew. It was the same answer every time. Because she hated him.

"Paul."

"Hmmm?" Paul glanced up. "Were you saying something?"

"At least come for Pippa's sake. She misses her uncle."

Paul laid the star back on the stand and went to the window. At least Bianca had left the star so he'd know she wasn't dead. That was something at least. If only he could have been here.

"I'm going to go pummel that Hartwith fellow until he tells me what went on!"

"Rupert . . ." Paul pinched the bridge of his nose. "There was a woman, all right?"

"A woman? All this is about a woman?"

"Yes." Paul walked to his desk and pulled out the chair.

"My little brother finally went and got himself in love? Who is she? Some Hebrew? An Arab girl?"

"No . . . She's from Ohio."

"She's a Yank?" Rupert took a moment. "Sink me and the ship I came in on." Rupert pulled a chair over to Paul's desk. "Was she one of the contest winners?"

Paul nodded and put his head in his hands.

"And where is she now?"

"Home, I assume. Probably married."

"You assume? I think there's a lot you're not telling me, as usual."

"It's complicated."

"Everything about you is complicated. Why didn't you bring her back here to meet all of us?"

Paul covered his face with his hands. "Use your imagination if you have one. We had a falling-out." That was putting it mildly. She obviously hated him so much that she stole the horse just to get away. He'd searched for her for two weeks.

"Did you compromise her? Did you take advantage of her?"

"Rupert!" Paul shoved his hand out and pushed the stack of teacups away. They shattered on the floor. "Why does everyone have such a blasted low opinion of me? Is there no trust left in the world?" Paul stood again and went to the fireplace.

Rupert walked to him. "What am I supposed to think? Here you are pining for some girl who's thousands of miles away and you haven't told any of us. You're either a coward or you're wracked with guilt . . . Have you written to her?"

"No." His eyes went to the crumpled letters in the corner. "I'm sure she'd burn my letters without even reading them."

"You're sure?"

"Pretty sure." Paul noticed the dust on the mantel for the first time. "Now, are you finished questioning me? I have things to do."

Rupert studied Paul's face. "Do you think I captured Charlotte's heart by pining away for her in secret?"

Paul rolled his eyes and ran his finger in the dust. "I'm quite sure I don't want to know about my stodgy brother's proclamations of the heart. I might not ever recover from that conversation." He pushed away from the mantel and headed down the hall. "Some things are better left alone, don't you think?" Paul went into the kitchen and put more water into the teakettle.

"Look, Paul." Rupert leaned on the counter. "If this Ohio girl isn't married, there's still a chance for you. Even if she is angry with you—and I can relate—a lot can change in six months."

Paul looked up and met nothing but sincerity in Rupert's eyes. He took a deep breath. If only . . .

"If you do love her, don't you want to be absolutely sure of things?"

Paul slammed the teakettle onto the stove. "You have no idea what I've been through. What I put her through."

"No, I don't," Rupert said simply. "But, since I am the stodgy barrister, perhaps you'd like to plead your case."

Paul sighed and ran his hand over his eyes. "What time does Charlotte want me to come on Thursday?"

Rupert put his hand on Paul's shoulder and smiled. "Seven o'clock."

I'm worried about her, Candace. More worried than I can say." Oscar Marshal pulled back the parlor curtain. Bianca sat on the tree swing outside, that stare on her face again. The one that meant she'd be crying soon.

"You should be worried." Candace looked up from her mending. "She doesn't even sing in church anymore." She plunged the needle into the cloth like she was killing something. "I told you no good would come of that godforsaken journey. All it did was push her farther into the world. She's too far gone." She shook her head and frowned. "She could've been married three times over by now. But you and her, you're just alike." She flashed her pale blue eyes at him. "Too good for anybody."

Oscar hardened his jaw and tightened his hand around the curtain. He breathed. He counted. He recited the Gettysburg Address. *Four score and seven years ago . . .*

"Betsy has three children and she's Bianca's age. She keeps a good house too." Candace ripped out the stitch. "Bianca can't even keep her room in order. Have you seen all those papers on the floor?" She stuffed the thread into the darning basket. "There's nothing to be done. You had to send her abroad. You and your easy money schemes and all your dreaming. It has ruined her. And now I'll never have grandchildren. I won't ever hold a grandchild in my arms . . . Oscar! Are you listening to me?"

Bianca lowered the pen, then raised it again. She'd broken her promise to Paul. She told him nothing would change after she knew the woman's name. Then she left him alone like they weren't even friends.

"One forty-seven Providence Street." Bianca spoke the words again, like so many times before. "Put ink to page and just send it. And then, if I don't hear anything, I'll know he really does hate me."

The wind rocked her gently on the tree swing. "If only Ashabel were here." Bianca touched the place where his necklace used to be. She closed her eyes and his kind face was there—auburn hair and hazel eyes, just like hers. The years fled away in her mind. She remembered him behind her, pushing her on the swing. *You're much too meek, baby sister.* He pushed her high and she'd screamed, her long hair ribbons spreading out against the sky. *Don't be boring. Life is only a vapor. Let go, Bianca. Just let go.*

And her hands had slipped from the rope, high in the air. "And I flew." Bianca opened her eyes to the place where she'd landed in a heap of laughter. There, by the purple irises. "Just let go," she whispered to the leaves of the tree. The wind blew again and the leaves shuddered, as if they agreed.

Mama had been right all those months ago. True love wasn't a feeling. And it wasn't some unending fairy tale where a man fulfilled your every desire. No man was the perfect romantic hero. No man could fulfill the aching, deep need within a woman's heart. That intimacy was for God. And God alone.

True love was about letting go. A daily choice. Knowing the worst about a person and sacrificing for them anyway. Choosing to love.

However, she'd also been right all those months ago. There were such things as soul mates—God's perfect will for marriage. But was that person your soul's mirror? Sometimes. Mostly, Bianca reasoned that God matched people up in how they could refine each other. Someone who'd teach you how to love God deeper and become the person you were meant to become. He'd given Bianca that choice.

God never promised the road was an easy one.

She lowered the pen to the paper.

Dearest Paul,

I do so hope you open this letter. I fear you might throw it into the fire when you see it's from me. I did not lie to you in Bethlehem when I said I would love you forever. I do love you, most passionately; that has never changed.

The pen froze in place on the page. The sunlight hid itself behind a cloud.

I think I'll die if you can't forgive me. I hate myself for leaving you. I know I don't deserve a reply, but ple—

The fountain pen jammed. Bianca shook it. Footsteps sounded behind her. It had to be Daddy, going to the garden.

She scratched the pen over the word again: *please.*

Daddy was walking closer, probably to check on her.

The pen exploded, all over her hands, her new dress, and the edge of the paper. She flapped the page in the wind, long rivers of ink coursed down the side. "I've ruined it!"

The footsteps stopped behind her. "Fountain pens are so unreliable these days."

The velvet tones of Paul's voice reached deep and shook her.

"Hello, Bianca."

Her body turned to soft fire. She turned. And there Paul Emerson stood, as real as the ink dripping from her fingers and the sudden tears in her eyes. "You're here."

"What were you writing?" His smile was like breathing after being submerged too long.

"I . . ." She lifted the soggy page. "I was writing to you."

"Were you?" Paul gazed at the paper and then her eyes again. "May I?"

As he read, his eyes changed. There was a look in them she'd never seen. The wind blew as a swaddling, pulling itself tighter before running its fingers through the leaves of the tree.

He was going to tell her that he couldn't forgive her. He must be in Ohio on business and thought he'd stop by. He was going to tell her how horrible she'd been. "Do you have a reply?"

"Yes." Paul stepped forward and brushed her hair away from her eyes.

His touch made her shiver. "I'm prepared. For whatever decision you've made."

Paul rested his hand on her cheek. He rubbed his thumb against her temple.

"I can take it," she whispered, the warmth of his hand stole her breath away. "Just tell the truth."

His eyes turned to the color of the greenest sea.

She knew that look.

Paul was going to kiss her. The realization struck her like warm rain. And candles in the darkness. And sonnets.

The noise of the leaves above faded.

His hand slid into her hair.

Bianca's gaze fell to his lips—those lips she had longed to feel against hers for so long. She was terrified. Completely and utterly terrified.

Paul closed the space between them and she could smell his shaving soap—exotic, spicy sandalwood.

He pulled her close.

And then Paul Emerson showed Bianca Marshal what it meant to be truly kissed.

Candace's mouth fell open. She put her face closer to the window. "Oscar! Oscar! Good God!"

"What is it?" Oscar put down his teacup and stood.

"There's a man kissing Bianca!"

Oscar raised his eyebrows and hurried to Candace's side. "Does he look like a historian?"

Candace dropped the curtain. "My socks and garters. How do I know what a historian looks like?"

"Is he tall?" Oscar shooed her to the side. "Does he look like he's from England?" He lifted the lace curtain. "Tall. Dark brown hair." He squinted. "Looks quite . . . capable." He smiled and dropped the curtain.

"Aren't you going to do something?" Candace pulled on his sleeve. "There's a man kissing your daughter out in the open . . . in plain view!"

"I knew she could do it." Oscar nodded and tears came to his eyes. "Come along, Candace." Oscar cleared his throat and put his arm around his wife's back. "I think we'd better tidy up a bit."

"Why would we do that?" She swatted at his hands. "Didn't you see? There's a man kissing Bianca."

Oscar looked in the mirror and straightened his tie. "Oh, my dear, how much you have to learn. That's not just a man." He turned back to her and smiled. "That's Paul Emerson. Bianca's soon-to-be husband." Oscar winked at her, something he hadn't done in years. "You're about to meet the father of your grandchildren."

"Well, good God!" A smile spread across her face. "Why didn't you say so?" Candace smoothed down her collar. "Good God!"

"Yes," Oscar fidgeted with his tie and then his hand stilled. "Yes, Candace." His gaze went to the figures outside the curtain. "*Good* God."

ACKNOWLEDGMENTS

For me, seeing this book in print truly is a miracle. *The Covered Deep* was a story fourteen years in the making. For every step of that journey, God placed special people in my life to help me along. They continue to be forever friends, constant encouragers, and some of the best people I will ever have the privilege of knowing. For them, I am truly thankful.

To my husband, Jim Vallance: Thank you for daring me to dream and for supporting me when nothing added up logically. It's not easy being married to a writer, but you have weathered it well. You make God smile in millions of ways. I so admire your courage. What is hard for others is often easy for you. I have seen your faith move mountains. Jesus always has more.

To my son, Abishai: You often make me laugh so hard I cry. I am so proud of who you already are. You are a true gentleman. Never stop being curious and continue to ask the hard questions. Don't forget Proverbs 3:5–6. You are going to change the world for the better.

To my daughter, Eleason: No one fills my heart with joy like you. You keep me young and invite me to dance. Your songs heal and your smile makes everything better. You are one of God's special ones. I love you around the world and back again. Never forget that your prayers are powerful.

To my brilliant critique group partners—Bob Spiller, Julia Allen, and Cindi Madsen: I couldn't have done this without you. Some of my fondest memories will always be those years we spent laughing, commiserating, growing as writers, and living each others' stories. You are all treasures. Thank you so much for helping me find Paul and Bianca's deepest truth.

To fellow writers Evangeline Denmark and Carla Laureano: You are two of the biggest gifts God has ever given me. It is a privilege to be in the trenches with you. Your bravery is unparalleled. Keep writing scenes that scare you and remind me to do the same. Our writing will make a difference.

To Jackie McKnight: You believed in this story when no one else did. Here now is the evidence of that belief. Your encouragement kept *The Covered Deep* alive.

To Connie Donahue: All of our deep conversations over the years continue to resonate. I have seen God do amazing things through you and I know He will do more. Many of the world's problems have been solved over our cups of tea. Thanks for always listening and for bringing me Starbucks when I was in a pinch.

To Marci Wagner, one of the best prayer warriors I know: Thank you for holding me up when the battle was raging. You are a true friend.

To Angie Geyer: Thank you for being sensitive to the Holy Spirit. Your kindness helped me cross the finish line those last two days.

To my literary agent, Rachelle Gardner: There's a reason you have the reputation of being the best in your field. You are amazing. Thank you for believing in me and for fighting for what I believe in. I'm so glad *The Covered Deep* gave you that "feeling" all those years ago. I'm excited for all the books ahead.

To the Christian Writers Guild and Worthy Publishing: Thank you for making one of my biggest dreams a reality. For me, this was a perfect circle. Waiting for God's best is never the wrong choice.

To Pikes Peak Writers: Your support through the years propelled me forward and made me a better writer. Some of my fondest memories come from PPW workshops and conferences. You continue to be an unfailing guide for thousands of writers. Thank you.

To everyone who ever wrote me a note of encouragement, prayed for this book, or was a part of my cheering crowd: Many thanks. Each and every one of you made a difference.

And finally, to my Redeemer, the One True Living God: You saw me during all those long nights of writing. You heard all the prayers. You have memorized me and You are the lover of my soul. This book has always been Yours. For the fourteen years and all the gifts along the path, I am thankful. Take me deeper, and continue to call me out upon the water (Hebrews 11:6).

ABOUT THE AUTHOR

Brandy Vallance adores history and frequently has to be told at museums that it's closing time. She loves to travel, plays the cello, and thinks all teacups should be bottomless. In 2011, she fulfilled a lifelong dream and went to England, Scotland, and Wales. Being a complete Anglophile, it was difficult to bring her home. Bribes may have been involved.

Brandy fell in love with the Victorian time period at a young age, fascinated by the customs, manners, and especially the intricate rules of love. Since time travel is theoretically impossible, she lives in the nineteenth century vicariously through her novels. Unaccountable amounts of black tea have fueled this ambition. Brandy hopes to avoid a similar fate as the writer Honoré de Balzac, who met his death via caffeine poisoning. At this point, the balance may not be tipped in her favor. Brandy's love of tea can only be paralleled by her love of BBC period dramas, deep conversations, rain, and a good book.

Brandy lives in Colorado with her adventurous missionary husband, a debonair son who has adopted her love of all things British, and a beautiful daughter who reminds her to pay attention to moments and never lose the wonder. You can visit Brandy on the web at www.brandyvallance.com or connect with her via Facebook, Goodreads, Pinterest, or Twitter @ BrandyVallance.

WORTHY·
PUBLISHING

If you enjoyed this book, will you consider sharing the message with others?

- Mention the book in a Facebook post, Twitter update, Pinterest pin, blog post, or upload a picture through Instagram.

- Recommend this book to those in your small group, book club, workplace, and classes.

- Head over to facebook.com/worthypublishing, "LIKE" the page, and post a comment as to what you enjoyed the most.

- Tweet "I recommend reading #TheCoveredDeep by @BrandyVallance // @worthypub"

- Pick up a copy for someone you know who would be challenged and encouraged by this message.

- Write a book review online.

You can subscribe to Worthy Publishing's newsletter at worthypublishing.com.

WORTHY PUBLISHING
FACEBOOK PAGE

WORTHY PUBLISHING
WEBSITE